Trini

Bilingual Press/Editorial Bilingüe

Address
Bilingual Press
Box M, Campus Post Office
SUNY-Binghamton
Binghamton, New York 13901
(607) 724-9495

Trini

Estela Portillo Trambley

Bilingual Press/Editorial Bilingüe
BINGHAMTON, NEW YORK

ISBN: 0-916950-61-1
Printed simultaneously in a softcover edition. ISBN: 0-916950-62-X

Library of Congress Catalog Card Number: 85-73394

PRINTED IN THE UNITED STATES OF AMERICA

Cover design by Christopher J. Bidlack

Back cover photo by Achilles Studio, El Paso, Texas

This volume is supported by a grant from the National Endowment for the Arts in Washington, D.C., a Federal agency.

Contents

To Megan Anne Copeland,
God's child,
beautiful and brave

Prologue

She was walking among tombstones when she saw him following her. The world was gold this October, leaves fluttering to the ground like substances of fancies, liquescent in a search among tombstones. She knew who he was, a gringo painter who had come to live among the Mexicans in Valverde. What on earth did he want? Only one way to find out. She turned and waited for him to catch up with her. Even now, he smelled of turpentine. He stood smiling down at her as he asked, "Waiting for me?"

His Spanish was soft and musical, almost like a native. She asked simply, "What do you want?"

"To paint you."

Why her? she wondered. With all the young and pretty girls around. She did not answer, but as they crossed Alameda, he asked again, "Will you pose for me?"

"Why?"

"I've watched you planting, behind your house. You know that broken hill behind your place? That's where I want to paint you."

Her eyes were full of pagan lights. She realized she had been the subject of his curiosity for some time. She bit her lip in thought, then she looked to the level of his eyes and with a little laugh agreed, "Why not?"

* * *

The canvas was finished. The background was done in red and yellow browns with great subtleties of shades, with infinite degree of line. The figure of Trini on canvas was painted into the light, almost as if it had appeared out of the depth of rocks and earth. The whole body was a movement of strength, sustained, yet free. There was something mystical about her eyes, dark, looking to the level of the living, yet seeing beyond. The hair flew loose and long with the wind. The most amazing thing in the painting were the feet, bare, brown, seeming to grow out of the earth itself.

"Now, tell me, Trini, isn't that you?" Chale was behind her, his voice full of excitement. Yes, thought Trini, it is me. What I am inside. How did he know? He's only painted me, not known me. She had seen many women like herself, who had crossed a river illegally into the United States. So many brown women faceless in the world. Yet, here she was. Only she, a life etched in an unpoised moment, in a fragment of continuous change, all spelled out to its very beginning and all the beginnings to follow.

"Chale."

"Yes?"

"It is me."

1

El Bultito

Matilda, heavy with child, stopped halfway up the slope. They were where the giant palos blancos stood, heavy with white flowers, air sweet with the smell of orange blossoms. From the top of the hill, Trini turned to look at her mother, half-sensing something wrong. Matilda was swaying unsteadily on her feet.

"Mamá?"

Matilda closed her eyes for a second and bit her lip, but quickly shook her head. "I climbed the hill too fast. Go, catch up with the little ones."

On the other side, Buti and Lupita were digging under trees that shone like glass. Deep in the marrow of the soil, by the side of the hill, pochote grew. Trini turned to her mother again, but Matilda gestured her away. "Go on, I'll rest right here."

The mother sat down on a heap of stones, leaning her head against a tree; at that moment a flurry of wind rained white blossoms on her. Trini watched her, breathing free.

"Trini," called out Lupita, "Come help."

Trini hesitated, looking at Matilda surrounded by fallen blossoms, a fairy ring of whiteness, plotted, pieced, by chance and wind. She'll be alright, thought Trini, turning and making her way down the side of the slope where her brother and sister piled white bulbs on the grass. She sat down to help them dig, the scent of secret moist earth heavy in her nostrils. They took turns using their one spade to break the greenness, digging bulbs with tiny tendrils of hanging root. There was full concentration on this effort until Trini looked up to see Matilda coming down the slope to join them. She was beside them now. "Here, I'll dig."

The mother took her billowing skirt, making a knot in front around the knees, sitting on the ground, her long, thick braids touching moist spring grass. She helped the children scoop the rich brown earth. Holding the spade, Matilda sat back every so often to rest, eyes closed, one hand against her arched back. Then she took a small knife from her apron pocket, cutting into the heart of a bulb, gripping it, fingers pressing in rhythmic strokes, softening the pulp. She raised the softened pochote over her face, her pink tongue catching the sweet milk; she bit into the fruit. "Good . . ."

She softened some pochotes for the children, her bare feet half-covered by the red, warm earth. Buti was talking about Sabochi's cave. They listened to the excitement in his voice. A soft laugh was spilling from the mother as she picked up a handful of earth and let it pour through her fingers.

"Why can't we go, Mamá, why can't we go to the cave?" begged Buti. "When he comes back . . ."

"When he comes back . . ." The thought floated in Trini's mind. Sabochi, a Tarahumara, took mysterious trips into the Barranca del Cobre. In the shadowed silence of his cave, he spoke many times about the world outside the valley of Bachotigori. All of a sudden, Trini saw pain cross her mother's face, eyes deep in the pain, one hand, fingers spread, falling on her stomach. With difficulty, she tried to stand, straining. Trini ran to help her. Her mother grasped Trini's shoulder for balance, her breathing thick and hoarse. "Run, get Papá."

"The baby?" Trini asked in a frightened voice, standing frozen, undecided. But then, she turned to Buti and Lupita. "Get Papá, get Papá . . ."

The two little ones ran down the slope toward the path that led into the valley. Matilda collapsed, falling heavily on Trini, head limp to one side. Time froze as she looked at her mother's limp form fallen to the ground. She whispered, half-sobbing, "Mamá, can you hear me?"

Her mother lay on the grass, eyes closed, mouth slightly open, a deadly pallor on her face. Trini knelt, then drew her mother's head upon her lap. Now the rhythm of her mother's breath came softly like the wind that touched the palos blancos. Amidst tears, Trini became aware of the life around her, trees with their showering clouds of blossoms, wild flowers in the brightness of bloom, and a sky so blue that the blueness hurt. She looked down again at the wind-blown figure of her mother.

"Mamá, can you hear me?"

She looked into the still white face gleaming with the cold perspiration of unconsciousness, frail bones sweetly visible through her stretched skin, one hand still lying across her stomach as if to protect the child she carried inside her. Then Trini noticed the blood forming a pool, turning the grass darkish purple She touched the knotted skirt around her mother's knees. With one free hand, she awkwardly undid the knot and smoothed her mother's skirt as she avoided looking at the growing pool of blood. She bent and pressed her lips to the cold forehead as if wishing to give her mother life, and she whispered, "Mamá?"

* * *

"Why must you lock the gate, Papá?"

Trini felt the injustice of it all. After all, she was thirteen and quite capable of looking after Buti and Lupita.

"It is safer now that your mamá . . ." José Mario's voice trailed off. No one wanted to think about Matilda's death, the baby's death. Now that Matilda was gone, Papá locked them inside the yard before he went off to the mines. All of them had lived in a mist of pain. But it had affected her father the most. The state of loss was still in his reflexes, his seeing, his hearing, as he moved mechanically through the days. Matilda had been dead for six months. Pain was revived in the children's eyes at the mention of Matilda. Their mother was gone.

"I have to go." José Mario touched each child's head, hand lingering, shoulders bent. After that, he turned away, a sadness in his step. He made his way across the huge yard, locking the gate behind him. Trini and the little ones followed to the gate, their eyes focused on the trudging figure of their father. It overwhelmed Trini, watching her father make his way to the turn on the hill. She felt the same kind of helplessness when José Mario sat in the dark. Her heart would cry, oh Mamá, we need you so! She wanted to reach out and comfort him, to stroke his hand, to put her cheek against his as Matilda had done, but she never could. Her father felt her presence and that was enough. Now she watched the lonely figure take the turn.

"Let's watch for Sabochi on the rocks," Buti suggested. The late morning was before them. Why not? thought Trini. Sabochi had come after Matilda's funeral. Shocked and full of grief, he had left almost as soon as he had come. He had promised to return again soon to help and to try to be the children's "mother." His promise hung in the air each waking day for Trini. But then, Matilda could never be replaced. But Sabochi coming home! There was happiness in that. He came, always bringing with him stories of the outside world. The three of them sat on the rocks that looked upon the hill. They could see Sabochi's cave from where they sat on a pile of rainbow rocks, rocks gathered by José Mario from all across the mountain and valley. The pile spoke its own stone language, of time making beauty, purple pinks and orange golds mixed with the contours of brown rocks, well veined in green. There was the glassiness of dark, glinting rocks gathered along streams. This was the place where the rainbow lived. After baptizing the sky with rain, the rainbow would pour itself into the rocks and rest there until the next rain storm.

The breathing valley rose eagerly along the curve of mountain. Inside the yard was the freedom of space and sun changing season. The leaves of a fig tree tangled the morning's quiet. Buti and Lupita had already found a new interest. Buti was stalking, following a darting lizard; he squatted in complications of moss, calling out, "Chapulín, chapulín, sin, sin, sin . . ." The lizard darted under the huge pile of rocks. "¡Allá va!" screamed Lupita, pointing.

They waited quietly for the lizard to reappear. He was gone. The sun was burning against her face, so Trini found the shade of the fig tree where Buti and Lupita were already stretched out on the grass.

"Let me braid your hair, Lupita," offered Trini.

Lupita pushed herself up to a sitting position, then sat cross-legged, rocking to and fro, following the dance of the fig leaves' shadows. Trini's nimble fingers braided hair as Buti poked around for the lizard. They sat in happy silence under leaf-shaped shadows. Then Buti's whisper was against her ear. "Who's that?"

They were looking at a little man, naked except for what seemed to be a red cloth around the groin and a gold earring in his right ear. He looked properly human; still, there was an air of the unreal about him. His lower lip was extremely full and widened into a smile, a comical expression. His eyebrows were heavy and peaked, yet his head was very round and bald. His marble eyes, quick and full of mischief, darted from one child to another. Only his hands seemed inordinately large, with long, tapered fingers. His nose and thighs were those of a tiny gladiator. He inclined his head to one side to observe them, put a finger to his lips, then clapped his hands in merriment as he ran toward them. The children could not do otherwise. They clapped too and followed him as he ran around in a circle. Now he was going around the fig tree, pointing up at the leaves.

"It's too late for figs," Trini informed him. "We picked them all." He shook his head and kept pointing, then he scampered up the tree effortlessly with those sturdy, muscular little legs. He shook the tree. Figs rained down on them. Did we forget to pick them all? wondered Trini. She still remembered the last of the figs—the empty tree. Where did all these figs come from?

Buti was turning somersaults and stuffing his mouth. Trini did not question any more, but sat down with Lupita to eat figs, watching the little man climb down. He sat down next to them, looking at them, head tilted. He began to eat figs with great concentration. The little man picked each fig, examined it, smelled it, then popped it into his mouth, showing his enjoyment by nodding his head and rolling his eyes. Buti had to do the same ecstatically.

"What's your name? Where do you come from?" asked Trini curiously. The little man smiled and pointed to the purple rocks. He handed Trini a fig. "How did you get in? The gate's locked. We didn't see you come over the fence."

He merely nodded an answer and invited Buti with gestures to do more somersaults. Lupita, open-mouthed, stared at the little man. While El Enano and Buti were turning cartwheels all over the yard, she ventured to ask Trini in a whisper, "Is he magic?" Lupita, seven, and Buti, six, knew about magic from their mother, who had spoken of duendes living in the circle of hills. "Is he a duende?"

"I don't know. Es un enano."

"What's the difference?"

"Un enano is a very small person."

"Is he real?"

"I think so. This is the first time I've seen one."

"He's magic. He came from the purple rocks." Lupita was sure.

Trini felt a thump on the head. El Enano was behind her, asking her to play with pleading gestures. An old game came to mind. Trini led them all into a circle and began to sing, "Naranja dulce, limón partido . . ." They showed El Enano how the game was played, El Enano swaying to and fro to Trini and the children's singing. He wove between each of them, playing the game, tagging each of them, and letting himself be chased around the yard while the others shouted in excitement.

After a while, they fell exhausted to the ground, eating the rest of the figs and counting fig leaves. Trini went back to the rainbow rocks and pointed out Sabochi's cave to El Enano. There it was, where cardones and pitayas grew alive in yellows and pinks.

"You can't speak, can you?" asked Trini as El Enano explored the colored rocks. He shook his head and seemed sad, but only for a second. He pointed to his ears, his eyes, and afterwards wove patterns in the air, fingers making hieroglyphic sense. Buti was tugging at Trini's hilpa. "Can he get us some cheese, please, Trini?"

"Why not?" Trini climbed down from the rocks and motioned for El Enano to follow her. He ran with rhythmic little soldier strides, following Trini and the children into the kitchen, then into a pantry where a wooden table was used to make cheese. José Mario, when making cheese, always kept part of the milk. Trini helped with the heating of the milk and the draining of the whey in a canoa. Matilda had pressed the curds and cut them on the table. The cheese was stored in molds, sarsos set on open shelves built around the pantry. José Mario sold part of the cheese in Batopilas.

The sarsos were too high for the children to reach, but it was no trouble for El Enano. In the dark, cool pantry, with its smell of chile and dried meat, Trini handed a knife to the dwarf and pointed to the cheese. El Enano put the knife between his teeth with a flourish that delighted the children. Then, balancing himself along the edge of a shelf, he climbed from one to the other with great agility. At the top, he pulled a sarso out and sliced off a chunk of cheese. He held it high over his head and grinned down at them, poised on one foot on the edge of the top shelf. The children held their breath. He winked and made a gesture of a drop to Trini, who held out her hands to catch the cheese.

But the little man did not climb down. Something held his attention. He reached behind the sarso and pulled out a bultito, holding it high over his head as he had held the cheese. There was the pose, the wink, but he did not drop it. He put the blue bundle between his teeth and the knife inside his belt and made his way down to the children. Trini put the cheese on the table and held out her hand. It was Matilda's blue bundle. El Enano gave it to her with great seriousness. Her eye caught the yellow sprig embroidery stitched so carefully. Trini knew full well what it contained. Sitting on the wooden table, Buti and Lupita were around her as she untied the bundle on her lap. There they were—delicate spirals, woven strips of spider forms, tiny pieces of silver and gold. These were not the deliberate openwork design of goldsmiths. These were natural falling formations of metal grains, spontaneous sprinkles of melting metal. Through the years, one piece at a time, these had been gifts from José Mario to their mother, for in the past he had done his own founding. Trini remembered how as a little girl she had watched her father straining gold dust. It was not his gold and silver, for it belonged to Mr. Johnson, the mine owner, but José Mario kept some of the ore in the house to melt for the americano. There had been cotencias full of silver ore and gold waiting to be melted. Trini remembered playing dishes with the piles of trochados, the silver dollars used by José Mario to pay the mine workers. That had been so long ago. The delicate designs in the bundle were not worth very much, but they had been precious to Matilda because they were gifts from her husband.

"¡Miren!" José Mario would say, holding the most exquisite and fragile of labyrinths, more complex and mysterious than the one built by Daedalus for the Minotaur. Matilda, busy in the kitchen, would come in to watch the quick happenings in silver and gold. When the forms hardened, José Mario would hold them up, then put them in Matilda's opened hand. As he dropped them silently in her palm, their eyes would meet, and he would say, "Pa' la mamá." Matilda's eyes would light up with contentment.

Now they were on Trini's lap, bits of silver and gold, memories without sadness, love breathing whole. The children laughed and talked about Mamá, precious, funny little incidents, surprisingly not forgotten. After a while, Trini took the tiny molds and put them back in the bultito.

From a distance, El Enano watched the children fingering their memories. In his own eyes was the feel of centuries. The newfound intimacy belonged to the children alone. He did not intrude, but slipped through the kitchen door and walked across the yard. Lupita looked up, the first to notice the absence of their new friend. He was gone.

2

Sabochi

"Chihuahua belongs to the Indians," José Mario was telling Sabochi, his eyes distant, his voice solemn. "But then the white man came . . ."

"Not to Cusihuiriachi," laughed Sabochi.

"Long ago, the Indians in this valley looked upon the light in the barranca as the sacred ground of gods. Over there, near the mines." José Mario pointed to the mountain east of the valley. "There was a pure light shooting up from the gash." He sighed. "Turned out to be gold, only gold."

They were sitting and smoking on the high terraced milpas where the whole family had come to seed the cleared land. Clearing it had taken two weeks. The seeding was easier, for plowing the milpas in Bachotigori was not necessary. The tropical climate on high ground made the earth giving and rich. The people of the valley planted after the winds of February, everyone sharing the crops for miles around. No one person owned the land. José Mario's family had planted lentils, beans, and, around the hill where Sabochi's cave was, they had planted chile piquín.

The children sat in a rock enclosure on the edge of a ravine. A patch of sun touched Trini's face as she looked over to where her papá and Sabochi sat deep in conversation. Since his return, Sabochi had been the children's "mother." But, more importantly, the gate was no longer locked. Sabochi often took them to explore the hills, following paths that led to streams making their way to the mother river. Sometimes they would come across sweet smelling clusters of wild herbs. The most exciting thing to Trini was discovering silent, shadowy recesses of mountain similiar to Sabochi's cave. The whole valley was theirs when Sabochi was home.

"Times are changing," José Mario was saying. "There's no more gold now. Water is seeping into the mines. The gods have left the valley, Sabochi. Now, you watch the alemanes and the americanos leave Batopilas. The mountains will again belong to the descalzos. But it is a different mountain now." José Mario, his small, thin frame leaning against a rock, closed his eyes to visions past and future.

That evening Sabochi had his own news as he prepared huacavaques for the family. José Mario stirred the white pozole while Sabochi cut tripe. Trini mashed red chile into a pulp.

"I will be leaving for Quirare," Sabochi was saying as he expertly and rhythmically cleaved a knife into the long strips of tripe. "Isidoro came to my cave last night, all the way from Cusihuiriachi. My father is very ill. I must go back."

"For a long time?" There was dismay in Trini's question.

"I cannot say, pollito. I'll be back if . . ."

It hung in the air. "If . . ." He'll come back. I know he'll come back, Trini assured herself. He always comes back.

"Who's going to be our mother?" Buti asked. Trini felt impatience with his question. She ordered, "You and Lupita set the table now."

Lying on her petate that night, Trini stared into the darkness, restless, her pores alive to the balmy air of a coming spring. She whispered in the darkness, "I don't want you to be my mother, Sabochi. Not any more." She choked back tears, feeling a darkness enfolded in a deeper dark.

* * *

The sky lightened after the rain. The dark margins of the hills were now clearly bright. The scent of rain invaded the darkness at the entrance of the cave. The center of the cave itself was not dark, for to one side was another opening leading to the other side of the hill where chile piquín shone red. Large boulders served as a natural ladder out of the caracol. All shadows here were eaten by the funnel of light that poured into the cave. In the center of the cave was Sabochi's petate, while on wooden shelves built by him were canoas holding piñones, cacahuates, sunflower seeds, and sugar cane. He had cut, whittled, polished and varnished the round bowls himself. There were pots and some blankets stacked neatly in a corner. Sabochi was back. But he had come only to bid them "goodbye." The ahau, his father, had been released from breath. The pueblo of Cusihuiriachi had lost its chief. Sabochi was going back to the village in the Barranca del Cobre to take his father's place. He would no longer come to the valley to live in his cave. The world without Sabochi . . . Trini could not imagine it. Anguish burned in her blood. How can I bear it? How can I bear it? The thought pounded.

"I'm going to live here forever," Buti promised enthusiastically as his total concentration became a shelling of peanuts. He filled his mouth until he could hold no more. Every so often, he would hand some shelled peanuts to Lupita, who had taken a blanket and spread it out on the ground. She was lying on her stomach looking out with fascination at the piece of sky visible and blue from the funnel opening. The ground in the cave was covered with leaves that had blown in. The cave was full of a splendid shadowy silence. Sabochi was finishing some wooden animals he had made for them while Trini watched the deft, swift movements of his gentle hands working with the wood. His profile against light and shadow aroused strange new feelings in Trini, a tenderness that suffocated. Again the restlessness. Trini stood looking at the light coming through the funnel. She climbed the granite steps leading out of the caracol, feeling a need to be alone. Glorious dragonflies swarmed the thinning sun as Trini sat outside and looked at a wet world. The funnel's mouth led up to the side of the hill along terraced milpas that rose in linear symmetry. Around the hill was the dark ravine where the sound of water grew as if from a river of great depth. She felt strange new magical feelings. Sabochi called out:

"Pollitos, ready!"

Trini went back into the cave where Sabochi held the wooden animals on his lap. He handed each of them one, a horse, a snail, and a turtle, all with sleepy eyes.

"They look like Buti," laughed Lupita.

Solemnly, each accepted an animal and kissed Sabochi for his gift. The new feelings brightened in Trini as her lips lingered on his cheek. How feelings swim into one another! She wanted to hear the honey of his voice, the wisdom of his world.

"Tell us about the universe," Trini asked softly. She was the child again, full of wonder. Sabochi's voice, like surging gentle air, made nature gods quite real, and all distant things came near. She wanted him to speak of the wild wind, the one that woke the trees and made its path along the deep ravines and hillsides, the one that spoke to her at night. "Tell us about the wild wind."

"Gods speak through the wind. They speak of freedom, change, timelessness. They tell us to touch things lightly as the wind does."

"The wind howls and whips everything. It scares me," Buti complained. Sabochi nodded.

"There are times when the wind gathers in violence," Sabochi agreed. "It balances the wind's dancing touch."

"The wind hugs me sometimes." Trini's eyes were dark with excitement. "Sometimes the wind grows inside me."

"It grows inside," Sabochi nodded. "A feeling with things to be, not things gone."

"Is that a riddle?" Lupita asked. "I don't understand."

"Hush!" admonished Trini. She understood Sabochi's words, for she felt the words as she sometimes felt the wind's gentle touch.

"The wind moves without feeling." Sabochi spoke the words as if they were just for her. But she questioned silently. Move without feeling? She felt a stab of sadness as she stated, more than asked, "You're not coming back, are you?"

"I'm the ahau of Cusihuiriachi now, pollito. It is my father's turn to roam. We have exchanged places." He said it softly, urgently.

Trini wanted to throw her arms around him, to keep him from leaving her. Instead, the child in her made her lean her head against his chest to feel his warm safety.

"What shall I do without you, Sabochi?"

"Live!" Sabochi laughed.

"The wind doesn't feel, but I do." The plea fell from Trini's lips, half-caught in a sob. There was a need for silence as the gloom of early evening spread. With the darkness growing in the cave, Sabochi said, "It is time to go home."

"Are you coming home with us?" Buti asked.

"No." Sabochi's voice was final, wistful. "I have things to do before tomorrow. I shall come get you tomorrow morning. We shall all climb the hill to El Camino Real."

We shall walk with him for the last time, the last time, thought Trini. It was so hard to accept. Buti pulled at her hilpa. "I wanna stay here with Sabochi."

So do I! So do I! her heart said, but she spoke in a grown-up, practical tone, "No, we must get home before dark." Sabochi walked with them to the path that led down to the valley. Trini took Buti and Lupita by the hand, leading the way down the winding way worn by sheep tracks, turned red by a setting sun. Buti was persistent.

"Why can't I live in the cave by myself?" He suddenly sat down on the ground, refusing to budge. "The cave will be lonely," he insisted, his voice beginning to break.

"It won't be alone," coaxed Trini. "El Enano will probably come live in it. That's what Sabochi told us, remember?" She was trying to pull him up off the ground. He still did not move.

"You're a baby," accused Lupita, threatening in the same breath, "We're going to leave you here in the dark." She tried to push him. He sat still, refusing to move. Lupita warned, "El Enano won't come live in the cave if you don't mind Trini."

"He will too, won't he, Trini?" Buti asked Trini, half-convinced.

"Might not."

"Why did Sabochi say he would?"

"He was supposing."

"Is that like lying?"

"Of course not," Trini explained. "It's like wishing." She pulled at the reluctant Buti one more time. Everybody knew what wishing was. Buti got up, apparently convinced.

Scattered carpets of violets happened along the descent until they came to the cauterized palos verdes, already budding, clustered along the path leading to the valley. At the bottom of the hill, they followed the willow trees, still bare. Buti, tireless, rolled himself down a slope, ran up again, then rolled down, again and again. A sadness still hung over Trini; they would say "goodbye" to Sabochi in the morning.

* * *

Isidoro was to meet Sabochi in Quirare to escort the new ahau back to his people. It was tradition among the Tarahumaras. Still, to Trini, the thought of the world without Sabochi was dark and ominous like the breaking storm that threatened. They were standing on the edge of the path that broke into the Camino Real. The air was scented with the coming rain. Such a smell had always filled Trini with a luminous excitement. But not today. She was solely aware of the thunder and the darkening sky. Sabochi sensed her mood.

"I will come back, pollito."

She did not answer, but listened for a while to his sure steps beside her. Tears came, slowly at first. She looked straight ahead at the haze of heavy clouds in the sky. There was another clap of thunder. With the instinct of a child, she reached for the nearness of Sabochi. He brought her quickly to his side. The clouds were hastening in the sky, covering the sun. Sabochi's voice broke softly into her ear. "The storm is just beyond the hill."

He pointed to the dark sharpness of the hill ahead. Trini felt a heaviness in her breath. "The storm is inside me, inside me." It was a thunder inside her that spoke of things to be lost. "Don't leave me, Sabochi!"

The words opened a flood of disbelief in the children, and they ran and wrapped themselves around Sabochi's legs. They began to cry.

"Here, here," Sabochi's voice was firm. "That's not the way to say goodbye for a little while."

"When will you be back? When?" the children demanded with begging sobs. "When?"

"When my heart is hungry to see your faces."

"I don't believe you!" Trini felt a lostness in her own voice. Sabochi drew her to him, demanding softly, "You must believe."

The neighing of the horses struck their ears. They sensed the nearing storm. Sabochi led the way with wide strides, holding the horses with a sure hand. The path opened onto a wide area of trees leading to the main road into Batopilas, away from the valley of Bachotigori. They could see the valley below them cast in the greyness of the storm. Lupita began to cry openly as Buti ran to Sabochi, clutching the bottom of the tilma that covered Sabochi's groin. The little boy was begging. "We go with you, please, please."

The thunder and lightning were now directly overhead. Sabochi picked up Buti, looking into the little boy's face, "Be strong, little man." He put Buti down, then picked up Lupita, putting his cheek against the little girl's hair. "Mind your sister, pollito." Lupita hugged and kissed him. He put her down, urging, "Go, go now!"

He stirred them down the path and watched them run. The sound of the little ones' voices came back in chorus as thunder struck again. "Goodbye, Sabochi; goodbye, Sabochi; goodbye, Sabochi!"

The children ran and slipped, and picked themselves up on the path, still calling out, "Goodbye, Sabochi; goodbye, Sabochi; goodbye, Sabochi," almost as if the echo of their voices would drown out the thunder itself. Trini did not follow the children. There was a ringing of her senses that touched every fiber of her body. She threw her arms around his chest, feeling the beat of his heart, holding him without words, until the lightning flamed behind the ravine across the way. She looked up into his face, wishing to find something . . .

She wanted to shout at him, "I'm a woman! A woman! Take me with you." She ached with the wanting. But there were no words. She touched his face, thirsting not to forget—line of jaw, the gentle mouth, the eyes so full of the universe. He had filled her life with wonder, and now he would be gone. She closed her eyes with the torment of the thought and let her head fall on the warmth of his chest. There she stopped to capture the new sensations she felt. She looked up again, wishing to find a revelation on his face, but saw only concern, kind and full of the love he felt for all of them. She had been his child for too long. His face told her that. But something in the tremble of his touch as he took her face to look into her eyes spoke of an unreached promise, a feeling growing . . . Was she imagining? Tasting her new sensation, she whispered:

"I love you, Sabochi. I love you so."

He held her close against his heart, his eyes clouded in a new confusion. His voice was sad, without passion. "I know."

What did he know? Where was the man wanting a woman? Sabochi was speaking to the child that he loved. She pulled away almost in anger, shouting against the thunder, "I love you like a woman loves a man!"

Again, the new confusion filled Sabochi's face. But it was full of pain, of question. All was unripe, untested. He could not accept. He was not ready to believe. His voice was serious, "What can I say?"

"Tell me that you love me, Sabochi, the way I love you!"

"I have always loved you, pollito."

"You know that's not what I mean!" The savagery of her voice made him draw her to him. Her breath came short in the tightness of his grasp. He held her close and she would not let go until the lightning struck dangerously near.

He held her at arms length and whispered to the rhythm of rain torrents, "Grow in stillness, little woman, grow in stillness." Then he turned her away from him and bid, "Go, go now."

She could do no more. She started down the path and did not look back. Her body staggered, her heart staggered as lightning charged the sky one more time. The rain was falling hard. Its excitement was her excitement. She opened her mouth to breathe in the wetness of the world, the discovery of herself, the greyness of a world empty of a Sabochi that would always be the thunder and the lightning in her life. The excitement grew as if the world were opening up to strange, terrible things, with such beauty! A gash of some glorious, bright wound, magestic, free.

3

Tonio and a Destiny

Trini had been sleeping next to an open window. She stretched, her body feeling the sunrise as the first light lent its pinks to darkness. The smell of night still clung to the breath of green things. She opened her eyes to notice that the leaves of the palos verdes outside the window were more than a shadow now. In half dream and half wakefulness, Trini heard the sharp and rhythmic sweep of an ax. Does Tonio ever sleep? He was already cutting wood in the yard. She did not like getting up so early to fix the morning meal, but if she lingered any longer, Tonio would come in and tease her. She leaned over Lupita's petate and shook her little sister. "Wake up!"

Lupita turned a tousled head and opened one eye. "It's night."

"Be quiet. You want him to catch us sleeping when he comes in with the milk?"

Lupita turned her back on Trini again and mumbled, "Tonio, Tonio, always complaining about Tonio."

Trini turned her sister over with some effort, shaking her again. Lupita fluttered an eyelid and attempted to sit up, only to fall back on the petate with her back to Trini again. "I can't wake up."

Trini slapped the humped buttocks. Now Lupita sat up with a start, rubbing her eyes. "You're mean." The eyes closed again as she held out a hand. "Gimme . . ."

"Get your own clothes." Trini was drawing an hilpa over her head. Lupita waited, humped, eyes closed, hands grasping at empty air.

"Bueno, you baby." An hilpa landed on Lupita's face. With eyes still closed, Lupita drew it over her head.

Trini made her way to the kitchen door. She opened the door slightly to see if Tonio were in sight. Her nostrils caught the smell of dew-wet earth and grass. Light glistened on tiny raindrops riding the veins of giant leaves on a tree just outside the door. The world was sensitized in a clean half darkness. No Tonio in sight. He must be milking Chula; good! She made her way to the pump. Lupita was behind her. Barefoot, the two girls walked into the yard. Trini felt the coolness of the early morning breeze as she pumped water into Lupita's cupped hands. The little girl splashed her face and hair, water running down her neck and wetting her hilpa. She ran back into the house dripping wet as Trini put her head under the pump and let the water run cold against her skin and hair. Its shock chilled her for a second, then the water became a soothing, fresh touch. She ran back into the kitchen to find Lupita vigorously rubbing her face with a piece of bleached burlap. She handed it to Trini who rubbed her own face and hair, feeling the warm tingle of awakened blood.

She made a mental note of things. Put water on the stove for atole, heat the corn tortillas from the day before, and if there were leftover milk . . . a treat, pinole from Batopilas! Tonio had brought some the Monday after his paranda. Parandero! Trini felt resentment rising. Tonio and his weekends in town! Sabochi had never locked them up in the house for the weekends as Tonio did. Papá had gone to San Mateo to look for his sister. He would bring her back to take the place of their mother. Meanwhile, Tonio was in charge. Tonio in charge—he worked everybody to death! Then, on weekends, he was off with his drinking and his women. He doesn't really care about us, concluded Trini. If only Sabochi would come back, or El Enano, to play with them. There was only Tonio. That Tonio!

After putting wood in the stove and setting water to boil, she remembered that the cannisters had to be washed. They had to be ready by the time Tonio finished milking Chula.

"Come on, slow poke, help me."

"It's Buti's turn," complained Lupita.

"You just mind. Forget Buti."

"It's not my turn. Wake Buti."

Trini knew it was impossible to wake Buti. "You know that takes forever. You can have double pinole this morning if you help."

Lupita followed Trini to where the cannisters were kept. Rinsed the day before, they now had to be scrubbed shining clean. The girls rolled them to the pump and scrubbed them until they shone, glinting in the sun. They left the cannisters out to dry and ran back into the house. The water was boiling. The kitchen was sunny and quiet. Papá was looking for Tía Pancha. In San Mateo there was snow in early spring. José Mario had talked about it when he left in late winter, promising to come back in late spring. Trini had never seen snow, for the sun shone the whole year round in Batopilas. The change of seasons came in colors, in harvests, and in winds. No Sabochi, no Papá, no El Enano, only Tonio. But then, she thought in all fairness, he makes us laugh.

Sometimes, Tonio would let Buti ride across the valley on his buckboard. She stirred the atole, wondering if Tonio would remember his promise, to take them to the river today. He had been full of jokes, and songs, and teasings all week. Now as he poured the milk he sang:

"En tus ojos tiembla mi destino. Y mi suerte en labios tan divinos . . ."

His voice was clear and strong, and Trini knew why he was singing. The weekend was at hand. Every Saturday morning he would leave, racing his wagon and shouting to Sarif, "Yuyuyuyuyuyu—ho!" He would return the same way, late Sunday night, hollering and singing his way across the valley. Sarif liked his singing, Tonio claimed, and he would do anything to keep his horse happy. Every Monday morning, he would grin sheepishly at Trini, eyes twinkling on a handsome face and exclaim, "I'm back."

He was so silly. Probably feeling guilty for locking them up like that. Tonio came into the kitchen whistling the love song.

"Chinita, you kids ready to go?"

He hadn't forgotten! He had been a slave driver all week. Every afternoon they had cleaned lentils and beans to store. They had dried chile and sacked it in the shed.

"Buti!" Tonio's shout filled the kitchen.

"He's asleep."

"Not anymore, he's not." Tonio made his way into the next room and hustled Buti out of bed. They wrestled playfully on the petate. Buti's muffled laughter rang out, "Hey, Tonio, awwwww, cut it out!" Tonio came into the kitchen pushing Buti in front of him. Buti's tousled head looked up at Tonio with evident worship as he scratched his belly button, then rubbed his eyes.

"Go wash," Tonio ordered.

"I don't wanna."

"Go!"

Buti reluctantly made his way to the pump as Trini poured the hot, steaming atole in bowls and set the warm tortillas on the table. Tonio was full of plans. "We'll swim out to the grotto." The grotto was hidden behind cascading waters about two miles down the river, close to the grazing grounds. It was a favorite place of Sabochi's. Trini and Sabochi had swum out beyond the waterfall many times. Now Tonio was giving her orders to take food along, for he planned to stay until the sun went down. The children ate in silence, anticipating the coming excursion. After eating, Tonio went to saddle Sarif for deliveries while Trini and the little ones quickly tidied up the kitchen.

The rest of the morning hummed for Trini. The river! The sweep of river light, the murmurs, the silence, all were familiar, happy things to Trini. By noon, the day's heat quivered on the ground, and the sound of Tonio's wagon returning drew the children out into the yard. Trini stood watching from the doorway, catching the flash of Tonio's smile in the sun.

"Ready!" His shout resounded in the hills.

"Yes, yes, yes!" Buti and Lupita scampered into the buckboard. Tonio jumped off to help Trini into the seat beside him. Then he turned the buckboard around and coursed the path that led to the east hill.

"I can swim all the way out to the rocks!" boasted Buti, his eyes gleaming, his body squirming on the wagon floor. Lupita was leaning her head out on the side of the wagon as she shouted, "Hear the river! Hear the river!"

Yes, Trini could hear the singing currents. Halfway into the valley the rumble of the wagon melted into the distant roar of a waterfall. Her hand clutched the edge of the seat. Tonio was racing Sarif as usual, Buti and Lupita screaming their delight.

"What's the matter, chinita?" Tonio asked Trini. She felt his eyes on her. "You're so quiet."

"Do I have to shout like a child?" Her voice mustered a little dignity, but she felt the warmth of blood rushing to her face. He grinned, then let out a howl, "Yaaaaaaa!"

There he goes again, thought Trini, he's a coyote. The howl bounced from hill to hill. He was teasing again, so she calmly and deliberately raised her chin and looked out toward a valley that lay deep and wide in greens. They were on a road made by goat tracks, and the sound of water clung in the air. The edge of the river had broken the land; a quiet streamlet had pushed the land to reach the river again. Next came the hill washed clean by flows of water pouring from secret recesses and, beyond that, a small waterfall hiding the grotto.

Tonio stopped by the streamlet's edge; the children scrambled off the wagon, running off to play and splash in the water. Trini waited primly for Tonio to help her down. She gave him her hand, but he grabbed her by the waist and swung her around.

"Put me down, Tonio!"

"OK, OK . . ."

Her feet were on the ground again. Feeling somewhat embarrassed, she ran off to join the others at the water's edge where Buti and Lupita had already peeled off their clothes and were busy watching bees among the rose laurels that lined the water's edge.

"Don't go out too far," warned Trini. "The current's strong."

She sat down under a palo verde to watch. Tonio was behind her.

"Going in, chinita?"

"In a little bit . . ."

"I'll take them out," Tonio offered as he took off his shirt. He waded the long curve of the stream where it met the river, then motioned the children to follow him. She watched him dive into the deeper water then come up for air as the children made their way to him.

"Come on, Trini . . ." Tonio's voice was like an echo, teasing.

"I'll sit here for a while."

Her voice sounded tight. From that distance, she could not see Tonio's grin, but she knew that he was grinning and why. I hate him, she fumed. He knew that she was too shy to undress before him. Somehow she could no longer be as free and open as Buti and Lupita. Tonio did not press. He dove into the river water again, and the children followed. Soon they had disappeared around the curve of the hill. She would go into the water when she was good and ready. She would do it privately and alone. The aloneness was nice. She looked up at tree branches that swayed a message—No more, Sabochi; no more, Sabochi. Her throat closed, and she felt the coming tears. No, I'm not going to cry, she told herself.

She found a secluded spot among the laurels and took off the hilpa. Then she went into the water. The sun played its flame on slow ripples dimpled in light. Soft and gentle, the water carried Trini with the pull of the current. The flow of water from the hill filled her with excitement. The thought of a departed Sabochi left her, and she became part of rushing rhythms that wildly filled the splendid, shadowy silence. Far off she heard Tonio and the children laughing and shouting. They had probably reached the grotto, and soon they would start back. She floated in the silence and gave up the thought of joining the others. . . .

That evening after supper, when Buti and Lupita had been put to bed, Trini sat on the porch steps and listened to Tonio sing his love song as he looked up at the stars through the shadows of treetops: "En tus ojos tiembla mi destino, y mi suerte en labios tan divinos . . ." Tomorrow he would leave for his usual weekend to Batopilas.

"You're going to lock us up again?"

"For your safety. You have a big yard to play in."

"You're mean; Sabochi would never lock us up."

"What would he do?"

"Stay with us."

"You don't want me around."

"Not if you make us work, but we could go to Sabochi's cave."

"That's not a good time; I need girls, music, beer!"

"You're a terrible person!"

"You think so?"

Silence, then the song again. She questioned, "You mean that?"

"From the heart."

"Your destiny trembles in a woman's eyes?"

"Why not?"

"I'm not going to talk to you any more, Tonio."

"Look at the stars, chinita! Don't be so serious." He began to sing again, "My fortune is a lady's lips . . ."

Why didn't he stop! She felt lonely for José Mario and the silences they had shared together. Papá, Papá—soon, soon, he would return. She called out "good night" to Tonio and went into the house wondering if Tonio ever made sense. As she undressed for bed, she remembered Sabochi with the gentle eyes. These feelings she had for her old friend were new, almost frightening. Her thoughts returned to Tonio and his wild insanity.

* * *

"He doesn't come any more, Trini."

Buti was sad, looking up at a bare fig tree. They had been locked up in the yard again, and Tonio had taken off for the weekend. Inwardly Trini sensed the reason for El Enano's disappearance. They were growing up, and life was no longer a mere design of colors and dreams like the rainbow rocks. The dreams of waiting for Sabochi, of the coming of Sabochi, the dreaming of Sabochi were anticipations that filled her life. She had little hope that El Enano would return. Tonio had brought a brusqueness with him, a tie to small realities that filled the day. Sabochi was far away. El Enano? Where was he?

All she could say was, "We're growing up."

But Buti still stared at the rainbow rocks, waiting. Trini realized that she, too, was waiting.

"Maybe if we all close our eyes and wish real hard," Lupita suggested, screwing up her eyes. Why not? thought Trini. Sometimes wishing hard enough . . . She closed her eyes and wished for the coming of El Enano. There was only silence and a locked gate, and the feeling of something lost. The rainbow rocks gleamed, but their little friend failed to materialize. Buti came up with an answer to cut the sadness in the air. "He's living up in Sabochi's cave. He's so busy eating up all my cacahuates and piñones, he doesn't want to come any more."

"He's not a pig like you," Lupita accused. Buti pulled her by the ankle, and she fell off the rock where she was sitting.

"Stop that, you two." Trini scolded, then offered, "We can watch for Papá."

"Papá, Papá, Papá," screamed the children. Then they scurried off to look for Buti's turtle. Trini gazed at horizons, a world moving without feeling, without thought except the murmur of life sounds. She looked up in the direction of Sabochi's cave on the south hill. It all came back so clearly, so hungrily, the last time he had returned. . . .

It had been after the finding of Mamá's bultito. She remembered Sabochi waving at them from his cave, standing tall, the wind blowing his long hair. She had run to the end of the yard fence and waved frantically back. Buti and Lupita had danced about with glee. Sabochi had come back! That had been the last time before the death of his father, before he had had to leave the valley for good. Trini ached to see Sabochi before his cave again. There was no one. She closed her eyes and reenvisioned that last time, that last time still joyous to her senses. He had come back from the great river, and, from his cave, he had made his way down into the valley. Lupita had pointed toward the turn on the hill, where Sabochi was coming down the path; then his figure disappeared behind the turn to reappear on the floor of the valley. The children waited at the fence. Now the figure was following the path leading to the house. Sabochi's tall figure walked in irrevocable sureness, the brown of his body gleaming with a splendor. His muscular movements of descent into the valley danced on his lithe body covered only by a tilma. All along the valley the shouts of the children echoed, "Sabochi! Sabochi!" He began a slow run that gained speed as he came nearer, a rope around one shoulder. Once he had reached the fence, the noose of the rope was thrown around the pole close to the fig tree, then laden with fruit.

"Keeee—keeeee, Sabochi," Buti chanted. "Keeeee!"

"Keeee—keeeee, Buti!" the answer came from behind the tree.

Trini and the children watched him climb over the fence with a dancer's grace, stepping on the high tree trunk and then swinging himself down to a lower limb. A drop to the ground and Sabochi sat down under the fig tree.

"It's hot today, eh, pollos?"

They had fallen on him in joyous welcome. Buti rolled on the grass with Sabochi until the Indian sat the boy on his chest.

"Ah, you are big, Buti."

Lupita clasped her arms around Sabochi's neck and would not let go. He rubbed his chin against her hair from side to side. Both children claimed him in happy laughter.

"That's enough, Buti, Lupita." Trini's happiness rang in her voice as she sat next to them. Sabochi sat up, reaching for her hand, then he drew her to him until her head was on his chest.

"Ay, pollitos, I have missed you."

They were all silent, melting into a oneness like the sound of a leaf sea. After a while Sabochi assumed a serious tone to ask them, "Have you gone to the river to bathe?" He lay back on the grass and looked from one face to another. "Your faces are dirty."

"We wash every morning," protested Trini.

"Tomorrow we go to the river."

Trini could see that Sabochi was hot and tired. "I'll get you some tea." She ran into the kitchen for a bule, soon flying out with it in her hand, headed for the pump where she kept mint tea in a jarro wrapped in wet hilachas to keep it cool. Tea spilled from the bule as Trini hurried back with a full bowl which she handed to Sabochi.

"Dios te bendiga, chinita."

"Amen."

He drank the tea quickly and eagerly, a few drops trickling from the side of his mouth, falling on his broad chest. When he finished, he lay back on the grass again and closed his eyes. "You were expecting me?"

Trini sat down beside him and in a breathless voice assured, "For days and days and days. The first thing, the first thing, every morning I—I look to your cave . . ."

"It's good to be home."

It was good to have him there, to have him close his eyes and lie still, aware of their presence. She had so much to tell him, but she wanted the restful silence by his side. She reached for his hand and opened up his fingers one by one. His eyes were still closed. Even the children were quietly looking on. She had to share the good things.

"We have a new friend." There was a soft excitement in Trini's voice. The heads of the children went up and down vigorously.

"A visitor?" Sabochi opened one eye.

"Un enano, un enano," the children informed him excitedly.

"He just appeared from the rainbow rocks like magic."

Sabochi sat up with interest and looked toward the rainbow rocks. "He comes often?"

Trini nodded. "When we are lonely, and that is often, he comes to play in the afternoon. He can't speak. He found Mamá's bultito."

A glimmer of light came into Sabochi's face. He shaped the word with his lips, "Matilda." The feeling fell gently among them, and Trini understood the rush of light in Sabochi's face, for Matilda had meant much to the young Indian. Trini wanted the reasons for his feelings. She recalled, "She was special to you."

"Very special." Sabochi had caught the distance of the light and was looking back to a time with Matilda. The story was in his eyes. Trini did not disturb his memories. Matilda had found a very young Sabochi half-dead from a fall and had nursed him back to health. He had been suspicious of mestizos at first. Indians had little faith in white men and less in those Indians who had mixed with the white men. Sabochi's real name was Ambrosio, but when he had referred to José Mario's family as chaboches, the Indian name for mestizos, Matilda had fondly renamed him "Sabochi." The name Sabochi stuck, and so did his closeness to the family. For a moment Trini felt uneasy. Sabochi coming alive at the mere mention of her mamá's name. Was that love? She disturbed his memories.

"You loved her."

"Always. I became Sabochi because of her. I am part of you because of her. I have tried to be your 'mother' because of her . . ."

Trini could see that he was treading on memories again. She breathed deeply through half-opened lips. Her thoughts were about

Matilda too. I miss you so. I miss you so. But you're with me, aren't you? Like earth and sun, never to be lost. Sabochi had not seen Mamá's bultito. "You want to see the bultito?"

Words came out softly, floods of memory in his eyes, "Matilda's bultito!" He looked off toward the house as if expecting Matilda to appear at any moment. Trini ran into the house and brought out the bultito, placing it in his hands with great care. He opened the little blue bundle, laying out the cloth gently on his lap and picking up and touching each metal piece. Matilda was very real, far beyond my realness, thought Trini, far beyond his own realness. Such were the histories of the heart. Sabochi broke the spell. He tied up the bundle slowly and handed it back to Trini, then jumped up and looked at the laden fig tree, exclaiming solemnly, "Mmmmmmm—figs! Get the ladder, Buti."

"Me too, me too, me too!" Lupita was jumping up and down.

"You too," agreed Sabochi, laughing.

Buti ran around the side of the house with Lupita following at his heels. Trini went to the kitchen for a bowl. In the quiet of the kitchen, she paused to sort out her feelings. In her hand was the bultito. It was hers now. José Mario had given it to her. Sabochi loved Matilda. Feelings mixed and pulled in opposite directions, love, envy, loss, all one in her special loneliness. From the kitchen, through the window, she watched Sabochi take the ladder from Buti and Lupita, out of breath from lugging it across the yard. By the time Trini came out with a tazón for the figs, Sabochi was high and hidden among the branches pregnant with the sweetness of the earth. The figs were falling rapidly to the ground. Buti was eating them as fast as he gathered them.

"He's eating them all," complained Lupita.

"Stop now," scolded Trini. "You have to wash them first."

"In here." Trini had placed the tazón in front of him. Buti didn't argue. He obediently started to put them in the tazón. After a while Sabochi's voice fell from among the leaves. "¡Basta!"

They all agreed; they had more than enough.

Enough—enough. Memories were not enough. Trini felt the old restlessness rising. She didn't want to wait for El Enano anymore. She didn't want to be locked up in the yard for the whole of a weekend. She needed someone other than her brother and sister. She watched the children lying on their stomach watching the turtle snugly hidden in his shell. She looked out towards Sabochi's cave—empty, empty, empty. She slid down from the rocks and went into the house. The front room was shaded and cool. From the cupboard she took out the bultito and opened it. Little silver happenings, evoking mysteries! Mamá's gone. Sabochi's gone. Memories of spun silver, leaf sea, figs, and the magic of Sabochi. So long ago! Or was it that time stretched out in her impatience?

She picked up a piece of a mirror and looked at her reflection, eyes somber, a trace of womanliness in the shape of mouth. Still a child's face, a face wanting so many things unhad.

4

Goodbye, Wild Wind

Tía Pancha, austere virgin of thirty-three, stared down at the children. They knelt before her, looking straight up her nose.

"Buquis, inquesen! Pídanle a Dios gracias, y pidan que les ilumine el pensamiento."

Mouthing words, one on top of the other, the children did as they were told. They thanked God, asking Him to illuminate their thoughts. Buti fell on his haunches, then straightened up only to fall again. Trini's knees felt tender, not being used to kneeling for so long, while Lupita gave up altogether. She sat cross-legged on the floor looking dejected.

"Up, child, up!"

Lupita struggled to her knees, wobbled, then went back on her haunches like Buti. Tía Pancha looked at them disapprovingly, sighing in resignation. I wish I understood the God Tía Pancha brought with her from San Mateo, thought Trini. She had never seen such passion for a God before. Her aunt stood fervently before them, strangely gaunt and tall, attempting to awaken the clay of spirit and body. She began the rosary prayers:

"Holy Mary, mother of God, blessed be thou among women and blessed be the fruit of thy womb, Jesus . . ."

So many Hail Marys and Our Fathers in one rosary! The long string of beads had to make one complete circle back to the crucifix. All eyes were on the crucifix, the stop sign, the sign for them to groan themselves out of their kneeling positions. Evening prayers were twice as long as morning prayers, the sharp timbre of Tía Pancha's voice arousing new feelings.

Her words on human worthlessness were a new experience for the children. I'm a sinner, Trini pondered, tainted and weak, like Tía Pancha says. I must learn to be meek and humble and to ask forgiveness every day. All things, Tía Pancha told her, were the result of Divine Will, and if they were not sorry for their sins God would plunge them into Hell. Trini watched Buti's eyes open wide with the frenzy of Tía Pancha's sermons. I should be like Lupita, Trini thought, overwhelmed by all the praying and kneeling and the beating of the chest. Lupita's face told her that Tía Pancha was simply tuned out. So many "thou shalt nots!"

They were two Our Fathers and one Hail Mary away from the stop sign when José Mario walked in from the kitchen glancing casually at the proceedings. Buti shifted the weight of his body to his other knee as Tía Pancha pointed a long, accusing finger at her brother:

"José Mario, kneel and pray! Be an example to your children."

José Mario turned a deaf ear and walked out into the evening air.

"Pagan!" shouted Tía Pancha after him as Trini secretly wished they could be as brave as Papá. In answer to his defiance, Tía Pancha went into a flurry of ruegos to beseech forgiveness for her sinful brother. The children watched her antics with great fascination. Tía Pancha's flair for the dramatic was unsurpassed where religion was concerned.

Trini remembered Tía Pancha's other passion, cleanliness. Right next to Godliness! Demanding the same frenzy! Aside from all this, Tía Pancha was a loving, kind woman who showed it in many ways. Trini and the children waited for Tía Pancha to finish the last prayer. When the crucifix touched her forefinger, they scrambled, getting off their knees and climbing over one another. Then they stood obediently before Tía Pancha, waiting for her command:

"Come!"

They followed her into the kitchen where she gave each little Christian a piece of dulce de leche. She kept the candy in a huge glass jar. They had watched her make it, mixing pochote milk with Chula's milk, adding nuts and raisins, beating the mixture until it peaked. It was the best thing about praying, the dulce de leche. Tía Pancha patted each one on the head, handed out the candy, and reaffirmed the faith.

"There you are, my little savages."

We are savages, thought Trini.

Tía Pancha had stormed into their lives ten months before, well supplied with her plaster saints, religious calendars, crucifixes, scapularies, missals, clothespins, a scrub board, and a huge tina. Never had they seen such a tub.

"In it," Tía Pancha explained, "we wash and we bathe."

"Bathe?" asked Buti, unbelieving.

"Every night."

"Every night!" shrieked Buti in falsetto.

Tía Pancha pointed to a mountain of dirty clothes piled in a corner of the room. "When do you wash?"

"When Papá or Tonio takes us to the river."

"River! I suppose you spread the clothes out to dry on the rocks?" Tía Pancha glared at them suspiciously. They nodded. Tía Pancha took out her scrub board, sighing in relief. "Well, never again. We wash like civilized people, and your pagan father can string up a clothesline for us."

It was a marvel to see. Clothes hanging on a line, the wind blowing them every which way. It was their favorite thing to do, hanging out the wash. While they hung out the wash, Buti and Lupita would shout, "Oh my God, I am heartily sorry for having offended thee. . . ." They had been ordered to learn their act of contrition. Afterwards, they watched the clothes blowing in the wind.

There was the making of bread. The children had never seen or tasted white bread, only tortillas. Now Tía Pancha would knead dough and put it in long square pans, covering it to rise overnight. Trini and the children would scramble out of bed in the morning to see the miracle of risen loaves. They would help Tía Pancha bake, drinking in the smells.

Anticipation of their first communion made the days exciting. Tía Pancha had found a church in Batopilas. Attending Mass was a hardship since the valley of Bachotigori was not within easy walking distance of Batopilas, certainly for early Mass each Sunday. Tía Pancha apologized to the priest for the unchristian behavior of her brother and promised to instruct the children at home in hopes of preparing them for their first communion. In the next breath, she reprimanded the priest for not building a church in the valley of Bachotigori, claiming the Indians needed Christianizing the most. When Tía Pancha returned home she was beside herself. "Descalzos! Pagans! Where is God in this valley?"

"All over the hills," Trini told her.

"What?"

"The Indians have little gods in secret places. They take flowers and wine and sing to the little gods." Trini was defensive in her praise of Indian ways. But Tía Pancha loved to be scandalized, "Their gods drink?"

"They like it." Trini explained.

"Oh, my little ones, I came just in time!"

And she did too, thought Trini. She remembered the expression on Tía Pancha's face the day she arrived, one of utter dismay. All had been disarray. Now there were baths, a clothesline, and salvation. Funny, thought Trini, they all feel good. She was as excited as the children about making her first communion. "Dos clases de gracia, actual y sacramental . . ." Trini would recite as she washed dishes. Sometimes she would sit around with Buti and Lupita to count sins, for they needed sins for a successful holy communion.

In a moment of confidence, Buti told their aunt about El Enano. Buti assured her, "El Enano is living in Sabochi's cave. He's eating all my cacahuates."

Tía Pancha pursed her lips, her tongue clicking disapproval. "You play with a dwarf?"

"He's our friend." Trini felt a pang of loneliness for the little man who never came anymore.

"They bring disease, bad luck!" Tía Pancha warned with a shake of the head.

"He's wonderful. He's like . . . like dreams," defended Trini.

"What do you know, child?"

What do I know? wondered Trini. It seemed as if many things that mattered were being erased from her life, forbidden by her aunt's beliefs. Even Sabochi. Tía Pancha decided that Sabochi was responsible for their wild ways. They were forbidden to visit the cave anymore. She also disapproved of Tonio, especially when he came home drunk after his weekend spree. Tonio, who was José Mario's best helper at the mines, ignored the aunt. Now that Tía Pancha was there to take care of them, he stayed in Batopilas for longer periods. He claimed that Tía Pancha's saints had taken over the house and they were giving him the evil eye.

"Don't say that, Tonio," admonished Buti. "It's a sin."

Tonio winked, "What isn't?" But Tonio came less and less to the house, and when he did, he avoided Tía Pancha. Sometimes the children would long for the old way of life. They would sit on the rainbow rocks and hope for El Enano's return. They watched the wild wind carrying leaves across the valley, scattering seed, bending trees. I am the valley, Trini decided, more than a Christian.

* * *

"I have been offered a job in San Domingo, to work in the mines there."

The news came brusquely from José Mario one February day. He came home earlier than usual and gathered the family around the table. With head lowered eyes grave, and words that came slow and uncertain, he told them that the mines in Batopilas were to be closed. The pits were submerged in water and the mines were no longer safe.

"Leave the valley?" Trini's hands shaped a gesture of surprise. The valley was part of her being. The seasons were inside her, the winds, the warm moistures. If they left the valley, what would they become?

"Where is San Domingo?" Tía Pancha asked.

"Past the mountain of Japón, through barranca country," José Mario told them. Tía Pancha was apprehensive. "Barranca country! So many white people never come out alive from the barranca, José Mario! You want your children killed?"

"Many white people have crossed the barranca." José Mario spoke calmly.

"Many have not and you know it!" insisted Tía Pancha, then she demanded, "Why don't you farm the land? Can't we live off the land?"

"It's not ours, woman. Whatever grows in this valley is claimed by all the people; it is not enough." His eyes found light with a wish. "If only we had stock . . ." In silence, everybody wished with him. After a while, he said resignedly, "We have to leave."

His decision was punctuated by a dry, hacking cough. It bent him over as Trini held his shoulder to stop the spasms. "Papá?" Trini saw her father's face, wet with perspiration, heavy, like his body, with decision. He seemed so worn, so lost.

Now, a long dangerous trip to San Domingo.

Tía Pancha was adamantly opposed to José Mario's decision to take Tonio along on the trip.

"We need his wagon and his horses, so hush up." José Mario never listened to Tía Pancha anyway, so Tía Pancha resigned herself to the inevitable. Chula and all the possessions that could not be taken on the trip were sold. The buckboard and pack horses were loaded with clothing, blankets, cooking utensils, and food for the journey, sacks of chile, cacahuates, piñones, cheese, and dried meat. Tía Pancha's huge tub sat on the wagon, holding the food and all her saints. José Mario carefully stored bags of seeds under the buckboard seat. Someday, he told Trini, they would own land and plant the seeds; she was one with her father. The seeds were something in the blood, the love of the earth, the ways of the valley.

"The sun will be up any time now. That borracho better get here or we'll travel in the heat," Tía Pancha lamented, as she secured the tub with a rope.

All had been done, and the children sat on the rocks waiting for Tonio to appear around the east hill. Trini was scanning the familiar hills. "Goodbye, wild wind," she whispered, watching a mass of clouds sail swiftly across the sky. She remembered the same sky full of mists, storm, wind. How many times had the sky matched the many colors of the rainbow rocks? There was a catch in her throat. "Goodbye, wild wind." She would take the valley with her. She would take the seeds and her father's dream.

Trini saw Lupita sobbing in Tía Pancha's arms. "We won't have our first communion." Tía Pancha was stroking the little girl's hair, comforting her. "What's the matter with you? There are churches in San Domingo. God is everywhere." Yes, Trini believed that, anywhere where there was sky and hills and wind gathering leaves. Buti was pointing, "There's Tonio!"

He came around the turn of the east hill, riding Sarif, waving at the children wildly. "He's here, he's here," shouted Buti as they scrambled down from the rocks and waved back.

Shortly after, Sarif was harnessed to the wagon. Tía Pancha frowned and shook her head as she watched Tonio stack liquor bottles on the floor of the wagon. "He's going to drink us into trouble."

Tonio made a grab for her waist. She stood her ground and pushed him away. "You're drunk already."

"Not a drop, Pancha, not a drop."

"You're going to drink all that?" asked Buti admiringly. Tonio grinned and tousled Buti's hair. "I'll need them, kid, before this trip is over." Buti was looking at Tonio with avid curiosity. "Did God make you out of clay like us, Tonio?"

"Sure."

"With more than a touch of the Devil," added Tía Pancha under her breath.

José Mario was closing the gate for the last time. He stood looking at the house he had built for Matilda; then he walked slowly toward them, shoulders hunched, steps reluctant. José Mario led them out of the valley. Trini and the children rode on the back of the wagon, while Tonio and Tía Pancha sat on the seat. José Mario did not turn back to look at the house once he had taken the reins and headed east. I know how he feels—Trini could feel his pain, a lifetime of memories being left behind. As they started across the valley, the house grew smaller and smaller. The hills were orange with the face of the sun. "Goodbye, wild wind, goodbye, wild wind . . ." became the rhythm of the wagon wheels, the rhythm of Trini's heart.

When they came to the edge of the valley, José Mario told them, "From El Camino to Quirare, then we take the highways to Creel before we reach Nedia country." Nedia country was the beginning of Tarahumara land.

Green hills rose and sank as the wagon rounded the hill that led to El Camino Real. The valley of Bachotigori, leading to cemetery hill, moss overgrown on headstones. Borders of grape hyacinths spread out along the wide edge of the road. From cemetery hill, Trini looked down at the town of Batopilas some miles to the east. A slight haze mixed with the brightness of the sun blotted out farmhouses, stores, the church, all familiar shapes. I want to stay, I want to stay, Trini told herself. She looked at the other side of the hill and there lay the valley of Bachotigori, with Matilda's house standing empty. The wagon came to a standstill. José Mario was making his way to Matilda's grave at the foot of the hill overlooking Sabochi's cave. I never noticed, Trini thought, but Mamá's grave is the only one that far down the slope. All alone. Mamá buried between the hill of the dead and the living valley. Papá was by her grave, pulling out weeds, touching the ground as if to touch Matilda herself. The graves never needed flowers, for the hills were bursting full of different blossoms, different kinds for different seasons. Now it was the time of the grape hyacinths. Papá looked across the valley to the house one last time. There was hurt in Trini's throat. He was so alone without Mamá. But he never gave up. Duty, love, courage, all mixed together. The children ran to the grave to sit by Papá. Trini also went to him, quietly sitting down beside him, placing her head on his shoulder, whispering, "She goes with us, Papá." After a while, José Mario shaped a question, soft like the wind. "Matilda?"

They all walked back in silence to the wagon. Then the sound of grinding wheels on gravel rounded cemetery hill and the valley disappeared before them. El Camino Real stretched out before them.

A day's travel on the highway took them from green fertile hills to brush hills jutted with red stone, and the brightness of the sun faded gradually, colors breathing in and out until the dusk invaded as they neared Quirare. There they camped on open ground, built a fire, ate, then fell into a tired sleep.

* * *

Seventeen kilómetros from Quirare they came upon the mountain road. It climbed perpendicularly. It still smelled of night as morning seeped in at its leisure. By late morning, they were halfway up the barranca where the road ran very close to the top of high cliffs. The copper canyon. The feeling of peril was thick as the wagon made its way alongside abrupt chasms that looked down thousands of feet. Trini looked over to see the joining of two great rivers.

"Look, Papá!"

José Mario held back the reins. "The Basiquari and the Urique." She looked down at the long windings of rivers. Along the sides of the mountain were written tales of time, waves and currents of centuries captured in rock. Where the strain of rock had been of silver light in Batopilas, now the reflection of the light against the rock was one of multiple colors.

"The rainbow lives here too. Look! Look!" Buti was shouting in surprise. An enormous giant of a rainbow, Trini decided. From a distance she saw, between cliffs, convoluted passages leading up to nature-made turrets; again, time spilled into stone. Then there were the rising mists filling an endless darkness. She melted in the bigness of things. Up, up, the mountain; then, at the next turn, there appeared an immense stone arch of reddish hue wavering on one side of the hill.

"It's falling," Buti hollered.

"It's been like that for centuries." Tonio informed them.

"What's centuries?"

"More years than you can count, kid."

Inside the arch, tall green pine rose, perforated by white light. Such bigness! Such beauty—all the work of God. Trini glanced at Tía Pancha to see if her aunt felt Him too. Yes, it was in her eyes. Then a sudden ridge appeared where foilage was dark green and thick and a field of nardos found its way into a cleft in the hill. Trini looked up, seeing something she had never seen before, white mountains. Buti and Lupita stared in amazement.

"Snow," Tía Pancha spoke in a knowing voice.

They reached the top, a narrow road where the pine forest thickened. Then the descent, and far below Trini saw an Indian village scarred by a silver creek. "Is that where we're stopping?"

José Mario shook his head. "No, we go to the next mountain, up to the village of Umira, then from there, forty-five kilómetros to Creel."

"We'll get there by noon tomorrow," Tonio estimated.

They rested in a paraje where a spring suddenly appeared at the side of the mountain. It was much cooler than in the valley now, so Trini and Tía Pancha unfolded blankets and Tonio built a fire from pine branches. The smell of the smoke was delicious. Food tasted so good; after supper, Trini wrapped herself in a blanket and looked up at a cool blue sky.

"I'm sleepy," murmured Buti from under a blanket.

"Is the barranca this beautiful?" Trini asked Tonio, who was sitting by the fire next to her.

"The green will disappear. Most of it is desert."

Trini tightened the blanket around her and thought about Sabochi's village. She looked toward José Mario, who sat against a tree smoking in the darkness. "Papá . . ."

"Yes . . ."

"Sabochi's village . . . We'll go there, won't we?" She was full of the old dreams. José Mario was silent for a moment, his eyes glinting, his words coming hesitantly, "It's out there. I've never been."

"Sometimes the Indian villages are lost so deep in the barranca that no white man has ever been there." Tonio told them.

"Cusihuiriachi is not one of those!" Trini protested with desperation. "Please, Papá, we have to find it."

"Yes," promised José Mario, "people can tell us. The Indians will know."

"God protect us!" Tía Pancha's dismay hung in the night air as she took out her rosary and flung her prayers into the dark.

5

The Goat

During the days that followed, the mountain became less steep and the vegetation less dense. From Umira, they headed toward the lowlands, passing pueblos of mixed population. The first pueblos were inhabited mostly by mestizos, but as they made their way into barranca country the mestizos became scarce. The numbers of Indians grew in comparison as they headed east of the main settlements. These were not primitive Indian villages. They were settlements with fountains in the middle of the plazas, Catholic churches, and stores. The mestizos had won out; in the last settlement before Indian country, José Mario stopped to buy supplies and ask for directions. Trini saw ancianos going into a church and children playing around the fountain. Buti pointed at a lazy cat sleeping on a muro as José Mario asked the storekeeper, "Can we buy supplies from the Indians?"

The storekeeper shrugged. "Depends. Sometimes they sell, sometimes they kill, sometimes they give away. Who understands descalzos!"

Tonio had been sipping away at his sotol. Tía Pancha made a point of it, "He's going to drive us off a cliff."

"You're a cruel woman," Tonio lamented. "Here, have a drink. It'll make you kind."

"You're shameless!"

"Sure." Tonio sniffed the air and avoided Tía Pancha's accusing eyes. A nervous journey for Tía Pancha, for the fear of Indian country and Tonio's drinking gave her little hope of coming through the journey alive. This had driven her to constant prayer. She made the children kneel and pray with her whenever they camped. During these times José Mario and Tonio would disappear in a hurry, leaving the children at the mercy of Tía Pancha. Hands tightly clasped, head lowered, she would beseech, "Keep us in your care. Save us from the savages, dear Mary . . ."

"Look, Tía," Trini pointed at a sunset during one of the praying sessions.

"Hush up and pray," ordered her aunt, still very much in the midst of her fears.

Outside of Carichic, the travelers sat around a campfire cooking atole for an early supper. A few miles back, they had picked apples from wild trees, and the children were slicing them for supper.

"I wish I had a rifle," Tonio exclaimed.

José Mario shook his head. "The Indians must not see us with weapons."

"We could kill some game."

The sun had not yet set as they rested and ate their corn atole and apples. It was cool in the paraje covered with mulberry trees. Next to their camp was a muddy stream where the children waded. Tía Pancha washed her hair with clear cannister water, for at every mountain stream the cannisters were refilled. Tía Pancha was drying her long hair in the sun. Then she began to plait it with quicksilver fingers. Tonio watched her with a smile on his face. "You're a good looking woman, Pancha."

"Be quiet, borracho."

"It's the truth, mujer."

Tía Pancha took to braiding her hair more quickly than ever. Trini wished that Tonio wouldn't tease like that. Suddenly, from the hill, hundreds of birds burst forth, soaring and shining in the face of the setting sun. In a cluster they circled happily, then disappeared behind a bluff as swiftly as they had appeared.

"If only I had a rifle," Tonio wished again.

Tía Pancha stopped braiding her hair to watch the birds. When they disappeared, there were tears in her eyes. "So sudden, all that beauty, so sudden. Now, it's gone."

"If I had a rifle, we'd have some for supper," Tonio repeated.

Tía Pancha crying like that! It stayed with Trini. Tía Pancha, not so apprehensive, not so much with her saints, but with beauty. Matilda would have cried too, Trini thought.

"If I'm not mistaken, if we go north, we'll come to Cusihuiriachi." José Mario was scanning the horizon.

Trini's heart skipped. "Are you sure?"

"If we keep east of Carichic."

Cusihuiriachi! It was a deep note, orange-mellow like the sun.

Tonio was looking at her curiously. Trini knew he sensed her happiness. He smiled, "Sabochi, eh?"

She nodded, warm in her feelings. He teased, "What does a chavala like you know about love?"

José Mario noticed the dwindling food, and the thought of Indians who hated mestizos made him uneasy. "I hope it's Cusihuiriachi. We could use Sabochi to guide us out of the barranca."

The grass-covered crags on the high ground led into a valley, Trini watched a herd of goats grazing. They must belong to someone—who? she wondered. The road had become very narrow, gradually being consumed by a tangled, growing ravine. It was the beginning of a sea of arbustos polvorosos, for the lush fertility of the high mountains was fast disappearing along the river. The caravan, too, was following the river. The settlement or pueblo would be found close to the river, hugging a life force as the sun beat unmercifully on land red and powder-dry.

There were no longer any commissaries, stores, or tienditas owned by mestizos. This was the land of the descalzos, and the caravan had been in the deep barranca for five days. Still no Indian village, only a river that at times narrowed to dry patches surrounded by mud and more arbustos polvorosos, a defeated river giving in to sun and dust.

The journey had taken its toll on the travelers too. The beating sun, silences. The rhythm of the wagon was painful to bodies now numb and cramped, numb to the jolts that shocked the tense stillness of their limbs. The only food left was a sack of corn, half-full. No more water from the river. And before them, as far as the eye could see, the endless red desert. Trini had never imagined Cusihuiriachi as a barren land. So Sabochi had given up the valley for this!

"We'll see life soon," José Mario hoped aloud. "We have to buy food."

"Cusihuiriachi?" That was the only word on Trini's lips.

"I hope it is." José Mario's voice was strained, worried.

That afternoon, in the shadows of the setting sun, they rested in a paraje. They saw a man coming toward them, an old raramuri riding a mule leading two other pack mules. José Mario went to meet the rider.

"Ave María . . ."

"Sin pecado original . . ."

The greeting involving the Virgin Mary was a customary one among Christianized Indians. José Mario breathed a sigh of relief.

Christianized Indians seldom had quarrels with mestizos. Perhaps he came from a village that would sell them food and guide them to Cusihuiriachi. Perhaps he was from Cusihuiriachi. The old raramuri looked at them with suspicion.

"You are chaboches?"

"We're travelers seeking to buy food," replied José Mario.

"You are brave, traveling through descalzo country."

The raramuri scrutinized each face, slowing turning from one to the other. His eyes lingered on the children. He finally seemed satisfied.

"I will rest with you."

With this he took out a pouch full of an aromatic powder; from another pouch he took dry pieces of corn leaves. He filled the leaves with the sweet-smelling powder, handing one to José Mario, another one to Tonio. Then he poured some powder on a leaf for himself, rolling it tightly, screwing the tips, placing it on his lips, and while it hung there he took two pieces of flint from inside the sarape around his waist, rubbed them vigorously until they sparked, then tightened his lips on the cigarette before he lit it. They smoked in silence.

Tía Pancha held the children back from the man, knowing the ways of Indians. She took some peanut oil and cleaned Lupita's and Buti's faces. Trini cleaned her face too, the taste of dust disappearing. She was hungry and thirsty. Soon Tía Pancha would cook some corn in muddy water. As the men talked, the aunt, Buti, and Lupita gathered brush and branches to start a fire. Trini listened to the conversation as she helped make the food.

"Is your village nearby, holy man?" José Mario asked. The old man was a raramuri—indicated by the three deep diagonal scars on his chest, signs of a mystical trial of indoctrination into a holy order among certain Tarahumara.

"I come from the north. I go to Tumuac to sell my loads."

"What are you selling, holy man?"

"Lentejas and calabazas."

Lentils and squash! Trini felt a sudden hunger.

"Will you sell us some?" José Mario ventured.

"What's mine is yours. No money."

With this the old man rose and went to the packs, heavy on the mule's back, and untied a sack. Tía Pancha handed large canoas to the children who ran to have them filled. The raramuri filled each one with large yellow squash and a rain of green-brown lentils. What a feast!

"We are beholden to you, holy man."

"My pleasure."

After supper, the raramuri took out a bottle of chicha. Beer! The men passed the bottle among themselves until it was empty. Trini wished she could taste something besides the muddy water, but it was not offered to the women or children.

The old man went to the cabaldura and took another bottle. They drank and smoked as early evening cooled the paraje almost to a chill. Tía Pancha unfolded blankets. The cooking fire had dwindled to a dying ember ash; the men were still deep in conversation:

"Who does not hate the white man?" the raramuri asked.

"The white man, too, is afraid of the Tarahumara."

"You are chaboche. You are part white."

"We are part Indian too," José Mario countered. The raramuri laughed, "Habla derecho y seremos amigos." True, the Indians did not enjoy or accept flattery or lies. Friendship was based on honesty. The old man continued, "I have lived for a hundred years and have seen the milk of our women full of bile and the pestilence of the white man passed on to our children. The white man steals everything, land, women, honor, and they tell vile lies. They think words cleanse them of deeds. No hablan derechos."

"The Tarahumara have killed many a white man," José Mario countered again.

"We only kill to keep what is ours. We do not deceive. White men are the plague."

Tía Pancha was praying silently on her rosary. Trini wondered how men could hate each other so. The raramuri was speaking again:

"It is the gobierno now." There was futility in his voice. "In the name of a white man's government, they try to destroy what we have had for a thousand years."

Tonio jumped up. "A song, holy man. Shall we sing for you, holy man?"

The old raramuri looked at Tonio and slowly a smile came to his face. Tonio beckoned the children. The raramuri nodded pleasantly as the children gathered around Tonio.

"What shall we sing?" Buti asked, ready and eager.

Tonio glanced at the raramuri, asking, "You have a favorite?"

The old man became pensive, then a smile. "Do you know the marriage of the fleas?"

"El piojo y la pulga!" Tonio grinned. "Isn't it good that the Indian and the mestizo have the same song?"

The old man nodded. Singing voices rose in the dark shadowed by the cast of a half-moon:

"El piojo y la pulga
Se van a casar
Les pregunta el cura
Si saben rezar . . .
Todito sabemos
Y nada sin falta
Contesta el ratón de su ratonal . . .
Que haga la boda
Yo pondré el maíz . . ."

Somehow the little song about two fleas who must pray if they are to be married, about an old benevolent mouse's offering of corn for the wedding feast, all nonsense, melted old rancors and angers. The old man clapped his hands to the rhythm of the music. Again, thought Trini, Tonio's joyous insanity has won out. She felt an admiration for her teasing friend.

The raramuri shared their fire, their songs, and their bed that night. The next morning, they broke camp and the raramuri took his leave. José Mario asked him before he left, "Do you know the village of Cusihuiriachi?"

The raramuri shook his head. "I have heard of it, but I have never gone east. That is where you're going?"

"Yes, holy man. Thank you for your kindness and your friendship."

"I am richer by it. Ave María."

"Amen."

They watched the old raramuri's straight figure disappear down the trail leading south. Then, they started on their way east. It was another morning of red sun and endless desert. By noon, Tonio decided to ride on ahead while the rest waited under the shade of cottonwoods that bordered the dried riverbed. Tonio had spotted a hill a few kilómetros away. He rode out with the sun directly overhead.

José Mario dozed off under the shade of the cottonwoods and Tía Pancha kept busy rearranging pots and pans in the sacks slung to the horses' backs. Trini watched Buti and Lupita climb a contorted cottonwood with a wide, open trunk. Sometime later, she looked toward the hill, wondering where Tonio could be. He had been gone for a while now. Had he found a village? Cusihuiriachi? José Mario woke up.

"Pancha, how long did I sleep?"

"Never mind. You rest."

"Is Tonio back?"

"No, he's been gone a long time."

José Mario walked a way in an attempt to spot him, but came back into the shade after a while. The sun was too hot. It was late afternoon when Trini saw Tonio riding toward them. Tía Pancha was cooking the last of the calabazas and some corn for an early evening meal. Tonio was over the bluff now.

"Tonio has a goat!" Buti called out.

Everybody rose to meet him. Sure enough, he had a goat slung over Sarif in front of him, its feet securely tied.

"You found a pueblo? Cusihuiriachi?" José Mario asked, walking toward Tonio.

"There's a village. I don't know what place it is." Tonio dismounted.

"Didn't you ask?"

"It was deserted. Horses, stock, fires were burning, but no people. I looked around."

"No people?" José Mario's voice was puzzled. He looked at the goat. "How did you get it?"

"I took it. I left money for it."

"You took it?" José Mario's voice was incredulous. "Don't you know descalzos by now?"

Trini watched the uneasiness on Tonio's face. "I thought we needed meat . . ."

"You fool!"

José Mario's anger was heavy with worry. The goat gave a bleat as if to confirm Tonio's guilt. José Mario looked out into the distance, grasping for solutions. "We have to take that goat back before they find out it's gone. Are you sure the village was deserted?"

"Yes, I'm sure." Tonio's voice was tinged with guilt.

"Strange." José Mario was still puzzled.

He ordered everyone into the wagon. They broke camp and Tonio wasted no time getting back on Sarif and leading the way. As they turned the hill, Tonio made his way north. While they circled speedily, Trini noticed the river crawling southward in an opposite direction. To the north, she could see the shapes of the village huts clustered together and the swirls of smoke from the chimney fires cutting the late afternoon sun. To the south the river was lost in an area heavy with trees, huge boulders, and brush.

Suddenly, José Mario stopped the wagon, peering toward the river. Tonio, ahead, whirled his horse around.

"What's the matter?"

"Look." There was the beginning of distress in José Mario's voice. "People."

José Mario started on his way, this time picking up speed. Tonio led the way, urging the horse into a run. The murmur of the river began to fill the air even as they neared the village. It looked deserted. Dusk was falling and the breeze had the rawness of night wind. José Mario halted by the side of a storage shed in the center of the village. Around it were the corrals, one with horses, one with goats. Tonio pointed, "See, Chema, how can they miss one goat."

"You know better!" José Mario jumped off the wagon and shouted orders to Tonio. "Untie the goat and put it back. Now!"

Tonio quickly did as he was told, fumbling with the knots that secured the goat to the horse. José Mario led the horses to a water trough. Tía Pancha asked, "Is there time to fill the cannisters?"

"Are you mad, woman?" José Mario's voice was strained, desperate. "We must make a run for it now."

He was right. José Mario was looking toward the river. The whole horizon was enveloped by moving tangled figures. Trini felt her body jolt forward as José Mario turned the wagon around. Trini looked up to see Tonio running with the goat toward the corral, throwing the goat over, then making his way to Sarif. He leaped on the horse and led the way out of the village.

The supply horses were forgotten as the wagon made a sharp turn and followed Tonio in the darkness. Tía Pancha's tina and the cannisters teetered to the edge, then fell out, tumbling and rolling down the path. Trini could see the scattering of possessions along the road. Pots rolled, bounced, a desolate clanging filled the dusk. The box with her bultito lay in the dust! The clatter of falling things mixed with the growing shouts of Indians. She was too full of terror to think of loss. The night air hit her face sharply and the road heaved before her. She heard Tía Pancha's prayers between sobs.

They were racing in the gloom, heading toward the hills. Even the darkness could not save them. She felt the taste of tears and dust as she clung to Buti and Lupita, cowering at the end of the wagon, their little bodies shaking with fright. Trini reached out and put their heads down, as her body felt each twist and jar. Tía Pancha held on to the back of the seat. José Mario urged the horses to race into the darkness of the mountain.

When they circled the hill, Trini looked up to see rising boulders that covered the open ground. No one in sight. José Mario stopped and listened to the silent dark. It wasn't long before they heard it, horses' hooves like driving thunder. José Mario drove the wagon down a slope to open ground again and, from a distance, Trini could now make out a group of riding men amidst swirls of dust that rose heavy in the gloom. The wagon hung at a fork in a broken hill. Lupita began to cry.

"What do we do now?" Tía Pancha cried in distress.

"Everybody off." José Mario's voice sounded unusually calm. He pointed to trees at a distance. "Over there."

He ran ahead leading the way. Trini scrambled off, helping Buti down. Tonio was beside her now, leading Tía Pancha and Lupita toward heavy brush. Suddenly, Tía Pancha cried out, "Dios nos salve!"

She was pointing to the top. The shadows of horses and men covered the entire length of the hill, and riding toward them were still more dark bultos of angry men.

"Hide!" was the last whispered order from José Mario. Disoriented in the darkness, Trini soon lost track of the others. She found herself alone. Running along a trail overgrown with brush, she found her way to the shelter of a cleft between two boulders. She flopped to the ground and stretched out flat. Loud shouts hit the darkness. There was a blur coming toward her. Suddenly, she saw the figure of an Indian only a few feet away. She held her breath. She could make out an arm a few inches from where she lay. She saw the figure holding still to listen, then he turned and ran the opposite way as a scream cut the darkness. It was Tía Pancha. Now the voice of Buti crying, then the explosion of Tonio's angry curses as he struggled with his captors. Trini raised herself and made her way quietly out from the heavy brush.

From behind a boulder, she saw a shadowy group of men. One of them hissed an order, then they separated like fingers on a hand. Trini found her way to the main road. Her hands felt sore, scraped, and a tight sense of nausea filled her. She stumbled toward some kind of an ascent, heard the falling of debris behind her. She looked down to see the shape of a face looking up at her, and a hand that reached and covered her ankle. She felt herself falling, gasping for air. She lay, a tired heap upon the ground, then felt herself being lifted. She tightened her grasp on a man's arm, and in the darkness her teeth dug into his flesh. He cried out, cursing, and dropped her to the ground.

Trini tried to run, but another Indian grabbed her around the shoulders as she kicked and hit. They pushed her down a slope to where a group waited. There she saw Tonio struggling with three braves. She heard her father's long, drawn-out, gasping cough, and when she saw him he lay on the ground, breathing in little short whistles. Papá, poor Papá!

It was no use. They were all prisoners. Curses and cries punctured the night air as they were pushed and shoved into the wagon.

6

Gone!

"Salgazanos! Die!"

The Indian's face was smoldering with anger. He pointed to the two dead bodies hanging from a tree, two suspended shapes swaying slightly in the night breeze. Trini wanted to cry out, but found no voice. Lifeless, heads hanging, the two men lost shape against the looming, giant boulders in the background. A group of men held Tonio and José Mario. One man had José Mario's hands pinned back, another pulled his head back by the hair so that José Mario's gaze would fall on the hanging men. Tonio, struggling against the men who held him, was also forced to look at the dead men.

They were by the river's edge, where the Indians had led the wagon in the darkness. Tía Pancha and the children huddled in the wagon. The children emitted soft, frightened whines. Trini saw Tía Pancha turning their faces away from the sight of the two hanging sculptured bultos.

"It was just a goat, damn you," Tonio shouted, as a scudding howl of wind swallowed his words. A Tarahumara held Trini's wrists in an iron grip. He stood before her, erect with recoiled head. His face was in shadows, but bits of light, rained by a moon through trees, fell on the huge hands that held her. She twisted her body to make him let go. Wrenching pain. She looked to where her father stood between two captors. He stood wary, rigid. He turned his head toward the spokeman and asked sharply, "Is this Cusihuiriachi?"

There was no answer.

"You're not going to hang us!" yelled Tonio, suddenly raising his tied hands and hitting the man next to him on the side of the face. The force of the blow threw the man to the ground. Tonio broke free from his captors. He ran into the darkness in great leaping strides, three braves following as he cleared bushes and rocks. Then they caught up with him and dragged him back. The moon slid eerily behind a cloud; the hanging men were lost in the shadows of the gaunt, black rocks.

José Mario demanded, "Are you the chief? We can explain." The words were half-caught in the wind.

"Salgazanos!"

"We're not thieves! We put the goat back . . ."

The spokesman pointed to the dead men. "Salgazanos!"

"What did they steal?" José Mario's voice rasped tightly.

"A young woman, cowards!" A murmur of assent rose among the Indians.

"Is this the way of the Tarahumara?" José Mario asked. He repeated his earlier question. "Is this Cusihuiriachi?" He looked at the spokesman hard. "Is your ahau's name Ambrosio?"

"How do you know?" the spokesman demanded.

José Mario breathed a sigh of relief. "This is Cusihuiriachi, isn't it?" The man refused to answer again, but José Mario continued. "We know Ambrosio. He was my brother in the valley of Bachotigori."

Trini prayed in silence. Please God, let it be. The spokesman was wary, unrelenting. He ordered, "Take them to the village!"

They were shoved back into the wagon, José Mario still demanding, "Where is Ambrosio?"

Still no answer. The wagon made its way to the village where Trini saw a huge bonfire effortlessly deploying spitting red embers that cut into the darkness. The flames rose in the middle of the pueblo square next to the large storage shed they had seen that afternoon. Its low roof made of logs and sod caught the dancing shadows. Eyes followed them, bristling like the fire. Trini saw strange, stern faces, but Sabochi was not one of them. Tehueques shoved them toward the door of the shed. Holding on to Buti and Lupita, she followed the straight figure of Tía Pancha with José Mario leading the way.

Tonio resisted, again, turning and digging an elbow into the stomach of the brave guarding him; instantaneously, three men were upon him. Trini saw one raise a heavy stick and strike a blow that caught Tonio on the side of the face. He fell to the ground. José Mario tried to get to him but was shoved roughly into the storage shed.

The shed was full of grain sacks. Two large windows looked out into the orange flames of the bonfire that fed a dancing light into the room. The tehueques locked the door behind them.

Trini ran to the window and saw them pick up Tonio, who seemed dazed. The two men locked Tonio's arms behind his back, then led him toward the shed. The door opened, and Tonio was thrown to the floor. Trini ran to where he lay on his back, groaning.

Trini bent down to examine his blood-covered face. It was not a deep cut, but it had bled profusely. José Mario was working on the rope that tied his hands.

"They're going to kill us," announced Tía Pancha tremulously as she led Lupita and Buti to a pile of grain sacks in a corner. "Look at the children! Frightened, exhausted, falling on their feet."

Trini looked at the tired little faces. They were holding on to Tía Pancha's skirt, eyes half-closed in tear-stained faces. Tonio was now on his feet, rubbing his wrists. He looked around the room, then began to line up sacks for the children to sleep on.

Suspicious faces stared at them through the window as they piled sacks onto the floor, eyes fiercely steady. Then, all at once, they disappeared. Only the bonfire burned a dwindling dance. She felt Tonio's hand in hers. "Try to sleep, Trini."

Buti and Lupita were fast asleep, stretched out on the grain sacks. Tía Pancha had covered them with her shawl and was herself lying by the children's heads, legs drawn up, arms pillowing her head. Only José Mario stood by the window watching. Tonio urged her again, "Sleep."

The heaviness of exhaustion weighed down on her. She lay down, feeling the flames from the outside fire like waves, waves. . . . In fitful sleep she dreamt of El Enano running in open waves of fire, running, beckoning her to the cave, Sabochi's cave. Then the fire turned into fields of chile piquín, redness waving in the wind. Sabochi's strong arms were holding her, keeping her safe . . . until she woke up with the burning sun upon her face, Tonio sitting quietly next to her.

"Everything's O.K." His voice was soft, reassuring. She sat up and saw José Mario fast asleep, his head against the windowsill, sitting on grain sacks stacked by the window. She saw his body heave with the coming of a cough which filled the room. Outside, the bonfire was a pile of burnt ashes dispersed at intervals by small breezes. The square was empty.

"What time is it? she asked. Tonio went to the window, looked at the sun. "Close to noon."

"Sabochi?" Trini's question was a hope.

Tonio shook his head, looking out into the empty square. Suddenly, he turned to wake José Mario. "They're coming."

José Mario was on his feet. Lupita and Buti sat up, rubbing their eyes. Tía Pancha was praying silently on her rosary as the tehueques unlocked the door. The children ran to Tía Pancha who enfolded them in her arms protectively. José Mario steped forward.

"Where is Ambrosio?" he asked.

Again, José Mario's question was ignored. The spokesman of the night before spat on the floor, then commanded, "Come!" The prisoners silently did as they were told, filing out of the storage shed into the hot sun.

Pencil lines of smoke smoldered in the huge, burned pile in the center of the square. Women began to appear with children, dogs trailing, following the prisoners as they made their way down a path lined with huts. Someone called out accusingly, "Salgazanos!"

The crowd was growing, braves leading the way past a water pump and the corrals. José Mario looked about frowning, squinting against the sun. He stopped suddenly. "Where are you taking us? Where is Ambrosio?"

The only answer was a shove. Someone hissed again, "Salgazanos!" A murmur rose in the crowd. Another voice shouted, "Hang them!"

The crowd surrounded them, pushing and shoving in a definite direction toward the river. Trini remembered the dead men of the night before. Fear was bitter in her mouth. She grabbed Tonio's arm for courage. His eyes told her to be brave. She felt the anger in the hard hands that pushed her forward. Faces, curious, jumbled, strange; strangled angry sounds filled the air. Trini looked straight ahead, holding Tonio by the wrist. She could feel his beating pulse against her fingers, a transference of strength. The thought of Sabochi was something vague, lost, distant now. The spokesman stopped and ordered, "Men, come! Women, stay!"

"No!" Trini cried out. "I stay with my father, with Tonio!"

"Keep the girl back," barked the spokesman. Two tehueques held her back as men hurried José Mario and Tonio toward the river. Trini struggled, catching sight of Buti and Lupita hiding their faces in Tía Pancha's skirt. She was breathing with convulsive effort, heaving and thrashing to make the braves let go. Words came hoarse from her throat, "What are you going to do to them?"

No answer. They shoved her roughly toward the village, Tía Pancha and the children following. For an instant, Trini twisted herself free to turn and see the figure of her father and Tonio lose themselves in the huge group of men making their way to the line of boulders that fronted the river. Trini stopped to beg, "Please, please, let them go!"

She was on her knees, hugging the thighs of a tehueque, pleading. He merely stood and waited until she was cried out, then he pulled her to her feet and shoved her ahead of him.

* * *

They crouched inside a dark room where the only window was boarded up; the smell of burning green branches filled Trini's throat. They had been thrown into the room without ceremony. Tía Pancha and the children sat in numb silence on the floor. The only light came from a doorway without a door. The dark was soothing to Trini. Nevertheless, she crawled into the sunlight streaming through the doorway. She leaned her head against the jamb, feeling a throbbing pain in her head. She saw an old woman, a man, and some boys working. Dear God! how strange to see people calmly doing things when such terror invaded her body. Her nerves were taut, her body tense, her eyes burning with tears; she placed her head on her knees and stared out without really seeing anymore. Behind her, she could hear Tía Pancha's gentle voice leading the children in Ave María.

"Ave María, ruega por nosotros . . ." Trini sobbed silently. Oh, yes, Sweet Virgin, don't let them kill Papá and Tonio. The prayers set a rhythm of hope beating in the dark room. Outside, the workers walked around small burning pyramids. The smell of burning cepas had the taste of ashes and made her eyes burn.

"Ave María, madre de Dios . . ." Trini watched two boys throw the green cepas into the fire.

"Tía, are they preparing graves for us?" she asked in a whisper.

"Don't frighten the children. It's just a cocedor de cal, that's all." Her aunt's voice assumed a lightness. Tía Pancha pointed, "See, Buti, and Lupita, the man is putting limestone in the well."

For a little while, curiosity clouded fear. Tía Pancha continued, "See, see how he sets the green branches on fire in the well?"

"What are the boys doing?" Buti asked, his eyes intent on the workers.

The Indian boys took out swollen rocks from one of the pyramid wells. The rocks looked like huge sponges. Tía Pancha told them, "Cal, limestone."

They watched the old woman sprinkle water on the swollen stones, then take one of the stones and tap it lightly with a flat stick. Instantly, it pulverized and fell like a dirt avalanche into a chiquihuiti. Tía Pancha pointed again. "They put it in the basket."

When the children's interest waned, Tía Pancha told them a cuento about aves. They listened for a while, then Buti remembered El Enano. It was a temporary flight to happier times. Tía Pancha began another prayer, "Dios te salve, reina y madre . . ." The children joined in with light, trusting voices. Trini watched her aunt with the children, thinking, she's so wonderful, giving them no time to be afraid. But I'm so afraid. Her aunt's attempts to distract them had not pushed back despair for Trini.

Papá? Tonio? A void overwhelmed, a dreading, numbing fear. She stood by the door and looked up at a relentless sun, a fire without pity. She fell on her knees, seeing the workers' fire as a killing fire, the pyramids were waiting graves, Papá and Tonio were hanging bultos on a tree . . .

Oh, God, she sobbed quietly, putting her head down to the floor, her body curved in sorrow. A shadow crossed the door, and in the darkness of herself, Trini felt someone. Her heart pounded a joy. She looked up.

"God, my God, Sabochi!" She knelt with arms outstretched, reaching for him. He picked her up and held her for a long time, stroking her hair, assuring her in whispers that all was well. She believed him. God was good. He answered prayers. She raised apprehensive eyes to him. "Papá? Tonio?"

"They're safe, fine . . ."

She laughed, cried, clung, floating in happiness. She could hear Sabochi's heart. He was holding her. "Sabochi, Sabochi . . ."

* * *

They stood by the goat corral, Buti in Sabochi's arms, Lupita by his side. Isidoro was cutting the goat from the herd, and José Mario was asking, "You can find the exact goat we took?"

Sabochi laughed. "Yes, each goat is different, like people."

Isidoro held a goat by its feet for them to see, then he put the bleating little animal under the curve of his arm. He went to a horse and tied the goat to its back, then mounted his horse, waved his arm, turned, and led the horse with the goat out of the village.

"Where's he going?" Tonio asked.

Sabochi's eyes followed Isidoro's trail of dust. "He's taking the goat to the hills."

"Why?"

"To free it there, so it may roam the hills. It no longer belongs to us. It never existed."

The gesture was one of grace. If the goat never existed neither did the theft. Sabochi now turned to them, smiling, "My family, this has not been a good welcome."

"Why were those men hung?" Tonio asked.

"Two strangers. They raped one of our young girls."

"Is it punishable by death?"

"All crimes are, where the strong attack the defenseless. It was also a matter of honor."

Nothing more was said about the hanging. Trini walked up to Sabochi and looked up into his eyes, so appreciative of his family's presence.

"I found you," she whispered, a happy softness in her voice.

"I am glad all of you are here, pollito."

"I would like to stay here with you." Her words said so much more. They spoke of a loneliness, a happiness, a dream.

"Stay?" Sabochi seemed bewildered.

"With you, Sabochi." Trini's statement hung in the air. There was something in Sabochi's eyes, something without joy or acceptance. How could he not want me when I have been his all my life? Her eyes told him this, and he turned away. Why did he turn away?

"It is a different way of life . . ." Trini heard Sabochi's words as if from far away. He had not said them. He cleared his throat in awkwardness, and spoke other words, kindly, deliberately. "It cannot be."

"Why?" Anguish drowned her. "Why?"

"There's someone you must meet."

For a fleeting moment their eyes met and Trini looked desperately for the old magic, but Sabochi quickly walked away toward a cenote, turning, nodding for them to follow.

The group followed him around a cluster of huts that circled the storage shed, Trini hesitant, behind the others. Little children ran naked in the sun. Sabochi's words—'It cannot be—It cannot be'—curled and contorted in the same sun. The laughing children were there and not there. The turmoil was spending her, making her blind. But life was all around her. A man was spreading corn to dry on a roof. Women bent over cooking fires. "It cannot be—It cannot be." Words, pain thickening the blood.

Sabochi stopped before a hut where a huge half-woven yucca basket leaned against the wall, where old, discarded pots lay around the yard, and an old rack made of rope held long strips of drying meat. Sabochi went inside. This was his house? wondered Trini. He was back, standing at the door. When he stepped out, a young woman followed him with a baby in her arms. His house? Who was she? The young woman smiled shyly and held out the baby for them to see.

"This is the first born of Ambrosio."

Trini stood and stared and did not choose to believe. How could she believe? She was hollow, years spilled into nothing. Trini turned her head away as Tía Pancha held out her arms for the baby.

"A boy?"

The mother nodded proudly. Trini faced them again, looked past the girl, past the baby, at Sabochi whose eyes were on her. Tears welled, a wild glistening. She choked back sobs. Sabochi stood immobile. She turned away and found Tonio beside her. Good, sweet Tonio, to hold on to, to stifle the hurt. She felt Tonio's arms comforting her.

Gone, gone, gone . . . Sabochi was beside her. He whispered, "Trini . . ." She felt an urge to laugh. Sabochi had never called her Trini before. It had always been those childish names. Changes had taken place in the universe. She ran from him toward Tonio, begging, "Take me away."

He took her hand and led her away from the group. She followed with her eyes closed, stumbling, holding tight. Where was he taking her? She opened her eyes. They had come to the well along the path to the arroyo. She could not go on. She had to face things. She must not be a child any longer. "Let's go back."

"Are you sure?" Tonio's voice was kind.

Trini nodded, looked up and smiled bravely. They went back to Sabochi's hut. Sabochi's wife was setting out straw mats in front of the house. Again, Trini was there and not there. Talk, gestures, things were out of her range of consciousness. Little bits and pieces took the shape of realness. Her mind photographed, her ear recorded—Sabochi's wife's name was Chimac—she offered food—she served them—Sabochi put wood into the cooking fire—Chimac took out a breast to feed her baby—Trini felt the rising of a suffocated scream. She stirred atole in her bowl aimlessly, tried not to hear, not to see, not to feel. She pushed away from the bits and pieces, then she felt Tonio's hand on her shoulder. No, this time she did not want his sympathy. She went up to Chimac blindly, stroked the baby's head, asked in an alien voice cut with hurt, "What's his name?"

"Chirachi, Chio."

Chimac's contentment tore at her; a flood of anguish, strange invasions filled her. The sun burned pain, spirals of blue and orange light glassed her sight. I mustn't faint, she told herself. She turned away from the young wife and in confused defiance called out, "Come on, Buti, Lupita!"

She broke into a run, the children following. Soon she had left them far behind. She stopped, waiting for them, noticing that their little faces were wet with perspiration. She led them down a path, slackening her pace. Buti's chatter came through, "They're playing ball, look!" He was pointing to a noisy dusty game with boys holding long wooden scoops that kept the ball in the air. Trini did not want to look; the noise was bruising. She quickened her step again toward the curve of huts that led to the arroyo, passing an old man making a parrilla of iron tubing. Trini's eye caught a trail of goat droppings snaking up to the old man sitting in the sun. She laughed, her laughter caught in a whimper. Nothing has happened. What I see does not exist. My valley must be near. Where are the hills? Remember the hills, Sabochi? Remember the fig tree? This is empty, empty land. It is not home, said her empty, empty heart. Faint veils of vapor rose from cooking pots, and ashes scattered in the wind before her. Buti was yelling, "You walk too fast!"

She didn't answer. She wanted to escape them, to go back to Batopilas. A whirlwind grew in her, something she could not stop. Yes, yesterday there had been no Chimac, no Chio, no Sabochi. No Sabochi? Gone, gone, gone . . . She swallowed her desperation, running and running against the dirt wind. She was past the arroyo now. She ran far beyond it with eyes closed, with a mouth of dust. She ran until she could run no more, her lungs about to burst.

Finally, she fell to the ground and cried like a little child, sobbing loudly, her sobs mixing with the howling wind. She cried until she was spent. Then she sat, knees drawn up, held by her arms, head to one side, and stared blankly ahead. Her body opened up to peace, floating, silence restoring the world. Sights and sounds came back. The horizon. The river. She got up and continued her way aimlessly toward the river.

Gone, gone, gone. Tears again. They came silently this time. Now she was by the water's edge, the rustle of leaves and the beating of birds' wings moaned, gone—gone—gone . . . Another whimper grew inside her, but she stifled it. The sun blazed—gone—gone—gone . . . She looked around and soon recognized the spot. There before her were the trees backed by huge boulders. She remembered the dark bultos against the moon. She looked up, frightened by the tree limbs, now bare, that danced to the wind's whine. The men were gone. Gone—gone—gone . . . The face of farce again! She wiped her quiet tears and tried to think of Chimac and the baby with calm. Vapors dissolving like the sponge, pulverizing. Death and life, green and desolate, cut by pain, loss and gain. Recovery sang in her veins, for no other reason than the surge of new energy in her body, the mind seeding new hope. Nothing stopped, all things went on, and with an elation born out of the sadness, a resilience born out of blindness, she turned back, feeling almost lightheaded.

She was el pollito, the little girl kicking dust along the road. She picked up a stone and threw it in the air. Then she looked for pretty stones, colored ones wearing the shades of her rainbow rocks. Every time she found a pretty one, she rubbed it clean on her skirt, putting it in her pocket. The sound of instinct hurrying in the blood. A name came to her lips—Chimac—Chimac—Chimac . . . What a pretty name. Like music. And the pain? Gone—gone—gone . . . almost gone.

Chimac, Chimac, Chimac—it was like the waterfall in Batopilas. She ran past the arroyo. She found herself in the midst of cooking fires, naked children, lean, starved dogs, milling people at their labors. She began to walk faster and wondered what had become of Buti and Lupita. When she came to the cenote, she looked around for them. They were not in sight.

She would walk back to Sabochi's house. She looked up to see Chimac walking toward her with Chio in her arms. Chimac smiled and called out, "Trini!"

Trini pulled back the blown hair from her face. One hand still held the colored stones. Their eyes met. Dear God, I must move without feeling, she told herself. Chimac was before her holding the baby against her shoulder. Pretty Chimac. Trini opened her hand and Chimac looked at the colored pebbles, then Trini let them fall out of her hand, like a spilling rainbow, one by one. They both laughed; Trini asked, with great seriousness, "May I hold Chio?"

Chimac put the baby in her arms, and they both walked back to Sabochi's house in silence.

7

Land of the Tarahumara

Four men stood talking at daybreak. The wagon had been loaded with comestibles for the long journey ahead. Isidoro and Tonio were tying a goat to an extra horse.

"You cannot kill it for food," Sabochi was explaining to José Mario. "The goat is a message to the ahau of Bucoyu. It says you are a friend."

Trini, sitting in the wagon with the children and Tía Pancha, noticed the early morning light dissolving in the air, meeting on the earth. The village was still asleep, except for Sabochi's braves. Sabochi was going on a journey of his own. He would ride toward the peaks of the canyon tiered by some past life of waterfalls now gone. He would ride by sober rocks cut vertically for miles up and make camp at the bottom of the canyon. He would ride in an opposite direction from them. But Isidoro was accompanying José Mario's party to Bucoyu.

"He's a good fletero," Sabochi nodded towards Isidoro. "He knows his mountains."

Sabochi's tehueques were mounting their horses. Goodbyes were easy, simple.

"Sabochi, old friend, my eyes hope to see you soon." José Mario's hand lingered on Sabochi's shoulder.

"I shall see you again, old friend," promised Sabochi. Buti and Lupita held out their arms for a final goodbye. Trini stood aside, feeling a new awkwardness. Sabochi's eyes were on her now. No chosen point in the heart to reach between them—only a desertion that was solely her terrain. He did not intrude. She lifted proud eyes to him, but said nothing. "Time to go." Tonio said. He came to her side, took her hand.

The silence between Sabochi and Trini was broken by a shout. Sabochi's tehueques were ready to go. Trini saw Sabochi mount his horse, slap his thigh, and raise an arm as a signal to his men. His eyes met hers for a second, then he turned his horse and rode out into the growing red light of morning.

"Goodbye, Sabochi," whispered Trini as she watched him lead his men toward the high terrain of the serranía. He was gone again, but this time it was a different Trini watching him go. Her eyes lingered on Sabochi and his men as they disappeared beyond the arroyo, past the river, into the mute imminence of the hills. In a little while, the quiet village would spring into life, the square would fill with sounds. Chimac would wait for Sabochi to return. Chimac had much more than dreams.

"Yaiiii, Sarif!" Tonio shouted. He was leading the way in an opposite direction, toward El Cerro Minaco, a three days' climb up a mountain that circled upwards, a barren mountain where nights were unbearably cold. The first three days were hard days of straining wagon, tired horses, and a climb perilous and cruel. When they camped at night, Trini listened to echoing winds and felt herself at the mercy of an untamed monster. After the third day, the ascent lost its sharpness, becoming easier. The red earth mountain had curiously, little by little, become pure, clear rock. The desert mountain was left behind, for between rock and stone, a vast greenness rose. Trini noticed that the rocks and stones had taken on the color of blue.

Light rose like a cathedral where hills were thick, and cloistered within lay a great level field lavishly sprinkled with polished slabs of blue, flat stones of gigantic size. They lashed through the thick grass until the grass disappeared altogether and the ground became pure blue, each stone carefully laid side by side to form a floor. Trini heard the glassy tinkle of water somewhere beyond. As the wagon clattered over the stone floor, it became a loud water world. Suddenly, Trini saw water falling from a break in the stone. It caught the blue reflection of the rocks and even the trees that grew on the edge of the pool were blue-hued.

José Mario stopped the wagon and Isidoro crossed himself in silence, afterwards explaining, "Peña azul." Rocks, trees, water, sky, all blue! Isidoro led the way on foot to a place where the blue stones made a natural path in the narrow break of mountain. Here, he knelt down and crossed himself again. He touched the stones reverently, then looked up to explain:

"The Virgin came to this place." He pointed to a circle of blue slabs that ran into a narrow silver-water spring. "The footprints of Her burro are over there."

On the alejo, true enough, could be seen what seemed like footprints of a burro leading to the spring. Isidoro recounted, "Shepherds from these mountains tell how they have seen Her riding, holding the baby Jesus." Tía Pancha was kneeling now, next to Isidoro, touching the stones, awe on her face. She crossed herself and clasped her hands to her bosom. "Bendita sea la Santísima Virgen."

The sky and the trees and the water seemed to melt into one another. Tía Pancha motioned for everyone to kneel. "We will pray." She took out her rosary from her skirt pocket, her fingers nimble and sure on the beads, her eyes closed, her voice ringing with a clarity of blue. They all knelt and followed her lead. Prayers danced and flew in the blue-hued silence. A whole rosary was prayed effortlessly, with blue reverence.

Afterwards, Buti and Lupita ran to the spring's edge and looked at their reflection flecked in sunlight, then they made a game of tracing the tracks of the Virgin's burro with their fingers. Tía Pancha went to the wagon, found a jar in the tina, then filled it at the spring. "It is blessed," she whispered. "I feel better with holy water along."

"We must cross before dark," Isidoro reminded them. "Up those mountains." He showed them the winding road. "The crosswinds are treacherous. They suck up everything."

"Is there another way through these hills?" asked Tonio.

"Only this way to Bucoyu."

"Then that's the road we take," agreed José Mario.

"The road is wide, but we go slow. The wind is the enemy," Isidoro warned.

They began the climb into the green darkness on a wide road with thick pine growing sentinel-like in long rows, up to an unseen top. The travelers stopped to rest and eat in the late afternoon. José Mario observed, "A good place to camp for the night."

Isidoro appeared troubled; he looked up furtively from time to time toward the pass, listening to the winds for long intervals. He held his chin, rubbing it in thought as he looked up toward a darkening sky.

"No," he decided staunchly.

"Why?" asked José Mario, curious, intent.

"The way the winds touch me . . . There's anger. The gods do not like the fact that we are here. Listen."

They all listened. Trini heard a cracking, slithering moan of wind.

"Gods?" questioned Tía Pancha with pointed disbelief.

"They command the whirlwinds." There was worry in Isidoro's somber voice.

"There are no mountain gods," exclaimed Tía Pancha.

"They are jealous of travelers who use the mountain." Isidoro looked at Tía Pancha, his eyes crinkling in puzzlement. "Why do you not believe in mountain gods? You believe in the Virgin."

"I'm a Christian!" answered Tía Pancha, somewhat indignant.

Isidoro's right, thought Trini, there are gods on this mountain. I feel them. She followed Isidoro to the ledge, looking down into an awesomeness of depth and up to a summit lost in clouds. Isidoro stood by her side, listening to something in the air, perhaps to something inside himself. Words came from him, urgent, quick, "The anger thickens. We must try to pass beyond the summit now. Now, before the winds begin. We must go beyond the beehives."

Beehives? Trini was amazed, curious. What beehives? But no one questioned. They quickly broke camp and soon were on the steep climb toward the beehives. Trini found it difficult to breathe. Was it heavy anger in the air? Was that what Isidoro felt? She looked up to see clouds, grey tatters of rags hanging onto the peak before them. No one spoke. To the left, Trini saw the abyss stretch like a vast river of ink.

The beginning of sounds—thin, crackling, growing. Before them was a peak turned brown with the thickness of giant hives, bigger than a man, which hung like aphids to sharp cliffs. The sound came from thousands of bees. A fearful thing, bees clinging to hives. Reflected in the sunset, they were like one huge red pulse. The buzzing sound grew louder, filling the world. Tring covered her ears as José Mario whippped up the horses and the wagon gathered speed. The horses strained their way upward. Suddenly, a swarm of giant bees rushed from an old hive and clustered on a tree limb. The line of fleeing bees seemed endless. Isidoro shouted, "The winds are coming. The bees know!"

José Mario urged the horses into a run, but the steepness of the climb made it impossible. The continual tortured moan of wind and bees became a terror. The sky darkened and the whirling of a dark storm filled the hollows. Isodoro's strong voice commanded, "Lead the horses between those trees!"

Off the wagon, toward the trees—a difficult task because the wind swept them toward the abyss with growing force. Trini saw the whirlwinds swirl up in an inky spiral. Her ears caught the sound of tearing bushes, the splintery smash of torn branches. As the wind ripped off bush and sapling, it sucked them into the howling circle of its wake, lifeless dust riding before the wind. It choked Trini as it swept her along. God, she had to hold on to something! something!

A brown tentacled hive was torn violently from the cliff. It hit a rock over Trini's head and the shreds of the hive flew wild, a dark cloud of bees filling the air. Bees dispersed, confused, lost. She saw José Mario tying the horses to a tree, the horses' flanks fallen in as they neighed. The wind slithered, scythe-like, strangling her breath, violently forcing her body toward the edge. She smothered a cry as she slid down, straining as best she could against the wind. The wind turned and jerked her body to one side with great force. Before her was a huge tree. She reached for it as dust and bits of rock, caught in the breath of the growing, violent spiral, beat and cut her body. She fell at the foot of the tree, her arms encircling its trunk, her nails clawing into the bark, bracing herself against a wind that insisted on tearing her loose.

But she clung, eyes closed against flying debris, breathing exhaustion, the wind sweeping her body like a broken branch. She lost her grip on the tree and her body rolled toward the ledge again. Helplessness overwhelmed her as she rolled freely, effortlessly, into the darkness. Now she was the wind, black and violent. All at once, she felt the weight of a body fall hard on her. She was being held fast to the ground. Between her own heavy breaths, she heard Tonio shout, "Hold on! Hold on!"

She opened her eyes to see him straining, one arm around a boulder buried in the ground, a tooth of the mountain, jagged, sharp. He pulled her body under his, inching closer to the rock protrusion. His mouth was open, gasping for air as the rush of wind hit him. But they were now close against the rock, Trini reaching for a hold, finding it, clinging. The weight of his body saved her from the tearing impact of the wind. They held on for a long time. Little by little the wind dwindled in its force. Then Trini's arms let go, her body limp, immobile; only Tonio's hold on her remained. She had become the whirling blackness, time stretching out to an abstinence, exhausting itself, left without breath or strength. Then there was silence as she lay face down on the ground.

But she felt Tonio raise himself; she felt his hands smoothing the tangle of hair that covered her face. She heard his voice. "It's all over Trini—you feel O.K.?"

She turned over on her back and lay there looking up at the dark silhouette of his face. He lay down by her side, holding her hand for a long while, then enfolding her in his arms. The world was peaceful again. In a timelessness of their own, they breathed in the night heavy with the scent of pine. The gods had spent their anger. Trini felt warm and safe in Tonio's arms.

Suddenly, José Mario's voice rang clear in the night air, and voices called out in answer. Everyone was safe. Late at night they formed a circle under the tree where Trini had clung for safety. Isidoro and José Mario saw to the animals while Tonio looked for firewood. He built a fire to kill the chill. Tía Pancha, looking exhausted and weary, was still apprehensive, "It's not safe here, up so high, in this darkness."

"It's safe. The bees have sung their death song. The gods have found us worthy of their anger." Isidoro spoke into the calm.

Tía Pancha gathered the tired children around her, laying out blankets in the dark. Tonio sat next to Trini to watch the flames dance in a slight, calm breeze, heavy with dew. She lay her head on his shoulder and fell into a tired sleep.

* * *

The sky was swept in pinks as the wagon made its way slowly into the village of Bucoyu. People gathered around the wagon, watching the travelers curiously, for it was not often that chaboches came to their village. Soon the travelers were sitting with the old ahau in front of his hut, as Isidoro presented the bleating goat. A tehueque sitting next to the old ahau stood and took it from Isidoro with great ceremony. The old ahau bent low, inhaling from a long reed pipe, swaying from side to side.

At a distance Trini could see green-patched mountains that seemed suspended from the sun. Her scrutiny fell on the ahau. His skin had the texture of red, coarse clay, dried by the sun, leaving tiny little canyons of water-hunger. The wrinkled skin sharply outlined the strong face bones, the deep-socketed eyes. It seemed to Trini that he had sprung from the earth, and, with time, sun and wind had etched him. Trini's ear caught strange words coming from her father's lips. He was speaking to the old ahau in his own language! She had never heard her father speak the language of the descalzos. A few phrases, a question, yes, but now his voice rose and fell in deep conversation with the old ahau. The ancient chief seemed to be listening with his eyes as well. The ahau answered in a dry, cracking voice with sparse words, with eloquent hands. Fingers—jutting, sharp promontories of bones—filled the air with gestures, like edifices; at times the old one turned his head to where Trini sat, smiling at her puzzlement.

They were to leave before the sun was high, so, soon after, the ahau rose and spoke with some of his men. The wagon was filled with comestibles for the journey ahead. Again, the ritual of the goat. It was the ahau's turn to present José Mario with a new bleating animal, a message to the ahau in the next village. After guiding them out of the village, to the lowlands of the red desert, Isidoro bid them goodbye.

"We shall share time again," he told them solemnly. Then the three men drew mountains and rivers and deserts on the sand. Isidoro was showing them the way out of the great barranca. After mounting his horse, he turned sharply with hand upraised. "Benditos sean." They watched him ride west into an endless horizon.

Six weeks of travel through land of shallow humus and low ranges lay ahead. As they traveled north, tall trees gave way to smaller trees and thornier underbrush. The sparse country had little to give. José Mario rationed food and water. When they stopped to rest behind the shade of giant boulders or among a cluster of straggling trees, Tonio would tie a rope around the goat's neck and let Buti and Lupita hold it while it grazed. No river was sighted for weeks! On the first day of the sixth week, they marked their journey along a dry riverbed that snaked its way northeast. The land was rising and winds were strong. Dust swirls burned and lashed and swept, adding to the travelers' fatigue. Along the river, water seeped through sand. Trini saw signs of spring. Was it April? She had lost track of time.

"See along the river—field daisies." She pointed them out to Tonio, who sat next to her on the driver's seat. "It must be spring." He looked at her sideways with a smile, keeping his eyes on her. He agreed, "I felt it last night. I looked up at the stars . . ."

"And thought of all the girls you left behind."

"No, I thought of you."

Their eyes met, but she turned away. She no longer felt like an awkward child with him. Her eyes followed the brave colors along the river's edge. José Mario rode up to the wagon. He had been scouting ahead and now came with good news. "There's a village ahead, about four kilómetros to the north."

Tonio nodded toward a greening mountain, pointing to sharply outlined trails leading to the top. On top of the mountain a finca gleamed white. Sun spiked the newly awakened vegetation that engulfed the huge ranch sitting alone on top of the mountain. It was like a different world from the desert below. Isidoro had spoken of the fincas belonging to the rich hacendados who raised thousands of head. José Mario shaded his eyes and looked at a man's dream, his eyes thirsty like the desert. Trini knew he was wishing for ganado, for stock and land.

"Someday, Papá . . ." the words caught in her throat. She wanted to promise the greenness of a future to her good, tired, father, but she could say no more. It was he who comforted her. "We'll plant out seeds some day, chinita."

"On our own land!" A dream had urged the words she spoke. José Mario looked up again at the finca with tired eyes, then urged his horse north, leading them to the village.

At the edge of the village lay a cornfield where gusts of sandstorms had choked the earth. Here and there signs of moisture clung. It must have rained recently, for this was not pliant earth, but hard and dry. It was the unprolific land of the iguana, sacred to the Indians. Beyond the cornfield they saw a cluster of huts. Trini turned to her father, who was looking at the sad cornfields. Resignation lay heavy in his voice. "A life's struggle, for that."

"Not like Batopilas, Papá," Trini recalled. "We just threw seed in the ground. The land was kind."

"It was not our land," answered José Mario brusquely.

Trini reached under the buckboard and came up with one of the seed sacks; she gathered a handful, looking up to meet her father's eyes, bright with hope. She remembered the nights she had helped him pour seeds into sacks as he had poured gold and silver. They had tied the little sacks with fervent determination for a future time. Now it would be for a time out of the valley of Batopilas. The place will be our own land. She made a silent promise. How to put it into words for her father? It would only sound like a child's wish. Still, the wish came out. "We will never plant these seeds except on our own land." His face said nothing. It had the bleakness of the desert. Tears sprang to her eyes. She held them back and poured the seed back into the sack, tying it securely.

They drove into the village that melted in the glare of sun and red earth. She saw impressive, giant, bone-like trees at a distance, dividing river from desert. In her mouth was the taste of heat. There was a festive air in the village as the travelers rode in. In the center of the main square was a circle of women busily cooking, steam from huge pots curling in the sun. A young headman came out to meet them and the ritual of the goat drew a curious, happy crowd. They had come at a time of good omen, unexpected rain, manna to the villagers. The visitors had come with the winds of April, boundless, drifting. The young headman introduced himself as Tel Chen, howler-monkey, then he led the men to his hut, leaving Tía Pancha, Trini, and the children free to wander around the village.

Trini looked curiously at young women dressed in mantas tied under their armpits. She walked up to an altar and watched girls strew corn leaves before it. On the altar was a statue of the Virgin Mary and a brown clay figure of the goddess Tonantzín. Trini felt Tía Pancha's grip on her arm, a questioning frown on her face. Trini knew she did not approve of a pagan goddess being placed next to the Virgin Mary. The four-breasted goddess of fertility looked like a lump of earth compared to the pretty painted little Virgin. Something pulsed in Trini, a secret preference for the brown goddess that seemed to gather strength in the sun and open air. Tonantzín was like the old ahau of Bucoyu, a spirit sprung from the earth.

Trini looked up to see Tel Chen walking toward the center of the square. People were gathering around the altar. Some kind of ceremony was about to begin. Tel Chen told the travelers they had come in time for the feast of good planting. A chant rose among the people gathering around the altar; they sat, rocking to and fro to strange rhythms played on drums and reed pipes. A prayer began to the rhythm of the chant, a Christian prayer of thanks for seed and wind and rain. Dancers made their way to the altar in a dance of supplication. Tel Chen invited them to sit on the ground with the villagers. All did except Tía Pancha, who refused. She remained standing, her mouth a tight line, eyes blinking nervously as she clenched and unclenched her hands. Trini knew that her aunt was not about take part in a pagan ritual. Her aunt's lips trembled words coming in a furious rush, "Pagans, savages!" Tía Pancha turned away from them, making her way out of the circle, walking gingerly among the people. Then she stopped as if remembering something she had forgotten. She made her way back to where the children sat.

"Come with me." It was the stern Christian speaking. Buti and

Lupita did not hesitate, but followed her, hard as it was to keep up with Tía Pancha's strides. Trini stood, unsure. She wanted to be part of the chanting, the music, the benediction. She looked toward Tía Pancha, who stood waiting for her, Buti and Lupita by her side, then turned and looked toward the altar. Tonantzín was smiling at her! She sat down again and joined in the chant without looking back at Tía Pancha.

She was part of it now. Dancers, young males garbed in breechclouts and headresses with lofty plumed panaches, circled and swayed. Energy—faith—sun—wind. She was free of her own body. She was the dance, the earth breathing.

The dancers were searching to the words of the drum for arrable land, dipping, swaying in tempered movements, turning in hope, reaching for the sky. They found a place, cleared it of the flow of water, music of the earth. The drums were in Trini's blood now, finding tributaries carrying light into oceans, worlds whispering, seed waiting. Tonantzín spoke and she listened.

The dancing stilled. Trini felt truly blessed, truly free. A parade of children walked around the circle, then stopped in front of the altar; one girl held a white huitoch with an imprint of the Virgin. A child picked up a cajoncito that had been set between the statue of the Virgin and Tonantzín. She handed the small box to a holy man who prayed for the first seed. Communion had begun. Bowls moved around the circle, pinole for bread, chicha for wine, the blood and the body, instantaneous immolation, a unity. The ritual was over.

Trini went looking for Tía Pancha and the children. She found them under one of the manzanilla trees, waiting for her. There was a scowl on Tía Pancha's face. "I hope you're satisfied."

"Oh, Tía, I am." Happy sincerity flowed in Trini's words; Tía Pancha was taken aback.

"I failed, Trini, I failed to teach you Christian ways."

"No, Tía, it's not your fault. It's the valley of Bachotigori in me." She put her head on Tía Pancha's shoulder.

"You're the wild wind." She was smoothing Trini's hair. She could not admonish any more. Buti and Lupita laughed as Tel Chen approached, followed by José Mario and Tonio.

"Time for feasting," Tel Chen announced, extending his arms in ritual welcome. They went back to the main square. Tonio told Trini what Tel Chen had said. The rain had brought good fortune. It had come in torrents and brought ganado down from the mountains. There were sheep, goats, and pigs. These didn't belong to the Indians in the village. A flash flood had driven the animals from higher ground where they had strayed to graze. The ganado belonged to hacendados who owned the big ranches on the high plateaus. Sometimes the gachupines would come down for the lost stock, but many times it was not missed. Then there were those that did not want to meddle with the Tarahumara.

So the corrals of the village held a bounty. Women barbecued over a cigüeñal while the lonjas of a pig were cut into small cubes of bacon and fried in milk. Women, with soft, graceful, rhythmic pats, were rounding tortillas made of guamuchile, a masa of black beans. A young girl offered Trini a bowl with a milky, pink liquid. She tasted it. Some kind of fruit. Tonio told her it was papache, fruit from a spiny dwarf tree. Trini and Tonio filled their bowls with food, then he led her through the broadening redness of a setting sun, by fires that glowed in half-darkness, toward a cluster of rocks away from the crowd. The coming of dusk, a mystery in the veins. She walked beside him, then Trini let him lead her to a rock where the silence of centuries rested in its hollow curve.

They ate, listening to music and laughter coming from the main square. It's so beautiful from up here, Trini observed. The good earth of Tonantzín. She looked across at Tonio, who sat concentrating on the food. He looked up, grinned, then soberly put down his bowl to look at Trini in the half-darkness. He must have sensed her thoughts, for he called out softly, "Tonantzín!"

"I'm thinking of her—how did you know?"

"You are Tonantzín."

"Me?" There was surprise in her voice.

"Forever Tonantzín."

Tonio's words rang true.

His seriousness surprised her. She said nothing, but leaned against the rock and looked down at Tonio sitting slightly below her. She handed him her bowl and knew it for a fact. "I am Tonantzín."

* * *

The journey through Indian country had almost come to an end. Only two days' travel would bring them to the mountain of Japón. They were now at the end of the barranca in a village where there was no bounty. Here, the desert clawed at life, and the village with its humble destiny was scattered haphazardly in the bowels of the barranca's edge. As they rode into the village, Tonio brought his horse alongside the wagon where Trini sat with Buti and Lupita.

"Did Chema tell you?" he asked.

"Tell me what? She looked up into his hot, dusty face.

"I'm staying in Japón. I have a friend. We're going to look for gold."

"Gold? Why gold?"

"I could ask the same thing. Why land?"

To each his dream, she thought, but the world without Tonio? "Stay with us!?" It was the pleading of a child.

"I made plans a long time ago."

"First Sabochi—now you!" There was a catch in her throat.

"Who will you miss the most?" Tonio asked, half in jest.

She looked at him, half-confused, wanting to say something, but couldn't. They were in the main square of the village where the ritual of the goat was repeated. It was the last ritual. The goat was a welcome gift to the poor villagers who had so little. There were no cornfields, no corrals with stock. In this sun frugality, it was the snake that meant survival. Trini walked through the village, and on the walls of the huts she saw hanging snakes, despined, all sizes. She stared at the snakes impaled on the wall. Her thoughts were with Tonio. A world with him was a world despined. She tried to shake herself free of sadness.

The ahau of the village invited them to a meal. As they sat in front of his hut, she looked around at the rows and rows of hanging snakes, baking in the sun. Someone handed her a dish with snakemeat, salmon pink, and dry tasteless tortillas made of mesquite. She tasted the food to be polite, swallowing the meat quickly, a piece of dry tortilla sticking to her throat. She coughed, and an old man reached out, asking, "You want tea?"

"Oh, yes." The thought of tea was delicious. He handed her a bule with manzanilla tea, hot, fragrant. It was so good! She listened to the old man explain about the snakes. The only snake that was not eaten was the coral, for the poison permeated the body. It was different with rattlers and boas. The poison from the rattlesnake, the cascabel, could be removed by cutting a handspan from head and tail. The poison could be removed from the boa by cutting off four fingers from each end. Trini drank her tea in silence, listening to the conversation, thinking of the manzanilla trees. How strange that the manzanilla tree grew on such dry land. She asked the old man about the trees and he told her that it was a miracle from the Virgen de Guadalupe. She looked at the bone-like branches of a tree near by, prospering. A miracle? Why not? Again, the secrets of the earth could well provide the moisture. It had its ways, perhaps a subterranean stream . . .

Trini was startled by a roar in the sky. Buti and Lupita yelled, "Look! Look!"

They ran to José Mario and Tonio to hide their heads from the roar and what they saw. A sense of disbelief overwhelmed Trini, a puzzled fear, for in the sky she saw a flying metal bird, a monster, glinting, roaring. She felt a coldness in her pores. What was it?

José Mario knew what it was. "It is an airplane." Trini and the children looked up at the sky and watched the metal bird roar by. José Mario was explaining. "The white man makes these metal machines that fly."

A metal machine that flies! A new kind of fear clutched at Trini, the fear of a world not of earth and simple things. The children watched in awe. Tía Pancha was explaining how she had seen them cross the skies in San Mateo. She shook her head. "They are evil things."

José Mario explained, "Progress . . ."

"What's progress?" Buti asked.

"People building machines."

"Why?"

José Mario shook his head. "I—I do not know why." His eyes seemed troubled as he looked around at his family. Worry fringed his voice. "There are new things, new dangers beyond the barranca."

"Times are changing," Tonio told them. "The alemanes have boats that swim under the ocean and people can talk to each other across the sea with a machine. There are cars."

"What are cars?" Buti asked, fascinated by what he was hearing, squinting his eyes to catch sight of the airplane now lost behind a hill.

"A wagon without a horse," Tonio explained. Everybody laughed.

"I'd rather have Sarif," said Buti in disappointment.

The plane had turned as if circling for a landing behind the hill, and the children watched excitedly. José Mario asked, "Why do airplanes come here? Do you know?"

The old man nodded, pointing to the hill. "Behind that mountain the bird comes down."

"What's behind the mountain?" José Mario asked curiously.

"Marijuana. The americanos come for it to take back to their country." How strange, thought Trini; those americanos with all their machines, so rich, like her papá said, came here for the weed of the desert! The world was hard to understand. There was a sense of fleeting dismay—the world without Sabochi, without Tonio—the world despined.

* * *

The caravan came to the cable bridge that spanned the mountains, the crossing point between the world of the Tarahumara and the world of whites. Ahead of them was the mountain of Japón. The bridge, before crossing, looked endless to Trini. It swung loose and trembled with the wind. Tonio crossed it first, the wagon rattling, swaying as it made its way across. Tonio returned, his lean tall figure, slightly stooped, hugged by the wind, his steps wide from the edge. He was beside them, taking Buti in his arms. "Ready, little fellow?"

Buti nodded, and as they made their way across, Trini saw Buti looking down miles into the river, closing his eyes as he clung tightly to Tonio; José Mario followed with Lupita in his arms. Trini followed the thin figure of Tía Pancha. Each step she took felt the momentum of the swinging bridge, the roar of the river rising, resounding in her pores. Halfway across Trini looked over the side, down into the chasm where the river carved the land below. Small whirlpools bubbled on the river's surface and Trini recalled the story of the river. This was the place where the seven-headed serpent lived, where it swallowed whole accidents of living things that crossed its path. Trini held her breath and felt the beating of her heart. The roar of river and the swirled gleams of light, the shadows of distant trees below seemed to shape for Trini the racing serpent's heads, seven strangely twisted knots, jerking spasmodically in flickering lights. Trini rubbed her eyes. It was all imagination. She looked away and saw the figure of Tía Pancha already safely across. On the other side, Buti and Lupita looked across the bridge at the world they had left behind and called out, "Goodbye, Sabochi, goodbye, Sabochi, goodbye, Sabochi!"

Trini felt a draining in her veins. Then she called out ever so softly, "Goodbye, Sabochi."

* * *

The last day's travel brought them to the outskirts of the mountain of Japón, where they stood looking down upon a town while Tonio made ready to go.

"The wagon and Sarif are yours, Chema."

"No, Tonio, we cannot take such a gift."

"It is not a gift. We are family. I won't need them. Please, Chema, give me the pleasure of leaving Sarif with you."

Tonio patted the horse one last time and gave the reins to José Mario, who took them and shook Tonio's hand in farewell. His eyes were full. "It is like saying goodbye to a son."

"Thank you, Chema." Tonio picked up the children in a playful goodbye and promised to see them soon. The next moment he had Tía Pancha by the waist, whirling her impulsively before he put her down. He grinned. "You'll miss me, Pancha!"

Tía Pancha nodded, trying hard to hold back tears. "I will miss you."

Tonio turned to say his final goodbye to Trini, but she was making her way down a hill, crying freely. When Tonio caught up with her, he made her stop. "Where're you going? San Domingo's the other way."

"I don't know. Who cares?" She was catching sobs in her throat like a child.

"I care."

"What difference does it make? You're going." There was bitterness in her voice. She sat down, her back to him, and from the top of the grassy knoll looked at the town below. "You're going to live there?"

"Nope. Just getting supplies, picking up my friend, then up the mountain." He pointed to a far-off peak outlined in the southern sky. "Trini . . ."

"Yes?"

"Who are you crying for, Sabochi or me?"

"I don't know." Her sobs were hard and desolate.

She felt the touch of his fingers on her hair and heard his voice, soft elastic:

"I'll claim you, someday . . ."

A heaving storm. She placed her head down upon her drawn knees and cried in abandon for a long time. When she was cried out, she listened to a silence opening up to engulf her in her loneliness. She turned to find Tonio gone.

8

San Domingo

"The mines in Batopilas, eh?" The manager of the office tapped a finger on the letter José Mario had given him from Mr. Johnson. Trini and José Mario, both the color of bronze, stood before him. There was a silence, then the manager stood up and walked to an open window where he stared out for a moment, turned and vaguely focused on the two people before him. He scratched his bald head with the nails of the right hand, observing José Mario's calloused hands, the thin body and the long hair. "Indian, eh?"

"We are Mexican," corrected José Mario. Trini was looking around the small dark cubicle of the office where a girl sat before a machine that made a clacking sound. The pretty girl got up and put some papers on a desk and as she did, Trini noticed the neat patent leather shoes. Shoes, pretty dress, short fluffy hair; how pretty, thought Trini. Like a picture on the calenders she had seen in a store in Batopilas. She looked up to catch the amused glance of the girl. Trini smiled, and the girl smiled back. The manager was back at his desk where he sat down heavily.

"No openings now," he sighed, then added, "but if Johnson wants you on, you're on."

"Gracias." There was relief in José Mario's voice. The manager dismissed it with a wave of the hand. "Report to Gómez in tira three at six-thirty." José Mario nodded, then, prodding Trini in front of him, made his way out of the office. At the door, Trini whispered, "They wear shoes."

"All americanos wear shoes."

The Tarahumara came to mind, los descalzos, yet she had never been conscious of the fact that she herself never wore shoes. "I wonder what it's like, wearing shoes, I mean."

"We have no need for shoes, girl." There was a streak of impatience in José Mario's voice. True, thought Trini, glancing back at the girl in the office, they had no need for them, still . . .

"Hurry up, girl," her father called. He was already on the buckboard and Tía Pancha was asking anxiously, "You have work?"

"Of course I have work, woman. Would I have come this far without the promise of work?"

The Mines Office stood isolated on a dreary, interminable grey hill that broke into open desert, several miles out of the town of San Domingo itself. As the buckboard made its way to the town, Trini saw the knife–sharp hill diminishing. Excavations, bleak and bare, were soon left behind; the road widened into a descent. In view was the town clustered around a hill, the usual mining town with its one-story wooden buildings. As they drove into the town, a company store with a hitch stump stood in view. A stunted cottonwood tree grew before a livery stable where an old rusty Model-T sat in a maze of yellow-flowered weeds. On a long building with scaly white walls hung a huge sign in black letters, CLÍNICA. The town square was almost deserted at this time of day. A brown dry world.

Trini's eye caught sight of a hill, green, with gabled roofs of enormous houses gleaming in the sun, a world set apart. José Mario was now at the turn. When they had rounded the hill, José Mario stopped in front of an adobe hut, the first of many. Next to a rain barrel was an old man with red hair and red beard standing in a doorway.

"Good afternoon, friend," José Mario called out. "Is this where the miners live?"

"Down there, in the arrabales." The old man was pointing to the descending gulch.

"We are looking for a place to stay. We have come all the way from Batopilas."

The pouches around the old man's eyes tightened. "Through Indian country?" He shook his head, then asked, "You don't know anyone in this town?"

"No," José Mario admitted. "But if there is an empty house, a room . . ."

"You have rent?"

There was worry in José Mario's voice. "We can pay some." The old man walked up to the wagon and scratched his beard. "Most of the houses belong to Don Maximiliano." Then a thought came. "Wait, Angelino died three weeks ago. His house is empty."

"Where is Angelino's house? Who do I see about it?"

"It belongs to Sebastiana, his niece, unless she already sold it to Don Maximiliano."

"Who's this Don Maximiliano?" asked José Mario curiously.

"He owns all the property. Much good it does him! He's in the asylum, went batty."

"Well, then, where do I find this Sebastiana?" Trini sensed the weariness in her father's voice. He began to cough in long, jerky spasms. "Are you alright?" the old man asked.

"Yes, yes, it's nothing." José Mario straightened up on the driver's seat. The old man turned and walked a little way down the road, pointing to a tiendita that stood at the beginning of the gulch.

"She owns La Puerta del Sol."

"Gracias."

As the wagon started on its way, the old man called out, "Sebastiana, she don't look it, but she's rich!"

Around the hill were the arrabales, El Barrio. Along the descent the mud houses became more numerous. The descent was a bumpy one, full of holes and heavy mud formations where little adobe boxes stood with lanterns glowing from windows. The huts were built along various levels of excavations and on the natural, ancient contours of mud, they looked like myrmidons resisting gravity. In some places, the pitted mud was filled in with coarse gravel until the next rains came; it seemed as if everything hung from precarious foundations, the houses melting together in the curvatures of mud. The rain's purpose, perhaps. Small children spilled from an open doorway as the moving wagon made its way to the store. An old woman watched them pass, eyes well hidden in a maze of wrinkles, her bare feet the color of mud. Before them was La Puerta del Sol.

* * *

"I'm not rich!" assured the woman who stood before them in the dark, sweet-smelling little store. She was bending forward to get a good look at the tired strangers. Trini saw before her a small, thin woman with only one bleary blue eye. The other was staring glassiness, half-covered by a sagging lid. She was leaning on a mop inside a pail. A grainy dampness and the tang of lye soap exuded from the floor. "Esteban told you that? That old redbeard! He hasn't been right since the tragedy." She gave a huge heaving sigh, then she invited them to the rooms back of the store.

Behind the counter was a door covered with a dusty green curtain. She led them into what appeared to be the kitchen. "I'll get some food." She made the offer, them went about banging pots and pans.

Soon she had served them bowls of stew made of chicken and garbanzos. She brought in an armful of beer and opened each bottle on the kitchen table before handing it out. Tía Pancha frowned, taking the beer away from the children. Sebastiana stared at Tía Pancha for a second, then shrugged. She drank half a bottle of beer, gulping freely, before she asked José Mario, "So? The Indians didn't hang you, eh?"

While they ate the good stew, José Mario talked of the journey. Sebastiana listened intently, nodding her head every so often. By the time José Mario finished, Sebastiana had drunk six beers, with Tía Pancha watching her disapprovingly. Sebastiana's one good eye was very bleary. She looked around the table good-naturedly, made a decision, then slapped her knees. "You can have Angelino's house and welcome."

"How much is the rent?" asked José Mario hesitantly.

"Angelino's smiling in heaven because his house will not be empty."

"How much is the rent?" repeated José Mario.

"Rent, rent, who wants rent?" Sebastiana sat back on her chair and challenged José Mario with a slow, deep smile, her bleary eye twinkling. Trini was getting used to the one eye. Somehow the woman's face, so eager in its interest, was alive with a beauty that made the eye unnoticeable. "It's your house!"

Her statement was final and she made her way to an icebox for another beer. She was shaking her head when she came back. "Did I tell you about Esteban? Let me tell you about the redbeard."

Tía Pancha was full of interest. "You said a tragedy?"

That was Sebastiana's cue. She heaved another sigh and took a long drink from the bottle. "Poor man! He had a son, a son you would not believe. Handsome, talented, broke all the girls' hearts. But full of pride. He paid for that." Sebastiana finished her beer.

"How?" Trini's head was up from the table where she and the children had half-fallen asleep.

"All the girls were after him, but he loved no one." Sebastiana looked into her apron pockets and found a pack of cigarettes and matches. "Well," she continued as she lighted a cigarette, "he went off into the hills, where the springs are. You saw them when you came into San Domingo."

Before the black mountains of the mines, a few miles out, there had been green hills, hills that had made Trini's heart glad. Trini was wide awake now. "We saw them!"

Tía Pancha motioned her to be quiet, as Sebastiana drew in the smoke of her cigarette and let it come out her nose. "Terrible things happen on those hills . . ."

"What happened to the boy?" asked Trini impatiently.

Sebastiana, taking her time, sat back, a foot across a knee, elbow on hand, flicking ashes thoughtfully. "Well, he went to those hills one day, fell in a crevice, broke a leg. He lay there for three days, hungry, in pain. Then one night he saw a pack of wolves coming toward him along the narrow path where he lay . . ." Sebastiana paused for effect, her eyes reaching deep inside her for memories.

"What happened?" asked Trini excitedly.

"Stop interrupting, child," Tía Pancha scolded.

"He got back home safe and sound." Sebastiana lighted another cigarette and sat forward, looking at one face, then another, waiting for someone's urging. There was only waiting silence, so she continued:

"The wolves saved him! After that, when a full moon rose, he would disappear into the hills again. One night a man from the barrio was walking home late through the hills when he saw the boy making love to a beautiful woman. He stopped to watch, naturally. But she saw him and ran away, leaving Esteban's son sitting on the grass. Now the man, he might have been drunk, or maybe not, but he claims he saw the woman change into a wolf."

Sebastiana sat back in her chair and watched their disbelief with great energy. "The boy returned to the village with a broken heart. He would never see his lady again. That didn't stop him though. He went back to the hills again and again, until one night he came home and told his father he was leaving forever."

Sebastiana sighed and looked at José Mario's empty bottle. "Want another beer?" He shook his head as she made herself comfortable, putting her feet on an empty chair, lighting another cigarette. "The woman had come back, made love to him one last time, telling him she would never return—not as a woman, anyway. But she could turn him into a wolf, that way they could stay together."

"He agreed?" Trini's voice was a near whisper.

"Of course," nodded Sebastiana with great wisdom. "That is the way of love. Poor Esteban hasn't been well since." She slapped her knee one more time and put her feet down from the chair. "I talk too much. You are tired. We go to Angelino's house." She led the way with a lantern.

* * *

"Will I go to Hell?" Lupita's eyes were full of tears as Trini cleaned the broken skin on the little girl's leg. The sobbing was more from repentance than from pain, though she squirmed and held her breath as Trini swabbed the wound with mercurochrome.

"You going to tell Tía Pancha?" piped the little girl between sobs.

"Do you want me to?"

"She'll make me kneel for hours because . . . because . . ."

"Because you took something that wasn't yours." Trini's voice was sympathetic. "No, we won't tell. Tía has enough on her mind."

Change—change—change. Papá was no longer with them. A rope had broken when José Mario climbed down a shaft. He had been taken to the clinic. The fall had not been a bad one, but at the clinic Dr. Henry had discovered that José Mario was suffering from tuberculosis. Poor, poor Papá, with his tearing cough and thin body! The company had sent him to La Clínica Lozoya in Chihuahua. His stay was to be indefinite! Everything was indefinite now. Tía Pancha had accepted it with resignation. "We must fit ourselves to what is."

Nothing is! thought Trini in desperation. But ways were found, new little certainties that would perhaps, in time, erode too, like the mud of the barrio. Life was different in San Domingo without Papá. They had to find a way to earn a living, to keep going until Papá came back. Papá, tired, dirty-black, sweating after years inside the mines, Matilda dying young, perhaps from overwork, and now Tía Pancha assuming the care of all of them. But I can help, Trini decided. I am old enough. Papá had told her that struggle was a pulling forward and could fill a life with meaning. Papá's words consoled, but they were only words. She envied the rich people on the hill.

She watched Buti and Lupita playing with the clown that had caused Lupita's tears. I can't take it away from them, Trini told herself. They've never had a toy. They took it from an empty house full of dolls—so what? She decided to let them keep the doll. She mused over the children's adventure, up on the hill . . .

* * *

Buti and Lupita were beyond the arrables and had climbed the loma of La Colonia Burgos, the residential area of the wealthy in San Domingo. It was inhabited by Germans, Americans, and gachupines, all in some way connected with the mines. Because El Barrio had sprouted in the dry gulch behind the loma, the only way to walk to town was to follow the paved white road leading up the hill, cutting across well-kept lawns and huge mansions, them down again into the town itself. The barrio people seldom did that. They would take the longer way around the hill, a hard, rocky footpath, eroded by mudslides, that took twice as long.

Buti and Lupita often did what was seldom done. This day they had gone up the hill, intrigued by the huge lawns and trees that concealed great white structures with pointed roofs, gardens, terraces. On the hill the children met a woman selling oranges. Trini had given each of the children a penny. Lupita bought an orange from the woman, but Buti held the penny tightly in his hand. It was not often that he had a penny. Now they were walking through an area where the houses had fountains and elaborate patios. Most of the houses were empty because the owners spent most of their days in Mexico City, Acapulco, and other resorts.

As the children sauntered through a grove of trees, they recognized Esteban with the red beard. He was a gardener for the rich and was setting up sprinklers when Buti and Lupita came upon him.

"Can we have a drink?" Lupita asked. Esteban pointed to a running hose and both children ran to it, pushing and shoving each other, taking turns to drink from the hose. When Lupita finished, Buti grabbed the hose and turned it on his sister. She screamed.

"Stop all that noise," scolded Esteban. "You're not supposed to be up here."

The children did not answer him, but started running toward the most palatial house of all, the one belonging to Don Maximiliano. They lost sight of Esteban as they went into the silence of a hillside lawn leading up to the house. It was green as far as the eye could see, the house on top of the slope, away from all the other houses. Lupita began to peel her orange.

"Gimme," coaxed Buti. Lupita, biting deep into her orange, shook her head. "Buy your own."

Where oranges had been plentiful in Batopilas, they were now a treat, for they had to be bought with money. It was not the simple matter of picking them off a tree.

"Just one bite," coaxed Buti again.

"No."

They were sitting on the lawn of Don Maximiliano's house and the house was empty. It looked empty. They knew about a housekeeper, but they had never seen her. The children ran to the back of the house, which had a huge patio of red and blue mosaic. The back piazza had a white domed roof. Through an enclosure, Lupita and Buti saw the inside filled with huge colored urns and large earthen vases holding tropical flowers, and all along the domed roof were puppets strung from long ropes of braided yarn. It was a beautiful array of clowns and ballerinas and horsemen grinning with painted faces and huge round button eyes. They swayed slightly in the wind. This was Buti and Lupita's favorite spot. They often came to look at the wonderful sight through the patio's gate.

"Door's open." Lupita was pointing to the doorway of the piazza. She turned an excited face to Buti, extending her hand with the orange. "You want some orange?"

"Gimme!" Buti made a grab for the orange, but Lupita took it away.

"If you climb the fence and go in there and get me a doll, I'll give you some." She made a slushing sound deliberately as she bit into the orange again.

"Tía Pancha will beat us for stealing," Buti cautioned, his eye on the orange.

"I never had a doll." Lupita's little face was against the iron gate. "They're so lonely up there."

Buti stared at the puppets, then back at his sister, who pleaded, "Don Maximiliano can't play with them because he's in the crazy house." She turned and watched Buti's face to see if she had made a point, then added, "He shouldn't have them all. Sebastiana says he sold his soul to the Devil."

Buti pressed his face hard against the iron gate, thinking. He countered. "He went crazy because he had too much money." He felt his explanation was not as exciting as Lupita's.

"Sebastiana knows better than anybody."

Lupita's reason was more exciting. The puppets grinned on. Buti noticed a sleeping dog in the patio. "There's a dog."

Lupita took another slushy bite of the orange. "He's tied up. He's so old he can't walk."

"You're eating it all up!" complained Buti, making another grab for he orange. Lupita held it high over her head, taunting. "Are you going to get the puppet?"

"You're dumb," said Buti, then reluctantly, "O.K."

Lupita quickly handed him the rest of the orange and Buti ate it in no time at all. When he finished, he complained, "It wasn't even half."

"You promised!" Lupita reminded him.

"What if the dog wakes up?"

"He's just an old dog."

"Andale pues."

Lupita gave Buti a boost and held his weight while he got one leg over the iron gate. He hung there, face down, still questioning the enterprise.

"What if the old lady comes out?"

"Nobody's home and you already ate my orange."

Hanging upside down, Buti could see the beginning of tears in Lupita's eyes. He curled himself up and went over the fence, then jumped down and ran toward the door. He climbed up on the white wooden siding and held on to a column beside it. He was now on the same level as the puppets. He called out. "Which one do you want?"

"El payaso!"

Buti made his way to the clown wearing a yellow suit and orange hair. He untied it, keeping his balance precariously. Lupita decided to help. She climbed over the fence. Buti was now now clutching el payaso in one hand, making his way down with the other, when he saw Lupita looking up at him. "What you climb over for?" he asked.

"Cause I want."

"Let's go."

They were making their way to the gate when they heard a snarl. Lupita hung on to Buti as he tried to appease the dog. "Good doggie, good doggie . . ." Buti shoved the doll into Lupita's hands. "There's your ol' doll."

Lupita clasped it to her bosom as she followed Buti to the gate. There was a fateful, almost hesitant bark. Both children stood still. The next thing they heard was the beginning of a growl.

"Run!" shouted Buti as he scampered up the gate, over, and down.

He saw the old dog advancing with newfound confidence, barking wildly as Lupita screamed and grabbed the iron railing, but not before the old dog had taken a snap at her leg. Lupita was crying as she made it over the gate, still clutching her precious payaso.

Once on the other side, they looked around. Silence. Then Buti looked at Lupita's leg. "It's nothing. Just a little blood."

The mention of blood started Lupita howling.

"Cut it out, don't be a baby," scolded Buti.

"The dog didn't bite you," Lupita reminded him.

"Maybe the Devil made the dog bite you." Buti liked his idea very much. Lupita hollered louder.

"It hurts." She was sniffling now, examining the doll, her face brightening as she hugged the grinning clown. She had forgotten the pain. They walked soberly through the soundless neghborhood. Esteban was nowhere in sight. When they came to the grove of trees, Lupita sat down to examine the wound.

"I'll clean it for you when we get home, but we better not tell anyone," Buti warned.

Lupita was whimpering as Buti plopped down on the grass beside her. "Why are you crying now? It doesn't hurt much."

"I'm crying because of Papá, that's why."

Buti was silent. He felt like crying too. The children looked up at the giant trees. There was no more speckled sun. A cold blue dusk was upon them.

"We better get back," Buti said as he helped his sister up. Tears were still streaming down her face as they ran down the path. They were now at the foot of the loma. Buti hurried down the footpath that led from the main street into the arrabales. It led into a tortuous callejón full of mudholes, thorny weeds and broken glass. After that, they passed the church, then the public bathhouse. Mud everywhere. The day's sun had left it crusting after the rain's softness of the night before. Past the public baths were several small shacks with open doors. A woman was scolding a small boy as she wiped his face clean with a cloth. The smell of cooking corn invaded the slight breeze that searched the shadowed walls of houses. Some women stood talking with poised, soft fingers, spelling the doings of the day. Two girls sat outside a doorway drying each other's hair in the last rays of the sun. The two children trudged to the high edge of the gulch. Lupita was limping. "It hurts."

Buti led the way through brittle grass sprouting out through the mud. They were now in front of Angelino's house. Buti waited for

Lupita to catch up, and then took her hand protectively. "I'll take care of you."

They went into the house.

* * *

"You'll manage." Sebastiana's voice had a ring of reassurance. Tía Pancha sat at the kitchen table looking skeptical. "I don't know." Her voice was worried.

"We can do it, Tía." Trini agreed with Sebastiana. Now that José Mario was no longer the breadwinner, plans were taking shape with the help of Sebastiana.

"Angelino used to deliver spring water to the people on the loma. Even people down here buy it. The water trucks are too irregular. You have a wagon and horses, cannisters, and I have a list of his customers."

"That won't be enough." Tía Pancha was still distraught.

Sebastiana was not one to give up. "You make your white bread and sell it. No one has seen white bread around here. You'll have more orders than you can handle."

Tía Pancha began to brighten, catching on to the spirit of planning. "Also, the hills are full of yerbas. I know them all. I can gather and sell them."

"Good," Sebastiana agreed, slapping her knee.

"We'll be alright until Papá gets back." Trini believed it. She had to believe it. Dear Sebastiana! She had asked Trini to work at the store. Sebastiana was doing it to help them out with groceries. Trini wondered if she were really needed. "Your daughter, Kata, doesn't she help you at the store?"

"That good-for-nothing. Always pregnant. Five children now!" Kata was not a happy subject with Sebastiana. She really loved her daughter and grandchildren, but could not stand her lazy son-in-law. He had been responsible for the loss of Sebastiana's eye. One day she had interfered in one of their fights, and he had come after his mother-in-law with a gun. Of course, he had been very drunk. The bullet was still in Sebastiana's head, for Dr. Henry had refused to take it out, claiming that it would kill her. She had lost one eye, however, and any love for her son-in-law. Kata's fights with her husband were regular. She would leave him for a while, staying at her mother's then go back repentent only to get pregnant again. Sebastiana claimed the bullet was part of her brain now.

At this moment she sat, grinning broadly, on the edge of a chair with the palms of her hands flat on her knees. It was a thinking pose for Sebastiana. "If you package those herbs, Pancha, I know a yerbería in San Miguel where they'll buy from you."

Sebastiana always had an answer and a solution to things. Go to the springs for water, bake bread, help Sebastiana at the store. A way of life . . . was that all? Papá was not coming back for a long time. Dr. Henry had said two years. Two years! But Dr. Henry should know. "Is he a good doctor, Sebastiana?"

"The best," Sebastiana assured her. She took her thoughtful pose again, head turned to one side, palms hard on the knees. "In spite of what he did . . ."

Trini and Tía Pancha waited. Sebastiana was in her glory again. She leaned back and crossed her arms, to make a grand accusation.

"He murdered his wife."

"Murdered his wife!" Sometimes it was hard to believe everything Sebastiana said. Still Trini and Tía Pancha listened intently.

"I speak the truth, as God is my witness." Sebastiana's voice rang clear.

She spoke of Dr. Henry fondly—a shy man, dedicated to doctoring, to helping the poor. A good man, but diabolical too—he had managed to get rid of his old wife. The wife had believed in spirits, claiming she was hexed. Dr. Henry believed that had been the cause of a long illness. One night she had walked out of the house and gone to the hills, never to return. A search party failed to find her. No traces of the wife were found, ever. Dr. Henry's words were never doubted.

"Why do you say he killed her?" asked Trini.

"Ah—ha!" Sebastiana almost jumped out of her chair, raising her finger in the air. "After the wife had been gone for a month or so, guess what he did?" Sebastiana paused dramatically, not waiting for an answer in particular. She smiled broadly. "He went to San Miguel and brought home a girl. Young pretty thing. She's his housekeeper—housekeeper, indeed!"

Sebastiana assured them that her opinion was the consensus of the whole barrio, but she still insisted, "He's the best doctor we could have." She sighed. "Men will be men."

Tía Pancha agreed.

* * *

Trini was crying softly as she washed dishes. Tears fell into the dishwater forming little soapy circles. She was thinking of Chimac, the baby and Sabochi. She wiped her eyes with the back of her hand and decided to be sensible. She looked at the beans cooking on the stove. They were done. She took them off the fire and put them aside. It was time to start out for La Puerta del Sol. Trini went into the other room to remind the children she was leaving.

"Tía Pancha will be home soon," Trini told them in parting, as the two little ones sat on the floor playing with el payaso. Tía Pancha was out making her bread deliveries.

Once outside, Trini walked close to the edge of the houses. The shade created by the roofs gave her a narrow cool path. It was a five minute walk to the store, but this time of day was not for walking. Such a hot afternoon! She felt sticky, dirty, and desolate. The neighborhood ladies were coming to the store to play cards today. Trini enjoyed hearing them talk.

As she came to the front entrance of the store, pigeons flew off the roof. She watched them scatter in the sky. No one was in the front of the store when she went in. She went through the green curtain. Sebastiana was sitting at the table playing cards. She was playing her usual solitaire, flipping the cards expertly and placing them with swift movements in the rows spread out before her. Trini saw Kata stretched out on a petate on the floor. She lay with her arm over her eyes, her stomach already a round gentle slope. Her children were scrambling around with a ball, using the sleeping bulk of their mother as part of the game. They shouted noisily; Kata sat up, scolding. "For God's sake, can't you be quiet?"

She sat awkwardly with feet spread out before her and reached for a magazine to fan herself. Sebastiana looked up from her cards, observed Trini through half-closed lids, then returned to her game, asking, "Want a pop?"

"A bath, that's what!" Trini blew the hair from her forehead.

"Sounds good." Kata had an idea. "Let's go to Lin Wang's." Lin Wang owned the public baths.

Delicious, thought Trini. She had never been. She asked Sebastiana, "Is there time before the ladies come?"

"Sure, sure, sure . . ." shouted Sebastiana with eyes on her cards.

"I'm leaving the children here, Mamá," Kata warned as she struggle to her feet.

"Sure, sure, sure . . ." repeated Sebastiana, oblivious to the children's shouts and Kata's warning.

Lin Wang bowed low as Kata and Trini went into the public baths. Lin Wang was one of the few people in the barrio who had running water. The girls put their coins in the box that read Pague aquí and went into the two empty cubicles with overhead faucets. Trini undressed and turned on the water, feeling its coolness like a caress. She closed her eyes to the luxury. After showering, she wrapped her body in a large piece of muslin that Kata had brought along. She felt much better. She waited for Kata on a bench in the small humid space outside the showers. She was drying her hair with the edge of the cloth when she saw the old Chinese man come toward her. He bowed politely and with a big smile told her, "You beautiful young lady."

Trini felt somewhat embarrassed by the sudden compliment. She murmured, "Thank you." He bowed again and left. Trini went back to the shower room to dress. When she came out, Kata was waiting. As they walked toward the door, Lin Wang came up to them again. This time a pretty girl about seventeen followed him. He bowed low again and pointed to the girl. "My wife."

Trini found it hard to believe. She was so young and the old man must be a century old! As they walked toward the door, Lin Wang called out, "You very beautiful girl."

"Why does he say that?" asked Trini curiously.

Kata laughed as if it were a very funny thing. "He was probably looking at you through one if his peep-holes while you were bathing."

"What?"

"He does that, especially with girls new to the neighborhood."

"You didn't warn me!"

"And spoil his fun!" Kata laughed, then added, "He's harmless."

"But . . ."

"But what? Don't begrudge the old man a simple pleasure."

"That girl?"

"She married him because he's rich."

"He's a terrible old man!" accused an indignant Trini.

"Don't be a prude. He's a nice little man."

Trini and Kata laughed. Then Kata offered another piece of information about Lin Wang. It seemed that he bragged to the whole town about having twelve wives in China. Supposedly he had outlived six wives since coming to Mexico. "Can you imagine?" No, Trini couldn't imagine.

Sebastiana was still playing cards when they returned. The children seemed to have disappeared. Kata asked, "Where are they, Mamá?"

"I sent them off to look for bottle caps. Whoever finds the most, gets a free pop."

"That was clever, Mamá, but they're not outside." Kata was somewhat impatient with her mother's ways.

"I told them to go down the gulch a way."

Kata took off mumbling under her breath. Sebastiana was still glued to her game. Trini sat down to watch, thinking that Sebastiana's sly, ingenious concentration demanded respect. Sebastiana was taking a puff from her cigarette, placing it in a saucer already full of cigarette butts. Without looking up, she reached for it again to take another puff. Trini always knew when she had a problem with her game, for the old woman would forget the cigarette, letting it dangle precariously from her lips as if it were pasted there. Light from the high window in the kitchen fell on the sightless eye, giving it a look of eagerness, an owlish look. Finally, Sebastiana looked up, stretched, and put out the stub of cigarette. Then she stood, scratching her stomach, and went to the icebox for a beer.

Trini heard the voices of Doña Paz and Señora Ortega inside the store. Sebastiana yelled, "Come out here where it's cool!" She had set out chairs, tables and glasses on the back porch where there was a cross-breeze between two side doors.

In an hour's time, six ladies were gathered talking about the latest gossip in San Domingo. Trini was sitting behind the counter in the front of the store. She could hear the conversation through the curtained entrance.

"Have you heard about the girl?" Señora Ortega asked breathlessly.

"What girl?"

There was the sound of someone shuffling cards and the pushing back of chairs. Another lady was asking, "Do we play bingo on Friday?"

"Let's make a pot of twenty centavos each and add twenty more on Friday."

"If you're rich!"

"I don't have any money."

"Put up your husband as the stake. Ha! Ha! Ha!"

Laughter rose, then Señora Ortega raised her voice deliberately. "Have you heard about Raquel's new girl?".

All the ladies seemed to be listening now. Señora Ortega continued, "Raquel found her, starved in San Morales. An Indian. The poor girl says she has no name."

"Did you hear the story from Raquel?" someone asked.

"I don't talk to the likes of her!" answered Señora Ortega indignantly.

To be seen in the company of Raquel was demeaning to the ladies of the barrio. Much less to speak to her, for Raquel was the local Madam, a rich one. As a girl she had been Don Maximiliano's mistress, and he had rewarded her by giving her a piece of land alongside the highway leading to the springs. Here, Raquel had built herself a very profitable brothel composed of a motel and a beer garden. Don Maximiliano had sent for a huge neon sign all the way to a city in the United States called Chicago.

Sebastiana knew Raquel to be the Devil's favorite. Raquel didn't simply sell her soul to the Devil, in fact she flaunted it, and the Devil could not refuse. The deeds attributed to her were many. Raquel recruited virgins at High Mass, and she knew how to repair maidenheads when virgins could not be found. She was well connected with politicians and many of the rich and powerful came out of her motel with loosened trousers. She kept a pimp by the name of Héctor who herded and guarded her girls and who drew her bath and cut her toenails.

"How did Raquel get her hooks on the poor girl?"

"The child was lost and alone, sitting on a street corner. Seems her people went back to the barranca without her."

"Is she a virgin?"

"Not anymore!"

A virgin! Tía Pancha had often admonished Trini's playfulness with Tonio. On discovering that Trini already had a "monthly" and no one had enlightened her on how babies came to be, Tía Pancha had sat her down one day and with bountiful Christian duty, explained the importance of virginity. A girl must be very careful and remain unsullied up to her marriage day. She must go to her husband pure and dutiful. Then Tía Pancha proceeded to explain how babies were made. Now this Indian girl had been violated. She was impure. How terrible!

"¡Que Dios la ayude!"

Trini sat at the counter and thought about the Indian girl, frightened, alone. She thought of Chimac. She wanted to run, to find her way to Raquel's place, to burst through doors and help the Indian girl. If only I could do something—anything. She felt so helpless, full of an injustice, as she sat listening. Why did they make a joke of it? It was so sad. In the blackness of her mood, Trini heard Sebastiana calling out. "Hey, Trini, come have some guacamole!"

9

The Girl With No Name

It was just before dawn. The moon, disdainful of the dark, moved among wisps of grey. Trini was leading Sarif in a cautious ascent through the gulch, up toward the road leading to the springs in the hills outside San Domingo. It was an hour's trip. When she came to the road, she got on the buckboard and took hold of the reins. She called out softly, "Andale, Sarif!"

The horse reared its head slightly, then made his way down the highway outlined by the moon. The empty cannisters clattered as they were jostled by uneven ground. Trini felt uneasy during these rides in half darkness. She had made many trips to the springs, but even so, the feeling was still there. A job that had to be done. The ride was a long one, and she had to get back to make deliveries early. Half an hour's ride on the highway, to the right, Trini saw Raquel's famous pasture, the open field with its tall swaying grass. It curved out of sight as a cluster of trees came into view. Beyond them was El Jardín de Venus. The notorious neon lights were not on, but she made out the outline of the huge square sign high on the roof of the motel; it was set back from the road.

Huge trees circled the beer garden, then grew in a serpentine fashion toward the highway. What was that? A darting small shadow was weaving through the trees, coming toward the highway. Who could it be at this hour of the morning? Trini felt a prickle of fear. She urged Sarif to go faster. The horse broke into a run. Trini was not going to wait to find out who was running toward the road. From a safe distance, she looked back.

Trini made out the figure of a girl running after the wagon, crying out thinly, "Please, please, help me!" Her heart pounded as she pulled back the reins somewhat reluctantly. Was she doing the right thing? Of course she was. The girl obviously needed help. The girl was waving frantically, running toward the wagon. Trini sat waiting, her hands nervously twisting the reins.

She heard the girl's hoarse, frightened voice as she came up to the wagon, "He's after me!" Instinctively, Trini turned to see who was following, her eyes darting from trees to pasture to road. She saw no one. The girl scrambled up the wagon as Trini quickly urged the horse into a run. It gathered speed. Trini looked back again. This time, out of the corner of her eye, she saw the figure of a man shaking his fists at them. Dear God! The girl had been right. Someone was after her. Was he going to follow? She halfheartedly assured herself that the wagon was too fast for him. She turned to see him stop, shaking his fists at them, then turn away toward the trees.

"Who is he?" Fear crowded Trini's voice. The girl beside her was crying, face down, long Indian braids dangling past the buckboard seat. Trini let her be. After a while, the girl looked up, eyes opened wide and fearful. She gulped the word, "Héctor . . ."

Trini recognized the name. Raquel's pimp! She was grim, concentrating on the road. Shadows sank and rose as the wagon climbed the hill and the road narrowed. They were coming to the springs. Along the way, the girl looked back furtively. It was light now. Trini breathed freely as they neared the water.

Trini knew who the girl was, the girl with no name, the one Raquel had found in Gran Morales. They were on a side path. The wagon climbed for half a mile to the huge boulders that led to the springs. Trini looked at the girl from the corner of her eye. She was not crying anymore.

The early morning air was tinged with moisture—the taste of the springs. No more fear—all washed away. The sky was so near. Trini wondered if the girl felt as relieved as she did. No. Her small body was tense, her frightened eyes full of pain. She's no longer a virgin, thought Trini. She needs to be with her loved ones. "Where do you live?"

"Miriachi."

"That's deep in barranca country."

"Help me." The girl was crying softly, helplessly.

"What can I do?" Trini felt very helpless herself. The girl's eyes pleaded, "Help me get back home."

"I have to go for help. There's a cave beyond that hill," Trini explained. "It's covered over by bushes; you hide there just in case and I'll go back to town."

"Hide?" New fear rose in the Indian girl's voice.

"Yes, I'll show you where. It's beyond the spring. You can help me fill the cannisters."

"Yes—I'll help." The girl wiped her eyes and smiled trustingly. They carried the cannisters up a path leading to a break in the hill. Beyond the break, they came upon a hill whose imperceptible folding and faultings had formed passageways for the secret waters that ran through it. It reminded Trini of Bachotigori. The silence was interrupted only by the current's turbidity. They rolled the empty cannisters up the smooth rocks until they reached a pool of crystal water. Here, on the edge of the pool the whisperings of water had carved into the stone for thousands of years. Here the water welled, almost silver in its clearness. They filled the cannisters, then they sat down to rest on a huge boulder.

"I hide—you come back?" the girl asked hesitantly.

"I promise. I'll be back. I'll bring someone who can help you get back to Miriachi."

"I can go back with you now."

"No, he might see us."

"Héctor?" There was terror in the girl's voice.

"Yes. I don't think he will stop me if I'm alone. I'll go very fast."

The girl did not protest. She walked toward the edge of the water and looked down at its silvery clearness. Trini came up behind her and asked, "You have a name?"

"My name is Mahki. I give you my name."

I give you my name—that was another way, thought Trini, of telling me that she trusts me, that she puts her fate in my hands. She reached out and touched Mahki's face. "I will get help, I promise." Her voice was sure, determined. They sat down by the water's edge, Mahki trailing her hand in the water, her eyes mirroring hope.

* * *

Before she reached the pasture, Trini checked to see if the cannisters were securely tied to the wagon. If she had to race the horse past the pasture, the water musn't spill. All the way down the mountain, Trini felt apprehensive. When the dead neon sign surrounded by the cluster of trees loomed before her, she took a deep breath, then tugged the reins: "Yaiiiiiiii!"

The trot became a gallop, the gallop became a run. Sarif raced easily on the open road until they reached the half-moon turn. Suddenly Trini saw it. A wagon across the road. Dear God—a trap! She reined Sarif hard off the highway to avoid a collision. Sarif snorted, wheeled and turned toward the pasture. He was headed for El Jardín de Venus through tall swaying grass! As he raced through the pasture, the wagon jerked and bounced as if it were coming apart. She pulled hard on the reins, the leather cutting into her palms.

"¡Para! ¡para!" she screamed. The horse slowed to a stop. The motel was in front of her. She caught her breath in fear, but immediately gathered her wits. With quick, deft movements she tugged at the reins. "Go back, Sarif, back!"

The big horse did not swing around fast enough. She recognized the man running toward her in the tall grass. Héctor! Panic exploded. She would ride hard, right over him, if necessary. She closed her eyes as she came close, praying, "Please, God, let me get to the highway."

She saw him crouch as the wagon approached. Trini's breathing was a painful rasp. The wagon would go over him. She was so close she could see the defiance on his angry face. But as she came close, he sprinted to one side, then jumped into the wagon.

She kept on going, running Sarif from one sharp turn to another, hoping that the zigzag momentum would throw him off. Please, please, let him fall, let him fall! No. He was next to her now on the buckboard seat. She could see him from the corner of her eye, his face mottled as he heaved his weight against her, attempting to throw her off balance. Trini felt herself falling, a whirring of speeding wheels, tall grass weaving, drowning her, then the hard ground. She fell and rolled and seemed to crumble. The ground tore and scratched, and the whirls of dust choked her nostrils. She lay face down and screamed into the dust. Then her hand touched something hard. She opened her eyes and saw her hands already digging at a piece of wood buried in the dirt by rain and moving mud. Between a rhythm of deep sobs and heavy labored breathing, she dug with her fingernails until she wrenched it from the ground. She stood up and looked around. Yes, he was coming toward her. She would run, but first she must hit him hard to get past him. That would give her time.

He ran toward her with arms outstretched. He would try to grab the piece of wood from her. She waited until he was near enough, then she raised the heavy, muddy piece and struck him on the left side of the face. She ran and ran and ran, never looking back. Then she heard heavy breathing and cursing behind her. She did not stop. Her feet were heavy, her ankles ached. She saw the highway just ahead. Suddenly, she felt a heavy hand digging at her arm. She struggled to get free, but could not. He was before her now, blood running down his face. She bent her head and dug her teeth into his arm, tasting the salty sweat of his skin.

He struck out with a closed fist that caught her on the jaw. The sun turned black, then red, then she focused blurrily on his face as he flashed down upon the piece of wood in her hand. It flew out, leaving her defenseless. He pushed her to the ground and fell hard on top of her. She could breathe no more. She managed to wriggle out from under him, scratching him across the eyes. He cursed and hit her twice with closed fists as he pushed her down; her head hit something hard. Pain and darkness took over.

* * *

Trini woke up in a room full of shadows. Slanting sunlight drifted in from a high window. Her head throbbed and she felt swelling on one side of her face. Her body was sapped. She lay face up, body lax, arms flung out on a small hard bed. She did not want to get up, but she had to get up. Her mind told her to get up. A muscle in her leg jerked in pain. She felt as if her head were too heavy to lift up. With difficulty, she raised herself on her elbows, her head thrown back, a crushing, painful weight. She saw the door. How far away it looked, wavering at a distance. She had to make her way to the door, but she could not stand the weight of her head. She fell back in bed and closed her eyes, waves of nausea weaving through her body. Am I going to die? she wondered. No, no, no, her mind said. Then she floated into a blackness where body and time were forgotten . . .

After a while she woke up again with a start. The headache was still there. She turned over on her stomach, breathing deep, looking at the door. I must get out of here—out of here—out of here. Her body was not ready to obey. There was a ringing in her ears as if her whole being were one loud neverending bell. It's the beating of my heart, yes, the beating of my heart. Pieces began to fall into place: She must get to the door to escape. The door—the door. She forced herself to a sitting position, her feet catching the weight of her body. Steady, steady. A seething ache rippled through her. With effort, she made it to the door, clutched the doorknob, turned it, shook it. The door would not give. She slid to the floor and cried. She stopped and sat numbly for a while, then she made a mental note of the fact that there was still sunlight. How long had she been unconscious?

If the door wouldn't give, there must be some other way! The window was too small and too high, but she would try.

Disregarding the soreness of her body, she put her weight against a chest and dragged it to the window, climbed it, then worked on trying to pry the window open. It was useless. The window would not give. She was breathing hard, blood awakened, warming up her body. Trini made her way to the door again, pounding, pounding, calling out, but there was only silence. She put her ear to the door, attempting to catch some sound. Nothing. Another thought came. The doorknob—the door was locked, but she could hack the wood around it—it might give—it might give. She needed something sharp. She searched—the chest—a night table with drawers. Her eyes fell on an ashtray full of cigarette butts, a man's pair of shoes on the floor a shirt thrown carelessly in a corner of the room. A man's room!

With a growing fear, she looked through drawers quickly, feverishly. She found an old rusty canopener. Clutching it, she closed her eyes to ease the throbbing in her head. She made her way to the door again. She hacked and hacked, but found that only splinters chipped off. She realized it was an impossible task. She let her body fall to the floor by the edge of the bed.

She wanted to give in to tears, but held them back. This was not the time. She must do something, something . . . All she could do was to give in to the ache again. She must be calm, drown out fear. She breathed deeply, watching particles of dust swim a skein of sunlight. She almost fell asleep again watching the threads of light. . . . The sound of footsteps woke her up. Her body tensed, her mind froze. She heard a key in the lock. She knew who it was. Terror ran through her as she rose and made her way to the shadows behind the door, pressing her body against the wall to disappear, the canopener still clutched in her hand.

The door opened. Héctor entered, his eyes darting slits; on his swarthy face he wore a gold-toothed grin from which spurted twisted, hot profanities. Trini began to shake convulsively and confusion scooped and scattered in her body as Héctor turned and saw her.

She felt a dried, burnt sensation in her throat. His eyes mocked. She swiftly threw the canopener, aiming at his face. He ducked and made a grab for her. His arm was a vice around her throat. She crumpled, but he held her up. She could smell liquor on his breath. She could feel herself tremble. The trembling grew. She struggled, digging her teeth into his arm. He cried out in pain. Again, curses. She backed away from him until the back of her knees were caught on the edge of the bed He pushed her violently onto it. Her screams came in shuddering gasps. They ricocheted in the room, back and forth, up and down. She tried to push him away, but it was impossible. He held her down with all his weight. The heaviness of his body splintered her breath. With a violent pull he tore her dress, and when she tried to scream again, he covered her mouth. There was a terrible thrust that made her wince, then all things were blurred by a thick, nauseating misery, a tongue of pain, the lift and fall of his sweaty, heaving body. Her eyelids closed in helplessness. In the shallow shadows her eyes photographed the coarse contours of his legs, his face distorted, formless. Her nostrils caught the black smell of his sweaty armpits, then her senses folded into nothingness.

* * *

The door was open. Héctor was gone. She lay stunned. The shape of hurt grew and bounded. It became the whimper of a lost child. She wanted to die. The uncleanliness of things overwhelmed her. There was a stench she did not recognize. Awareness ripened in her senses. A cold night breeze was chilling her body. Reflections from the blinking neon light made strange, mocking patterns on the wall. She told herself—get up—go, go, run, run, run. She was suddenly conscious of her naked limbs, the torn clothing. She sat up in bed and pulled a sheet off it to cover herself. She went to the door and saw the light of the neon turn the pasture a garish red that blinked itself into a green, then a purple—a dirge. The door led directly into the open pasture. She was in the last room opposite the beer garden. She heard voices and music behing the heavy vines that covered the trellis around the garden.

She ran toward the highway. The tall grass and leaves from the enormous trees swayed blithely in a cold wind. She looked back once and caught the lights of the neon sign flashing and winking like a mechanical Satan. The night's descending winds carried her swiftly through tall grass that seemed to sway in sadness. She stumbled on one of the cannisters that had fallen off the wagon. The beginning of a wave of hysteria sent a shivering through her body. The cannister gleamed a coldness that knifed her very bones. Then she was out of the pasture and on the road.

* * *

Tía Pancha prepared a hot bath for her. Her eyes were rimmed in red as she went about helping Trini, smoothing her hair, weeping silently, speaking in soothing tones.

"My poor, poor child, get in the water, wash off . . . wash off . . ." Tía's voice broke. A rage, a pendulum motion of anger and sorrow swelled in Trini. Tía Pancha was holding her. "He could have killed you, my child."

"I wish he had!"

"No—you're lucky to be alive," comforted her aunt.

"Alive? After what he did to me?"

"Yes." Her aunt's voice was steady, sure.

"What's to become of me now?" Trini said bitterly.

"You go on with your life."

"I'm dirty!" Trini's voice rose in passion. "He must be punished for what he did!"

"It's not easy, my child . . ." There was resignation in Tía Pancha's voice.

"I'm not a virgin anymore, am I?" Trini whispered.

"It doesn't matter."

"You said it did. You said it mattered very much!" Trini was hysterical. "I'm dirty, dirty, dirty . . ."

"Sh! Quiet down, child. Here, get in the water."

Tears streamed down Trini's face as she let her body drop into the warm soothing water, its warmth a kind of forgetfulness. The clawing emotions subsided. She closed her eyes and felt the unfolding of fatigue. She was suspended in a sea of grey, a kind and safe harbor. She wanted to stay in the water forever. Safe, safe, safe . . . She was falling asleep, the pain melting in a buoyant warmth. She opened her eyes wide, startled, when Tía Pancha touched her on the shoulder. The water was now cold. "You'll get chilled," Tía Pancha whispered. Her aunt was holding a clean piece of burlap. Trini slipped out of the tina and wrapped it around herself. Her pores tingled with cleanliness. Suddenly, she thought of Mahki, she had promised Mahki—Mahki was waiting. She clutched Tía Pancha's hand, words falling heavily. "Help her, the Indian girl. Get Sebastiana, Tía, she can find Esteban, someone to help Mahki, please . . ."

"Tomorrow, Trini, tomorrow."

"No, now, now!" Trini's voice wore hysteria as an undersurface, muffled by her will.

"It is three in the morning, child."

Trini shook her head. "It has to be now, now."

"Tomorrow. Be sensible. Tomorrow."

Trini sat down at the kitchen table, the cloth held tightly around her, her body shivering, her voice a mere mumble, "Now, now, now . . ." Her head was down on the table. Fatigue took over, she was asleep.

* * *

When Trini woke up, a shivering of the mind jerked into focus the events of the night before. She was lying, warmly covered, on her petate; before her, Sebastiana's feet paced the floor.

"The girl's gone. We combed the hills. The Indian girl is simply gone," Sebastiana was saying. "Six of us spread out and combed those hills until the sun went down . . . not in the cave. Not anywhere."

Until the sun went down? How long had she slept? They were talking about Mahki. She was gone. Gone where? Trini stirred. Sebastiana was beside her, bending down to stroke her cheek. "Pobrecita inocente, may his soul burn in hell!"

Sebastiana knew. Everybody would know soon. Trini felt engulfed in shame, the old helpless anger rising again. She spoke calmly, asking, "How long did I sleep?"

"A whole day, practically."

A whole day! They had looked for Mahki all day. She asked, "You didn't find her? I'll go with you . . ."

"It's no use, child. I know those hills like the back of my hand. She's just not there." Sebastiana paused, then shaking her head, she predicted, "She either made her way back to Gran Morales and went off into the barranca by herself, or . . ." She paused again, her tone ominous now, "Héctor found her."

"No, no, no . . ." Trini was crying in huge heaving sobs. She remembered the trust in Mahki's face. "I promised . . ."

" It's not your fault, child. After what happened to you . . ." She knew that Sebastiana was trying to console her, but her words held the brunt of the nightmare she wanted to forget. Shame–shame–the face of Héctor–the gold tooth grinning. God no! Would she ever forget? Sebastiana's own angry voice was planning some kind of action. "Pancha, you must report this crime to the authorities. Hell, la policía is in with Raquel, but we must have a hand at justice . . ."

"What's the use . . ." Tía Pancha's voice sounded hopeless, bitter.

"Pancha, it's your duty."

"Yes, yes, yes," sobbed Trini, "He must suffer as I suffer."

She was sobbing wildly in Tía Pancha's arms.

* * *

The palacio municipal, where the office of the police chief was, had been an old fort. The building was in need of much repair. Trini and Tía Pancha walked through the long hall looking for the office marked JEFE. People passed them in the hall, but Trini looked straight ahead, avoiding their eyes. A nervousness suffused her as she followed her aunt into the Jefe's office.

A huge electric fan was whirring over a desk where a man, wearing a uniform, sat. In a firm voice, Tía Pancha asked to see the police chief. The man looked at them curiously since people from the barrio seldom came to see the Jefe. The man went into an inner office and after a few minutes reappeared. He motioned them to follow.

In the inner office, the Jefe sat at his desk, drinking something in a tall glass. He took a handkerchief out of his pocket and wiped his brow. He, too, looked at the two women quizzically. "Yes?" There was irritation in his voice.

Tía Pancha stood tall and stern as she repeated the crime committed against Trini. El Jefe shifted his gaze from Tía Pancha to Trini, who told herself, don't be ashamed, face up to him. But she was unable to look him in the face. She heard his voice, gruff, unsympathetic, "Are you sure it was this, eh, Héctor?"

Trini nodded in confusion.

"It's a serious accusation, you understand." His voice was menacing.

Dear God, he doesn't believe me! Anger overwhelmed Trini. Why? El Jefe was saying, "Raquel is an influential citizen. Idle accusations should not be made against one of her employees."

"He's a pimp!" There was angry scorn in Tía Pancha's voice. But Trini knew that they were wasting words. The ways of the world were cruel. The thought bound her to her own agony. El Jefe was addressing her now. "Have you ever been to El Jardín de Venus before, eh, girl?"

Again, an accusation more than a question. She clutched the edge of the chair where she was sitting until her knuckles turned white.

"Speak up!" His voice was loud and rude.

"I—I have never been there before."

"How old are you?"

"Fifteen . . ."

"Did you tell your aunt here the truth?"

Trini looked up and saw the Jefe's expression, suggestive, lewd. She felt the blood rushing to her face. She stood up and gestured helplessly, her eyes bright with bewilderment. She turned and ran out of the room, out of the office, through the hall, into the street, into the alley where Sarif had been secured. She struggled into the wagon and sat there, hunched in misery. Her whole body was shaking. What now? What now? she asked herself. No! She would not spend the rest of her life crying. What happened, happened. There was nothing she could do about it. It was so unfair! El Jefe had insinuated she was to blame! Through the agony, words came to her, words that were a strength—Sabochi's words—"Grow in stillness, little woman, grow in stillness."

"Can I, Sabochi?" she whispered to the empty corner of the world where she sat. Her Tía Pancha was getting into the wagon. There was bitterness on her face.

"We are only women, Trini, poor women from the barrio. There is no justice for the likes of us!"

They were both one painful chrysalis of helplessness and anger.

10

Revenge

"My baby's going to die?" The words were hardly audible. Trini walked to a window in the reception room of the clinic and stared out at a cold bleak day. She peered out gloomily at a pile of adobe against the side of the wall and felt an impalpable force bearing down on her. The weight of the world. A vague terror paralyzed in silent hysteria began to rise in her. She bit her lip hard, teeth refusing to let go, until the taste of blood touched her tongue. She closed her eyes and held her throat with open hands as if to crush out breath.

"Are you alright?"

Dr. Henry was behind her, his voice kind, restrained. She nodded, still not turning to him, feeling his hand on her arm. "Sit down, Trini. I'll get you some water."

"No. I'm alright." She let him lead her to a chair. She sat, hands on knees, fists clenched. She could not look at him. She could not look at anyone. His voice was heavy with sympathy. "I wish I could tell you there was a chance. But there's not. It'll be over any time now. The baby never had a chance, Trini. What's wrong with her happened before she was born."

Before she was born! before she was born! She looked up, eyes moist with pain, whispering, "May I stay with her until . . ."

"Of course. Do you want Pancha with you? Anyone?"

She shook her head, pausing for a minute to get her voice under control. "No, no."

"I'll take you to her."

The room was dark and quiet and the baby lay in a crib against a window covered by the steel-grey branches of a willow. She had been with her baby only a few minutes before Dr. Henry had come to tell her the baby would not live. Now, she sat watching the little sleeping form, tiny little hands jerking in the stillness that was harshened by the bare branches outside the window. She took the tiny little hand for a moment, then quickly let it go to stare out at the misshapen, skeletal branches of the willow. "Are you punishing me, God?"

The question filled the room. She leaned her head against the window and stared at the grey of sky and tree. It's because I didn't want the baby at first, not at first. If only I could push the fear of death away. Perhaps the thought of life . . .

* * *

The door burst open, letting in the gloom. Trini stood outlined in the doorway. She was unkempt, dirty, her hair falling wildly around her shoulders, her face wearing the greenness of the day now gone.

"Where have you been?" questioned Tía Pancha.

"Planting Papá's seeds."

"Where?"

A burning savagery shone in Trini's eyes, "The hills." She walked to the table, reaching into a pocket, coming up with a few seeds in her hand. She put them on the table and spread them out with her fingers. "I promised Papá I would plant his seeds on our land." She paused, a certain regret in her eyes, but then went on, "But in the hills, I felt the earth wanted seed, enough to make the earth glad . . ."

"Are you alright?" Tía Pancha's voice was apprehensive.

Trini sat down at the table, spreading out her hands to look at them. They were dirty and scratched, her fingernails clotted with earth. She laughed softly to herself. "I will watch the seeds grow. Papá will be glad to know. I'll write and tell him." The excitement in her voice wavered at the thought of Papá. Now, she pleaded, "When is he coming home?"

Tía Pancha only shook her head. There was no need to discuss José Mario. They all knew that he would be gone for a long time. The aunt turned worried eyes toward Trini. "You shouldn't stay out in the hills so late, not in your condition . . ."

Trini winced. She did not want to be reminded. She still could not accept the fact that she was pregnant. Héctor's child! She bit her lip and stared blankly at a flickering lantern, then put her head down on her arms. Tía Pancha changed the subject. "Look what I bought in town today."

It was seldom that they had any money to buy anything. Trini looked up. Tía Pancha had a package in her hands. She unwrapped it on the table. It was a pair of shoes. Trini remembered the girl in the Mines Office so long ago. Now, she reached out and fingered the stitching somewhat disinterestedly. Tía Pancha suggested, "Try them on."

Trini glanced down at the rough soles of her feet, crusted with the years. "I'm a descalza!"

"The roughness will go away when you wear the shoes."

"Corns never go away."

"Now, who told you that?" Tía Pancha asked, rather surprised. "What we Indians have on the bottom of our feet is natural. Nature put it there so we could walk. Only the blisters made by shoes never disappear. Those are corns. You don't have those. Your skin will be like a baby's once you wear shoes."

"Soft as a baby's . . ." Trini touched her crusty soles, then tried on the shoes. They fit. Her eyes gleamed with wishfulness. "All I need now is a store-bought dress."

"You're getting too big. Look at you!"

The reminder again. She was too big now with a child she did not want. It was a sour thought, like the memory of Héctor's rancid mouth. She glared stonily at the flickering wick, then blurted out, "I hate it! I don't want a baby!"

With a sudden swift gesture, she savagely swept the table clean of paper, string, and seeds, then she pounded on the surface until the sides of her hands felt a tingling hurt. Her face was tortured, contorted with the thought, her mouth an open moan that would not stop. "I . . . don't . . . want . . . the . . . baby!"

"That's enough, Trini." Her aunt's voice was stern. "The baby is God's miracle, no matter how conceived."

Miracle? She stared, with the shape of the moan still on her lips. The dancing flame of the lantern spoke of treachery, not a miracle! The seed of a pimp—the seed. Suddenly, she felt ashamed. Her tía was right. The baby was not to blame. There was nothing more beautiful in the world than a baby, a baby. The seed was beautiful. She remembered her papá's seeds. She had held them so reverently in her hand, cleaned and weeded the land, broken the earth with a shovel, placed the seed into the breathing earth. Her face softened, but her nails still dug hard into the wood of the table.

* * *

It was a soft rain, the kind that is breathless in its silver flow, the kind that melts clouds until the light smells warmly moist. Trini had opened a window to smell wet earth. She looked down at her sleeping baby, who was breathing easier. She moved a chair up to the window where the bare willow reached for the rain. Her lips formed a prayer:

"Sweet Mother of Jesus, feel for me. Don't let my baby die. I love her so now. I've loved her since that Christmas, your Christmas, when the world was white."

Trini looked out a a vastness interwoven by bare branches, the sky hinting a whiteness, tears falling into open plams. She called out to her mother who would hear. "Oh, Mamá, intercede for me. I feel you so near, here, now. I felt you then, that Christmas when my baby was still in my womb . . ."

There was comfort within her being. Matilda was near. She was with the peace of the rain, with the silence of the room, with the sleeping baby . . . just like last Christmas.

* * *

Christmas! An early snow had crusted the ground on the day of La Virgen de Guadalupe. There had been a kermes at the church. Sebastiana had her friends in charge of the bingo game and had devised a way for Trini to get the prize. Sebastiana had rigged the game.

"What would Trini do with a sled?"

"Enjoy it. She's still a child."

"The baby's almost due. You're crazy, Sebastiana."

But Sebastiana would not be put off. The bingo game was held. Trini won the sled. It was fire engine red, and Buti and Lupita were in ecstasy. Sebastiana nodded approval when she saw Trini and the children in the snow. She turned to Tía Pancha and confided, "In the Christmas raffle, the prize is baby clothes."

"You are outrageous."

"It's what the barrio wants."

"It will embarrass Trini."

"Not for long."

Before the Christmas celebration, Buti became the expert in handling la arrastra down hills. Trini and Lupita took his lead, but couldn't keep up. Finally, Buti insisted that Trini ride with him. In spite of her awkwardness, they flew down the hill. Trini saw it flee before her, white, with tiny drifts like angel swirls. Oh, soundless winter! Trini laughed and tumbled in the snow with her brother and sister, sometimes stopping to feel the warmth of the child inside her. The baby had created the shape of a new existence, moving inside her in its own silent, dark universe. There was a glowing energy in her veins and tumbling in the snow with Buti and Lupita was part of the new life flow.

Watching Sebastiana make her famous revolijo in the kitchen on Christmas Eve, Trini confided, "Oh, Sebastiana, I want my baby very much." Sebastiana nodded as she mixed sweet bread, nuts, cheese, and raisins in a baking dish. Then she held a bottle of rum under her arm and waved Trini away. "Keep your distance."

"I know how you make it, Sebastiana. You told me this morning."

"I did?" Sebastiana raised the eyebrow over her one good eye. "So I did! So I did!" With that, she unplugged the bottle cap with her teeth, took a drink of the rum, then poured it indiscriminately into the revolijo. Trini watched her with a glint in her eyes.

"You put rum in your bacalao?"

"Sure. Rum's good for everything. Of course, no one knows how I make my bacalao."

"You told me this morning." Trini laughed.

"I did?" Sebastiana scratched her head, taking another gulp from the bottle. "You're going to enjoy this pastorela!"

"This is my first."

"It is good. You're like the Virgin, heavy with child."

"I'm helping Señora Ortega," Trini informed her friend.

Sebastiana shook her head, taking another drink. She stared at Trini with what seemed to be compassion. "You poor child!"

The pastorela . . . Around the bend was the church of San Angel.

Trini breathed the clear air as she looked around at a world of blue crystal, reflections of a sun turned purple. Trini felt the wind, thin and dagger sharp against her face. From the barrio street, she saw snow-covered hills, skeleton trees with barren boughs sprinkled on the hill like talking fingers, all directed toward heaven. There was an air of festivity. From roofs, high windows, and makeshift posts hung piñatas and lanterns, awaiting the procession. As she approached the lighted courtyard of the church, she saw the stout outline of Señora Ortega.

"Ah, you're here! Thank Heaven!" She looked at Buti and Lupita beside Trini, a shepherd and an angel. "Go, join the others . . ."

Trini handed her a box from the sled.

"The halos! You finished them." Her eyes shone in expectation. "Twelve of them? You've been such a help, Trini. Of course, they don't deserve halos." Señora Ortega sighed wearily.

A rush of angels bounded out of the entrance. They seemed to be chasing St. Michael down the street, straight into a snow bank. In no time they were all piled on top of him. Señora Ortega touched her temples and moaned. "It's been like this all morning. Wild creatures! You look after them I'll take care of the shepherds, and both of us will keep our eye on the Devil." The poor distraught señora was looking every which way.

The angels were now around Trini, pointing at St. Michael. "He stole tamales out of the kitchen. Pig, pig, pig . . ." St. Michael's mouth was full. He stuffed the last of a tamale into his mouth before the angels could snatch it away. Señora Ortega ordered: "Everybody, into the courtyard!" They rushed past her. Señora Ortega stared at them ominously. Trini followed. Before her was the haystack that would serve as a background for the play.

"Nobody gets within ten feet of that haystack, you understand?" Señora Ortega threatened. The Devil, dragging a long red tail, ran past them. The señora grabbed him. "The tail's too long. It has to be cut."

Oh, no, thought Trini, she shouldn't have said that. One of the angels was already snipping off the Devil's tail, inches at a time. A shepherd shouted, "Cut his ass off . . ."

"There . . ." said the snipping angel.

"Awhhhhhh . . ."

"Your tail hurts, Diablo?"

To be a child, thought Trini. Hadn't it been only yesterday? Señora Ortega was threatening to beat every one of them. Trini passed the halos among the angels as the Devil grabbed the snipping angel and threw her into the haystack.

People were streaming into the courtyard now. Tables were almost full. Three goats wearing mistletoe and red ribbons and two sleepy sheep were being led toward the front.

"Señora Ortega, look, the goat's eating the table!"

"He's just licking up beer," an angel chirped.

Trini finished putting on the last halo as Señora Ortega clapped everybody into place. The pastorela was about to begin.

The story was a new one to Trini, one that Tía Pancha had missed in her religious training. It was a contest between St. Michael and the Devil. The scene was a shepherd's inn. St. Michael, with his angels singing in the background, pits his wits against the Devil. St. Michael persuades the shepherds to pay homage to the Child, the Devil dissuades them. A duel ensues. St. Michael wins, and the shepherds kick the Devil off stage.

At the end, Señora Ortega came up to her, pleased as punch. "All went well. No one hit anybody over the head with a sword, and no one set the haystack on fire. Thank heaven, it's over!"

Señora Ortega was right to be thankful. The sword fight had clattered at a proper pace. The only thing that Trini noticed was when the Devil was thrown off stage, he no longer had a tail, not even a stub.

People made their way to the church. Trini looked for Tía Pancha and Sebastiana to join them. It was time for family. Lighted candles filled the sides of the aisles all the way to the manger. There were prayers and communion. After the service, everybody filed out into the courtyard again. In the courtyard, protected from sudden snow by tentlike strips of canvas, food was being served. The winning ticket in the raffle was being announced by Sebastiana, who waved the raffle number at Trini. Trini blushed. She guessed what had happened because everybody was cheering and clapping. Tears came to her eyes. When she opened the prize, she found an assortment of baby clothes contributed and knitted by the ladies of the barrio. She whispered a "thank you." Sebastiana smacked her on the cheek. "Smile, we want a smile."

"Yes," everybody chorused. "We want a smile."

Trini smiled, feeling the warmth of glowing faces. Mariachis were now playing as boys placed brimming pitchers of beer on the tables.

After the feast came the posada through the main streets of the barrio, with people opening doors and lighting lanterns in the houses where the pilgrims were to seek refuge. Young people played the part of the pilgrims, going from door to door seeking shelter. Trini stepped out into the dark, where snowflakes drifted downward. Sebastiana took her hand and led her to the others. Trini was hesitant, embarrassed by her heaviness. "It's for the ones who . . ."

She did not finish the sentence. How could she say, "It's for the ones who are innocent, like the Virgin?" Standing in the snow, heavy with her burden, she could not bring herself to join them. A crimson flush covered her face, her lips trembled. Sebastiana pushed her toward them, then the boys and girls rushed to her. Sharp light from the lanterns, reflected on the snow, showed their faces, eyes seeing her as one of them. Laughter cut the cold air, and the singing began.

They carried her along in their midst, keeping her warm, protected from the wind, for she was with child like Mary. There was a balance now, a white delight stirring in Trini. She breathed the cold as if breathing in clean life. The whiteness was no different from the greeness of seedlings, free and open to the sun. All was earth. The child in her was earth. The Christ Child was earth. She began to sing, one of many voices.

The procession made its way down the main street. Lanterns were lighted in tienditas and houses along the way. Even Lin Wang had lanterns outside the bathhouse. Trini saw him smiling and bowing, waving a piece of mistletoe at all the pretty girls. He wore a crimson mandarin gown of festive silk, as colorful as the piñata in front of his place. The sides of presidios and houses were full of snow, beautifully outlined by the light of the paper lanterns. The singing rose among the pilgrims walking, seeking refuge for the Virgin Mary. "In the name of Heaven, give us refuge, for my sweet wife shall be the Mother of the Sacred Child . . ."

From inside the houses, innkeepers answered. "Go away. You are a thief. You cannot stay . . ." From house to house, the pilgrims went, each time making a plea, then hearing a refusal. Finally doors were opened from all corners of the street. Voices rose simultaneously, "Welcome, blessed pilgrims. Find refuge in our hearts. Welcome . . ."

That was the time for the breaking of piñatas in the snow. The festooned earthen pots were strung on wire around the main square. Children broke the piñatas, one by one. Candy and gifts fell into the snow. Gifts for the children from the Christ Child.

Lights, people, laughter, talk, snow, sky, stars—God in his heaven—observed Trini. All the gods of the earth are close. She had felt them as she had harvested her beans and squash, when she smelled the glorious giving earth and heard the silver crystal fall of water against rock. Now, it was in the snow air quiver. Such a gladness in her! Somehow she had ceased to be merely herself. Her fiber was something far more, a holiness outside of feasting, harvest, and Christmas. She was part of a mysterious force, a mighty pull, along with all other life. Holy, holy, holy, the falling of snow, the greening of life, the Child of Innocence. She stood aside watching for a while. She put her hand to her stomach and felt her baby kicking.

* * *

Then a New Year's miracle! Trini had left the warmth of Sebastiana's kitchen. Stars and an icicle of moon hung low, and the world was still frozen silver. The old twist of the hill leading to the arroyo was before her. Halfway up the hill, she stopped to rest. She inhaled cold, sharp air into her lungs. Her body felt unusually cumbersome and uncomfortable after the heaving effort up the path. She stretched her neck, eyes closed, mouth open, then she opened her eyes wide to see the silver moon again. The first night of a new year, she thought, a new year. She tried to see and feel the coming of new days, but felt nothing. Why is there no hope? Because I'm afraid? I mustn't be afraid, she told herself. Having a baby will not kill me. She stopped abruptly and looked up at the moon again. Yes, it looked like a silver falling, a little happening from her Mamá's bultito. Mamá! She had died in childbirth. No, Mamá, not me. I feel fine. It's just so hard when the time nears. The baby would be a beginning, like the new year. Somehow the thought of Matilda's death did not bring sadness. The silver of moon made her sense that Matilda was far from dead. She was watching the moon somewhere. Trini laughed in the silent darkness.

Her step was lighter now as she made her way along the edge of the arroyo. The light from windows melted into the raw, twilight mists. A tall figure approached her. There was something familiar about the rhythmic striding of the man, for Trini could make him out now. She could not see his face in the darkness, but the penciled mists through reflections from lighted windows outlined his head. For a broken, confused moment, she felt her cheeks pale. She did not have to see his face to know who he was. Her body found a sudden guileless freedom as she ran to meet him. She cried out, "Sabochi!"

Sabochi, Sabochi, Sabochi! Her heart sang as she stood before him. Her laughter was pouring into the cold air. She was in the realm of his warmth and strength. She was the wild wind cleaving to mountain, and her happiness rose and sprawled in the whiteness of the world.

"How? Why?" Trini's voice was fringed in happy incredulity.

"It was time." Sabochi's voice was still the same, a serious, gentle song. "Isidoro's grandfather died and left him a pig farm in La Junta. I came with him. I told myself, my family is not far from here."

She did not question more, but in the blue dark found the cradle of his arms again. She raised her lips without hesitation. His mouth was warm, giving. She would not let go. She could not let go. The mists cloaked them, isolated them, in their moment. Then, they walked in silence toward the house, a moon sliver lost in changing mists.

Tía Pancha opened the door, a hand rose to her heart in surprise. There were already questions in Sabochi's eyes as he observed Trini's heaviness. By lantern light, a story was unfolded. Sabochi's face became heavy with anger, but all that Trini saw was his presence. She held his hands, every so often kissing his palm in her happiness. Sabochi and Tía Pancha talked. When the talking was done, Sabochi's eyes burned with a fierce fire. Trini wanted to tell him that nothing mattered except that he was sitting across from her, looking at her, talking to her, but words did not come. She looked down at her heavy form, helpless and lost.

"Does Chema know?" Sabochi's voice tore the silence.

"My brother knows." Tía Pancha answered. She tried to change the conversation. "How long will you stay?"

"Until Isidoro comes . . ."

Blood had drained from his face as he suddenly hit the table with his fists again and again. A terrifying anger seemed to grow in his body, filling his every gesture.

"This pimp, this Héctor, he goes unpunished?"

"What can we do? Raquel has influence," Tía Pancha said with bitterness.

Sabochi sat at the table cloistered in a lonely, ponderous mood. He looked off into space for a long time, not seeing anyone, not asking any more questions, refusing food. Trini felt like crying. How could happiness be tainted so? She begged, "Please, Sabochi, let's just be together."

She put her arms around his neck and sobbed like a child. His eyes filled with tenderness. "Don't cry, little woman, I shall take care of things."

"It's not so terrible now, Sabochi." She raised her eyes to meet his. "I want the baby. You're here. What else matters?"

There was no agreement in Sabochi's face. It was sphinx-like, a mask revealing no more than eyes in flight, a movement without feeling. Trini knew from long ago that Sabochi in stillness was all feeling. Now there was a void, a chasm.

"It is late." Tía Pancha's voice was tired. Sabochi nodded. "Can I sleep by your side, Sabochi?" Trini's eyes pleaded.

Tía Pancha started to protest, but Sabochi made a gesture for her not to interfere. Tía Pancha shrugged and made ready for bed. Trini, like a happy child, unrolled a petate next to his. Sabochi's face was still masked, sullen. He watched her pillow her head in her hands and lay down beside her. She wanted to stay awake, to feel his nearness, but sleep was overwhelming.

Dozing off, she felt the touch of his hand on her cheek and she was borne into dreams. She and Chimac were running in the snow, tumbling in its softness. A light seemed to carry them like a huge wave. Trini heard herself calling, Sabochi! Sabochi! Then Sabochi was before her, not seeing her. She put out her arms, but he only had eyes for Chimac and the baby in her arms. Again the snow drifts breaking like waves, turning into spring water, the face of Mahki laughing as Trini pulled and tugged at rich tomato plants. She saw a streak of pain turn green and orange, carrying her along, drowning her in a waiting darkness . . .

On a cupboard she and Tía Pancha had built there were rows of pans with rising bread. Tía Pancha had kneaded and prepared two dozen loaves the day before. She must now put them in the oven. Trini put wood into the stove. Her body felt sore, her breath coming short in gasps as she moved around the kitchen. Where had Sabochi gone?

For a while the chore totally absorbed her. When the fire was ready, she placed four loaves into the oven. The bending sent a sharp pain running down her legs and, as she straightened her body, she felt a rise of nausea. Holding tight to the back of a chair, she told herself—It must be time. I must finish the baking. From a box she took square pieces of burlap and put them on the table. Again, the nausea, swimming. It passed, leaving her face wet with perspiration. She sat down at the kitchen table until the smell of the baked loaves told her she had to take them out, put some more into the oven. The heat of the stove revived her. She took out the crisp brown loaves and wrapped them in burlap squares. By the time she had done the last batch, a roll of pain struck again. She opened her mouth to breathe deep and help the pain go away.

She heard the sound of the wagon. Tía Pancha was back. She would know about Sabochi. From the window Trini saw Tía Pancha making her way to the house after telling the children to unbridle Sarif and feed him. At the door, Trini caught her aunt's anxious glance. "How do you feel? You were moaning in your sleep."

"My back. Pains all morning."

"How often?"

"I don't know. Often, I guess."

"It's your time. I'll have Lupita get Sebastiana."

"You sure?" Pain came upon her as she asked, consuming her body. She was sure.

"It's time." Tía Pancha helped her to a chair.

"Where's Sabochi, Tía?" The words shivered lke her body.

"I don't know. He was gone when I woke up."

There was the beginning of fear. "You got up at dawn. Did he leave in the middle of the night?" The fear grew in waves. Her senses began to throb with it. She closed her eyes and a picture clicked in her mind. Two men swaying in the breeze by a river in Cusihuiriachi. Two bodies lost in the shadows of boulders.

"God, no!" Trini's voice was wildly shrill. Tía Pancha's eyes wore the same thought as she made her way to Trini, who was again bent with pain. Trini looked up, breathing hard. "He wouldn't, would he, Tía?" Her voice came thickly.

"He would." Tía Pancha's words were a finality.

Trini closed her eyes, her lips shaping a prayer. Please, God, let him come back soon. I need him. A brittle, caving pain rose. It bounded and sprayed. She moaned.

"It's time, Trini."

It was her time and the hours to follow were full of pain that came in undifferentiated rhythms. There was no time for worry now. The pain demanded all of her. In the midst of a red haze, she saw Buti and Lupita looking at her. She heard Tía Pancha telling Lupita to get Sebastiana. The pain was molding its own world. She now belonged to a red world that lifted and fell, that rested in sudden stops as perspiration poured down her face. Her mouth was so dry . . . so dry.

The baby was born when the sun turned red against the mountain. She felt only a drowning fatigue. Someone placed a breathing warmth next to her. She was so tired, so tired. She fell into a dreamless sleep.

* * *

But dreams came—how much later? Whisperings in a vastness. She felt the smoothness of the rainbow rocks, rain pelting them. When it stops, thought Trini, the rainbow will leave the rocks and go into the sky. Where is El Enano? She felt herself touching the rocks that were melting into rain, melting into light, the colors of the rainbow; from far away she saw her old friend running toward her with little soldier legs, a finger to his mouth, a twinkle in his eye. She laughed, and the laughter tinkled and bounced. The dream was shattered by the rasp of a whisper, then another whisper. The edge of long sleep still clung.

Drowsiness was all silver-blue, then the name of Sabochi shocked her into wakefulness. She opened her eyes and saw Sebastiana and Tía Pancha looking down at her. Their eyes were like a wire tautly pulled. Worry clouded Tía Pancha's face. Trini knew something was wrong.

"Sabochi? Sabochi?" Her mouth carved the thirsty words.

"Here." Sebastiana held a cup with some steaming tea.

Sebastiana was beside her, holding up her head, placing the rim of the cup to her dry lips. The smell and taste of yerbabuena were warming, smooth. The tea revived her. She fell back on the petate, asking again, "Sabochi?"

Tía Pancha and Sebastiana looked at each other as if harboring a secret. Her aunt stared down at her for a moment, then turned to Sebastiana with a nod, crossing herself. After an anguished pause, Sebastiana sat down next to her. She smoothed Trini's hair back from the forehead, then told her a tale of revenge:

* * *

"Sabochi told me, Trini, he told me after I saw the police hold him down and bind his hands. I left the crowd in the jailhouse and made my way to your Indian. He told me what happened, right there in his jail cell.

"He got up in the middle of the night, caught in a night wind that carried him to the shed where he saddled his horse and made his way to El Jardín de Venus. All by himself he would seek justice! Ah, when he told me, I knew he was a man of great courage. Well, he came to Raquel's place with its garish flashing lights that blink the work of the Devil; he slipped the horse down the open field, thick with mud and melting snow. Then, in the cluster of trees, he dismounted, feeling branches, measuring their stoutness, their height. Such cunning! When he found a massive limb that protruded like a dragon's head, he tied a noose on one end of the rope and threw it around the limb. Then he waited and waited on his belly behind a clump of scrub.

"He heard the sounds of music, laughing, jingling money, shouts from that whore's place, den of iniquity! Finally, when the wind died down and a coil of morning light snaked through the sky, he saw the door open. Raquel, no less, came out, bidding good-night to some fat customer, the mayor, the police chief, who knows! And right behind them both was the coward, Héctor, scraping and kowtowing. Well, when the customer left, that witch with man-fingers told her pimp, 'Check the rooms.'

"I can see Sabochi now, holding his breath, piercing the darkness to follow Héctor with his eyes, his body poised and waiting. Raquel went back into the building, the door swallowing the noise and lights. Only Héctor stood in the darkness, flapping his arms to ward off the cold. He made his way to the motel rooms. That's when Sabochi ran after him. He broke the shadows in the path of Héctor, who stopped in alarm as Sabochi appeared in his path.

" '¡Cobarde!' The word 'coward' from Sabochi's lips rang in the night.

" 'Who are you?' growled Héctor.

" 'Your name is Héctor.'

"Héctor stood uneasily, seeking an escape. His glance caught the shape of an owl flying between trees.

" 'Remember the young one named Trini?' Sabochi's question hung in the air with savagery.

"Héctor stood confused, trapped, a hissing sound escaping from his throat.

"'Here!' Sabochi unsheathed the knife from his belt and threw it to the ground before Héctor. 'Pick it up, coward! I give you a better chance than you gave her!'

"Héctor slithered to the ground. His hand found the knife. Then he stood and faced Sabochi with legs and arms spread, his body bent. He began a series of jerky little jumps backward, away from Sabochi, but he was no match for the Tarahumara, who moved like lightning. Sabochi thrust down on Héctor's wrists. The knife flew out of his hand, glinting in its dive. Then Sabochi held Héctor's body against his arm, neck twisted, arms every which way. He dragged him, half-sliding in the mud, toward the trees. Héctor struggled helplessly against the strength of the bigger man. When they came upon the dragon limb, your Sabochi swung the gasping Héctor sideways, then placed the noose around his neck. Héctor let out a scream, laden with the terror of the world. It was too late. Sabochi pulled the rope up, up, up, then tied the other end to a low sharp stump. Drowning, gurgling sounds escaped from Héctor's throat. His legs kicked until the body hung limp. An owl cried. You have been avenged.

"Ah! That is real justice. I know it. Sabochi knows it. But the police? The stupid fools call it murder. He tried to get away, your Indian. He rode away on his horse, but they caught him. I was in town when the police brought him to the jail. Six men could not hold him down, though they beat on him, tied and defenseless as he was. He stood proud, that Indian of yours, made the others look like worms. I tell you, it was something!

"Your Indian doesn't want you to worry. Somehow, he said, he would get word to his tehueques at La Junta. Tarahumaras never stay in jail. They are like the wind. Your Sabochi is a clever man, you'll see. They plan to take him to Chihuahua where the jails are strong enough to hold him. Ha! He will escape!

"This morning I rode out to Raquel's place to see if Héctor's body had disappeared, to see if Raquel cared enough about her pimp to cut him down or, if she's a witch, to see if she cut out his liver and his heart for demon's brew. The body was still there. Nobody seemed to care! Poor, poor, Héctor. His head hung down from the dragon's limb. I could see his teeth behind a purple tongue grinning at me. So, I cut him down and laid him on the grass, closed his eyes and mouth and said a prayer for him though his soul is doomed to hell."

Sebastiana smiled down at Trini and stroked her head. "Rest now, little one. It is in God's hands."

Trini lay stunned. She held the baby close, love flowing from her body to the tiny miracle of life. Yet tears ran down her cheeks, tears she could not stop. Sabochi in jail! To be taken to a Chihuahua jail! He, who was like the wild wind, like the stallions he caught, a freedom. Locked up! The weight of the thought drained her body of all joy. I will go where he is, I will try to help him. She was torn again, for the child in her arms came first. It was an instinct of the earth, and to that Trini was bound.

* * *

Perhaps it was the rain stopping—something had broken Trini's reverie. A luminous stillness filled the room. Trini reached out and touched her baby's forehead, but even before she felt the cold little body, she knew. Dear God! She knew. She picked up the little form in her arms. So much pain every which way! Her heart screamed, but death had come without a sound. She knew her little girl was gone, but she rocked her and talked to her, and tears fell on the tiny face.

"Baby, baby, baby. I love you so!"

She held her close for the last time. Silence for a long time, then, all at once, she felt a rush of milk fill her breast to overflowing.

11

The Lamb and the Wolf

"They say these hills were full of wild turkeys once," Tía Pancha informed Trini while they rested on the flat surface of a boulder washed pink by spring water. Starting with the first light of morning, they had come to the hills where massive fringes of green herbs grew among the rocks. Tía Pancha sat surrounded by the herbs she was busy sorting.

"Where are they, the wild turkeys?" Trini asked. She stood, holding her skirt form the blowing wind that carried scents of spring.

"Gone. But the mountain of Japón still has flocks on the high sierra."

The mountain of Japón! Trini looked toward the blue-grey hills where boulders rested like sleeping giants. Japón! Tonio! Trini drew in her breath, lips slightly open, touched with life, senses extended. So many things had happened that the thought of Tonio was poised in an old dream. Ambiguous feelings rose: Sabochi, Tonio, both gone, both a part of her life, yet unreachable. But it was Sabochi who needed her, who had avenged her, whom she must try to help. Trini caught Tía Pancha's curious glance. Trini informed her, "I have to go to Chihuahua. To see Papá. To find Sabochi. I have to go, Tía."

"Chihuahua is not like San Domingo. What can a mere girl do?" Tía Pancha asked resignedly as she sorted herbs.

"Seeing Papá well—being with him—that will give me hope."

"Hope for what?"

"I will find Sabochi." Trini's voice was determined.

"That's easier said than done, I'm afraid." Tía Pancha's voice was skeptical. "You have no idea where that Indian is."

"I'll look and look until I find him."

"Those are the words of a child," Tía Pancha sighed.

What could she do? Her tía was right. But the urgency to go was there. A kind of desperation swelled in Trini's blood. Tía Pancha kept on examining leaves, cutting stems, separating them. Trini pictured herself in a strange city, alone, without money, afraid. Yes, she was afraid. She thought of Sebastiana's offer. Sebastiana had written to her sister Celestina, in Chihuahua, explaining Trini's circumstance. Celestina had written back urging Trini to go to Chihuahua. Nothing ventured, nothing gained, the letter said. Sebastiana's sister had offered her a place to stay. Why not? She must do something! The thought of Sabochi in a Chihuahua Jail was too much to bear. She remembered their meeting on that cold, misty New Year's day. I did not have enough of him. I'll never have enough of him, she cried within herself. He needs me now . . .

"Come help me sort, Trini." Tía Pancha was still separating herbs. Trini searched her aunt's face, wondering if her tía had ever felt anything close to love. Had she loved anyone? Her aunt had always brought a dimension of security to her. Little else. Tía Pancha had never revealed anything about her past life.

"Well?" Tía Pancha's voice was insistent. Her hands were quickly and expertly tying las yerbas into small bundles. The different herbs lay scattered around her like mysteries, yerba de la víbora, yerba del cáncer, yerba colorada, la inmortal, la carcomera, el chuchupaste, la matarique. Tía Pancha knew them all. Yerbas with the power to heal or destroy. Like love and hate, thought Trini. Yerbas to warm, to boil in the blood, intoxicating, aphrodisiac, all from the earth . . .

"Stop daydreaming and come help." Tía Pancha sounded impatient. Trini didn't want to sort herbs. She wanted . . . She wanted to tell her tía that in the earth of her there was a seed, dark and passionate, waiting. How could she say it? It was all pain, this growing up, this loving. Being a child had been so easy. . . .

"What am I going to do with the likes of you?" Her aunt was tossing bundles into a basin. Trini sat by her side, putting her hands over her aunt's busy ones. "Stop. Tell me about you."

"Tell you what?" Her sane, reliable aunt listened.

"Have you ever loved a man, Tía?" The words were said. Tía set the herbs aside, eyes grave and contemplative. She whispered, "Does it matter?" Looking at Trini, the aunt knew it mattered. "Yes—I suppose every woman has loved a man once. . . ."

"The way I love Sabochi? I mean, he has Chimac."

"That can't stop love."

"Oh, Tía, you understand!"

"What you feel without him—the emptiness—it's of your own creation."

"No." Trini protested, unbelieving.

"Yes. It is. But you are too young to understand."

"All I know is I want to be with him."

Tía Pancha laughed softly. She raised an unconscious hand, a half gesture in the air that spoke of time as redeemable. Then she began her story. "I ran away from San Mateo when I was a young girl, Trini, away from a cruel father and cruel brothers. No, not José Mario, not your father. He was kind, but he did not stay around very long. I was very lonely." Tía Pancha paused, memory quivering in her eyes. "I remember, my brother and I were looking for a lost lamb one day, and I came across a wolf. He was eating the lamb. The wolf had such yellow eyes. They stayed with me, those eyes."

There was an interval of silence. The thought of the wolf was an imminence, something breathing in the air. Tía Pancha continued, eyes turbulent:

"Sometimes I shaped distortions in my loneliness, Trini. The wolf's yellow eyes would appear as whirling fires. I knew it was all in my mind. In that isolated house in San Mateo, I would hear the wind explode in wild laughter. I shrank from my vision and, in my madness, I heard the helpless bleating of the lamb. One evening, I watched my brothers and my father at the supper table. I was suddenly filled with horror. Little by little, like moving shadows changing form, I saw them turn into wolves."

The memory came in a rasping voice. Trini took her tía's worn, thin hand in hers to stop the fear that still crowded Pancha's inner life. She continued:

"I ran away before I went completely mad. I walked all the way to Mesadura. With frozen feet and a shivering that would not leave me, I begged in the streets; when it grew dark, I huddled in a doorway to escape the cold, and there I was discovered, delirious, sick."

Tía Pancha's voice became a warm excitement; her hands fumbled with the folds of her skirt, her eyes dissolved into the past:

"I do know what it is to love a man, Trini. The man who found me on his doorstep, his name was Chale. I loved him. Oh yes, just like you love Sabochi. Chale kept me in his house until I got well. You see, I had pneumonia. He had come from Uvalde to help old Paco, the blacksmith, who had gone to San Felipe to have his cataracts removed. Chale was saving the money he earned at the forge to take back to his wife and children."

Oh, Tía! Tía! You too? You loved a married man! How strange! thought Trini. A past swirled unabated into a now. She listened to her aunt's story with pain and joy interfused:

"What can I tell you? We did things for one another, little gentle things. We were one energy in the same house. We became lovers, passionate, passionate lovers . . ."

There was the running and the rising of remembered desire in her aunt's intoxicated cadence, in her eyes. She leaned forward, eyes bright.

"I lived each day to be loved. Everything about him was a sharp, incessant fire. Oh, such heavy love!" Tía Pancha reached out, taking Trini's face in her hands. Her voice was now soft, secretive. "Let me tell you something, Trini. I let him go. I let him go back to his wife and children. It was something I had to do because I loved him." A soberness came into her eyes. "My only regret is that after that I did no more than wait for him to come back to me. For eleven years!" Tía Pancha covered her face with her hands. The dream was spent. When she looked up at Trini, the tormented waiting of lifeless times was in her eyes. She whispered, "He never came back. I should have known. Life is not for waiting." She suddenly reached for a stem of copalquín, picked its leaves, then stared at the empty, bare twig. "I had created my own emptiness. The little time I had him should have fulfilled me . . . but I waited."

Trini felt her own tears, warm against her face. She wanted to comfort her aunt, to hold her, but she could not. Instead, she walked away to the edge of the pool where water flowed through an open arch of stone. She took off her shoes and put her feet into the water, feeling its coolness. She looked up at a tree with a golden throat against the sun; a short distance away, herbs shone a deep purple. She felt as if perhaps she knew little of passion, less of love. She had wanted more, much more than what her tía had had. She turned to see her aunt looking somewhat gaunt, hands gripping the side of the flat stone where she sat. Oh, the bareness of things!

A honey silence, evanescent, evocative, filled the air. Curves of shadows softly moved among the rocks and trees, the sound of water, lapping, lapping. She walked back to her aunt, took her hand in silence. That was enough. Tía Pancha's eyes were like water over broken stone. She seemed to be running out of her body into the old happiness again. Chale was with her, in the air, in glittering moss, in mountain subterranean silver water, whispering . . .

12

The Blue Cottage

In the patio of La Clínica Lozoya, voices converged into hurried whispers. Nurses were gathered around an old man in a wheel chair. He was being revived, cleaned, after a sudden coughing spell; blood gurgled in his lungs. The corruption of his illness now shook his thin frame. His eyes were closed, his mouth jerking at the sides, skeleton hands grasping the arm of a nurse. Trini turned her eyes away. She did not want to see. She knew that her papá was cured. Trini had arrived in Chihuahua the night before. The first thing was to visit her father. Celestina gave her careful instructions on how to get to the clinic, still urging her to wait a few days, but Trini could not wait. "I haven't seen Papá for two years!"

Trini took an early bus from La Colonia Murguía where she was to live with Celestina, her two daughters, and two grandchildren. As the bus crossed the bridge that spanned the Chuvisear River, memories erupted—the figure of Papá coming home from the mines, his small, thin frame spelling such loneliness! His letters were so brave, so full of concern for their welfare. The next bus left her almost at the entrance of the clinic, a square, white, unpretentious building with green lawns.

Now she was in the patio, waiting, looking piercingly at the orange sunlight flooding half the room. The old man had been wheeled away. The feebleness, the blood, the helplessness, it had all unsettled her. She had watched the old man gasp his desperation alone, trying to help, running for the nurses. The ritual of the nurses was over, the old man wheeled away, but the sense of his loneliness stayed. Her papá had been in this clinic for two years, without his family. Oh, dear God, he must have been so lonely!

She wiped tears away and went into a garden, silent and empty except for the occasional chirping of birds, the whirring of sprinklers.

Trini found a bench and sat down, only half-aware of city sounds from a far-off distance, the bigness of the city affirming itself. Chihuahua was very different from San Domingo. Suddenly, she heard Papá's voice, "Trini!"

She looked up to see the figure of José Mario waiting. He looked so well! His gaze clear and strong! She ran to him and held his thin warm body against her own.

"¿Papá?" It was a question asking many things, saying many things, remembering all that had happened in his absence. Warm and safe in his arms, she opened her eyes to see, over his shoulder, dandelions spreading themselves down a walk across a wide lawn. How simple is joy! Her papá—dandelions. His eyes, too, were asking, wondering, moist with the happiness he felt. He wore a shirt of roughed blue. His face had lost its brownness, giving way to the prescribed paleness of hospital life. The mountain was temporarily out of José Mario. The harshness of cavernous undergrounds had been softened. She almost sang his name, "Papá!"

Papá would be going home soon, back to what he was, what he knew how to be.... He held her at arms' length.

"You've grown so, Trini. A woman now ... Seventeen?"

His words startled her somewhat. A woman now ... the thought wove itself into the new mystery of herself—Papá was well. He would be with his family soon. Dear, good Papá! They sat on a stone bench in silence, close to one another. There was eagerness in Papá's voice. "Only four weeks now, Trini. We go home together."

We go home together? Home? She must tell Papá. She must tell him there was nothing for her in San Domingo. She must convince him of her need to find Sabochi. "I have to look for Sabochi, Papá. I cannot go back without finding out what's happened to him."

"You have four weeks to look."

What if she didn't find him in four weeks? She would stay until she did. But there were so many things they had to say now to bridge the absence of two years. She must tell José Mario that the family was waiting for the return of the man of the house, that she still had Mamá's bultito full of his love gifts. They talked about seeds waiting to be planted and the dream of a future, a piece of land, all theirs. She promised her father she would someday own a piece of land and it would be his.

They talked until dusk, then walked back along the path, full with the sense of family.

* * *

Trini waited for three long hours and twenty minutes before they led her into another office. Mr. Soto was the fifth person she had been referred to in her search for Sabochi. At the beginning of the search, when she had entered the first tall, authoritative building, she had been hesitant, awkward, and fearful. But now, having experienced the indifference and confusion of the people inhabiting the cadaverous offices in the court house and in La Presidencia, she was angry, tired, and hungry.

She had been shuffled from one office to another, a maze of cubicles with impressive front desks where self-important clerks seemed to know nothing more than the sifting of papers and looking through files. She had come up with nothing more than someone else to see in another strange office. Now she was being led into an office where a Mr. Soto sat behind a desk. He was already turning papers over, one by one, wearing a suit frayed at the elbows, and the few hairs on his head were plastered down against his skull with oil. Trini listened to the tiredness in her voice as she told the story for the twentieth time. "... and he was sent to the jail here in Chihuahua to be tried."

Mr. Soto took out a cigarette and lit it, then after the first puff looked at her from behind thick glasses. He rattled off the names of several offices. "You've been to all these places, eh?"

Trini nodded despondently. "Yes, every one of them! No one seems to have heard of a Tarahumara named Ambrosio or Sabochi."

"Indian," muttered the man. "A plague ... This one from the canyon, eh? Few of those in our jails." He leaned his head over the desk. "And why are you looking for him?"

"He's a friend ..."

The man grinned, exposing some missing teeth. "That, you think, is going to help? Very unlikely. You have money?"

Trini shook her head and looked at him with pleading eyes. "Please, please, let me look for him inside the jail."

He shifted the weight on his buttocks. "Impossible. Not allowed. If he were on the roster and you came to visit, that's another matter. But just to look for someone who does not exist ..."

"He does exist!" She checked her anger, her voice becoming soft, supplicating. "You can manage it, can't you?" Her hand clutched his sleeve.

For a minute or so, he looked at her appreciatively, then he put his hand over hers. "Yes, I have influence."

She drew her hand away but forced a smile. His eyes were suggestive, lewd. "You will be grateful, eh? After we look, a little dinner, then . . ." The lobes of his nostrils quivered with anticipation.

"Yes," Trini blurted out. The words had come in a breath of despair. A rush of hate filled her blood for men such as these—another Héctor!

Mr. Soto laughed, his lead-colored jowls moving gelatin-like. His marble eyes glowed faintly behind his glasses. He patted her hand. She drew it back convulsively, a smile frozen on her face, as he made a phone call. She closed her eyes, jolted by the anger that suffused her, but she still prayed, "God let it be . . ."

Trini rode in Mr. Soto's car, not recognizing any of the streets or buildings along the way. Every so often he would place a thickly veined hand on her knee. She drew away and pressed herself against the door, muscles tense, fists clenched. He parked the car a prudent distance from the city jail, and in a few minutes a jailkeeper was leading the way through corridors, turns, doors and more doors, until they came to a desk with armed guards. The guards unlocked a door; it led to a room that in turn led to another room lined with cells on either side.

She peered anxiously, expectantly into faces. So many of them! Some pallid, sick, angry, lifeless, others as anxious and expectant as her own. But there was no Sabochi—no Sabochi. With confused and fearful eyes, Trini saw looming shapes, sometimes savage silhouettes. She heard shrill voices shouting obscenities. The smells of unwashed flesh assaulted her senses. The acrid sharpness of urine filled her throat.

At the next turn, a closed fist suddenly came out of a grating. Then there were more eyes, round in their softness, narrow in their suspicion. A jailer unlocked another door. So many men. Sitting on the floor of the cells, playing cards, leaning against corners. She felt Mr. Soto's possessive grip on her hand. She heard a growling impatience in his voice. "Well, do you see him anywhere? Nowhere, eh?"

His grip was a vise. Hate overwhelmed her. She was caged as so many men were caged. She knew that if she turned to look at him, it would be the face of Héctor that she would see. She was perspiring freely and her knees were beginning to buckle when her eye caught the figure of a tall Indian in one of the cells. His broad, strong back was to her. Trini held her breath and her heart skipped as she ran and put her hand between the grating, reaching out ot him. "Sabochi!"

The Indian turned. It was a stranger! Someone grabbed her wrist and pulled her violently against the grating. She saw a mass of fingers, hands, arms, all touching her, pulling, scratching, mauling her. She uttered a cry and shrunk back with a desperate pull, then her body arched again as she ran from cell to cell. Sabochi? Sabochi?

They had come to the end of the corridor. There were no more cells. She turned helpless eyes to the jailer who was following behind her. He shrugged and shook his head in sympathy. Trini began to cry like a child, her sobs bouncing from cell to cell, exciting the blood of men eager for an outcry, any outcry. It was the tower of Babel abandoned by God, the palace of Pandemonium singing its chaos. The jailer led the way, pushing them in front of him. Trini ran, with Mr. Soto following, through corridor and turn, then corridor again. Doors were unlocked and slammed shut again. Finally they were out, breathing free.

"Well, are you satisfied?" gasped a tired, frightened Mr. Soto.

Trini knew one answer. She ran once more, never looking back to see the ridiculous and helpless figure of her benefactor standing with arms upraised, shouting for her to halt, and when she disappeared around the corner, he made his way to the car, shoulders hunched.

* * *

José Mario was going back to San Domingo without her. They were threading a steep side street leading to the bus station. She took his arm and hugged it reassuringly. It had all been said. It had all been talked out since the letter from Tía Pancha arrived at the clinic. Trini had read it and her world changed. She had sat at her father's feet, sobbing away old dreams of Sabochi.

Isidoro had been to San Domingo, the letter said. Sabochi had sent him to let them know that he was safe in Cusihuiriachi. His tehueques had freed him in La Junta after his arrest. He had never arrived at the jail in Chihuahua!

There had been a postscript, an afterthought on Tía Pancha's part, that purged Trini's dreams. But then, she thought, as she walked beside her father, why are my dreams part of someone who was never mine and never can be? Something in her disagreed. Something in her said, oh, but he is yours. He will always be yours. A dream? What was a dream anyway? Child's play, an empty bauble, like Mamá's little silver happenings. She reproached herself for making plans on the false substance of a dream—but isn't a dream the urge of all plans? Life was so confusing!

The words from the postscript still felt like an open wound. Sabochi had a new son! Even now, with her face to the sun, she felt the welling of tears. It was still not cried out after all the sobbing in the garden at the clinic. She had thrown the letter to the ground and stared at it, eyes wide, dark in their misery, until she had risen in a sudden rage and stood before her father. "I'm never going back, never!"

"It's your home. You are going back." José Mario's voice, severe, ungiving.

She had screamed out at him, at the world, "Never, never, never!"

Collapsing to the ground again, she had laid her head on his knee, reached for his hand, clasping it for steadiness. Then she let go whispering urgently, "I want to stay here, Papá."

"You're angry. It's not time for a decision."

But the decision had grown into a plan, a way out of old disappointments. As the weeks had gone by, she had been finding reasons why she should stay. She was in a city of mestizo ways, gachupín ways. She didn't want to love all that was Indian anymore. She would learn about the city, become the city, learn to prefer her white blood. But she couldn't explain this to José Mario. He would not understand. The meaning of a lifetime was already shaped and focused in his old eyes. He believed and lived by Indian ways, Indian rhythms of the blood. The seasons and the mountains had seeped through his being. I want to be a city girl, she told herself with a little bitter laugh. Do you? Do you? Do you?—some inner timbre questioned.

José Mario's attempts to dissuade her failed. "How can you live without your family, Trini?"

She had run into her father's arms, her body heaving in misery, "Oh, Papá, I'll miss all of you so! But, Papá, please, let me grow out of myself!"

He had relented. Now he was going back to San Domingo by himself. They had come to the end of the ascent. The street was now a sudden drop. Before her, a humpbacked bridge hung in the distance, blurred by the glaze of sun and dust. How like my life! thought Trini. The bus station was to the right, next to an old building with sagging hulks and rotting boards. As they went into the bus station crowded with people, she stopped and turned to José Mario, wanting so to tell him that she would bridge the distance some way, somehow. Words tripped over her feelings. All she could say was, "I still have your seeds. We'll plant them, someday, you and I, on our own land. I promise. I must go forward to find a way, Papá. Land—a piece of land . . ."

The hope of that promise was in his eyes as they made their way to the ticket counter.

* * *

Celestina had left Chihuahua to go to her new farm in Morentín. Trini had taken over her vegetable stall in the city market. She had been working with Celestina at the market for several months, watching the older woman's frustration over being an inquilina. Los inquilinos were vendors who rented space in the city market, buying produce from large farms. According to Celestina, they scraped out a living, owning nothing, not even the cash register. Trini watch Celestina scratch sales on long brown paper bags, dating each bag, then adding up the totals at the end of the week. By the time the cost of the produce and the spoilage were subtracted from the sales, there was a frown on Celestina's face. She chewed the end of her pencil and closed her eyes in mental calculation. For fifteen years she had been saving every penny she could spare to become one of the bien puestos. The bien puestos, the well-heeled ones, owned their own farms, their own produce, and all the profit. After fifteen years, Celestina had bought a farm, that is to say, a small piece of land that needed all her attention. She sniffed, "Los bien puestos won't be looking down their noses at me!"

She was determined to bring her unproductive, dry piece of land to life. Celestina was in Morentín and Trini had taken her place at the market. Trini lived with Licha, Celia, and Celia's children. Licha worked as a waitress at El Canario restaurant, and the gentle Celia had to take care of her two children while she waited for a dying husband to be brought back to Chihuahua. The husband, while working in the fields in Fresno, California, had neglected to wear a mask while sprayng chemicals. The poisons were eating away his body. Doctors in California had decided to send him back home to die.

Trini took care of the vegetable business six days a week, taking an early bus from La Colonia Murguía where she lived in los presidios Urbino, number twenty-two.

Today was Friday, and the bus was stopping as usual on Eleventh Street. As she got off, she saw Timoteo opening the market's wide doors. The old building covered a square block. The hollow of the early morning gathered sounds of growing activity. The parking of trucks and the shouts of the produce men melted into the sounds of merchants opening the small box stalls that lined both sides of the street outside the market building. Trini hastened the rhythm in her step, feeling the morning, as vendors zigzagged, dog-trotting with bultos on their backs, sounds splashing and sprinkling, the smell of clean, wet streets heavy in her nostrils, her ear catching car hummings at a distance. As Timoteo opened the door, Trini was carried along by a sea of vendors that appeared from every direction and flowed into the marketplace.

Trini's eye caught the figure of Señora Guzmán, trying to keep up with her, panting, turning her head from left to right like a bird. In a stall to the right, Trini noticed Josefino, one hundred years old, busy at arranging hand-tooled leather goods, belts, purses, holsters, shoes, placing each piece on a red sarape, carefully spacing them, standing aside to admire his work. The smell of the leather filled her nostrils as she waved to Josefino. The old man waved back, smiling, shouting a morning greeting, "Buenos días, chula!"

Señora Guzmán caught up with her. Trini prepared herself to listen to the old woman's usual complaints, for that was all that ever came out of Señora Guzmán's mouth, it seemed. She alternated woes from the weather to her son, from rising prices to her son, from the tricks of crooked politicians to her son, her voice resigned, punctuated by sighs and the clicking of her tongue. Today, she started with her son. "A new job, he said—ha!"

Señora Guzmán waited for a reply from Trini, who turned, eyebrow raised. It was enough reply for Señora Guzmán, so she continued, "His soul will burn in hell! I can't live with it. I threw him out this morning."

Whatever the job was, Trini could feel the tonal pleasure in the old woman's build-up to the tragic announcement, now declared. Señora Guzmán blew her nose and wiped her eyes for effect and then went on. "He came home with a camera. A photographer, he tells me. I thought my problems were over. So, I ask, son, what do you photograph?"

Señora Guzmán began to cry outright, her fat jowls dancing up and down with the heaving of sobs. Trini began to feel sorry for the old woman because her tears were so genuine. But then, she could never tell about Señora Guzmán. Jerkily, skipping into a run to keep up with Trini, la señora caught her by the sleeve, stopping her in her tracks, raising herself on tiptoes, whispering with horror in Trini's ear. "He takes pictures of naked women—in brothels!"

Trini tried to look concerned, feeling the beginning of a smile at the corners of her mouth. Before she could turn her head to sympathize, the old woman was gone. Trini saw her running toward another woman, waving her hands in the air. "My!" sighed Trini, "she'll tell the whole market by closing time."

Most of the stalls were still closed as Timoteo screwed the hoses to the water faucets to wash off the old broken tiles on the market floor. Some parts of the floor were simply dirt holes or makeshift wooden planks. He hosed down the floor, snaking between stalls, whistling and calling out greetings to the vendors who were arriving. Timoteo was very old. Trini wondered how many years he had been washing away the putrescent smells of each tired day.

From outside the market building, she could make out the lumbering motions, the purring of running motors, the produce trucks lined bumper to bumper. Soon the produce men began their rush, looming through the door, taking different directions to cover all the stalls. Trini prepared for the delivery of the fresh produce, carefully sorting out the stale vegetables and fruits from the day before and putting them into a basket. These were picked up by Simon later, for he bought the stale produce as animal feed. He came along every morning, flipping a peseta on the scale, making amorous sounds at the pretty girls, picking up his cajón. The not-so-stale fruits and vegetables were mixed in with the fresh produce after being washed and revived in fresh water. Salable tomatoes and aguacates were dried carefully after washing and placed on top of the new produce.

Trini saved the small green squash for special customers, favorites of Celestina. The smell of fresh chile, shockingly green, tickled Trini's nose as she made bundles of the small mountain of fresh cilantro, tying each bundle with a piece of string. Then, her deft fingers removed the outside leaves of corn and the loose scales of white onions. She had washed and arranged the produce attractively before the arrival of the first customer. Once that was done, she made her way carrying two pails to the faucets where a line of women waited; their conversations, gay, laughingly loud, were occasionally broken by barking orders from men in nearby stalls. The two girls in front of her smiled, including her in the conversation. "I was telling Rosa about my date last night."

"Tell Trini about your father."

"Well, my date got drunk, and I was late getting home. Papá was waiting. ¡Ay, ay, ay, Dios mío!" the girl laughed as her hands played skillfully in the air. "Papá was at the door with his gun! He put it right to Lalo's temple and told him to scat. Poor Lalo! He didn't even feel the gun! He opened one eye, looked at Papá, smiled and left. Just like that!"

Laughter filled the faucet area. A girl remarked, "I bet you got it from your papá."

She showed them a black and blue mark on her shoulder. "I got it good. Papá says enough beatings will keep me a good girl. It's very difficult to be a good girl."

"Are you a good girl?"

"Yes and no."

Laughter again. A black-haired woman with soft eyes announced, "I have a casita."

She was now the center of attention, for getting a casita was quite a doing. It was hard to find a man to set up a house for you, to pay expenses. Sometimes girls secretly admitted that getting a casita offered more advantages than marriage. An older woman broke the mood of the girls by passing along some practical advice. "The produce man from Ojinaca has to move his tomatoes. You can get them cheap."

When her turn came, Trini filled the two pails, then made her way back to the stalls, the talk around her becoming a hum. There were two customers waiting when she got back, one woman already weighing her purchase. She opened a straw basket into which Trini poured vegetables, onions after squash, cabbage before tomatoes. Trini was giving out change to another customer when she saw La Gitana opening her stall.

La Gitana did not deal in perishables—she sold baskets, love charms, and paper flowers. Most of the basket stalls in the market looked dusty and cluttered but not La Gitana's. Baskets were arranged in piles from the floor to the ceiling according to size and color, blues, yellows, and greens. On an opposite wall, a huge red laundry basket filled with tiny thimble baskets was the background for the counter. Here La Gitana displayed her specialities—love potions, fetishes, perfumed cushions. All these were free gifts for anyone who had his fortune told. The final artistic touch in the colorful stall were the flowers, all made by La Gitana. Some of the awkward, shaggy-leafed, huge blooms were very much like La Gitana herself, rakish, friendly. Trini's eye caught sight of the tiny, dainty, starched angelic bouquets of little nubes. No, decided Trini, those are certainly not like the gypsy. There's nothing angelic about her. La Gitana shouted from across the way. "Hey, Trini, two mangos for our breakfast."

Trini crossed over with two ripe orange mangos in her hands. She gave one to La Gitana with a smile and watched her bite into it with great relish. Trini ate hers slowly, wondering how old the gypsy was. La Gitana refused to talk about her age, but not about her countless lovers. Her passionate encounters were her favorite topic of conversation; as she spoke, her fingers found the elastic of the blouse hugging her shoulders. She pulled it down to inspect a beauty mark, creamy brown on her pale skin. She sighed, "This little spot makes men passionate. You have one, Trini, eh?"

"A beauty mark?"

"No stupid, a lover . . ."

They laughed, then La Gitana tossed her dyed red hair. The gypsy popped the last piece of mango into her mouth, looking with dismay at her sticky hands. She danced herself across to Trini's stall, face tilted, hands in the air, then she dipped them into the pail of water Trini used to wash vegetables. She shook her hands, wiping them on a piece of newspaper as she walked back to Trini. She placed her elbows on the conter, face on palms, to watch Trini with a mock solemn air, asking, "Why don't you have a lover?"

How could she tell the gypsy that the man whom she would have as a lover did not care for her? How could she tell La Gitana that sometimes she felt this hate for certain kinds of men? She wanted to talk of Héctor—to talk of the misery of her experience. Of how little she knew about making love. She had wanted Sabochi. Yes—she had wanted Sabochi as her lover. He was already a part of her being, would always be.

She looked at the gypsy with admiration. There were so many things about the seller of flowers that intrigued her, the flash of her smile, the buxom body sensuous in its freedom. La Gitana's exuberant confidence always gave Trini a lift. La Gitana tapped her hip, eyes narrowing, mouth pouting, still wondering, "How can you live without a lover? I'd die!"

Trini smiled and said nothing. La Gitana laughed, exposing big white teeth, taunting, "You don't dare, eh? What's the matter?"

Trini looked down at her sticky hands, open palms on her lap, then she raised questioning eyes to La Gitana. "Lovers? Maybe I could love one . . ."

La Gitana sighed. "The voice of inexperience."

Hagglings, barkings rose, tangled voices flung in midair. Trini noticed a customer at her stall. She waited on the woman, then sat down to shell green peas into little mounds, glancing up to watch La Gitana laughing and joking with some man across the way. There was something about La Gitana that reminded her of someone, the coquettish tilt of the head, the touching fingers, the softness of the voice—who? Then it came to her. Of course! Licha, Celestina's younger daughter, the one engaged to the proprietor of all those restaurants.

La Gitana never seemed to take men seriously. The gypsy had once told her with pain in the deep pools of her eyes, "That is the only way not to get hurt. Anyway, what man takes a woman seriously? You must learn to play the game the way they do."

Was love only a game? wondered Trini. No, it has to be more—like Papá's seeds. It's something rooted in good things, a nourishment, she told herself. She knew her feelings were childish and confused. She was just an Indian girl without experience. But her instincts told her she was right about love. Instincts could not be wrong, for they were of the earth.

At the end of the day, while Timoteo closed the mercado's huge door, Trini waited for the bus, thinking of Licha, lovely Licha, who was full of discontent.

The bus left Trini at the bottom of a hill that led up to the presidio Urbino. She walked two steep blocks without a break in her stride, then turned the corner leading to the entrance of the two-story building. There were twenty-eight units in the old L-shaped building; wobbly stairs led up to number twenty-two. She reached the top of the stairs and paused. Licha stood at the door, a scowl on her beautiful face. She was not looking at Trini but across to the street below. She wore only a scanty slip, the softness of her slender, curved body outlined in the shadows of the doorway. Her full round breasts were a creamy sheen on the lace edge of an expensive slip. Licha had beautiful clothes bought by Don Alejandro from fashionable stores in Mexico City. Trini heard dogs whimpering in the street. They were scratching on some door; children screamed and mothers called while a radio blared mariachi music into the hot sun. Licha's eyes were still beyond Trini, her voice petulant, impatient. She had a complaint. "It's scorching!"

She edged herself against one side of the door to let Trini enter, her eyes still in the distance. Trini did not answer but turned to see what Licha was so intent on watching. She seemed to be looking at the cottage across the street, the one painted blue with a picket fence and an apple tree in the front yard. It looked out of place among the dilapidated presidios that surrounded it. Trini made her way to the kitchen. The long dusty ride on the bus and the walk uphill had left her mouth parched. She drank a glass of water that tasted heavily of iron, then dropped herself into a kitchen chair, stretching out. Licha followed her and leaned against the wall. "I hate this place . . ."

Her voice trailed off, her eyes sullen. Trini shrugged then got up with some effort. She could feel the weight of fatigue as she made her way to the kitchen faucet. She took a rusty basin from a sideboard, filled it with water, and splashed her face and arms. She finally let the water run on her head, adding damp weight to the wrapped braids on either side. Trini reached for a towel hanging on a nail, rubbed her face and arms vigorously, then wrapped the towel around her head. The wetness and the scrub had left its tingle; her flesh no longer felt sticky and hot. She looked up to see Licha watching her, amber eyes full of mischief. "I have a wonderful idea . . ."

Trini had heard her complain about the rundown presidio many times before. She did not blame Licha, for it was hard, five people living in two rooms. The bedroom was cramped full with three single beds. There was a cot in the corner of the kitchen. In the bedroom, Celia's two children slept on one bed, Celia and Trini on another. Licha had the cot to herself.

But today Licha was doing more than complaining. She was planning something.

Trini was too tired to be interested, but she asked, "What idea?"

"Celia went to Morentín with the children."

"So?"

"We're alone." Her voice was full of conspiracy. "We don't have to stay in this place."

Trini unfastened her blouse, slipped it off, and crouched out of her skirt; she took a wrapper hanging on a hook behind the bedroom door and put it on. Clothes multiply like people in a big city, she smiled as she mused. She remembered la hilpa which had been her solitary garment in the hills of Batopilas. Now there were stockings, shoes, undergarments, skirts, blouses, even a wrapper. She had to spend what she earned for clothes in an attempt to be modern, citified.

Licha sat on the bed, hands clasped, legs tucked up. "Did you hear me?"

Trini humored her. "Where do you want to go?"

"The blue cottage . . ."

Trini slumped down beside her, unwrapping the towel from her head, placing its wet coolness against her face.

"The blue cottage?" Trini asked as Licha let herself fall back on the bed, her slip curling up over her thighs, full and long. It was obvious that she had planned something.

Licha smiled, a sly glint in her eye. "Let's just go live there!"

The blue cottage! Trini envisioned the tiny house that stood on alien ground in the poor barrio of La Colonia Murguía. It was back from the crescent road that led to the presidios and adobe chozas past the railroad tracks, close to the old dam. The blue cottage was a casita and had been built for the young mistress of a well-known politician who wished to keep his extramarital affairs sequestered. Casitas were sprinkled in all the poor neighborhods where they stood out like sore thumbs with their fresh paint, picket fences, gardens, and many of the luxuries the poor could not afford. This cottage had neat, wide windows and a shingled blue roof. But the lawn behind the picket fence was yellow from neglect. It had been empty for some time now.

"You have a key." Carlota, the last mistress of the blue cottage, had entrusted the key to her beautiful friend.

"You game?" There was daring in Licha's voice. "Let's get away from this smelly hole. I've wanted to for so long, but you know Mamá."

"It doesn't belong to us."

"Who cares! Mamá can't scream at us all the way from Morentín."

"I don't know . . ."

"You know you want to."

"It would be nice . . ."

"Well, then? The electricity is off, but we can use candles. Come on!" Licha's eagerness dissolved all doubt.

Why not? thought Trini. The feeling of space would be nice.

* * *

Trini and Licha were lying on a massive bed in the master bedroom of the blue cottage. Licha had taken Trini through the house, showing her everything, rugs, drapes, perfume bottles on a dressing table, tiled bathroom, dishes. They had laughed and giggled like two little girls as they ferreted around the house among the shadows of twilight. Later, they sat propped up against huge feather pillows with satin covers slightly soiled along the edges. Trini had never seen so many fine things.

"Everything's so dusty. Tomorrow we'll clean . . ."

"Clean!" protested Licha, throwing a pillow at Trini. "You do it, not me."

Licha jumped out of bed to look at herself in the large wall mirror by the side of the bed. She piled her silky black hair on top of her head and turned her face to study her profile. Then, she let the hair down and gestured around the room, saying in jest, "See how profitable sin is? But all this . . ." her voice was now dead serious, ". . . is piddling."

Trini did not answer. She felt awkward and dumb when Licha spilled over with assurances. She watched Licha take off her wrapper, then trace the outline of her body, laughing softly. Trini looked toward the open window. She had opened it to air out the mustiness of the closed house. She stood looking out at the apple tree in the center of the front yard. Long weeds hugged the edge of the porch, defined by a rising moon. Cricket sounds were woven into the apple tree. There's a sense to this, thought Trini. Sometimes she had the urge to run from Licha's complications. Licha was beside her now, soft and supple, rummaging in her wrapper pocket for a pack of cigarettes. She asked Trini, "What's out there?"

"Night."

"So?" Licha made her way back to the bed, flipping the pack onto a pillow. She sat down and picked up the pack again, tapping out a cigarette, holding it between her fingers, breathing in the dark. She ordered, "Come away from the window, Trini. Talk to me."

Trini did as she was told, finding a place next to Licha on the bed. Licha was staring at herself in the mirror, holding the lighted cigarette in her hand. After a while, she turned impatiently and snuffed out the cigarette on a night table. Then she stood and walked up to the mirror, a calculating look in her eye. "I'm lucky, Trini."

She turned around slowly, looking at herself from different angles. "I have a chance to escape the barrio, the stinking poverty. That's why I'm marrying Don Alejandro." She met her own eyes in the mirror, asking, "I'm beautiful, aren't I?"

Trini knew Licha had no love for Don Alejandro. He was the owner of El Canario and four other restaurants. Licha had worked for him before he asked her to marry him. Yes, agreed Trini, you are very beautiful. She said nothing because Licha affirmed it with her tone of voice, with the self-admiring twinkle in her eye.

Licha walked around the room, picking up a perfume bottle, a powder-puff, a jewelry box, putting them back a quickly as she picked them up. She sat down next to Trini and reached for the pack of cigarettes again. After taking one, she rolled over on her stomach, cupping her face in her hands, the unlighted cigarette between her fingers. She spoke slowly, deliberately, "This cottage is nothing compared to what I'm going to have."

Suddenly her mood changed as she began to tell Trini the facts about casitas. "They're battlegrounds. But what a delicious battleground! Lovers living the grand passion for a little while, then, poof!—the jealousies. She wants to know why he spends so much time at home, and he wants to know if other men visit the house he is paying for."

Trini listened intently as Licha talked out her argument with an amused smile. "Take this cottage, for instance. The furies of hell in this place! El político's mistress ran away with a lover in el político's car. They were arrested for stealing the car and landed in jail!"

Trini and Licha laughed, their voices resounding in the air. Licha rolled over on her back, crushing the cigarette in her hand and throwing it against the mirror as she continued. "The second mistress tried to kill herself when her viejito left her, and the third one . . ." Licha spread out her arms, then brought her fist up against her heart, "stabbed her lover on this very bed."

Licha put her arms over her head and stretched out from one end of the bed to the other, her voice feigning seriousness as she went on with her argument. "Carlota, well, Carlota was another matter . . ."

The beautiful Carlota!—the last mistress of the blue cottage. She had been the kept woman of a rich businessman whose wife found out about the affair and offered her husband an ultimatum—either he leave his mistress or she would have her father ruin him. What could the lover do? Give Carlota up, of course, but not before gifting her with the place as a peace offering, papers and all. Licha recalled, "That dumb Carlota. She followed the man to Mexico City–with a gun! She's probably somewhere in jail or dead! Ah, casitas!"

Trini fell back on the bed and stared at the ceiling. She could feel for Carlota. She asked softly, "Why did she follow him?"

"For love! Isn't that stupid?"

No, thought Trini, it's not stupid, but she remained silent as Licha continued, "Carlota's father lives in the barrio. He wanted to rent this place, but those who can afford it don't like the neighborhood, and the barrio people cannot afford the rent, so the poor man has no daughter and no rent. He has no idea where she is. He reads the newspapers from Mexico City looking for murders, expecting to see Carlota's face on the front page. But nothing. Love–ha!"

Trini visualized Carlota finding her lover, unable to pull the trigger, falling at his feet to beg for love again. She checked herself. How silly of me! Then she remembered how she had come to Chihuahua looking for Sabochi. The thought of Sabochi, Chimac, and a new baby suffocated her, made her turn over on the bed and hide her face. Licha sensed that something was wrong. "What's the matter?"

Trini did not answer, so Licha sat up, shaking her head. "It's that Indian, isn't it? You're as bad as Carlota!" Trini looked up at Licha, sitting there, smiling in the moon shadows, and wondered if it were true.

* * *

"Don't be a gutless ninny!"

Licha was scolding as she tried on her wedding dress in front of the mirror in the blue cottage. She turned to face Trini, who was putting the finishing touches on her bridesmaid's dress. Licha was insisting, "You know you want to stay here."

"Without you?" Trini was really questioning herself as she finished the last stitch on a buttonhole, clouds of soft, green tulle spreading around her.

Don Alejandro Sosa was paying for a very expensive wedding. There would be catering for five hundred people at El Casino Norteño, where the wedding reception was to be held. After the wedding, the bride and groom would fly to Buenos Aires. Trini had mixed feeling about the wedding. She was happy for Licha, but what would she do without her companion? Licha was the excitement in her life, for in her Trini saw all the things she would like to be—desirable, confident, gay. It had been a temporary dream studded with possibilities. Now Licha was going away. What will I do without her? Trini wondered.

"You stay!" Licha was ordering.

"I can't live alone in this place."

"You are a gutless ninny. Listen, I have the guts to marry that old man. That takes guts! What if he dies on me, in the middle of the honeymoon?" The thought became a joke to Licha. She started giggling, then it became laughter, laughter that wove itself into her whole body. She could not stop, but when she did, a soberness took over. "He's getting a good deal. I keep telling him I'm marrying him for his money, and he keeps telling everybody it's a love match!"

Now, they both laughed; the laughter was caught after a while in silent reflection. Trini fumbled with the idea of staying on at the cottage alone . . . no, of course not! Another thought came to her mind. "Why don't you live here with Don Alejandro, Licha . . ."

"Stop! I have bargained for much, much more—this is nothing."

Nothing? wondered Trini. She imagined living with Sabochi in the cottage—somehow the image did not materialize. No, with Sabochi, it was necessary to be near mountains, the old cave, riding garañones, the seasons, vivid and bright. That was Sabochi. She dare not stay alone in the cottage. She would go back to number twenty-two. She had her own plans to make. A piece of land somewhere in the world, was there such a piece for her? Where? How long would it take? She did not want to think about it now, or about living in the cottage. She hated giving in to her own sad resignation. She looked up to see Licha appraising her curiously. "You know you're quite pretty, Trini. Use it . . ."

"I'm not . . ." Trini had never thought of herself as pretty.

"Yes, you are! Do something with it in life."

Licha opened doors to new thoughts, but somehow Trini could not keep up or really believe. Licha knew how to work out all possibilities in her own life like a careful mathematician. But she? She felt like a seedless wind, restless, without direction. But then, in a strange, undefinable way, Licha was a seedless wind too, in spite of her beauty, her confidence, and all the things she said that time and again led to good fortune.

"What are you thinking?" Licha asked, slipping out of her wedding dress.

"I was wondering if you believed in love."

"Don't be naive. That's childish and foolish, stop being an Indian!"

A shadow crossed Trini's face. Licha was right. The dream of Sabochi had been false. She was done with a child's wishing. Maybe she should seriously consider Licha's way. Then she thought of Licha's sister, Celia, waiting for a dying husband. There was a substance to the older sister. At times when Celia talked of her husband, her eyes lit up with an old happiness, something that Trini recognized, something that was much more than Licha's nervous gaity. Funny, Licha seemed to have everything and nothing. Celia seemed to have nothing, yet everything. How strange. Loving someone made all the difference . . . then Licha broke into her thoughts.

"We're running late. There's a million things to do before Domico's tonight."

Don Alejandro was taking the wedding party to the most expensive restaurant that evening. Licha asked, "You have a dress for tonight? Of course you don't! I have just the dress for you! Tomorrow I get married! God help me!"

Trini scrutinized Licha's face. Was it really mock despair? Licha smiled serenely at her, "Come on, let's hurry . . ."

* * *

Alejandro's party had already had dinner, and Trini was sipping some after dinner brandy when she saw him. He wore a green waiter's uniform. He was writing up an order at a table where he stood talking and laughing. Trini held her breath in happiness. Yes, it was Tonio. She excused herself and made her way quickly to where he stood. She reached out and touched his arm. "Tonio!"

He turned and looked at her, not recognizing her. His handsome dark eyes questioned. It's only natural, she reasoned. My face is rouged. My hair cut and curled. Then there was Licha's expensive gown, making her look older, almost sophisticated. "It's me, Trini . . ."

Tonio stared at her, unbelieving, then the questioning broke into a smile. The orchestra started to play and couples were making their way to the dance floor. Tonio skirted the crowd, guiding her to the other side. The sense of the child arose in her, the one she always felt in the presence of Tonio. Tonio suddenly remembered the order in his hand. It took him only a second to plan. "I'll be back. Wait here."

She did as she was told, losing herself behind the potted palms next to the carved doors that led into the kitchen. She sat down on a red velvet chair and looked across the floor at Don Alejandro dancing with Licha. People were lounging, casually sipping drinks, waiters hurrying in and out with orders. After a while, Tonio came through the door with a tray high over his head. He passed her, the muscles of his body rhythmically pacing the way to the table that had ordered. In a few minutes he was back.

"Let's go." His voice was sure, commanding, like the old times.

"Where to?" She really didn't care.

"We'll ride around," Tonio offered.

She nodded, then remembered the wedding party. "I better tell Licha. Wait here." It was his turn to wait as she made her way across the floor. She sat down next to Licha, who was engrossed in a conversation with Don Alejandro's doctor.

"Licha . . ." Licha turned, raising an eyebrow, looking across at the waiting Tonio, then back at Trini. She asked in pleasurable approval, "Who's that?"

"Tonio."

"You never mentioned him," Licha reproached.

"Oh yes, I did."

"All you talked about was your Indian." Licha's amber eyes twinkled.

"I'm going with Tonio," Trini said without hesitation.

"Good for you! But for heaven's sake, don't be late for the wedding tomorrow."

* * *

Lights, embers, flames, passing symmetry—the world of night was illuminated by high rows of giant glows that opened up, flying on each side of the road. Trini felt a beginning. A beginning of what? Tonio was no longer just a memory but sat, very real, beside her. She watched him from the corner of her eye. The same old, dear Tonio, with life-renewing spirit, the old grin, the old gestures, driving the car like a city boy. Change—places, times, but not people.

Of course people change, she told herself, but Tonio seemed the same. He joked and laughed and sang in the old manner, driving the way he used to run Sarif, fast, free. He stopped at a little store to buy nieve raspada.

They ate the ices as the swell of life grew and diminished from the moving car. Buildings arched in tall silence, then folded in darkness; the car sped down La Avenida Colón as bancos, cathedral, el palacio, all whizzed by. Finally at El Paseo Bolívar the car followed the curved road to the park's high grounds. Tonio stopped. They sat in silence, looking toward the city alive with lights, Tonio smoking a cigarette, turning to her every so often, his eyes absorbing.

He took her hand and led her up the hill reaching for a million blinking stars. Trini felt the inarticulate sense of change, as if the running into life needed a complete stop to gather threads still reaching out from the past. The same stars had blinked at them in Batopilas, on the mountain of the giant hives. An expectancy leaped to her throat. . . .

"I never found gold. . . ." Tonio's words sounded absurd. She could not help laughing softly.

"What's so funny?" He was puzzled by her laughter. She hastened to explain. "I had forgotten, the gold, I mean . . ." She looked up, catching something lost in Tonio's eyes. She felt a little bit ashamed. Tonio had lost a dream and she had laughed. Her eyes were bright with sympathy. "I'm sorry, Tonio, about the gold."

He leaned his body back, elbows firm on the gound, shrugged and sighed. "It was a long shot." He turned to look at her, wearing the old grin. "What about your land?"

"I'll have it someday." Her voice sounded sure; was it silly to sound that sure?

"You'll always be a descalza, in spite of the lipstick and high heels."

"I *am* a descalza." She believed it too. "Batopilas, Mamá, they're a map inside of me. So many things . . ." Her eyes were searching for threads from the past again.

"Such as?"

"Mamá, the day she died—not the dying, more the way she looked that morning. We were on a hill like this one, and she was drinking pochote milk. I remember her tongue waiting for the milk. Her feet were buried in the earth, and I had the feeling she was like a tree . . ." The memory was caught in the flux of excitement as Trini found another rush of words. "I remember the dancing to the goddess Tonantzín. The Virgin was there, perfectly pink and beautiful, but I forgot her. To me, the brown goddess was like music. It's like knowing where you belong—what you belong to ..."

"What? Not who?"

"Yes, what. I can't explain ..." Prismatic feelings were growing inside her. Tonio reached out and slowly took off her shoes, running his hand along the side of her foot and ankle. She felt grass spears touch her bare feet. She spread out the folds of Licha's dress and looked at him solemnly. Tonio turned on his stomach, folding his arms under his chin, staring down at a blinking city. He spoke now half-seriously, half in jest.

"You are still Tonantzín."

"I think I am too." Her voice was serious.

"I think it's time to claim you."

"Claim me?" her blood surged.

"In a way, all these years, you have been mine." His voice was honey soft.

"I belong to myself, Tonio—people don't belong to others."

"That's a funny thing for you to say."

"Perhaps ..."

She lay down beside him, falling into his mood, made splendid by the night. Softly he began to sing his old love song. "En tus ojos tiembla mi destino, y mi suerte en labios tan divinos ..."

"Now, your love song's for me." To how many women had he sung that song? Yet, on this night with all its magic, the song was only hers—yes, only hers.

He turned to her and began to stroke her hair gently, then she felt the pressure of his lips. It felt so good to be kissed, but she broke away, confused, pulling herself to her feet. She ran down the hill. She stopped, wondering why she had run away from him. There was another part of her that wanted his lips, his arms. He was beside her. He asked, "Are you afraid?"

"It's all too fast." Was she afraid? So many things made them part of one another. She changed the subject. "I have a casita."

"Another man?"

"No, no ..."

She saw the puzzled look on his face. She promised, "I'll show you. I'll take you there now."

As they made their way south toward La Colonia Murguía, Trini spilled over with all that had happened to her, good and bad. She wanted to close the gap in their lives. It must be all there, there for him to know, her heart told her; the story grew. He listened in silence all the way until they came to the half-moon road that led up to the cottage. He stopped at the gate and they made their way up to the porch. The apple tree made a spider shadow on the shimmer of the moon.

"We have to light candles," she whispered laughingly as she led the way into the house. She led him by the hand to the room where she and Licha had spun so many dreams. The moon shone in reflection on the wall mirror next to the bed, where they sat, laughing together in the darkness. The silence was liquid, vibrant. After a while, she went to a drawer and took out two candles, lighting them, placing them on the night table.

"I've always loved you Trini." There was a new seriouness in Tonio's voice.

"As a child . . ." laughed Trini.

"You're a woman now. A beautiful woman, the earth-goddess, Tonantzín."

"And . . ."

"I want you . . ." He said it with urgency. "You love me, Trini. Sabochi was just a child's dream."

He gently pulled her to him, his lips on her mouth, pliant, warm, strong. All her loneliness was stilled as passion grew, emerged, spilled over, in the candled shadows and the shocking brightness of the moon.

13

Storm

Trini was running again. Loving Tonio, she tried to grow in stillness, easily weaving her days into his, projecting them into years. It had been like that to her. But not to Tonio. That was the reason she was running again. It was January, and she was leaving for La Junta in the morning. Isidoro would be waiting for her. Looking out at the bare apple tree, she reconstructed the events of the last two years. Time backed up like a well of tortured anger, thoughts rushing through her mind, thoughts of Tonio, of the wounds he had inflicted, wounds to the heart, wounds to the spirit. The romantic, tender Tonio. The first year had been good. . . . She looked at the sad, bare branches melting into a sad, grey sky.

She remembered that first year, waiting up for Tonio to come home. There was always the late supper with a special treat from Domico's. She listened to his stories, wild and absurd, until the wee hours, then watched him sleep late into the mornings. She would wake him in the quietness of the early afternoon. His dear, handsome face would break into a smile. He would reach out for her. Then they made love in a white sea of sun and stillness. Such love!

She loved to brush his uniform and iron his white shirts. It was done with so much care. Trini watched him dress before the wall mirror. Sometimes he would take her for a walk along Libertad Street, holding her hand firmly in his warm grasp. Trini felt the joy of belonging. She enjoyed the fabric of night life along the street because he enjoyed it, because she was with him. She would sit in the darkness of a cantina, watching him drink, play guitar, gamble. But always he would find his way back to her, to take her hand, to lead her to wherever he desired. . . .

He had loved her. He had come home on her eighteenth birthday with a piñata full of silly little gifts—a tiny doll made out of buttons, a bunch of wilted flowers sweet in their dying fragrance, a wisp of silk handkerchief some lady customer had left behind at the restaurant. The caring, the sense of belonging, the steady storm of passion in the afternoons, they were glad things to remember. Tonio, making love, his supple hands discovering with such mastery—Ah! the first year had been so good!

Then came the second year. One night in bed, sweet with the body smell of love, she had confided, "I'm pregnant, Tonio."

He had reached for a cigarette in silence and found none. He got out of bed with the pretext of looking for a cigarette. But she knew that he was not happy with the news. She wanted to tell of her happiness, but she swallowed the words in the darkness. She sensed a door closing between them. She wanted to cry out, "We are family, I want the baby, marry me," but there were no words, only darkness. He had found his cigarette and had come back to bed. She had watched the moving flicker of the red ash. She sensed the heaviness of his brooding.

He could not accept. He did not accept. She could only love him, and the distance between them would grow as her body did with the coming baby. During these months he frowned, impatiently left the cottage without her, leaving her alone for days and days, the beginning of a senseless time, a motionless time.

* * *

Licha was home in a new apartment on Quintana Street, an exclusive residential district. She had come back, distraught and bewildered by the inconvenience imposed upon her. Don Alejandro had had a heart attack in Acapulco. Licha, caught in the whirl of social life, spending her days on the long, sunny beaches, had been forced to pack up and come back to Chihuahua with her very sick husband.

Trini found her in her new apartment, with trunks full of pretty things still unpacked, pouting over her situation, but not without a new twinkle in her eye. She was now in charge of Don Alejandro's business, keeping accounts, talking to lawyers. Ambition shone in Licha's eyes. She speculated. "He has two huge insurance policies. If the poor man dies, I can remodel all the restaurants. His lawyers think it would be good business."

Licha! How can you plan such things, thought Trini. Maybe that is the way to be. When one does not feel, one is not hurt. . . . No, she could never be like her friend. She realized it was more a lack in herself than a criticism of Licha. To be like Licha was a talent, a terrifying talent, but a way of defying hurt. And all my days, thought Trini as she watched her companion's eager concentration on the accounts, are hurt and pain. Licha looked up from the accounts to observe her critically. Trini was very conscious of her cumbersome body, for her pregnant state was Licha's focal point at the moment. Her friend laughed somewhat derisively. "What else has your handsome man done to you, Trini?"

"I want the baby." It was the truth. She wanted the baby very much.

"You just don't learn, do you?" Licha shook her head, sighed, and went back to the figures in her account book. Trini wanted to confide in someone, but not Licha. Licha would only play the part of the cynic and reproach her for her submissive Indian ways. Then, too, she was too proud to tell her friend about the new distance between her and Tonio.

But Licha knew. She was clever enough to read symptoms. She knew men too well. Perhaps she had even planned to do what she did. One day, Licha surprised Trini and Tonio at the cottage. Laden with a feast of chicken, beer, and tequila, she had come to celebrate. "You and Tonio and the baby!"

Looking beautiful and bright, she had come into the cottage, embracing Trini, turning to Tonio, kissing him fully on the mouth, her hand lingering on his cheek. She took him by the hand, leading him to the car to bring in the food and drink. Later on, her hand fell on his shoulder or his hair too often as they worked in the kitchen.

Trini, nine months pregnant, was not in a festive mood, feeling awkward and ugly next to the blithe and lovely Licha. Trini fumbled with plates and glasses while Licha sat next to Tonio, listening to his sudden friendly chatter, answering him with a laugh, a slap on the hand, or fingers that lingered on his arm, his lap. Trini choked on the food. She watched Tonio and Licha sharing food with such pleasure, chicken caught hungrily between laughing teeth, with the delicious licking of fingers. Licha catching the quick foam spilling over a beer can with a pink tongue, curling, tarrying, her eyes laughingly saying the unsaid. It was like a transfusion for Tonio, the creation of small panics in Trini.

Walls of confusion, anger, helplessness rose around Trini. She had become the intruder, the unwanted. No, Trini had cried inside herself, I don't have your talent, Licha. I'm an awkward, ugly Indian girl that he doesn't want anymore. He's beautiful like you, Licha, but I love him too well, too much perhaps . . . The words raged inside her, meaning nothing to the two who planned their enjoyment without her. She left them then, running out of the house, making her way toward the swaying silhouette of an apple tree, full like herself. The barking of a dog filled the early evening. She was aware of the barking breaking the stillness, like glass at her feet. She leaned her head against the tree and knew that a time had been shed, that something in her life would turn and shift after today. An emptiness expanded and grew. She had to cry, she must cry. She cried herself out, then she wiped the tears away and listened for sounds inside the kitchen. There were none. Where were they?

She hurried back and found the kitchen empty. She walked slowly and reluctantly toward the master bedroom where she had known such joy with Tonio. Through the door, she could see them on the bed, sitting, looking at each other in the mirror as if they shared a secret joke. Trini stood in the shadows of the doorway, feeling a profound weariness.

She heard Licha laugh as she sprawled on the bed. She used to do that in the old days, thought Trini. It's all harmless. I'm imagining things. The sluggish air weighed heavily in her throat. She watched them in serious, intimate whispers, oblivious to her presence. As Licha talked, her ringed hands opened gracefully with excitement, at times a hand falling on Tonio's knee and staying there, and when he leaned toward her in response, again the rings caught the sparkle of reflections from the mirror. Licha's hand was resting on Tonio's shoulder; Tonio was more alive than Trini had seen him in a long time. Suddenly, through an open door, Trini caught the smell of dust and rain. A storm was breaking.

* * *

Trini gave birth to a little girl alone in the blue cottage. Tonio had simply not come home from Domico's one evening. He just disappeared, and in the days following the birth of her baby, she sat in the darkness by the window waiting for him to come home. Surely he wanted to see the baby. Surely he cared. But he did not come. When the baby was a few months old, Celia suggested that she go out and look for him in the old haunts.

Celia had asked to be the baby's godmother. The Sunday the baby was baptized, Celia urged Trini again to go and look for Tonio. She promised to look after Linda. Trini had put the beautiful, pink Linda in Celia's arms and had set out for Libertad Street. She took a bus to town and walked along the narrow street. It was already night and the sounds of mariachi trumpets wafted through the sudden opening of bar doors. She went into the bars and lost herself in corners, watching for Tonio. She scanned the bar stools, the tables, the dance floor. No Tonio. She asked familiar bartenders and some of his old acquaintances if they had seen him. No one had.

The round of Libertad Street became a routine for several months to follow. Fruitless, fruitless, until one evening she knew that she would look no more. What was the use? She would go home and make some sense of her life without him. That was all she could do.

That evening, as she was walking away from Libertad Street, she saw a familiar figure standing under a lamppost, next to a vending cart where the glare of a neon light fell on heavy glass jars holding watermelon juice. An old man was making gorditas, the sizzle of heat and grease in the air, and next to him was the thin, erect figure, a kerchief round his head, of Isidoro! Yes, the face was unmistakable. What was he doing in Chihuahua?

"Isidoro!" She was by his side.

He turned, eyes questioning. She saw no recognition in his face. Trini spoke with a soft urgency. "Trini."

He squinted in the brightness of night lights, then nodded with a smile. He had changed so little! People were passing by them, between them, Isidoro pointed to a small café across the street. "We can go there."

The café was almost empty. Only two people sat in a corner booth. Trini and Isidoro sat by a window bright with the language of outside life. Looking at Isidoro across the table, Trini became another person, the thought of Tonio suddenly gone. Old feelings had surfaced, old memories, and the first word on her lips was, "Sabochi?"

"In the canyon of Tararecua."

A waitress came by and they ordered coffee. Trini wanted more of Sabochi. "Are they tracking horses?"

"Yes, a big herd. I go with them in January."

"How long will he be there?"

"They track now. Camp by the mouth of the Tararecua all winter if there's a blizzard."

"All winter?"

"All winter—until spring."

Sabochi spending all winter in a camp by the Tararecua. There was a half-formed hope on her lips. "I wish I were you, going to the canyon—Sabochi."

"You go. I take you."

She shook her head, a memory clicking fresh and strong—Sabochi on his horse, Sabochi by her side in San Domingo—how the memories tutored her heart, the old magic improvising. But no, she shook her head. Why go to Sabochi? He belonged to his village, to Chimac. She had no claim. But to see him again! She needed him so. She needed him so. The glimmer of the thought hung in the air. A rush of words broke forth from Trini. "Isidoro, I may want to go with you. I may have to go with you. Where can I reach you if I decide to go?"

Isidoro wrote down an address on a paper napkin as the waitress came with their coffee. He folded the napkin and placed it in her hand. "I will be at this address in La Junta. Remember, I leave the last week of January."

It was an anchor, a hope. Her heart was light as Isidoro took her to the bus stop. There was a slight drizzle as she bid Isidoro goodbye, putting her arms around him, taking his hard calloused hand in hers. On the bus, drops of rain glistened bright against the window, reflecting light. The world was swift, passing shadows broken by swirls of colored lights. She cried softly all the way to La Colonia Murguía. When she got off the bus, she felt cleansed like the world was cleansed by the evening rain. The air sang, Sabochi, Sabochi . . . Sabochi, the waiting, Tonio temporarily forgotten.

But not for long. In bed, in the soft dark, her body ached for Tonio. It was Tonio that all her senses desired, a flame to be destroyed and restored; her want, alive, a soft brilliance untouched, somewhere, somewhere . . .

* * *

Trini saw Tonio at the funeral of Don Alejandro Sosa. He was with Licha, lovely in widow's weeds. Licha's fingers moved in tender pride on Tonio's arm. The widow's eyes revealed a tearstained satisfaction. Tonio's strong, handsome presence obviously infatuated. She leaned against him in bereavement, a sad, meek smile on her face. Tonio held her protectively. His eyes saw no one else.

Oh, God, thought Trini, shrinking to the back of the crowd, feeling a confused pain that snatched away all dimension, cruel, fierce. When it was over, Tonio led Licha away from the grave, clasping her hand, finger through finger.

Trini felt Celia's hand on her arm. It was Celia who led her away, for she was blinded by tears of anger, of shame. Later on, sitting in the kitchen of number twenty-two, the stricken Trini demanded, "Did you know?"

"Yes," answered Celia quietly, "but I didn't have the heart to tell you."

A soft moan broke through Trini's sobs. Celia spoke gently, "They've been living together all the time Don Alejandro was in the hospital."

"You didn't tell me!"

"What good would it have done?"

"I waited for him!" Trini stood very still, covering her face, then looked up at Celia with brittle calmness, asking, "What do I do now?"

"He won't come back, Trini, not now . . ."

"Will he ever?" There was a flat finality in Trini's voice.

"She'll leave him one day. That's her way."

He loves her so much, thought Trini. Poor Tonio, that day would be the day he would feel what she was feeling.

* * *

Trini moved back with Celia to number twenty-two, for she could not pay rent on the cottage. Celia had to leave for Fresno, for the United States, to bring back José—his life was nearing its end and he wanted to die at home. Trini stayed to take care of the children. It was a busy time. At night she would fall exhausted into a deep, fitful sleep, awakening the next morning to move, to clean, to feed the children. There was a numbness to life. She concentrated on the children.

Celia came back home with a dying José, a young man who seemed old—so thin and emaciated, only his eyes burned with an obstinate fire that denied his illness. Trini made it a point to keep the children away from the house in the mornings. She wanted to give Celia and José time to themselves, and yet there were days when Celia would insist, "He wants the children around him today."

Celia's eyes shone with biting despair, and Trini was to become part of that suffering in the time that followed. There was pain for José; only the hypodermic and morphine made existence possible. His eyes would flow into life at the sight of his wife as her fingers, now expert, filled the syringe and injected the numbness of peace into his thin arm. José was twenty-eight and resisted dying, a dark liquid fire of resentment shadowing his eyes.

Celia would lie by his side and together they would watch the sunrise. Or they would sit with the sleeping children in the room, silent and full of things unsaid. But the time came when José was no longer able to recognize anyone, his fingers weakly touching the edge of the sheet, looking for a grasp, fingers fluttering, then resting interminably.

Watching Celia and José in their closeness, in their despair, was a torment to Trini. She tried to be with Celia as much as possible, sharing the anguish that lived in the wife's every move, in her voice, and in the stillness of her body.

When this magnified Trini's loneliness, she fell into the old habit of waiting for Tonio. It was a hold. She sat and waited while her child slept, knowing well that he would not come, but still breathing expectancy, imagining how it would be if he did come.

And then one night he did come, but not of his own volition. Two friends brought him home to Trini, for he had passed out at a bar. With the help of his friends, she put him on the cot by the wall of the kitchen and sat watching him all night. A joy grew in the darkness. Tonio was home—Tonio was home.

When the day broke, she found herself still there, thirsting to touch him, but she did not move. She longed to lie by his side, to hold him, to feel the beating of his heart against her cheek. She held back, feeling exiled. Then Linda awakened. She dressed the child and played with her for a little while, always with the sense that Tonio was sleeping close by. He slept all day.

In the next room, José's struggle was the dissonant timbre of the day. He could not eat anymore. His bodily functions were slowly ceasing. They sent for the doctor. He shook his head. "It won't be long now."

Celia's tired face revealed no emotion. When the doctor left, Trini tried to make Celia eat something, but she seemed to be drowning in José's dying pangs, scarcely aware of the food Trini put before her. She sat at the kitchen table, her head in her arms, wrapped in the waiting for death.

Trini took the children for a walk. When she returned, Celia was asleep at the table. Trini did not awaken her, for it was a sleep of exhaustion. Tonio still slept, his back turned to the wall.

In the late afternoon, Celia closed the bedroom door to be alone with José. Trini was at the kitchen table feeding the children when she turned to see Tonio standing by her, watching. She reached out to touch his tired face, but he drew back impatiently. God thought Trini, he can hurt me so. He spoke, his voice sounding cold, confused. "How long did I sleep?"

"All day." She was surprised at the tone of her own voice.

"Any cigarettes in the house?"

There were none, so she offered to go to the store for some. When she returned, she found Tonio sitting dejectedly at the table, eyes lost, hurt, the children engrossed in their own game around him. Trini felt his private desperation. But it was beyond her. He reached for the cigarettes without thanking her, his indifference an armor, protecting the vulnerabliity of his own dark passions. She left him alone, hurt to the core that he had not sought out Linda. Not a word. Not a question. He fumed and walked the floor, wrapped in a misery Trini dared not understand. Then he was gone.

The despair was hers again. It disfigured and erased her hope. Something in her pushed and pulled for release. She wished she did not want him so. In the next room, life eroded. It was Celia and José who mattered now. They were suspended in a death dance, wretched shadows wasting the day, life betraying each breath of the dying man as death approached at leisure.

Suddenly Tonio was back, but he looked past Trini at Celia, who had come out of the bedroom to rest, to splash water on her face, to talk of other things with Trini. Tonio was suddenly beside her, looking savage. "Where is she? You're her sister."

"Licha?" Celia's voice came from some confused haze.

"Yes, Licha, Licha, my God, Licha!" Tonio was crying before them unashamedly. "Where is she?"

Trini watched his body shake with the thoughts of a love that burned his soul. Anger, sorrow, pain, all charred her own heart. He was stomping on her, more and more. Celia, as if waking from another existence, stared. Then she let out an agonized cry. "My husband is dying! How dare you come in here demanding?" She slapped his face. Tonio stepped back, caught in his own misery, then was gone again.

Early the next afternoon, José, staring into space, died with Celia by his side. The wife sat quietly by him for a long time, every so often stroking the peaceful, unlined face of her dead husband. Interlacing strands of light from the window played on the thin, still form.

"It's over, Trini." Celia, too, had been released. There was no answer from Trini. No words would do. She sat next to Celia, holding her hand in silence. In the dying afternoon, she sensed dark origins, the beginning of a new unknown in herself. Evening came. A star, like dancing death melting into life, congealed into a brightness, finding its way to the dead face.

Celestina came in from the farm to attend the funeral, but Licha wasn't there. She had gone on a trip with the doctor who had attended Don Alejandro. Tonio was there, looking for Licha, his eyes desperate, full of pain. Trini turned away, feeling the pain of his search. Poor, poor Tonio.

In the weeks to follow, Trini came to an acceptance. Tonio was gone forever. Celia had heard that he had left Chihuahua. He had gone to the doctor's house looking for Licha. He had fought with the doctor, attacked him, accused him of taking Licha from him. The doctor had pressed charges, so Tonio had left town.

That evening in the dark, Trini decided what to do. The next day she wrote a letter to Isidoro.

* * *

Now, in this motionless time, in this feeling time, she was giving some direction to her life. There were moments, of course, after writing the letter to Isidoro, when she was apprehensive about her decision. How could she leave her little girl, even for a while? But Celia urged her to go, to leave Linda with her.

"You know you want to go. Why would you have written Isidoro?"

"I don't know what I do these days."

"That's exactly what I mean, Trini. Go. Find some peace. Come back with some kind of purpose. You'll be a better mother to Linda. I'll take care of her as if she were my own, you know that."

Of course, Celia was right. This utter hopelessness, the endless crying, her constant forgetfulness, all were not good for Linda. It was best to go, to run . . . She laughed, admitting to herself that her attempt at solutions was always to run, to move.

The next morning she was on a bus to La Junta. Along the road, cold damp mists followed a hard rain. At La Junta Isidoro was waiting. He asked no questions. He had horses already packed with provisions for the journey.

It had stated to snow by the time they descended into barranca country. There was a white crispness stretching from the lowlands to the hills. Is running a better part of myself? Trini questioned. No, something told her, a journey is never enough. To grow in stillness, the seed, the root upon the earth. That would someday be the better part.

On their first evening out, no breath of air stirred as they camped for the night in a grove of cottonwoods. They built a fire and stars filled the heaven while they cooked corn. Isidoro took out a bottle of aguardiente. "Drink–it'll keep you warm." He handed the bottle to Trini, who drank, in time feeling the glow of the liquid heat. She looked at the outline of dark mountains at a distance. She loved the clear silence of the mountains and open space. She had begun to lose the tenseness, the sense of hopelessness. This was very much her element.

"Warm?" Isidoro asked, watching her from across the fire.

"Oh, yes. . . ." She could say no more.

Isidoro nodded, smoking, looking up at the stars. He was not a talkative man. They slept close to the fire, and when morning came Trini found herself under a blanket of snow, the sun breaking through a haze of clouds. She helped Isidoro put the blankets and the lonas out to dry on huge rocks. An old memory brought a smile to the face. Tía Pancha scolding her for putting things out to dry on rocks like an Indian. But I *am* an Indian, above all things. She thought of her family, a sense of guilt rising. If she had run, why had it not been to her family? She honestly did not know. The sun had come out from behind a cloud, its light vibrating in the snow. She knew why; Sabochi was the answer. She had lost Tonio, but had she truly lost Sabochi?

The afternoon turned cold, a wind rising, swift and biting. Isidoro warned her that the direction of the wind was an omen of the coming blizzard. By nightfall the snow wind whined and whirled down on them as both riders and horses strained to go forward. Exhausted, her throat burning with cold, she watched Isidoro make camp between huge boulders that sheltered them from the wind. Rolled in blankets, lying next to a frozen brush with stiff icicles webbing its branches, Trini felt the beginning of fear. What if they froze to death? No, she trusted Isidoro. He would take her safely to Sabochi.

The wind held sway. She fell into a heavy, tired sleep, at intervals waking with the moan of the wind in a darkness without moon. She lay awake. She was alone again. She always seemed to be alone. But there was Linda—warm and full of love—why had she left her? She realized her face was uncovered when tears froze on her cheeks. She rubbed her face vigorously, then slid down into her body warmth.

The next morning they set out to cross the lower slope of the sierra before they started on the last hard climb. The one-day trek was possible if they reached it before the blizzard hit. Isidoro had another plan.

"I'll take you to the cabin if the blizzard hits hard, and I'll go on alone. It is safer that way. Sabochi will come to the cabin for you when it is safe."

The storm hit hard by midday. They ploughed through loose snow all morning, climbing against the wind. Trini's body ached as she trudged heavily toward the pass. The horses sidled along against the force of the blizzard, Isidoro leading them. At midday they stopped to rest while the thin-flanked horses grubbed beneath the snow for dried grass. She sat against the skeleton of a tree, Isidoro before her, squinting his eyes to look out into the distance. A line of sun cut the grey, bleak air.

"Isidoro . . ."

"Yes?"

"You're sure he'll come to me. Why should he?"

"Because you came . . ."

Trini told Isidoro about Tonio, Licha, Linda. She spoke of her need for her old friend. "Oh, Isidoro, tell him what I've told you. Tell him he's the only one who can make me believe again . . ."

"He will come to you."

They sighted the cabin late in the afternoon. Leading the horses, they scrambled up the slope to the door. It was one large room, empty exept for a stone brazier. They stamped the snow off their shoes, massaging their frostbitten hands to help circulation. From the door of the cabin, Isidoro pointed out the pass. "Over there, beyond that mountain, is the camp. See where the pass climbs?"

Trini saw where the sierra gradually came together until it became a narrow penciled path. Isidoro went out again to stake the horses, coming back with a muleta holding provisions. "I'll start a fire."

Isidoro brought in wood and built a stong fire in the brazier while Trini made some corn atole. They ate the hot porridge sitting next to the fire, then settled down for the night. The next morning, Isidoro left before daybreak, warning Trini not to leave the cabin. She would wait for Sabochi in a world buried in whiteness—without storm.

14

Moonstone

After Isidoro's figure had disappeared in the implacable whiteness of the pass, Trini went back to sleep close to the fire. She slept all day and all through the night and was startled into wakefulness by silence the second morning. The fire was out. She could tell by the numbness of her face. Her body was warm under the blankets, but as she turned toward the window, a snaking pain of cold warned her about the numbness. She pulled the blankets over her face and began to rub it warm. It felt like ice against her fingers. After a while she felt the blood rising, though the coldness remained. There was also the hollow feeling in her stomach. She could not tell what time it was because there was no sun, but she knew she had to get up to build a fire, to eat some food.

The sky outside the window melted into a snow mountain turned grey. She got up with the blankets still around her and made her way to the brazier. Isidoro had left a pile of logs and branches. Blowing on her hands to keep them warm, she took a log and placed it in the open pan, breaking branches and twigs for fast burning. She scratched a match against the stone and felt the pleasant shock of its small heat. The fire took hold and soon she felt its scattered warmth. She fixed her gaze on the fire without thought, with only a feeling of peace—the relaxed freedom of a rested body—and a grey-white anticipation, out of mind, touching only the edge of her senses.

After a while, she felt the need of air, her mind beginning to shape questions. Why Sabochi still? Sabochi—Chimac, Tonio—Licha. She pushed the thought away. I should be with Linda, she told herself in reprimand, but then to avoid thinking about things she went to the window, her gaze falling on the horse staked a few yards from the cabin. I have to go out and feed it, she told herself. I'm hungry too. She rummaged through the sack of food Isidoro had left and found a bag of corn. She boiled corn over the fire for herself. While her atole cooled, she watched the flames rise high and free. Thoughts were lost in dancing flames.

She felt the need of air again. The brazier was meant for coal, not wood, so the smoke and the mustiness of the room were overwhelming. There was no exhaust. She went to the door and opened it for cold, clean air, then stood looking out into the vast white silence.

Something began to run through her skin, a glimmer of an old happiness, the stirring of a wild wind. Transfixed, she imagined greenness under snow, a sapling bent with white, straightening out its limbs to flower before her very eyes, and a splinter of light grew, dispersing the greyness of the sky. She had never left the valley or the rainbow rocks. From a distance where trees tufted on a small hill, she imagined the small figure of El Enano, golden playfulness flecking his eye, a finger to his lips, beckoning her. Yes, yes, yes, her heart said, run, find the days now gone, find the old, honey-golden expectations. You're still there, Trini. You're still there, Trini. . . . Where? she asked herself, standing by the door. Her eyes imagined El Enano turning and turning in the snow, running free from tree to tree . . .

The neighing of the horse broke her reverie, a magic dissolved. The splinter of light was gone, the sapling again bent with snow, and the whiteness of the mountain melted into the grey of the sky. The day seemed to be gone already. She had no way of telling.

By the time she went out to feed the horse, it was already turning dark. She shook the snow from its blanket and looked up at the grey sky succumbing to the night. The icy wind wedged its way, flurrying the snow on the dunes beyond the cabin. She had left the cabin door open. By the time she returned, the snow had found its way inside, forming a thin film on the floor close to the entrance. She closed the door behind her and returned her shivering body to the now dead fire. She wrapped the blanket around her and dozed.

The warmth of the room dissipated and the growing cold awakened Trini. She shivered; feelings, swift and mutable, were storming her heart, overwhelming her with loneliness. She put more wood into the brazier, started a new fire, fanning the few embers back to life. She watched the fire grow and burn while thoughts, mothlike, fluttered through her senses. I reach out—there's nothing there. What's the matter with me? Is it my fault? Desolation danced in the yellow flames. What drives me on and on and on? A fierceness seemed to rise in her, mute, indecipherable. She folded inward, her mind grappling for answers, for reasons. None came to the surface. Her eyes welled, her heart stumbled. Tonio and Sabochi had outpaced her, hurtling into lives of their choice without her, without needing her, without wanting her. She was like her father's seeds, without warmth of sun and earth, not belonging, unfruitful. She became immersed in a longing that gradually faded like the fire. She slept then, to awaken in the cold dark. She was in the radius of the flame's full heat. Easily, she fell asleep.

The morning light! There was a sun today—another day gone. The fire was out. She felt the cold inside the blankets. She put more wood into the brazier. The wood pile was dwindling. She felt the need of cold, clean air. She had to gather wood. She rummaged through the sack, looking for an axe, a machete, anything. She found nothing. There were logs out in the snow, but nothing with which to split them. Brush and branches would have to do. She went out into the vastness of the white world. A good, clean feeling shaped itself inside her, all entwined with cold air, sun, the view of bone-like trees at a distance. She fed the horse and watched it eat the corn out of her hand. She had to change its lona which was covered in a soft snow whiteness. She found a dry rolled-up lona Isidoro had left behind in the cabin. After seeing to the horse, she ran out into the snow to scan horizons. Where could she gather wood?

There was a pasture to the south. Here, the shreds of ivory-limbed trees were formed like ancient dancing gods praying to heaven. The trees were clustered on the edge of the pasture where a hill rose. She knew what kind of trees they were, the strange, intricate shape of manzanilla trees she loved so well. Oh, the prayer of hills and stillness! A small black bird dipped and pivoted in the snow, its little beak pecking frantically for fallen seed. You and I, little bird, you and I, she thought, are the only two creatures in the universe. The thought swelled.

She ran the distance to the hills where the trees looked like suspended apparitions, silver-pink. They were bone-bare and mystically statuesque. The prayer of trees. And everywhere, in an earth covered with snow, Tonantzín was feeding roots with the green blood in her veins. Tonantzín, sleeping under snow, waiting. Trini laughed.

She set about her task, picking up fallen branches and pieces of driftwood protruding from the snow. When she had enough, she tied the pile to her back. She made her way slowly back to the cabin.

Every so often, she stopped to straighten her back, to balance the weight of the pile. The wind lurched in the wide pasture, creating revolutionary swirls of snow that could easily sweep her off her feet. Halfway across the pasture, she saw the figure of a man leading two horses toward the cabin. Sabochi! Oh, the familiar stride! She called out into the pearl whiteness of the world. "Sabochi!"

The name rang clean and clear, the vortex of the sun drawing it into the light. "Sabochi!" He stopped to wave and watched her making her way to him, half-falling, half-running, calling out her gladness. "Sabochi! Sabochi! Sabochi!"

They stood face to face. What you are, what you want, is all enclosed in the brightness of this day, her heart sang. With fumbling fingers, she undid the pile of wood on her back. By this time, he was by her side. The pile had fallen, almost silently, on the snow. Trini's face was without secret. She was now enclosed in his arms, feeling the warm music of her racing blood. She was a child again. He felt it too. What madness. He scooped up snow and flung it at her; she in turn ran after him, catching him. Then they clung and whirled in a cold, white, netted world—moments caught in moving feeling, stillness growing.

Sabochi staked the horses, unfastened the maletas, and carried the provisions into the cabin. Trini noticed that the fire was out again. She shivered in the coldness of the room as she stood by and watched Sabochi build the fire once more. Warmth flowed, and she went rummaging among the sacks he had brought with him. Surely he had brought something else to cook besides maíz.

"Sugar! Coffee!" Her voice rang out joyously. "We can stay here forever!"

It was a wish, loud and deliberate. Forever, forever, forever. She made some coffee, and as they sat close to the fire, drinking the aromatic warm liquid, she felt the dizziness of her joy, an arrogance that sang sweetly—forever-forever-forever. She spoke to Sabochi about Tonio in words that spilled over; other words then came—about the death of her baby, about the birth of Linda. Sabochi felt with her. It was written in the ember changes of his eyes. And when all was said, she told him in all honesty, "I had to come to you."

He reached into his jacket pocket and took out a kerchief, unfolding it, holding it out to Trini. "For you."

Inside was a smooth stone, translucent, the luster of pearl. He explained, "A moonstone."

She ran her fingers over the feldspar, its pearliness reflecting delicate, concentrated colors. She raised her eyes to his and saw in them the memory of an old gesture come alive again.

"For your bultito."

Why was he doing this? Why? It was her papá offering a silver happening to Maltida because he loved her. Sabochi loved her? Yes. It was in his face. Nothing pierced the silence as she held the stone in her hand, looking at it for a long time, raising her eyes to Sabochi's in shy confusion. She went to him and found her place under the curve of his arm. Her voice pleaded softly, "Let's stay here. Just you and me."

"Until the snow melts."

"I hope it never melts."

In silence, he reached out to stroke her hair. He talked about the camp in the Tararecua. How the tracking would be fine as soon as the snow melted. He talked about the stone. "It's a gift from a white man who went into Cajui country in the barranca to dig up an ancient cemetery, looking for gold."

He paused, reached out and opened Trini's hand gently to look at the moonstone again. "I warned him he would be killed. He laughed and showed me his rifle. He didn't understand that the rifle was no good. He's probably dead by now. This fever for gold, I do not understand. But he was my friend."

His fingers were now closing her fingers over the stone, a pensive wonder moving on his face. Trini reached out to bring him back to her. "It's funny, isn't it, the way we come together, then part?"

He laughed softly, his eyes half-closed. The warmth in the room was a silken drowsiness. Suddenly, Trini realized how exhausted he must be. She got up and came back with blankets and then ordered, as she stood over him, "Sleep. You're so tired."

He did not protest but lay down to sleep the long sleep of exhaustion, while Trini sat watching the face of the man she loved. Her eyes followed the curve of his body, now relaxed on the floor. She felt the green blood of Tonantzín racing in her veins. The cold, hard moonstone in her hand was warm now, a little fire, like the one rising in her. All there needed to be in the world was this man breathing calmly by her side. She was to have him until the snow melted. Until the snow melted. A tear trickled down her cheek.The heaviness of the thought bent with Sabochi's steady breathing. Why? He belonged to Chimac. How could he forget that? But at this moment she felt like the wild wind, and he was the red hill. Wasn't that everything?

The fire was smoldering. There was need of air in the room. She opened the door, using a piece of rolled-up burlap for a doorstop. The cold briskness of the air filled the room. Then the harshness of the cold put out the dwindling fire. She closed the door and set about building another one. She opened the door again slightly to let the current of air feed the flame for a minute or so, then closed the door again. Afterwards, she sat next to Sabochi and watched the flame dance, struggling for its own red life, pushing, tugging, growing, like the flame inside her.

The sun was fading when Sabochi awakened. He opened his eyes. She still watched him, arms and chin on bended knee. He closed his eyes again and rolled over on his stomach, having lost the tension of fatigue. She moved closer to where he lay, reaching out to touch the hardness of his back. He did not speak, for he had fallen asleep again. The fire was no more than embers now. From the window, Trini saw a half moon rise, suspended in the dark. Without the darkness, she thought, the moon would not be moon. She took out the kerchief and untied it, then watched the light of the moon fall on the moonstone. She sat quietly looking from stone to half moon to the quiet figure sleeping by her side.

The fire had gone out one more time. The room needed air. She did not know how late it was but felt it was very late. She opened the door slightly, just enough to clear the air; the current was penetrating and cold. It awakened Sabochi, now well rested. He remembered the horses that had to be fed. While he tended the horses, she cooked some atole. They ate it in silence by the light of the half moon. Sabochi took a bottle of aguardiente from the maleta. Trini drank some of the fiery liquid, soon feeling a comfortable glow. Sabochi started the fire again. Amidst a new silence, she remembered the moon in the light of the stone. "Look—the moonstone—it could have come from the moon."

"Yes, a soft white fire . . ." His voice was gentle, like an echo of the old Sabochi in his cave, carving wooden animals. Half ashamed of old childish dreams, she attempted to erase them. "It's crystal, isn't it?"

"Yes."

She watched him put out the petates for the night. She remembered the night in San Domingo when she had insisted that he lie next to her. She would lie next to him this night. She would reach out for him. He should be a little afraid of me, she told herself.

I could keep him for always. Could I? Can I bind anyone to me, to what I am?

He lay down. There were no words, but the silence was heavy, potent; she knew that he shared her wakefulness. Was he waiting? She had wanted him as a man for a long time now. She lay under blankets, taking off her clothes, her nipples rising to fullness. Then wrapped in a single blanket, she went to where he lay in darkness. She could see the glint of the moon in his waiting eyes. She lay down beside him, finding his warmth under the covers, taking his head in her hands, the bareness of her body breathing against his. The wild wind had found the fire of the red hills. His lips were running the length of her body, vibrant, ecstatic.

Green blood glistened, throbbed, ran through arteries, cutting the moon, shifting the light, until the earth exploded, gaping wide for green waters, green blood, soft, soft. The earth was all inside her. All was body, beyond body, for body. He stroked her hair, belonging to her by the strength of her passion. But even now, in his amber, golden eyes, she saw and felt the growing of a new storm in him. The dream had been undone.

* * *

"The snow is melting." Trini did not take Sabochi's words too seriously. She was wrapped in the confident joy of the many weeks they had been snow-bound, lovebound. Why should she keep track of days? Sabochi loved her. Her passion had wrapped him around her like a fire. Then there were the times of sweet quiet when they searched the bone branches of the manzanilla trees for buds. They threw the handfuls of buds into boiling water and watched the flavor come to life. Unborn buds giving off life's flavor.

"The snow is melting." He repeated the words as if they were a struggle in him. She still did not listen, she didn't want to. She wanted only to feel. Her days were like the moonstone, pearl white, full of lights, smooth, lost days, new days, suspended days. At night, feeling the warmth of his body, the gentleness of his hands, she knew. He was lost in the earth of her. A gliding moon changed its face many times outside the window where he lay asleep beside her. Old moon, new moon, dark moon, half moon, how many times? It was never enough.

His eyes loved her with confusion now. He would shrink away

from her at times when her passion claimed him, as if he understood there could be no escape. But as she watched him touch the earth, moist and brown underneath the disappearing snow, she saw old hungers in his eyes. She had seen it before when she was a little girl, when the urge to roam grew strong in him. She understood the hunger, the hunger to return to what he was, to what he would always be, the ahau of Cusihuiriachi. His men needed him. His wife and sons needed him. The snow was melting. She saw him warring with his own feelings, saying nothing; when he spoke there was a thickness in his voice. She knew it was up to her to let him go. A part of her said, keep him—he's your life—he loves you in so many ways. No, she could not destroy him. She remembered Tía Pancha's words, "I let him go back to his wife and children because I loved him." She wanted to keep him near her, to forget the world.

Deep inside she knew she could not be cruel. She must send him back. The thought scattered all her sense; it was a furious plunging into nothingness again. These were sullen days, drizzling days, grey, cold, for both of them suddenly became aware of the bareness of the cabin. Their isolation was not life. They only had each other—why wasn't that enough?

One morning she noticed a lone spring flower shivering in the chilled air. Thistle plants swaying in a snow wind seemed to cry out, let him go, let him go. She could not stand it. She covered her ears frantically. She clung to him in desperation, their passion burning like a mournful song.

In the days to follow she saw delicate spears of green piercing upward from the snow, fringes of color spread between craggy ledges where she and Sabochi walked together hand in hand. Now, in his arms at night, she listened to the chanting of warm winds rounding the hollow of the mountain. The snow melting, a time melting, a moon demanding . . .

With a heart splintered, hesitant, one day she dared to say, "Go home, Sabochi."

"Yes." His answer came simply, full of love. Then he was swaddled in silence. She realized that impatience was growing in her. She thought of the little desert village that was Cusihuiriachi. No, she would never be happy there. She longed for a hot bath, the sound of radio music, the lights of the city. If she convinced herself of that she could anesthetize the pain. I have to be much more myself, more than just a woman in love. She was a mother who had stayed away too long. She longed for Linda so! She was part of the white man's world. Yes, she was—she was sure of it. There was the dream of land somewhere and Papá's seeds. So many things. But still she cried, lost in her misery. Sabochi reached out to comfort her. "I'll stay here with you. I can't make you unhappy."

She almost laughed her tears away. "No—neither of us would be happy. Go, go, go."

She could feel the gratefulness on his lips as he pressed them against her hair. "Grow in stillness."

"I love you, Sabochi. I always will."

"I too—love you."

This was their bond now, unbroken, whole; she would let it be. It was the best time, the right time to part. This way, she thought, we shall always be what we are to each other at this moment. Oh, the pain of it! Will I ever see him again? Will I ever hold him again? If I can only believe that there will never be an end to us. If . . .

15

Juárez

One part of Trini was staring at a yellow beetle making its way across the screen of the kitchen door. The other part of her was feeling a turbulence, muddled questions without answers, muddled feelings caught undefined in her breathing, in the nervous play of her hands. Her eyes, expanded, liquid, stared at and past the beetle clinging unperturbed to the screen. It was the beginning of a long twilight, one like a bursting dawn, sudden, consuming, reminding her sadly of the cabin and Sabochi, both far away. There was no stirring of wind in the dying afternoon where the sun still slivered the coming dusk. She wanted to cry, to scream, to find her way back to Sabochi again, to claim him no matter what the circumstance.

Her eyes narrowed as she bit her lip, her hands tidying her hair. She hated the place. Celia, the children, and she had come to Morentín to help Celestina with spring planting. Three women, plowing and planting in the harsh sun. The work in the fields started at dawn and ended at dusk. Still, the land gave little, for Morentín was a poor, barren little community dotted with small plots of vegetable farms, each claiming a small adobe shack and a well. Water was always low and never enough. It was an ungiving land. The heavy, exhausting work would make her fall on her bed, blessing sleep. Linda was, once more, by her side. That was Trini's only comfort. Trini reproached herself: your child should be more than just a consolation. But the emptiness was still there, and Linda felt warm and human in her arms. The child in her arms made the tiredness fly out of her body at the end of a day, when the emptiness began. With Linda, there was peace. Now, there was a yellow beetle clinging and her thoughts were with Sabochi. She was carrying his child. She felt the blood surge in happiness. When the feeling subsided, when the mind played with solutions and answers again, the thought of Tonio pervaded. He had been sending letters. They had reached Trini in Morentín, and this was the cause of her restlessness, her dissatisfaction.

Tonio had broken into the fullness of feeling for Sabochi and the child that would be born. Again, her mind went over Tonio's pleas. Oh, yes, he was begging. Trini had thrown the first letter to the floor with anger, hating him. But the feelings of resentment and hurt did not last. He had intruded, bringing with him a motley of feelings. She remembered his demands for passion. Oh, yes, they had been demands. His pleasures were always satisfied. A part of Trini accused, so what? His pleasures were your pleasures. The appetite for love had been the same. I am like Tonio in many ways, she told herself. But she did not want to forgive him. She was afraid to forgive him.

She was alone. So alone! She was somehow encapsuled in a fierce pride. It's all up to me, my life, without Sabochi, without Tonio. Just Linda and me. But I must do something—something more than accept these burning, empty, desert days—something. The letters jumped into her mind again. I want to see my little girl, Tonio had said. I want you as my wife—we'll get married like you wanted. Juárez has opportunities. Somehow, that stuck in her mind. Juárez has opportunities. Her eyes were back on the beetle again. She remembered seeing similiar yellow beetles swarming on a fallen hornet's nest that leaned against a tree stump by the side of the road. The beetle's stillness in the warmth of a ray of sunlight was not her stillness. She was looking beyond now. Celestina was coming up the road waving a letter. Another one! She flushed with anger but at the same time felt a curious excitement. How could she decipher all these feelings?

She sighed. Why not admit it? I've been waiting for the letters. I do care that he wants me. Perhaps he's changed. He says he has. I know better! Again the struggle, and then the thought—the world will have to be without Sabochi from now on. Instinctively, she touched her stomach, still smooth and flat. Thoughts began to explode softly, gently, as she remembered Sabochi in the cabin. Their passion had been so different from her passion with Tonio. It had been a giving without asking, a soft fire building to great heights, but with it was that love that had nothing to do with body. She wanted both—the body love and the spirit love. Sabochi understood the earth of her. To Tonio it was all the pleasure of the body. I won't go to him, I won't go, she promised herself, even as Celestina came in through the screen door and handed her the letter. "Another one."

The old woman's eyes were inquisitive, curious. "What do you want, Trini? He wants you. How many of us end up without a man?"

"There's more to life than a man!" objected Trini vehemently. Was there? Soon there would be two children. The words "husband" and "home" were security, safety. But these words were part of a dream, perhaps a silly dream. She had heard a sad seriousness in the old woman's voice. "Go, don't be a fool, go to him."

That evening Trini sat in the darkness by the kitchen door. All the chores were done, but the tiredness of her body did not still her thoughts. The heaviness of the heat became her impatience, but there was a moon, cool in the darkness. Oh, how it made her yearn. Her thoughts revisited the blue cottage, the wide bed, the mirror on the wall, the long nights of love with Tonio. It was all there, the grin, the sound of his singing voice. Sabochi was gone forever; she must build on something with someone. No, no, Tonio must not be a mere refuge. She hated herself for falling into the old pattern. Her thoughts were back to Tonio, the beginning of desire faint in her nostrils as she again smelled his uniform while she brushed it. Her hands reached out to feel again the two-day growth of beard over his cheeks, his sensuous mouth. Wanting Tonio—was that love?

By lantern light, before going to bed, she opened the letter. A money order fell out. She picked it up and read the letter, folding it carefully afterwards, placing it and the money order back in the envelope. One sentence from the letter was imprinted in her mind: I will meet you at the bus station on Saturday. She knew she was going. She knew she had to tell him about Sabochi's baby. Could she? Perhaps that was enough reason for going to Juárez—to give some kind of ending or beginning to their relationship. And there was Linda—Tonio was her father.

* * *

"¡Puta!"

Tonio hit Trini with the back of his hand. She fell back on the bed where Linda sat crying. The blow stung her cheek, but Trini did not cry. She said nothing. She had said everything that had to be said about Sabochi and the baby. Tonio's face was woven in anger and hurt. How could he understand? Trini reached for Linda to comfort her, knowing that the child was the one in the greatest need of comfort. But as she held the child, she began to cry convulsively. The little girl stopped crying and hugged her mother in an attempt to console her.

"You love Sabochi!" His accusation was bitter. Trini did not answer, knowing he was right. Tonio waited for her to answer, waited with hurt surging in his eyes. There was no answer. Trini knew what he would do. He would run away. He did exactly that, slamming the door behind him. He's gone, maybe for good, Trini said to herself, half in panic, half in regret. What am I going to do alone in a strange city? She must be calm. She mustn't alarm the child. Linda was breathing jerky little sobs, cradled in her mother's breast. "Chiquita, calla, it's alright."

But Trini didn't believe her own words. She picked Linda up and wiped the child's tears away. She made light of things by setting Linda on her lap, rocking to and fro. The room was dark and somber. Through a shuttered window, sounds seeped in. He'll come back. He has to come back, she assured herself. The two of them were enveloped in a dark waiting. What if he didn't come back? Fear flickered. Linda's little head drooped on her mother's shoulder, her eyes heavy. It was Linda who mattered, Trini reminded herself. The poor child was exhausted after the long bus ride. She was already fast asleep. Trini quietly unfolded the warm little body on the bed and lay down beside her. Her thoughts ran back to the morning when they had arrived in Juárez. It seemed such a long time ago! No—only that morning; Tonio waiting at the station . . .

From the moment she stepped off the bus with Linda, Tonio had placed an arm possessively around her as if nothing hurtful or painful had passed between them, as if time had stood still since that first year in the blue cottage. How like Tonio! But time had passed, and pain, and loss. She searched his face for some sign of it, but saw none. It was the old Tonio, laughing, confident, handsome, full of plans.

He took them to eat at a place where they served flautas, Tonio serving the wine as mariachis sang Juan Charrasquiado—"Not a flower left . . ." Big, impressive Tonio sat across the table making big impressive plans. She remembered how she had believed so long ago, like the child from Batopilas! It was Tonio's way. A man came over and pressed a bill in Tonio's hand, then whispered something in his ear. Tonio laughed and placed the money in his pocket. He moved his chair close to her side. "Monday we get married by el civil."

He looked at Linda dotingly. "She sure looks like me." Yes, Linda did look like him, Trini agreed silently, her eyes on the man who had given Tonio the money. "Did you hear me? Monday we get married."

She had hungered for those words so long ago! Somehow the words were not enough. What's the matter with me? She must tell him about Sabochi and the cabin. She pushed the thought away and asked him about the man. "Who was that?"

His eyes followed the man who had put the money in his hand. Tonio laughed. "My coyote. Owed me a bet. Has a contract for mojados with some outfit in California. I'm waiting my turn."

Trini held her breath. "You're going to California?"

Tonio laughed away her fear. "Not now, querida." He looked at her with liquid-warm eyes. "We get married. We live as a family, that's what I want most. Oh, I've missed you."

She felt anger rise to her throat. Didn't he miss Licha? Wasn't she the one that mattered in his life? No—she mustn't think that. The letters begging, hungering, were for her, for Linda. Licha was gone forever from his life—who else could there be? Blood rose to her cheeks as she remembered the passion they had shared. It was more than that. There was more to his wanting . . . She wanted to reach out and touch his hand, but she dared not . . . Perhaps what she had had with Sabochi . . . She erased the thought from her mind guiltily, then looked up to see Tonio drinking his wine. He impulsively joined in the singing of Juan Charrasquiado as he reached out to put his arm around a passing waitress, who laughed and hit him on the chest, pushing him away. Trini felt an old uneasiness. The next moment, he was lifting her chin, looking into her eyes, promising, "I've waited a long time, my wife."

My wife! The words stretched in light. My wife! The words bathed her in warmth. Somehow, the world seemed right again. Now, he was filling her glass. She drank the wine eagerly, wanting to feel it in her veins, wanting to believe that the warmth would last, wanting all her fears to dissipate.

"Let's go home." Again soft, secret words from his lips.

"Home." She repeated the word with wonder.

"Nothing fancy."

"Let's go home." Her words vibrated with anticipation.

It had been a mile and a half walk to the presidio in the arroyo where Tonio lived. As they walked along the heat-blasted streets, she told herself, I'm happy, I'm happy, content, hopeful. She would have a husband, someone to love her, claim her. A thought suddenly pressed her. She had to tell him about Sabochi's baby.

The red haze of the sun swallowed the earth walls of the presidios along the street. The street was similar to those in the arrabales of San Domingo, all makeshift, like her life. In corrales, rusty, broken salvage leaned against adobe walls—broken sinks, tires, an old carcass of a car, all useless, abandoned. They were following the natural curve of the arroyo, like the verge of a stream. Women talked outside doorways, and children yelled shrilly as they ran barefoot in the dust. Trini's eye caught the figure of a small, thin boy wetting himself, the wetness forming a circle in the dirt as he laughed. What do I do? she asked herself. Do I have the courage to tell him about the baby?

She was following Tonio across a street toward a block-long presidio with a black tarpaper roof. The smell of onions and peppers saturated the air. A pretty young girl sat on top of a car fender while a boy ran his hands secretly down her arm and rested on her thigh. Two old men walked in front of them, deep in conversation, words spilling from cracked, excited voices. Trini felt very much at home.

"That's it. Number twenty-seven." Tonio was leading the way. The rooms were cool and dark as if the sun had been suddenly stolen. Home was two rooms separated by a dull, faded yellow curtain; behind it was a bed and a chest of drawers. The rest of the apartment was the kitchen, shuttered and closed. Trini opened the back door, which led into a patio where she saw a woman hanging out wash while an anciana threw out dirty water from a basin. Two more women talked by the side of an outhouse. Tonio stood beside her. He kissed the back of her shoulder lightly, then turned her gently around. Yes, it was happiness that swam inside her, brilliant and full. All the old feelings were caught in the late afternoon. He whispered into her hair. "Sorry?" Linda was reaching for her hand, her eyes sleepy and tired. "I'm thirsty, Mamá."

Tonio picked up the child, smoothing the hair pasted to her little face by perspiration. She cuddled up against him, repeating, "I'm thirsty."

He set Linda down on a kitchen chair and made his way to the kitchen door. "Faucet's outside."

They waited for him sitting at the kitchen table, Trini stroking

Linda's hair. Then both parents watched the child fondly as she drank the water.

"Trini . . ." his voice was earnest.

"Yes?"

"We'll be happy."

Trini was silent, but there was the thing she must do. Tell him, about the baby. How would she begin? Anxiety tore at her throat. Linda was leaning her little head on the table, looking at them through drowsy eyes. Trini picked up the child and put her on the bed, taking off her dress, tying up her hair to cool her off. Trini sat by the bed, fanning the tiny face, eyes heavy with sleep. Tonio sat beside them, watching, the afternoon heavy in the room. Linda fell asleep, little beads of perspiration resting on her hairline. Trini's heart commanded—Now, now, now—but all she could do was turn her face away to look at her sleeping child. He sensed the tension. "What's wrong?"

The words had to come out. "I shouldn't have come."

"You did . . ."

"I know." The words choked her. Then the rush, freeing her. "I'm going to have Sabochi's baby."

It was done. She turned to look at Tonio, meeting his eyes, head lifted, then rose quickly to cross the room as if to find reasons at a distance from him. "After you left, I went to him, Tonio. He's always been there when I've needed someone—all my life." She stopped and repeated the words faintly, slowly, "All my life."

Tonio screamed the words across the room. "He wasn't there! You went to him!"

"I went to him." God! It was true. She looked up at Tonio. He seemed to have shrunk, slumping down on the bed, hands covering his face. I'm hurting him so, but he must understand. "I went to him after you left town—I had no one—you made it clear there was no one but Licha for you. We stayed in a cabin until the snow melted . . ." Why go on? It was enough—it was enough.

"You've always loved him, Trini." It was a statement of sadness, more than an accusation. But he was right. His next words were like the twist of a painful knife. "Sabochi is the only man you've ever loved."

"That's not true!" Trini was sobbing now.

"Do you still love him?"

"Yes."

He called her, "whore . . ."

Now, in the darkness, as she lay alone with her child, she still felt the blow he had struck. She felt the knifing accusation. Puta! puta! puta! It rang in the darkness, but it rang untrue. How long had she lain there fully awake, remembering? Every nerve in her body, every sense was waiting for him to come back. How short-lived the happiness she had felt that afternoon. What if he didn't come back? She was in a strange city with only a few pesos in her purse. The thought of returning to Morentín—no! What then, San Domingo? No. Maybe she could find work in Juárez. For how long? She was carrying Sabochi's child. I mustn't be afraid. That's the thing. I can't be afraid. She huddled on the bed, lying next to her sleeping little girl, waiting in the dark.

She drew Linda to her, holding her, stroking the hair of innocence and earth. Through the shutters, the light of the moon fingered thinly into the room. She went to the window and opened the shutters, letting the moonlight spill into the room. Such a beautiful spring night! Shadowy people sat in doorways. They knew nothing of her loneliness. She could hear muffled sounds caught in strains of music and laughter, shouts and whistles. She went back to Linda and held her close. The child stirred in her arms, then opened her eyes, whispering in the dark, "I'm hungry."

Was there any food? Trini went to a cupboard and found a can of peaches, a loaf of bread. She found a can opener in a drawer, then she opened the can and poured the fruit into a small dish, taking it to the child, watching her eat by moonlight. There was a lantern on the table, but she did not feel like looking for matches, and the dark was comforting. Between mouthfuls, the child asked, "Where's Papá?"

Contagions. Trini answered softly, "I don't know."

"Is he coming soon?"

Oh, Tonio, please, please, for her sake. She needs you so, she pleaded in silence. And then, as if in answer to her plea, the door opened and through the master shadows of the evening Tonio entered.

"¡Papá!"

Linda ran to him, arms outstretched. He picked her up, kissing her hard on the forehead. Then he put her down and sat next to Trini on the bed in the darkness. She felt a rush of love for him; she wanted to speak of it, but words did not come. She sat perfectly quiet, at times drawing her breath in sharply.

She heard his words, soft, thoughtful. "I wish it hadn't happened, but there are many things I wish hadn't happened."

"I love you." Her voice sounded helpless, defenseless. His head came to her breast as she stroked his face gently, the full moon singing their forgiveness. Linda crawled between them, exuding a happiness that warmed them. They sat listening to sounds outside the window for some time, and when the child slept, forgiveness was the passion they had shared together so long ago in a blue cottage.

* * *

"Twenty-four hundred pesos!"

Trini looked at the bank book in her hand. The words Banco Nacional de Méjico were engraved on the cover. The account was in her name. She looked at Tonio, questioning, as he explained, "It's just a little bit, but it's for land, the land you want."

"For land?"

"The piece of land you've always planned for."

"Oh, Tonio!"

"Save it—I'll send more."

They were sitting on a bench at the processing station at the international bridge. Behind Trini, a window framed a huge warehouse full of glistening painted machinery on the El Paso side. Tonio was leaving for Salinas, California, with fifty other braceros to work in the fields, to make American money. Monshi and Elia sat beside them. It had been Monshi and Elia, who lived in number thirty-one in the same presidio, who had always talked about the riches in the United States. Monshi, like Tonio, had been waiting for el coyote to find work for him. Elia urged Trini to cross to El Paso to work as a mojada while she waited for Tonio to come back. Now Monshi and Tonio were leaving. Elia had already found a job for Trini in El Paso as soon as they could get her across without papers.

"Hey, there's el coyote!" Monshi whistled and waved to catch the attention of the dark, burly man. He was herding workers into a bus, keeping count in a notebook. Trini watched the long line of braceros wearing sweat-stained hats. The coyote waved back disinterestedly, then returned to his business. Monshi asked Elia, "How many before us?"

"Two . . ." Her voice was the beginning of tears.

"Hey, woman, don't cry."

A little sacrifice for a future, that was the way Elia had explained it to Trini. Trini clutched Tonio's hand, the grip tightening when she thought of him going. Linda was sitting on Tonio's lap. California was a foreign land, an inaccessible part of the world to Trini. She cautioned, "Please take care."

"I'll come back—just a year, that's all. I hate to leave you with the baby coming."

"I'll be alright."

"Sure."

"Yes." She remembered how Linda had been born without Tonio around. He didn't remember. "A year, that's all . . ."

She loved him so. She would save money—enough to buy land, their land. El coyote was approaching, shouting, "All you green-carders, load number four. Get in line!"

Tonio picked up Linda, hugging her close. He put an arm around Trini. "I'll write."

"Yes, yes, yes," she whispered, kissing him over and over again.

Then they were gone. The women of the departing men waited until the buses filed down the street, circling over the streetcar tracks, making their way across the immigration bridge to the United States side. Then the buses disappeared. Trini's life was hazed once more, a blur in the future. It was time for her to journey again, to search, to find, to plan. An old guilt rose. She had to leave Linda once more to work in El Paso. When you're poor, she thought, all is given up, even your children. I mustn't be bitter. Someday . . .

"Now we find La Chaparra," Elia exclaimed in a practical voice.

"What?"

"To get you across the river." Elia was looking closely at Trini. "You sad about leaving Linda with me?"

"I would like to care for her myself. You're so kind to offer to take her."

"It's the thing to do—leave our children for the daily bread God does not put into our mouths."

"Don't."

"Listen, she'll be alright."

Trini suddenly felt tired, as if she had journeyed for centuries, her destiny still unshaped. An ache arose . . . Oh how she wanted to see Tía Pancha's face, to hear Buti and Lupita's laughter, to feel her father's arms around her. Now, she would leave Linda again. She looked down at her child's face, trusting, curious. The child would make do in her child's world. Trini's hand tightened around Linda's as she followed Elia along Juárez Avenue. Suddenly, she stopped determinedly and promised herself, "The money is for land, just for land."

* * *

La Chaparra, a small-framed, fiery-eyed woman of indeterminate age, told the group to follow her up the sandhill behind her house in El Arroyo Colorado, a poor barrio close to the river. Trini's shoes dug into the blistered red sand as she followed the others up the hill. She was one of eight people who were going to cross to El Paso, all mojados, without legal papers. There were three girls about her age, two Indians, and a man named El Topo who seemed to be well experienced in border crossings.

The Indians made it to the top of the hill before the others. El Topo warned the group when the Indians were out of earshot, "Cajui. Never go into white man's land unless they're running away. Probably slit somebody's throat."

Trini, apprehensive, noticed that El Topo's speculation was taken calmly by the other climbers. She glanced at the Cajui half-fearfully but couldn't help noticing how harmless and innocent they appeared to be. La Chaparra was at the top now, her brown skin shining against the old orange blouse snugly belted at her waist with a man's belt. She wore an old leather skirt that had seen better days, round dangling earrings, incongruous army boots, and a wide sombrero. Her face, washed clean and honest, turned slightly to watch the last stragglers catch up. La Chaparra sat down on the red sand made redder by the sun; everyone followed her lead.

Sitting on the edge of the mount, Trini caught a view of the river cutting the land thinly, vegetation spreading into the fields of tall yellow grass now amber in the sun. Beyond that were the shapes of buildings and miles of telephone poles. La Chaparra pointed at an old bridge, a converging point of river and railroad tracks. "El Puente Negro."

El Topo, sitting next to her, nodded. "Easy to cross. One guard. Not like old times," La Chaparra added.

"When there were many, it wasn't hard. We used decoys. They would wade across, the guards would chase them. Then the boys would circle back to the Juárez side." He chuckled, "Ha, pobres pendejos, couldn't keep up with us! Thirty, forty people running every which way, and those dumb guards going around in circles."

"Ever get caught?" Trini asked.

"Sure. Many times. They put me in the old cow sheds behind the Coliseum, then threw me back to dear old Juárez."

"Easy now," La Chaparra assured them. "Hundreds cross in a week's time."

"Like locusts coming from the north," El Topo agreed, mopping his face.

Trini looked across at shafts of sunlight forking down on the turn of the shallow river. La Chaparra took out a pack of cigarettes and threw them to El Topo. He passed the pack around. They were friends, those two, Trini observed. Tonio with a green card in his pocket! The land of plenty! "Tonio, my husband," she volunteered, "is working in California. He has a green card."

"You think that makes him special?" asked El Topo with a cynical laugh. "We're all the same. They call us taco, spic, greaser, mojado; we're nothing to them. You know where your husband is? In a choza with dirt floors, no water, no electricity. When I worked in the San Fernando Valley, there was a ditch carrying shit outside my window. Ah, sweet life! I picked melons, straddling rows, pulling vines together, from sunup to sundown. They think we're mules."

"It's money," defended Trini. She had no great desire to cross to El Paso to live among strangers—to clean other peoples' houses—but the money was needed.

"Money! It goes back into the gringo's pocket. The rent you pay for a stinking choza and lousy food takes most of it. The rest you spend for women, liquor."

"Stop whining, Topo," chided La Chaparra. "You cross all the time."

Trini's hopes began to ebb away as La Chaparra, using the long, untrimmed nail of her forefinger, mapped out on the sand the way to her waystation.

With steady eyes and steady deliberateness, she explained, "See that road? The one that leads to the tracks? We run it, all the way to the open fields east, after we cross El Puente Negro."

"Shit." El Topo flipped the stub of his cigarette. The river, under the old bridge that spanned it, lay in shallow water most of the time, heavy brush growing on all sides. A new bridge had been built to replace the old one; it was about two miles west, where illegal crossings were more difficult. There was only one guard on the abandoned old bridge, and people were frequently warned by the border patrol that the guards on the high tower still watched the old bridge.

Easy to spot mojados from there. But, with weary-worn experience in border crossings, they knew it was a bluff. They knew there was only one man up in the tower, with only one pair of eyes and many distractions. The sun would hit the high tower, which meant the guard would sometimes sleep. La Chaparra explained, "The guard eats, we cross one by one, ten minutes apart, you understand?"

The Cajui nodded their heads in agreement, not because they understood, but because everybody else did so. La Chaparra continued, "We wait till dark. I go last. There's no moon tonight. After we cross, we run like hell, heads down. Remember, low in the brush. We go north."

"Roll in the mud—squat—squat . . ." grumbled El Topo. "The gringo says that's what we do best, squat."

"We get across, eh?" La Chaparra answered with a mirthless laugh, then cautioned, "You girls leave everything behind except the clothes on your back."

They all stood silent now, looking out toward the bridge, until La Chaparra turned and found her way down the hill. Inside the house, the girls put on everything they owned, piling one dress over another while La Chaparra explained about the meetings at San Jacinto Plaza. "You two! You're going to work as barmaids?" She looked at the two pretty girls named Olga and Sarita. "Wait for Julio. He wears a red vest. Don't talk to anyone. Some of the girls sitting around that look like us—they're stoolies. They work for la migra. They turn their own kind in for a lousy ten American dollars."

"Muchachitas, watch out!" warned El Topo with a grin. "Julio with the pink hands is a pimp."

"Why barmaids?" La Chaparra teased.

"Listen, old lady, we're not going to do the dirty work for any gringos. We'll make more money our way."

"Not serving drinks!" laughed La Chaparra, then turned to Trini and the other girl. "Right out of the farm—good girls, eh? You have a gringa waiting for you at the park tomorrow?"

"Yes, I have—I have a name here and a phone number." Trini's voice was hesitant, afraid.

El Topo grimaced. "All kinds of alligators in the dirty pond, Julio, gringas . . ."

La Chaparra hit him on the side of the face with the back of her hand. El Topo fell back in a mock fall, chortling and pretending to be in pain. The Cajui huddled together looking confused. El Topo looked up at La Chaparra, grinning and rubbing his cheek. They're more than friends, thought Trini.

That moonless night, eight bultos trekked along the edge of El Arroyo Colorado, furrowed with gullies. Trini followed the short, stout figure of La Chaparra along a rocky, sinuous path that climbed steadily up to the llano leading to the old bridge. The Cajui seemed very much at home in the dark as they led the way with La Chaparra, never slackening their pace. They were in the open llano now, remote and silent. About half a mile north was the bridge. Behind them, to the south, the lights and sounds along Juárez Avenue blasted the darkness. In a cold half-run, Trini looked up to see tiny stars blinking in the heavens. Eight shadows ran and vanished behind brush to reappear again, to halt and listen, then run again toward the river's bank.

The bridge loomed before them. Trini slid down a wide shallow depression where the ground was soft and wet. El Topo had been right about the mud. They were now at the Juárez bank of the river. They waded across, staying close to the walls of the bridge. El Topo caught up with the Cajui who led the way, the girls following; La Chaparra stayed behind as a lookout. As she made her way across, Trini stopped, peering into the dark to listen. The guard was just overhead. A sluggish fear clung like the muddy waters swirling around her ankles, a cold open void. She shivered in the darkness, gulping, listening to the intake of her own breath. The others were already across, damp shadows waiting. She ran across and huddled among them, body chilled, clothes caked with mud. Foul brown water flowed over her feet and ankles as she and the others silently watched La Chaparra edge her way across, a burlap sack draped over her shoulder. She approached, a finger to her lips, motioning for them to follow her as she made her way through tall cattails and brush spreading on the edge of the muddy water. Suddenly, a flickering cigarette sailing down from the bridge broke the darkness. The guard! La Chaparra fell flat to the ground, gesturing quickly for them to do the same.

Trini went down flat into soft, wet mud smelling of manure; she felt the sharp cut of thicket branches on the side of her neck as she lay breathless, waiting, hair wet against her face. The guard turned away from the bridge and La Chaparra, half-crouching, motioned for them to follow her. They stumbled along through a field, then turned eastward, breaking away from the river. With the bridge behind them, La Chaparra broke into a run, then stopped before a barrow pit. She jumped in, barrel-like, rolling down. Everyone followed. Chaparra's panting was close to Trini's ear as she slid down, heels digging the soft earth. At the bottom she brushed her hand against the side of her neck to feel the warm, sticky blood from the cut on her neck. A floating misery choked her. She wanted to cry, but couldn't. Instead, she stretched out her pregnant body to delude the ache that overwhelmed her. The baby! Was the baby alright? She sat up, head down, and wrapped her arms around her stomach as if to protect it. She felt it stir.

"Safe." La Chaparra's voice rasped with fatigue.

For a while, eight bultos lay scattered along the pit. No one said anything. Then La Chaparra was up again, scrambling out of the pit. Everyone followed, running across a drainage ditch toward a rotten old water control gate away from the river. They came to a canal running east and west in the middle of emptiness. La Chaparra pointed to the outline of a shack past the control gate. They crossed a narrow wooden bridge that spanned the canal, then headed for the shack. When they reached it, La Chaparra opened the creaking front door, which was loose at the hinges.

Trini found herself in a huge, empty, musty room that smelled of skunk. She watched La Chaparra put down her burlap sack and fumble in it for candles and matches. El Topo fell heavily on the floor, whispering hoarsely, "Everything hurts . . ." He let out a long, soft howl of relief, then looked up at La Chaparra as she lighted the candles. "Woman of my life, do you have some liniment on you? Or better, whiskey?"

La Chaparra ignored him, putting the small velorio candles on a broken stool against the wall, the only piece of furniture around.

Everyone was exhausted. Here they would wait until the first morning light mingled with the dark. La Chaparra would wake them up when it was time to meet El Gordo, who would come for them in a car, then on to San Jacinto Plaza where they would disperse, each to his own fate.

La Chaparra lit the candles as each of them found a place to sleep.

Trini lay down on the floor among candle shadows, her hands pillowing her head. Tomorrow she would be in a strange world. . . . Sleep came.

* * *

She worked hard for her patrona in El Paso, speaking in gestures, grimaces, smiles, for la gringa knew no Spanish and Trini knew no English. She always felt uncomfortable under la gringa's scrutiny. Days of toothpaste smells and furniture polish; Trini caught la gringa watching her through the corner of her eye as she mopped floors and ironed clothes. She enjoyed working when she was alone, watching extravagant soapsuds thrashing away in the washing machine. Hot water, cold water, the measure of days. Pale and puzzled, she adapted awkwardly to the automatic order of her new world. She was very much alone, sleeping in a small bare room where her mind would spill over with hunger for the brazen colors of her own world. The smell of cooking beans, the slap of tortillas. She thought of Linda too often. She wanted the closeness of her child. Gringas were lucky to have so much money, what sacrifices did they make? At night, she imagined how la gringa and el gringo made love. Did he go to her bed, or did she go to his? Did they make love at all?

There were oddities—the plate, the cup, the spoon set aside for her use, la gringa's assumption that mojadas were dense. She knew that her patrona did not mean to be unkind, but it made her angry. Many times she was slow and clumsy because la gringa's eyes told her that she was.

The gringa's children followed her around, asking for the Spanish names of things as she fed and bathed them. Playing in the yard with the children one day, Trini found a robin building a nest. They watched together. Still, she remained outside the family's life. The gringo watched her too, his indifferent eyes narrowing when he looked at her growing body. The woman frowned, shaking her head.

One day la gringa told her, with hands gesturing a message about her pregnancy, that she could stay no longer. La gringa made some soothing sounds, then paid her for her work. The day she left, the children hugged her and la patrona gave her two grocery bags full of old clothes, then drove her to the Santa Fe bridge. At the bridge, la patrona told her with little pushes and strange sounds that it was easy to cross into Mexico. Simple, she just had to walk across. La gringa was right.

16

Perla

"It's full of old prostitutes," Elia was saying as she stripped the skin off a cooked chicken, warning Trini about the old mansion on the outskirts of El Arroyo Colorado. It was Trini's last night in Elia's apartment, where she had been staying after the job in El Paso. But Elia's family from Torreón was coming to stay. Elia insisted that she not go away, but Trini knew she had to make it on her own. Trini found an apartment in a neighborhood called El Terreno de Brujas, the witches' lair. It lived up to its name, consisting of two blocks of crumbling ancient buildings, half of them empty, desolate, with gaping windows and doorways. The old abandoned houses had been stripped long ago. A mile or so away from the city dump was the old mansion that housed the retired prostitutes. The debris of the world, stripped and quiet, continuing, decaying, forgotten. It was the cheapest thing she could find for Linda and herself. Tonio sent her thirty American dollars which she promptly put into the bank for land. Elia shook her head as she took a knife and cut off the chicken legs, still warning, "Juárez is a sin city, then you go to that place—it's like a ghost town except for them."

"It's like any other place. And besides, it's all I can afford."

"Do you know that Juárez is the ninth biggest sin city in the world?"

"Everybody sins. That's just a word, anyway," laughed Trini.

"Ha!" Elia sniffed righteously.

"They're like you and me, Elia, just human beings."

"Human, eh? You haven't heard about Perla."

"Perla?" Trini was curious.

Elia concentrated for a few minutes on cutting the chicken into small pieces, building up to her next pronouncement. "A witch, that's what she is, a consort of the Devil."

"That sounds impressive." Trini stopped peeling potatoes for the caldillo and gave Elia all her attention. Elia's eyes grew mysterious as they strayed from the chicken to Trini. "Some time ago she willed the death of the brujas who used to live in that house. Died like flies. Of course the Devil helped her kill them."

"Silly talk!" said Trini as she raked potato peelings into the trash.

* * *

Trini moved into the witches' lair, still wondering about Perla. The only person she had met was the rent collector, who looked at her suspiciously and warned her in one breath that the rent was to be paid in advance, and she had better have it on time. Her apartment consisted of one room, dark and airless, with the apparatus of a kitchen and one lumpy bed. The room opened onto an alley littered with garbage and broken bottles where a huge leaking conduit found its way to a nearby ditch. Among the debris lived hurrying old figures who came out into the sunlight, scurrying about with bucket and broom, tossing dirty water into the constant charcos in the corral—a daily ritual without words. Soon the doors were slammed shut, leaving the corral and the alley in weary silence. This newly found desolation seemed dismal and dreary to Trini. When she happened to come face to face with one of the women, they passed her by, never speaking. It was a living burial ground, this dilapidated building with its rotting beams and sagging doors. The city dump, half a mile east, filled the air with its heavy, putrid smells that choked Trini when she first arrived. After a while, the smells were forgotten, but the constant taste of decay remained in her mouth.

A hundred years before, the building had been an elegant mansion. After the revolution, it had been converted into a second-rate hotel; now it was a faceless tenement, ineffectually choking in its own rot. The only remaining sign of past glory was a patio on the side of the building. This area was enclosed by crumbling walls covered with ivy in profusion, where light and shadow played an intricate game. Trini had seen it in passing, but had never walked beyond its gate. Still, she had a feeling about it, as if it were something outside the sadness of the world.

Inside her bleak, dark room, where she tried to follow a sensible pattern of life with Linda, fears began to grow. Her money was dwindling. Tonio had not written. Soon there would not be enough food, much less money for rent. She had to find work of some sort, anything. But she was getting so big. Who would hire her? She refused to think of the savings for land in the bank as a way out. She would never touch the money. There must be another way.

One day, tired of the darkness of her room and the frenzy of her worry, Trini took Linda for a walk, making her way to the patio. She removed the latch of the old rusty gate and stepped into a strip of garden lost in time, a place suspended in golden autumn light. It was full of the song of the cicada. In the center of the patio was an immense elm, its dwindling leaves dipping in a soft wind. Next to it was a stone pond, small, circular, its brown, stagnant water full of floating leaves flushed in fall colors, flower petals lost in the clamor of the leaves. By the side of the tenement wall, an extended roof provided shade. All her fears were temporarily forgotten. What a beautiful place! Like Batopilas! A place to dream . . . Trini sat breathing in the golden light, letting it carry her like a sea while Linda played on the old mosaics. Why, why had she not come before? It was like one of those ancient hills in Batopilas where sounds melted into light. It was like a soothing secret never told. Here she could escape from her worries, the dreariness of her existence. After that, the patio became a daily habit in the afternoons.

One afternoon, while Linda piled dead leaves into mounds, Trini was startled by the sight of a little man wedging himself between two hedges. A madness overtook her for a moment. El Enano! The little man stood inside the patio now. Yes, of course, it was him, Trini assured herself. The place suddenly had the germ of magic and imaginings had substance. Why not? The little man was coming toward her. She felt time slipping away. The old tune of an old game came to her lips, "Naranja dulce, limón partido . . ."

The sound of her voice was hesitant, words tumbling out somewhat nervously. Linda looked up laughing, and the little man stopped in his tracks. His head tilted, a friendly, quizzical smile on his face; then, he made his way again toward the shade under the extended roof. There had been no recognition. Trini felt the drain of disappointment as she watched him examine the shaded area, ferreting about with familiar little soldier strides. She realized that he was different in many ways. This little man wore clothes and had hair, and she saw no gold earring on his ear. The smile was the same. The language of the eyes was the same. But then, he would have recognized her, remembered her, if he were a part of the old magic.

Trini caught herself. What's the matter with me? Magic? She laughed, the sound bouncing in the afternoon sun. The little man turned and joined in the laughter. Linda laughed in unison. The little man scratched his head and tilted it again, then turned away, making his way quickly to the hedges from whence he had come. He was gone.

"Mamá, who's that?" Linda asked excitedly.

"Someone I used to play with . . ." Trini hesitated, then continued in a practical voice, "I don't know. He looks like someone I knew once."

Tears came, falling into her palm, amber drops glinting light. Where was the world of wild winds? Of secret caves? Where was the something free and binding in the universe? Where?

"Don't cry, Mamá." Linda was by her side, burying her head in Trini's lap. Trini quickly wiped the tears away and stroked the little head. They sat quietly for some time on the edge of the stone pool, the cicadas blending in with the hush. Trini began to tell Linda about her childhood. "Buti and my sister Lupita were very young. There was a little man . . ."

The tale was interrupted by the little man, who returned through the gate, this time carrying a chair. And, following him, was the most astonishing woman Trini had ever seen. She was tall and seemed to float in a yellow fringed kimono; her skin was the color of ivory, like the Aztec women of Guadalajara that Trini had seen in magazines. Her bones were outlined monuments of a noble race, and she wore one long, heavy braid down her back. The little man ran before her until he came to the shaded area, where he placed the slatted chair; the woman sat, opening a fan with a quick twist of the wrist, the grace of music. It opened like a butterfly. Her arm extended, she held it in midair as she stared into space. The little man stood by her until she finally turned and looked at Trini and Linda with calm, cool, dark eyes, looking beyond. She whispered something in the little man's ear, and he scampered through the patio and out the gate, then disappeared. The woman beckoned to Trini with a rapid, graceful bending of a long forefinger. Trini, taking Linda by the hand, approached. The woman sat regally on the slatted chair with lifted chin and an unmoved countenance. She introduced herself.

"I am Perla, who are you?"

"Trini—this is my little girl, Linda."

"Oh, yes—you moved in some weeks ago."

"Yes." Trini could not help but stare.

So this was Perla! Trini had expected to see an old woman who had seen better days, more frightening than beautiful. This was the witch who willed people to death? I was right, Trini thought, it isn't true. She felt the woman's steady eyes on her. "Manuk is bringing chairs."

Sure enough, the little man was coming back with two chairs. He set them down in the shade, and with a sweep of his arm he invited Trini and Linda to sit down. Then he sat down on the ground next to Perla, crosslegged in the manner of El Enano.

Trini could not help asking, "Does he speak?"

"No," Perla answered. "He cannot speak, not with words. He's from Talpa. I am from Sayu, near God's ocean. He comes to make me happy when I wish for him."

Wish for him! It was magic.

Long ago El Enano had appeared to make her happy, too. How marvelously strange! But the ocean, the great one, was the farthest thing from Batopilas. She felt twelve again, then reproached herself quickly. I'm a woman of twenty-one. I'm not a child. He's not El Enano.

Still, Trini asked, "Did you give him that name?"

"No. He has had the name for a thousand years. He told me so. Look, he speaks with his hands!"

Manuk was weaving patterns in the air, touching arm, flicking fingers, turning palms, touching breast, eyes, and ears. How wonderful, thought Trini, for a thousand years! She felt a sudden regret. Perhaps El Enano had spoken the same way, and she had never known. Linda was engrossed in imitating his gestures. Perla interpreted. "He's glad to see you in this world, that we all have come together like the colors of stone."

Colors of stone! The rainbow rocks? Trini was caught in the magic again. It was all too much the same. She looked at Manuk with feverish intent, holding out her hand. "Do you remember Bachotigori? The fig tree? Did I play with you long ago?"

She finished breathlessly, eager for his answer. Manuk laughed and rocked himself back and forth, then wove an answer which Perla deciphered. "He says, we are all one."

Trini questioned, confused, "We are all one?"

Perla tapped Manuk playfully on the head with her fan, reprimanding, "Always riddles!" Then she turned to Trini, her eyes a deep scrutiny. "Something troubles you. You are tense."

What better time and place or person to ask for help? She met Perla's gaze and told her simply, "I have no money. I need work to pay rent, to buy food."

Perla's eyes warmed with sympathy, then she nodded, looking away for a while. She turned back to Trini and inquired, "Have you been to the park to watch the birds?"

Trini shook her head, somewhat disappointed. But Perla insisted in a calm, clear voice. "You must go. El Parque Borunda. The birds are marvelous."

How strange, thought Trini. Why did she ask about my problems? Manuk was winking an eye, approving of Perla's suggestion. Trini wanted to ask more, to hear more, but Perla was now absorbed in tracing time with one finger, touching the creases and blue vein channels of one hand, at times lifting her hand spread wide against the sun. Perla spoke again with a light, airy voice that rang finality. "You will come to the patio again, won't you?"

Perla was dismissing her. Trini nodded, at a loss, feeling adrift. But Perla's tone was clear. Trini took Linda's hand and walked back to her apartment.

* * *

Angelita, wearing a white apron, came with the first offering. It was a most appropriate name for the chirping, rosy little woman who stood before her, apologizing for not coming before. She handed Trini a bag of bakery bread. "From where I work. Would you like to go to Mass on Sunday?"

The surprised Trini thanked her for the bread and yes, she would like to go to Mass very much. After Angelita came others, each one with an offering of food. Trini knew that Perla had spoken about her plight, and that was the reason why they came. There was blind Margarita, tapping the ground with a white cane. She sold gardenias along La Mariscal, the same street she had worked for so many years while in "the life." Sara came next, wearing a neat white blouse and horn-rimmed glasses, looking very much like a bookkeeper. As a matter of fact, she had learned the art of good business in bed. Now she was a fence for stolen goods. Finally the twins, Lina and Lidia, smiling behind rolls of fat, offered her cigarettes and a bottle of gin. They played the lottery, choosing numbers only when they were very drunk; that was the way they picked.

On Sunday, Angelita came for Trini promptly at six in the morning. Linda, not quite yet awake, held on to Trini's hand as they walked the three blocks to the streetcar. It was a long ride to El Sagrado Corazón on the other side of town. Waiting for the bus, Trini confided in Angelita. "The landlord—he came and said I didn't have to pay the rent. You know why?"

"It's Perla's doing." Angelita was sure, nodding her head in approval. "She owns the building."

"Perla?" There was astonishment in Trini's voice.

The streetcar was clanging its way toward them. Once they had boarded and found a seat on el tranvía, Angelita began to peel an orange for Linda as the streetcar jumped and jerked its spasmodic stops and goes. Trini's thoughts were still on Perla. "Is she a witch, Angelita?"

"Yes—an angel too."

"Someone told me Perla willed people to death."

"It happened . . ."

The streetcar was now half-filled with early Sunday riders, old women with rebozos, also on their way to Mass. There was an old man asleep in the back, snoring loudly. Angelita gave him an indignant stare, then went back to dividing the orange in sections. She took one piece and held it high over Linda's face, ordering, "Open!"

Linda was halfway through her orange when Angelita began.

"The house was full of spiritualists once. They had quite a business going, cheating people, telling lies. Then Perla came. She, too, talked to people, but she did not tell fortunes or talk about the dead. She just spoke softly and sometimes said things that didn't make sense until much later. Her advice was free, so in time the spiritualists were out of business."

"They were witches?"

"The spiritualists? No, spiritualists are jokes—witches are real."

"I don't believe in witches," Trini informed Angelita.

"Why not?"

Trini couldn't say but she remembered how Perla had advised her to go see the birds. It hadn't made much sense at the time. She laughed softly as she watched swift images of life and place cast away by the speeding streetcar. Angelita was wiping Linda's hands. There was anger in her eyes as she continued. "Those jokes dragged Perla out in the middle of the night and beat her half to death, leaving her unconscious by the arroyo, the one with the whirlpool full of blood water."

Perla—dragged, beaten—poor Perla! Trini imagined her lying in the arroyo, her long braid in the red water. She cried, "I hope they suffered for it!"

"They did!" Angelita nodded. "Some say the Devil went to Perla's aid. That he made her sacrifice live chickens to him in the whirlpool."

"There were witnesses?" Trini was skeptical.

"Some people claim they saw her do it." Angelita's voice sounded impartial. "After that, the ones who hurt Perla died, one by one. Nobody knows why. Perla disappeared. The whole neighborhood blamed her. One day she came back. She had bought the building."

Trini could not visualize Perla making bargains with the Devil. There was a thoughtful silence until the streetcar jerked to a stop in front of El Sagrado Corazón. As they climbed the cathedral steps, Trini turned to Angelita and asked, "Was Manuk around when all this happened?"

"Manuk? Who's Manuk?"

"El Enano who visits her."

"I've never seen him."

Trini decided to say no more, but remembered Perla's advice. "Angelita, after Mass, let's go watch the birds in the park."

"If you want."

They went through the wide doors into the cathedral.

* * *

Trini waited for Don Fermín, proprietor of La Corona grocery store, to finish with a customer. He was weighing rice, pouring it into a bag on top of an old metal scale. He squinted one eye, the other one keenly concentrating on the still unsettled marker. He slowly rolled a toothpick from one side of his mouth to the other. Trini was bursting with her plan, clasping her hands nervously as she stared out the store window at an empty street. She had discovered the sense of Perla's words. She had gone to the park to watch the birds, and the plan had been born.

Angelita had bought three pieces of cream taffy from a candy vendor as they watched the birds trilling and chirping in the trees. Angelita was finishing her taffy when she exclaimed, "Not as good as the one I used to make. My first profession, making candy." She smoothed her skirt almost prudishly. Sometimes Trini could hardly believe she had been in the life. Trini turned to watch the vendor make his way to the corner of the park, children gathering around his cart as he shouted, "¡Dulce de crema! ¡Melcochas!"

The birds in the tree by the vendor's cart floated off from grass to tree again, then sailed off into an orange sky. Trini sat watching as the plan began to form. She asked Angelita excitedly, "Is it hard, making candy?"

"Hard work," she sighed. "That was a long time ago."

Angelita looked like the sweetest, most virtuous of grandmothers, soft-spoken, religious. Not once in their relationship had the old woman mentioned how she had fallen from grace, and Trini had no intention of asking. The thought of candy-making was foremost in her mind. "Angelita, will you teach me?"

"Teach you?"

"To make candy. Don't you see? It's a way to earn money. I'm too big now for anything else. Please, Angelita!"

Angelita was thoughtful for a moment. She watched the candy vendor, then her eyes came back to Trini. She had decided. "Why not?"

Trini was all plans now. "I'll sell it to the tienditas in the neighborhood—I'll get credit from Don Fermín . . ." Her voice trailed off as her decision firmed.

* * *

Trini heard Don Fermín clear his throat, a deep sonorous growl, as the bell on the door tinkled its goodbye to the other customer. Trini shook away her memory of the park, ready to confront Don Fermín with her plan. "Don Fermín . . ." She hesitated, watching him roll the toothpick from one side of his mouth to the other. He stood waiting, watching her with the one good, unsquinting eye, the other almost closed in impatience. The plan was still bright in her mind. She burst forth, "I need credit, Don Fermín. I'm going to start a business, and you will be my customer."

He stared at her somewhat incredulously, his one keen eye reflecting suspicion. Trini continued, "I know I owe you money. But how can I pay you if I don't earn some? If I make candy and sell it to you and other tienditas, then you'll get the money I owe you. But you must let me have more credit."

There! It was said, and it sounded like a fair plan to her. She watched Don Fermín as he went back behind the counter, scratching his head. He leaned over the counter with both eyes squinting this time and asked, repeating her words slowly and deliberately, "You want more credit, though you haven't paid your bill, then I'm to buy this candy from you?"

"Yes." She stood her ground, her eyes bright with the plan, her words steady, sure. Don Fermín stared at Trini's very pregnant body, the light in his keen eye, now opened wide, reflecting some puzzled admiration. Before she lost ground, she told him what she needed. "Sugar, piloncillo, two pounds of pecans, lard, milk, raisins . . ."

Don Fermín turned away from the counter, shaking his head, mumbling under his breath, "Crazy spunk . . ."

But he got all the ingredients, writing down the prices on her bill with the stub of a pencil. He put everything into a bag, then watched her leave, an elbow on the counter, the one keen eye following her, the toothpick moving slowly, pensively, from one side of his mouth to the other. She turned and smiled her gratitude. "I'll bring the candy in a few days."

Three days—and what days! When Trini got home from Don Fermín's, she and Linda divided the ingredients three ways on the small, wobbly table. Trini had decided to repeat the process three times, for that way it would be easier to knead the sugar dough. The next afternoon she cooked the first batch in a huge black pot borrowed from Angelita, who gave her meticulous instructions on how to make the candy. She stirred constantly to keep it from burning; its sweetness bubbled and, as the concoction thickened, the stirring got harder. At times the syrup spilled over the pot onto the small kerosene stove, filling the room with the smell of burnt piloncillo. Once it thickened sufficiently, she set it aside to cool. That was only the beginning, and she was already hot and exhausted.

Linda watched her mother silently, doing little things to help, cracking nuts, washing spoons. Trini looked out the window and noticed that the day was gone. She fed Linda some supper, the spice smell heavy in the dim room. She put Linda to bed, then by candlelight returned to the sugar dough. It was still warm, and soft and grainy. She took a large wooden spoon, began to stir and stir, round and round and round, at times beating little sections that peaked. The dough got harder and harder to beat. A rolling sharp pain invaded her back. Her arm muscles, taut and tired, kept up the pace as she put all her weight into the stirring, her hand attempting an arduous circle in the now unpliable dough. Suddenly, the spoon broke.

And with it, her efforts. She slumped down on the bed where Linda was asleep and cried. She scolded herself for thinking all things were possible. Kneading that sugar dough was an impossibility. The small kitchen table was too crowded, her body ached, the spoon was broken. She cried like a child, sniffling once in a while, wiping away tears with the hand that still held a piece of the broken spoon. Rest now, her body told her, rest now. She cried tears of defeat. She looked up to see a slant of moonlight on the wall. She stared at it numbly for a while, head bowed, mind gasping . . . there was a slant of moonlight on the wall! Her mind glimmered with a new plan. A new excitement caught at her throat. She no longer felt her fatigue. The wall, the wall! She could throw the sugar dough against the wall as she had seen Matilda throw corn masa against a metate in Batopilas. What better way to knead?

She began to hum snatches of Tonio's love song. Everything was possible again. The plan began to grow: she would scrub the wall clean, place a sheet on the floor to catch the dough—but she didn't own a sheet—she would borrow one, even if it was late—it didn't matter—she would knock on Angelita's door—she would have the first batch of candy done before morning.

By late morning of the next day the gleaming sugar dough had been rolled out and cut, ready for Linda to sprinkle nut pieces on top. Trini had finished scrubbing the kitchen wall in the middle of the night, placed the borrowed sheet on the floor and watched the masa of glistening sugar slither down the slant of moonlight onto the sheet until it became smooth and elastic. Then, she had fallen on the bed exhausted and slept.

* * *

The next Sunday after Mass, Trini took Linda to the patio. She had caught a glimpse of Perla walking toward the hedges when she was saying goodbye to Angelita. She wanted to talk to Perla again. The woman was sitting on her slatted chair as Trini hurried toward her, stopping, drawing in a deep breath. Perhaps she should not intrude, for Perla seemed consumed in a sun-stillness, arms relaxed against the sides of the chair, head back, eyes closed. Trini sat down next to Perla on a stump half-covered by overgrown ivy. She put a finger to her lips to let Linda know that she must keep still. A faint rumble of thunder far away touched the late morning.

"Do you know what a flower king is, Trini?"

Trini was startled by the unusual question. She kept silent. Perla laughed soundlessly, placing finger to finger, palm to palm, her voice running soft as if it were part of the sun. "There is an old temple in Sayu, Trini, where I was born. I used to climb it as a child, as the flower king had climbed it thousands of years before."

Trini had only seen temples in magazines, but her mind tried to grasp the reality of one. A pyramid pointing to the sky. She still said nothing. Perla began to raise her hands as if in prayer, open, supplicating, her eyes closed. Trini looked up at a sun hazed by its own brightness. She did not want to intrude. But then she felt Perla's eyes on her. Warm words came from her lips. "It's good to feel life, Trini."

Yes, it is good, thought Trini, warm blood surging as she placed her hand upon her stomach. Sabochi's child. The thought was like the thought of a long green river leading to the sea. Again, Perla startled her. "The women of my family were high priestesses of the temple in the time of the flower king."

"What is a flower king?" Trini asked.

Linda was listening intently to Perla's words too, her head on her mother's knee. Perla's words came as if from far away. "In the mists when the jaguar drank in peace with soft paws, the king would climb bearing a flower, five-leaved. This was the king before greed and power and lust . . ."

Perla was engulfed now in a new stillness. There was another roll of thunder. Perla was chanting softly, some strange musical Indian words, hardly audible. She stopped suddenly. "The flower king would climb the temple each spring to pray simply for life—life—and more life."

Life—life—and more life. How beautiful. Not a prayer for power or goodness or forgiveness. Not a prayer of fear or lostness. Just an asking for life. Trini felt caught in the magic of Perla's memories. But how had Perla become a whore? A high priestess from an Indian village unspoiled by white men? She could not visualize Perla in the arms of any man. The purity of the woman's grace belied the fact. She asked, "How did you end up in Juárez?"

"End up?" Perla's lips became a hard line, her eyes suddenly full of a wild pain. "You mean as a whore?"

Oh, God, why did I ask! thought Trini. But she did want to know, to understand the pieces of the heart belonging to this Indian from Sayu. She heard Perla's voice, now a hard coldness. "My own choice."

"I can't imagine . . ." Trini's voice faltered.

"Then you know little about life."

"Yes, I know little about anything."

"How beautifully humble you are, Trini. That could well save you."

"Save me?"

"Yes," Perla laughed. "Of course, you may never need saving." Her eyes were tracing the past. "I didn't want to stay in my village. A girl of thirteen dreams of excitement. I wanted to go to the white beaches of Talpa; I ran away. Cafés, music, men. It doesn't take long for an ignorant Indian girl to fall into the trap. But you must understand, I was selective because I could be. I was the most desired, the most beautiful, and I learned the craft of making love well. There were many satisfactions."

There was a clap of thunder. Thoughts of the flower king had been forgotten. Perla's eyes were questioning. "Can you understand, Trini?"

"Yes."

"Guilts melt sweetly in the mind, Trini. The important thing is not to live in dead space."

Trini remained silent, watching Perla's face lost in her own map of things. After a while, Perla turned to Trini and stated with finality, "Enough of the past."

"Yes," laughed Trini. "I went to see the birds." They were of one mind for an instant, then Perla asked, in a matter-of-fact voice, "You have customers for your candy?"

"Five, in all directions. That's my problem now. How to get around."

"Ah, what would we do in a problemless world?"

It will take time to think that out, thought Trini. Maybe Perla meant nothing more than the words she said. Maybe the idea of making candy would have come to her at home as it had in the park. One thing was sure. Perla was a marvelous mystery, like Manuk. She asked, "Where's Manuk?"

"Who knows!" Perla laughed lightly. "In Tapla, in a cave under the sea—or back in the circus."

"Circus?" Trini was puzzled.

"The circus of life, Trini."

Oh, the things of the world were mysterious. There was no more to say.

Her casual remark to Perla about her difficulty in getting around to customers brought Sara, the fence, to her door with a bicycle. "Perla says you need transportation. This has been lying around for months. Use it."

Trini used the bicycle for three weeks, packing her candy in boxes, securing them to the front of the bicycle in a basket, another basket secured to the back. The five tienditas where she delivered her candy were within a radius of three miles. She rode the bicycle down the streets, people gaping at her bigness, but she did not care. Still, the bicycle rides were tiring and long.

One afternoon, coming home with empty baskets and coins jingling in her pocket, she felt the beginning of nausea as she wheeled around a corner. She stopped to catch her breath as she felt a thick, heavy oozing streaming down her legs. She looked down to see a pool of blood at her feet. God! She waited for a few minutes until the nausea passed, then made her way slowly and shakily to the tenement, leaving a trail of blood. She could not stop. She did not know a soul. She found enough strength to get to her door. When Linda opened it, Trini fell into an unconscious heap.

It was Angelita who put a stop to the candy making. She made Trini stay in bed for a whole week. The baby was due any day now. There were to be no more thoughts about earning a living.

The Sunday after her recovery they went to Mass. When Angelita stopped to talk to some of her friends after the service, Trini and Linda stood by, listening. A woman who worked in El Paso was complaining about entry into the United States. "I waited two years for a legal passport."

"Haven't you heard?" someone else asked. "The American president Truman says parents of a natural born citizen can fix papers."

The same woman said to Trini in jest, "If your baby were born there, you could live in the land of plenty."

It had been said in jest, but Trini thought about it all the way home. When they got off the streetcar, she was already planning again. The land of plenty. Yes, the gringos had so much. To buy good land in Mexico was almost impossible unless you were rich. If there was so much money in the United States, surely there was land, good land. She stopped dead in her tracks. "There's good green land in the United States, isn't there, Angelita?"

"I suppose there's everything in the United States." She was watching Trini's face. "You're at it again. I can tell by the look on your face, ay!"

"Why not, Angelita? My baby born an American citizen. I will work, buy land, and when Tonio comes back, he will be so proud of me."

Angelita shook her head disapprovingly. "You and your crazy ideas—off you go!"

Maybe, maybe, thought Trini. But things had to be done. There was nothing worse than standing still. There was fervor in her decision. "I'm going. I'll cross the river if the Virgin tells me to."

The following Sunday, Trini remained after the service in the empty church. Yellow slivers of candle flame seemed to float in front of the altar, and the Virgin Mary glowed in yellow light. Trini rose from her seat and walked slowly down the aisle past dozens of pews toward the veladoras, flickering tongues dazzling, that reached up to the light the Virgin's face. Oh, Sweet Virgin, give me a sign, give me a sign. She was before the Virgin now. The Virgin's eyes were alive with compassion. Trini fell on her knees and prayed.

That night she dreamt of the Virgin, who wore the face of Perla. A light whirled before her. Was it the sun? Suddenly, from this same mercurial light, flowers rained, melting into a whisper, "Find my church on the other side."

Trini woke with a start. It was still night; Linda was fast asleep by her side. Trini sat up in bed and stared into the darkness until the first light faintly touched the ceiling. I must ask Perla what to do, she decided.

* * *

She knocked on Perla's door several times during the day, but the shades were drawn and no one answered. Late in the afternoon she tried one more time. A harsh, rasping voice called out, "Come in."

Trini went into the room, dark and stale, where she found Perla, not the visionary, absorbing light, but a woman lying on a couch in a drunken stupor. Trini drew back to make sure. It was Perla, her hair a webbed sea on a soiled satin pillow, eyes full of pain, face contorted. The next moment Trini felt the soft touch of Perla's fingers on her arm. Trini struggled with a painful confusion. Is this the high priestess? Her heart ached for Perla.

Perla lay listless and inert, staring the whole time at the ceiling; only the fingers on Trini's arm were alive. Trini covered them with her own hand, concern in her voice. "Can I do anything?"

Perla's mouth opened, shaping a soundless moan caught in her throat. Words were uprooted in pain, one by one, from some dark abyss, eyes at bay. "Every–thing–has–been–done–and–undone."

The swollen, painful words filled Trini with terror. There is no magic here, she thought. It was the dead space of which Perla had spoken. She wanted to run away, and she wanted to stay. She wanted to understand. This was not the little girl that had climbed the temple at Sayu to ask for life–life–and more life. Yet, even in her lostness, Perla exuded an energy; although stupified, broken, a fire coursed through her spirit.

"It's Trini, Perla."

"Wha–What?" Perla's voice was thick, heavy. The Indian woman sat up slowly on the sofa, jerking her head back, mouth opened, stretching the neck muscles taut, a breast exposed when her gown gaped open. She sat as if paralyzed. Trini sat down beside her, taking her hand. "Perla, look at me."

Perla turned to Trini, unseeing, then her head fell forward, as if she had no control of it, to stare at the floor. Trini pleaded, "Please, Perla."

This time the woman of good and evil fame looked at Trini with painful amber fire, a high priestess straining, trying, "The flower–king . . ."

"Prayed for life." Trini was sobbing quietly.

"Life–and–more–life," moaned Perla. "Why can't I die?"

"Wish for Manuk, Perla." She was trying to help. "Wish for Manuk. He will make you happy again."

Perla turned to Trini, eyes brooding, dazed, voice mocking, "Manuk? He's gone forever, I think, to the cave under the sea–" She stopped, cutting the air with a disenchanted gesture, then her head fell on Trini's arm. She still spoke muffled words, "Pull, pull, through the dark hole . . ."

Then she let her body fall back on the sofa. She was back in her abyss again, reality burnt out, anguish bursting. "I can't hear you, Trini. There's a roar inside me. My gods are crying."

Perla's eyes glistened wildly, hands raised again, haggard, splintering the air with fear and fury, dropping to hold her body, shriveling, another moan escaping, choked, rutted. The convulsion eased slowly, until she lay in a stretched stillness. She was the child again, eyes peering into the dusk, a whisper spilling helplessly as she covered her ears. "Don't you hear the crying? Oh, how they sob, my gods, my father, my mother . . ."

Trini held her, lips pressed against the suffering woman's forehead, the taste of body heavy on her mouth. Then there was peace, and in the coming dark, as Trini sat by her quietly, Perla found her old voice, strong, impervious. "Thank you for being here."

But Perla was soon lost again, this time in a calm of her own finding. She belonged to herself, and Trini could not help anymore. She kissed Perla lightly on the head and made her way to the door.

The next day Trini returned to the cathedral. Perla had not been able to help. She knelt before the Virgin whose eyes were Perla's sweet pain. Trini cried softly in the empty church. In the stillness, velvety soft words shaped themselves in her mind. "Find my church on the other side."

17

The Pilgrim

Trini walked with stumbling feet behind La Chaparra. They had followed a network of alleys through El Barrio de la Bola overlooking the western bank of the Río Grande. The adobe choza on top of the sandhill gaped empty, roofless, without windows or door. A gaunt cat sitting on a pile of adobe stared at them with the frugal blank eyes of starvation. It was unusual to see a cat in this barrio. They were usually eaten by the starving people who lived in the makeshift cardboard and tin huts scattered along the hill. La Chaparra, her back against the wall, slid down to the ground, out of breath. The barrio ended on top of a hill that overlooked the smelter across the river on the United States side. Trini, tired, brooding, followed the path that led to the river with her eyes, shading them against the harsh sun. La Chaparra had brought her to the easiest crossing. The boundary between Juárez and Smeltertown in El Paso was no more than a series of charcos extending about fifty feet.

"You sure you want to do it?" La Chaparra's voice was skeptical. She muttered under her breath, "You're crazy, no money, having a baby in a strange land—you're crazy."

Trini turned to reassure the seasoned wetback, though her body was feeling the strain of the climb. "Everything will be fine, now that I know the way, thanks to you." She would wait for the pains of birth, then her pilgrimage would begin to the Virgin across the river. Somewhere in El Paso was a church, el Sagrado Corazón. She would be led. Things had been taken care of haphazardly. Tonio had sent her forty American dollars which she promptly gave to Elia for Linda's keep. This time, Linda, she promised, this time will be the last time I shall leave you behind. I will find land, and there we'll stay. The dream stifled her guilt. For her, destiny was an intuitive pull, a plan with a dream, sometimes without practical considerations. But practical considerations were luxuries in life. She could not afford to think of the dangers ahead, the suffering. She must just go. Pull, pull through a dark hole, Perla had said.

On the way back home, La Chaparra cautioned her of the dangers—watch out for la migra, stay away from the highway. If they catch you, you might have the baby in jail if they don't process you back soon enough. Day crossings were easier through El Barrio de la Bola. La Chaparra wished her well and left her at the entrance to El Arroyo Colorado.

Perla came to say goodbye. She was leaving for Talpa. Not Sayu, for she could not look into her father's eyes. But someday, she had confided to Trini, she would go back to Sayu to die there. She would climb the temple again to pray like the flower king. Now she was going to the sea, to wait for Manuk to come to her.

"Will he know you are there?" Trini had asked.

"He knows everything." Her voice was wistful, then her eyes flamed with a fever. "I cannot stay here any longer, Trini. I need faith again, not so much in God as in people."

"You seem so sad."

"I am lost. What am I? a witch? the whore? the high priestess of a lost world? Perhaps the whiteness of the beaches . . ." Her voice was soft again as it trailed off in thought.

"I'll never forget you, Perla."

"And I will never forget you. The mystery will always be there for you, Trini."

Again, words to make Trini's heart leap. They went to the patio in the afternoon for the last time together, sharing a long silence with the sun. That was the way Trini wanted to remember her, Perla, the priestess of light. Yes, things went out and beyond in all directions with secret, dark-light visions that made all time one, all people one. Yes, Perla made her feel it. Trini kissed her friend goodbye and left her still sitting there.

The birth pains came before dawn a few days later, a soft, late autumn dawn that wove its mysteries for her between pains. She took a streetcar at six that left her on the edge of El Barrio de la Bola. From there she walked all the way down the sandhill through the arrabales leading to the river. The river was not a threat. Most of the water had been banked upstream into irrigation ditches that followed new-found fields converted into farmland from the desert.

This was the point of safe crossing, safe from deep water, if not completely safe from the border patrols who made their morning rounds on the highway that followed the river. Still, her chances were good. Her pains were coming with regularity, but at distant intervals. From the Juárez side of the river she could see the small, humble homes scattered in the hills of Smeltertown. She rested under a tree on the edge of the river, her pores feeling the chill of the coming winter. She leaned her head against the tree, a lilac tree, of all things, in the middle of nowhere! For an instant, she seemed to feel a force from the earth, from her hold on the tree. She laughed, then pain cut sharply through her body. It sharpened and focused her instinct. Failure was impossible.

She took off her shoes and waded across a shallow area until she came to a place where the water was flowing uniformly downstream. She made her way carefully, looking for sure footing, her toes clutching at cold sand. Brown mimosa seeds floated on the surface of the water. Then, without warning, she felt herself slipping into the river. As she fell, a pain broke crimson, a red pain that mixed and swirled with the mud water that was up to her breasts now. She had lost the shoes she was carrying. Her feet sank into the deep soft sand, and she kicked forward to free herself. The steady flow of water helped pull her toward a dry section of riverbed. She was but a few feet away from the American side. Then, she was across.

Shoeless, drenched through and through, holding a wet rebozo around her, she made her way, breathless and cold, to a dirt road leading to the main highway. She looked both ways for any sign of a patrol car, but saw none. She sighed with relief, searching around for a place to rest. Ahead, she saw an abandoned gas station with a rusty broken-down car by its side. She could hide there until a bus arrived. She sat behind the car with the highway before her; looming across the highway was a mountain carved by the machinery of the smelter, contoured by time, veined with the colors of a past life. Its granite silence gave her comfort. She understood mountains. Like trees and the earth, they bound her, gave her their strength. Pain again. It consumed her as she clutched the edge of a fender, the metal cutting into her palm.

While the pain still wavered, she saw a bus approaching far away along the stretch of highway. She wiped the perspiration from her face with the wet rebozo, her body shivering, her vision hazed as she fixed her eyes on the moving, yellow hope that came toward her. Her blood was singing birth, a fading and then a sharpening of her senses. She felt weak as she raised her heavy, tortured body and made her way to the edge of the highway. She stood, feet firm, arms waving. Oh, Sweet Virgin, make it stop! She waited, eyes closed, until she heard the grinding stop. Thank you, Sweet Mother. She opened her eyes to see the door of the bus swing open. When she got on, she saw the driver's eyes questioning. Words came out of her mouth; the clearness of her voice surprised her. "I have no money, but I must get to a church."

For a second, the bus driver stared at the pregnant woman, muddied and unkempt, standing her ground. He simply nodded, and the bus went on its way. She saw that the people on the bus were mostly Mexican like herself. Their eyes were frankly and curiously staring. A woman came up and helped her to a seat. She asked with concern, "Is there anything I can do?"

Trini looked at her with pleading eyes. "Where is the church?" She was breathing hard against the coming of another pain.

"A Catholic church?"

Trini nodded. The pain came in purple streaks. She bent her head, her face perspiring freely.

"It's your time," the woman whispered. "There's a hospital near."

"No, no, no, the church." Trini's plea swirled with the pain. She whispered, "The Virgin told me."

"¡Jesucristo!"

It seemed that the bus driver was going faster without making his usual stops. No one protested. The church was the destination now. Trini leaned her head against the window, hardly conscious of buildings interlacing light and sounds. At a distance, a church steeple rose south of the maze of city buildings. Someone said, "Over there, El Sagrado Corazón."

Joy danced on the brink of Trini's pain. El Sagrado Corazón! She had been led. She had been helped. She was certain now that her child was meant to be born in the church. The pain pierced, bounced, and dispersed. Then she breathed freely. The bus had stopped. The driver was pointing out directions. "Just go all the way down the street, then turn left."

The woman helped Trini off the bus as voices called out words of sympathy and good luck. As the bus took off again, Trini's legs gave way. She fell on bended knee on the sidewalk. The pains were almost constant now. She looked up at the woman with pleading eyes as the woman cleansed her brow, encouraging, "Just a little way now, pobrecita."

"I have to find the Virgin . . ." The words were dry in her throat.

"The rectory . . ."

"No, the church." Trini shook her head in desperation, breathing hard. "The Virgin."

The woman said no more, bracing herself to hold Trini's weight. Through a wave of nausea, Trini saw the church before her. Ave María, Madre de Dios, bendita seas entre todas las mujeres. The prayer came like a flowing relief. They were climbing the steps slowly. Happy moans broke from Trini's throat as her legs wavered and her body shook in pain. She could feel herself leaning heavily on the woman. The woman opened the door of the church, and they walked into its silence. Before them were the long aisles leading up to the altar, a long, quiet, shadowy path. The woman whispered, "Can you make it?"

Trini looked up and saw what seemed like miles before her, but in front of the altar to the right was the Virgin Mary holding out her arms to her. The same smile on Her face as when she had looked down at Trini in the Juárez church. The pain was now one thin tightrope made of colored ribbons that went round and round, swirls of red and black. Reflections from the stained glass windows pulsed their colors, hues of mystery, creation. Colors wavered and swam before her eyes, the Virgin's heartbeat. Yes, she would make it. She stretched out her hand, feeling for the side of a pew to support herself. There was peace now in spite of the pain. The candles flickered, dancing a happiness before the Virgin. But now her body made its own demand, one drumming blow of pain. She fell back in a faint, and the woman broke her fall to the floor as two priests ran down the aisle to see what the matter was. Yes, the Virgin had been right all along . . .

* * *

Trini held the piece of paper in her shaking hand. It was in English so the words meant little to her, but the name Ricardo Esconde written in black ink stood out bold and strong. Her eyes, radiant in her triumph, looked for a second into the unconcerned eyes of the clerk, then flickered away. "Gracias."

Thank you, God—thank you, clerk—it was all over. Her son's birth had been registered. She walked away unsteadily, the weight of the baby in her arms, the paper held tightly in her hand. She made her way to a chair in the corner of the office, a queasiness commanding, stomach churning, the taste of vomit in her mouth. She let herself fall into the chair as she tightened her hold on the baby. Her breath came in spurts. She raised her head, throwing it back, mouth half-open to draw in air, her body withstanding many things—fear, hunger, fatigue. She had run away from the priests. Her mind retraced the time of her escape as her shaking hands carefully folded the birth certificate.

It was now in the pocket of her skirt. She had run away, not because the priests had been unkind. They had helped with the birth on the floor of the church, angry questions lost among sympathetic murmurings. After that, sleep overtook the pain. When she awoke, the priests placed a son in her arms, clean, wrapped in a kitchen towel. She had smiled her gratitude and had gone back to sleep. Later, she eagerly drank the hot soup and ate the bread they offered her, the baby close and warm by her side. But then the priest who spoke Spanish told her that the immigration people had to be notified. It was the law. The woman had told them that she had crossed the river.

When they had left her alone, she had simply taken the baby and walked away, out of a side door into an empty street in the early afternoon. She had walked south. When she could walk no more, she sat on a corner bench to rest. A Mexican woman sat next to her, waiting for a bus. She looked at Trini and the baby with interested eyes but said nothing until Trini asked, "Where do I register my baby as a citizen?"

Instantly, the woman understood. She shook her head as if to push away the futility of things, but answered, "City-county building." The woman was pointing north. "It's closed now."

"How far?"

"About twelve, thirteen blocks north, on San Antonio Street." The woman's eyes were troubled. "Just walk up, then turn left, but watch out for la migra. You look like you just came out of the river."

The bus stopped before them, and the woman disappeared behind its doors. Trini looked around and saw warehouses with closed doors, parking lots yawning their emptiness. She had the urge to cry, to give up, but the sun was falling in the west, and the baby in her arms told her differently. She sat numb, without plan, without thought as buses came and went, loading and unloading passengers. She sat on the bench until dark, putting the baby to her breast before she set out again. How insatiable was her drowsy, grey fatigue. She set one foot before the other without direction as gauze clouds were swallowed by the night. The night had swallowed her and the baby too. She made her way to an alley, away from the wind, and there in a corner slept, the baby clasped tightly in her arms.

* * *

That had been yesterday. Now it was all over. She had found the building—the baby was registered. A thought came to her like the climbing of a mountain, steep and harsh. What now? What now? She caught the stare of a woman waiting for the clerk. Then Trini noticed the clerk's eyes on the baby. The man was clasping his hands, then unclasping them, then tapping his fingers on the counter as if he were deciding to call the authorities.

Wan and pale, Trini drew the baby closely to her and made her way to the door marked "Vital Statistics." Her hands were trembling out of weakness and fear. The baby began to cry as Trini made her way out of the building, shouldering her way through people, avoiding eyes. She was a curious sight, a muddied, barefoot woman with wild hair and feverish eyes, holding a baby, running for dear life. She ran along the streets that took her away from tall buildings, from uniforms, from American people. She was going south again. Her mouth felt dry and raw, and the towel the baby was wrapped in was soaking wet. Oh, my baby, I have to change you, feed you, her heart cried. But still, she ran until she could run no more, standing against the wall of a building to catch her breath, avoiding the curious stares of people. Before her was a street sign. The words were distended images, visions of hope: "Santa Fe."

Holy Faith! The name of the street was Holy Faith! An omen—a guiding force—a new decision. The hope was as feverish as her body. She would follow the street to its very end. She started on her way again, feet heavy, body numb, the baby now crying lustily in her arms. People had been left behind. Only one man passed her, unconcerned. Before her was a railroad yard, across the street a bar, beyond that an old familiar bridge, El Puente Negro! Strange, the circle of her life. The end of Santa Fe had brought her to a dead end. She did not want to cross the bridge. She did not want to go back. She had to find a place nearby to rest, to look after the baby's needs.

Behind a warehouse was a lumberyard fenced off with sagging, rusty wire. She made her way through one section where the fence had sagged to the ground, her feet stepping over a desiccated piece of lumber, half-buried in dry mud. She sat down against the wall of the building and hushed her baby with soft tones of love. The baby had to be changed. She raised her skirt and jerked at the cotton slip underneath. It did not give. The baby lay on the ground crying harder. She pulled at a shoulder strap, tearing it, repeating the process until both straps gave. She pulled the garment from the knees, stepped out of it, then tore it in pieces to make a diaper. With quick fingers she unpinned the wet towel, flinging it over a pile of lumber. Afterwards she placed the dry pieces of cloth on the ground and lifted the baby onto them. He was whimpering in tired, spasmodic little sobs. Her breasts were hard and sore in their fullness. Now she rested against the building, picking up the baby and turning him tenderly toward her. The nipple touched his lips. He took it eagerly, drops of milk forming on the sides of his little mouth. Then she dozed with the baby at her breast.

After a while she awoke with a start, aware of the greyness of the day. She sat quite still, the baby fast asleep. Her arms felt cramped and stiff, so she laid the child low on her lap and stretched out her legs.

Through half-closed lids she saw El Puente Negro at a great distance, like a blot against the greyness of the day. Her mind was a greyness too, things not yet clear or distinct. Thoughts ran: a world in circles, a black bridge standing, pulling through a dark hole, Santa Fe—faith, faith and the burning of a fire, a plan. Perhaps it was all useless, this trying. She felt as if she were a blot lost in space. All she wanted was a chance, a way to stay in the United States, to find a piece of land, to have the family together.

It had taken Celestina fifteen years to buy a thirsty, ungiving piece of land in Mexico—fifteen years! No, there was a better way in the United States where the poor and hungry did not have to stay poor and hungry. Something had pulled her to this country of miracles. It was all still shapeless, meaningless, beyond her. But things would take shape. She would give them shape. A blot in space was the beginning of many things in all directions. She looked down at the sleeping child, Sabochi's child, a son, Rico.

Her blood was racing with new energy, her mind grasping at possible solutions, possible ways. She must find a vecindad, people who had come over for the same reason, people who could speak her language, help her. She took the baby in her arms and slowly made her way back to the street.

Then she saw it, a patrol car. Two men were standing next to it. One sat on the fender, smoking a cigarette. The other tramped back and forth, looking at both sides of the street. Wild imaginings invaded her mind. They were looking for her. The priest had reported her. Furtively, she looked for a place to hide, noticing the boxcars in the railroad yard. She would be safe there until dark. She ran with the baby toward a long string of boxcars, crouching, looking for an open door. She saw one, ran to it, and placed the baby on the floor of the car; then with great effort she put her palms firmly on the edge to pull herself up.

The boxcar was empty except for some bales of hay and a heavy odor of cow dung. She sat by the side of the door waiting for the patrol car to leave. The baby was still fast asleep. Flies swarmed in the hollow of shadows. Trini found herself without thought, with only the waiting and with an anxiety that carved itself into her fatigue.

Again she dozed, and this time she was awakened suddenly by the sound of a train whistle and a rude jolt. She felt the movement of the car, halting, grunting. Oh, God, the car was moving! Her body jerked forward, the impact throwing the weight of her body on the baby. She quickly rose to her knees. The baby was crying. There was no thought of getting off. She fell back on her knees and picked up her son. She cradled him and moved from side to side to pacify him. She put him to her breast. While the baby nursed she watched blurred images beyond the boxcar door as the train gathered speed. Where was it going? How far? She felt apprehensive about her plight, woven purely out of chance, out of daring. A growing emptiness in her stomach! What if my milk dries up! Buildings flashed by as the train turned and swayed. Bump, bump, bump—the pattern of the beat was a curious mixture of hope and fear. She felt it to her fingertips. The train began to slow down. It wasn't going far! Trini heard the traffic melting into the metallic slowing rhythms of the train. Was it stopping? She waited, teeth biting her lower lip. It stopped.

Trini rose to her feet and went to the door. What she saw was an alfalfa yard enclosed by a series of sheds. There was not a human in sight when Trini looked out the door. Only piles of bales lay scattered throughout the yard. The train might start again any minute. She placed the baby by the door, then jumped off, feeling a numbing shock run up her leg as she hit the ground. She reached up for her son and then walked quickly past the bales toward a shed that opened onto a street. Outside the yard was another street sign, Virginia Street.

Street of the Virgin! Hope rumbled. Too hungry, too weak, and too afraid to feel excitement, she seemed to be borne forward by some strange pull. Before her, a barrio sprawled, vibrating with life. She hastened her step toward the familiar sounds. Her ears caught the blare of music from a Mexican radio station, conversations in her tongue sprouted in the sun. The day had lost its greyness. Children screaming, women yelling, shuffling up a rutted path that curved into an alley between two tenement buildings, ruins scarred by time and neglect. Boys slouched against the walls next to cardboard boxes and cans full of garbage. A pervasive, acrid odor rasped her throat.

A terrible loneliness descended on her. Thoughts of Tía Pancha waiting at the door, Buti and Lupita running toward her—she was so alone. Her eyes filled with hunger as she looked at the sad, limp curtains on the screen doors that she passed. The moving silhouettes that spilled from the open places were all strangers. The last rays of the sun had receded to the broken back roof of one of the buildings. Trini watched some boys huddled in conversation around a streetlamp still unlighted in the coming dusk. She walked around a caving depression sprouting broken glass and tin cans as an old dog sniffed her legs, his tongue hanging out. She watched a fat woman, hair ill-kempt, in shapeless clothes, talk in a hurried monotone to another woman, who was nodding in agreement as her hand slid down one leg, scratching where ants had found a path between her bare toes. They stopped their conversation to stare at Trini and the baby.

Maybe they'll help. I need food, a friend. Saliva began to fill her mouth, a wave of nausea overwhelmed her; her knees buckled. Concern for the baby gave her the sense to break the fall as her knees cracked on the hard ground, the impact of the pain vibrating to her jaws. In half-consciousness, her trembling hands automatically tightened around her son, then she curled into a limp bulto on the ground.

* * *

She was in El Segundo Barrio, Second Ward, in a tenement called Los Siete Pisos a la Muerte, seven steps to death. It was a chaotic barrio, the product of abject poverty. Eusebia, the old woman who had rescued her, spoke of miseries with a toothless grin—one outhouse for eighty families, one communal sink, people found dead in dark rooms of starvation, disease, old age. Cockroaches and rats burgeoned amidst a sense of decay—decaying life, palpitating, multiplying, seven steps to death.

Trini sat in a corner of the room nursing the baby while she watched Eusebia peer at the boiling tea. She was boiling anís, yerba buena, and canela. She added rum. She would sell the concoction for ten cents a cup after midnight. The "alkis" would line up in the dark, narrow callejón, the passage cutting to the back of the old woman's apartment. Her one door opened to the alley.

Trini had been helping her serve customers for several weeks now. She served the dark bultos along the walls of the alley. The first night had been a frightful one for Trini. They were mostly men, all ages, strangers hidden in the dark, stepping forward one by one to reach for their drink.

They stepped out from the dark into the lantern light. It fell only on their faces, strangely severed from the dark bulks of the bodies still hidden in shadows. A face with a dead tongue, slushing moans. A hand reaching out, shaking with palsy for the cup of calientito. A mouth gulping the steaming liquid, afterwards coughing harshly, saliva spraying on Trini's face and hands. She stepped back, disgust in her eyes, a brittle fear sprinting through her body. But she was no longer afraid.

She learned to joke with the regulars. They had smiles, dark eyes full of knowing. There was a sort of gallantry about the line of bultos leaning on the alley wall, waiting for their calientito.

This evening Trini sat on a mattress laid out on the floor. The room held only an oil burner, a table, one chair, and the mattress. A rope strung across the room served as a clothesline. It perpetually held wash, for Eusebia did not hang wash in the back yard. It would simply be stolen. Trini watched Eusebia put the tea aside to steep. Trini set the baby down. There were beads of moisture on his face from the warmth of her body. Eusebia's eyes glowed faintly in the semi-darkness. With a twist and shuffle, the old woman came forward with a plate of boiled sweet potatoes. Trini took one and bit down hungrily. They only ate one meal in the morning, then

Eusebia would give her something to eat before the customers came late at night.

Trini ate with some discomfort. Eusebia was watching her, cackling softly, chin trembling as she too helped herself to a potato. She stuffed it into her mouth, mashing it with her toothless gums, her bony jaw clamping and unclamping, an ooze exuding from the sides of her mouth.

Gulping noisily, she goaded Trini. "You going to marry one of my alkis, eh? The one that tried to kiss you last night?"

Trini disliked the old woman's goading, but she had been kind. She had taken her and the baby into her house. The old woman had stopped the hemorrhaging that had ebbed away Trini's life for many days. Somewhere underneath a heavy, horned crust of hardness, Eusebia had a heart, though she had a sense of humor that was sometimes cruel and cutting. Trini had seen her cry with her alkis. She sometimes fed them and let them sleep in the little room. She would sit despondently on the floor and curse God for so much suffering in the world. Then she would laugh like a mad woman and talk about the plots to burn the misery down to ashes.

"One huge bonfire—he, he, he, he, he, he, he!" Eusebia's eyes told Trini she had taken the seven steps to death and survived them all.

At midnight, Trini was already pouring the hot drinks for some early customers when Eusebia nudged her. "Pssss, you want to go live with people who can get you land?"

Trini did not answer because she simply did not believe her. She was digging again. Eusebia chuckled as she poured some canela for herself and Trini. She handed a cup to Trini, urging her to drink.

The canela had a sharp, good taste. She smiled at Eusebia. Something told Trini that Eusebia was serious. Did she really mean it? Eusebia was chanting, "No more, no more seven steps to death for you!"

"Where? When?" Trini anticipated, eyes eager.

"Tomorrow." Eusebia chuckled and nodded, her body lost in its mirth; then the furious wrinkles softened as she patted Trini's hand and turned away.

18

Valverde

Pancho's head was inside the hood of the touring car, an old phaeton with the metal bows and canvas of the convertible top tied down to the sides. His galvanic movements with screw driver and grease rag made Panchito, his oldest son, lean forward to observe his father's operation. Pancho's head popped out from under the hood. "Hand me the oil can."

The nine-year-old scampered down from the observation point, the top of a wooden fence, and ran to the back porch steps where the oil can sat. Three-year-old Bobby was sitting on the top step nursing a scrape on his knee, a serious look on his face. He stopped when he saw Panchito pick up the can, then followed his older brother to where his father was half lost under the hood. An outstretched arm reached for the oil can, remaining poised in the air until the head came out, eyes squinting, face bright with sweat. Pancho announced, "It's fixed." He gestured toward his tool box, commanding, "Funnel, funnel, funnel . . ."

Panchito rushed to the tool box and came back running, the funnel in his hand. Pancho placed it on the oil duct, pouring the oil while he wiped his face with the edge of his rolled up sleeve. The two boys watched with great respect as they always did when their father was "fixing". After a while, Bobby picked up the empty can and poured the last few drops through his fingers into the dirt. Pancho frowned, then yelled, "Trini!" He waited, then yelled again, this time through the window, "Trini!"

Trini rushed out the kitchen door, well versed in the ways of the family toward the man of the house. Pancho was holding Bobby high by the arm; the little boy's toes seemed to barely touch ground. Pancho ordered, "Here, wash him off."

Trini took the little boy and made her way back to the kitchen. The kitchen with its bright yellow walls and flowered linoleum was the sunniest room in the house. Delfina, Pancho's wife, was draining the grease off some sputtering chorizo. She glanced over her shoulder at Trini, who was carrying the little boy, his chubby little legs kicking the air. "What did he do now?"

"Got oil all over his hands."

Trini made her way through the hall into the bathroom, then held Bobby over the sink and washed off the oil. Bobby, docile and curious, watched her scrub his hands, but as soon as she dried them, he squirmed out of her hold, dashing into the living room, then out the front door. Trini watched him go. She made her way to the small bedroom in the back of the house to have a look at her own sleeping son. The room had been part of the porch once, but Pancho had enclosed it. Delfina's favorite topic of conversation was her proud boast that Pancho could do anything. The house had been a ruin when they had bought it three years before. Since then Pancho had put in electricity, new plumbing, new floors, built the extra room, painted the whole house, and had even planted some fruit trees.

Pancho commanded his family to fetch and clean up after him in harsh, gruff tones. Most times he was a gentle, quiet man who left the running of the house and the disciplining of the children to Delfina and her mother, Mamá Chita.

The family had escaped El Segundo Barrio when Mamá Chita sold her small grocery store and bought the house for Delfina and Pancho with the money. They had moved out of the barrio for the sake of the children, Pancho informed Trini. The run of Florence Street where they lived held modest, small homes, the surrounding streets boasting more expensive homes belonging to gringos. The Fierros had been caught in the cross-current of two cultures.

Pancho was Pancho to his Mexican friends and Frank to his new acquaintances, mostly fellow workers with the railroad. Part of the escape from the defeat of the barrio had been finding work with the Southern Pacific Railroad as a "scab" during a union strike. Even after the strike, he had been kept on and within two years had become a mechanic.

After work, while Delfina and Trini washed the supper dishes, Pancho sat in his favorite chair, listening to his favorite American programs. He never missed the Jack Benny Hour. While he listened, he read the *Post*, eventually falling asleep. Trini would turn off the radio, and the living room was quiet except for the rhythmic, lusty snores of the man of the house.

Delfina bought most of her groceries in Juárez because the dollar stretched farther in "peso country." Still, she would buy bacon and Campbell soups at the American supermarket. She had bought an orange squeezer to feed her family fresh juice in the mornings. Both Pancho and Delfina conversed in broken English unless they were angry or excited, then Spanish became the rapid fire of exchange. Mamá Chita always spoke Spanish in her soft musical, Castilian tongue.

Trini had been with the Fierro family for nine months, thanks to Eusebia. The old woman had informed the family, "This waif has a crazy idea about finding land. For her sanity, find her some land." It had been said in jest mixed with a solemn sobriety. Pancho had scratched his head skeptically, but he never gave up any challenge. The money in the bank was not enough for land, but Trini would talk of nothing else.

Delfina obtained a legal passport for Trini and Linda, but Linda was still living in Juárez with Elia. For a little while, only for a little while, Trini assured herself; soon we'll find a place of our own. The Fierros were a generous lot. They wanted Linda with them, but Trini waited. Tonio had not sent any money for some time. There were no letters from him. So, it was up to her to find land, to support her children.

During her weekend visits to Juárez, she and Linda would talk about having a "home."

Even now, looking at the sleeping Rico, she wished for it. She bent over, touching his forehead with her lips. He gave a silky little sigh, his lips curving into a smile, a chubby little arm outflung, fingers curled. It was up to her to find a way of bringing her family together. Rico had opened the door for all of them into the United States. But it was not easy for immigrants from Mexico. Trini sighed. I guess it's the same all over the world. The poor were always at a standstill. But she refused to accept that. Soon she would have a plan, a way . . . Somewhere a piece of land was waiting for her papá's seeds.

She missed Tonio so . . . come home, come home, I need you, her heart cried. His last letter had been an angry one, complaining of injustices. He had asked about the baby. Tears came to Trini's eyes as she looked at the sleeping child, whispering, "Your father will come home soon."

She needed Tonio's warm hardness, the touch of another human being, to be restored, to feel the lightness of heart that a woman can feel with a man. At night she talked to Tonio as if he were beside her: Oh, Tonio, is it all running to nothing? I'm outside of everything, Tonio. I want my own. I want you . . . Her whispers halted in the darkness and she listened to the emptiness. She reached out to cuddle the sleeping baby, to drink in the sweet, pungent baby smells. They made her whole again. She touched the baby's wisps of hair so gently.

Mamá Chita was at the door, smiling, holding a container with hairpins and a comb in her hand. "Have you seen the girls?"

The girls were Delfina's two small daughters, eight and nine, who usually, at this time of day, crawled through a maze of grapevines in search of their little friend next door. Trini offered to go get them. She found the two girls and walked back with them to Mamá Chita, who sat waiting on the front porch. The anciana spoke in her soft rhythms. "Come, let's comb your hair. We are going to Valverde."

Trini knew that the trip to Valverde was because of her. They were going to look at land.

Pancho had heard about a strip of land south of Evergreen Cemetery outside the city limits. Pancho talked about it as Delfina served a late breakfast; Trini listened while making sandwiches for the trip.

"The river used to change course every two or three years. One morning people woke up on the American side, another morning on the Mexican side, until they built Elephant Butte Dam. Now the course is steady. No one could buy the land until boundaries were settled. Morley bought most of it. Stole it at fifty cents an acre. Now he wants to sell at five hundred. That's what Scrubbs says."

Five hundred dollars an acre! Trini made some mental calculations. The twenty-four hundred pesos and the seventy dollars Tonio had sent were less than five hundred. She couldn't afford it. It didn't matter. Looking at land would keep the dream alive. Maybe less than an acre . . . Questions crowded in on her. What will you live in? How will you survive? Land is only a beginning. But the word Valverde rose in her mind. The green valley. Oh, green rivers of desire, green hills of dreams! Oh, the mysteries that were taking her home!

* * *

"The land is not for sale." Cowboy Scrubbs spoke in English in a cold, flat voice. Trini's expectant eyes fell on him. His tone and manner were denial enough, so that Pancho did not need to turn to Trini to translate. Pancho scratched his head and thrust his head sharply to one side to scan the land, all property of L. Morley. The overseer stood by the door of a long wooden compound; the Morley ranchhouse sprawled in the background. Cowboy Scrubbs stared at Pancho, finality glinting in his eyes, catching the reflection of the sun like steel. His right hand went into his pocket and came out with a handkerchief. The white cloth found his nose, which was emitting hard, violent, vacuous explosions. He wiped his nose with a fanning motion, then jerked his head back up and looked past Trini, speaking to Pancho. "Try the hermit. He's dying, maybe already dead. Wants to sell his place, I hear, to pay for his funeral. Scrap of land, maybe an acre."

They left Cowboy Scrubbs standing, looking after them, as the car created swirls of dust, making its way through a neatly graveled road. Young pecan trees claimed the land for miles. After a full circle around the property, the farm's gravel road became asphalt. They were leaving the valley and heading back toward the city. Trini's eye caught the rush of large fields set off at a distance, the expanse of large, expensive properties, and, when the fields dropped from view, the sudden appearance of a country store, a filling station, and a cluster of small adobe houses. They were in the small town of Ysleta with its one movie house and few stores. Then the town disappeared as suddenly as it had appeared.

Trini sat silent, squeezed against the door, the baby on her lap, Mamá Chita holding Bobby next to her, and the two little girls on the other side. Pancho, Delfina, and Panchito sat in front; Panchito was poking around the picnic basket, proclaiming his hunger. Pancho swung the car off the road onto a dirt path. They swayed to the lurching of the car as it made its way down toward a narrow gulch to the south. Delfina asked, "Where are we going?"

"To the hermit's place."

"We're close to the border," Delfina observed.

"It's still Valverde. The hermit bought land on the Mexican side. Now it's on the American side."

Trini noticed that Pancho was driving the car along the edge of a gulch. She asked excitedly, "Will he sell?"

"Needs the money to be buried with." Pancho explained.

Houses had become less frequent, and soon there were no houses at all, only fields of tall grass and river brush. Then the fields gave way to an ancient grove of giant elms that thickened, creating light shadows on the road. Pancho pointed to the horizon, lavender-pink in the haze of the sun. "There's Juárez. We're on top of the old river."

Greenness overwhelmed Trini. The place had the feel of Batopilas. Let it be, let it be, let it be, she begged, eyes closed. She, a blot in the universe, would find roots. All around her she heard the sounds of invisible birds, the hum of crickets. She looked up to see treetops fleeing in the sky. How beautiful. Land, seeds, family, all in this beautiful valley. Don't let it be a dream. Not anymore. Let it be home.

* * *

They sat around a giant elm, eating their picnic lunch, sharing it with the hermit. Trini looked toward the small frame house which sat at a distance, at the glint of sun on rustling grass, at brown sunflower stalks halting before the elm, and her eyes fell on the hermit with fascination, her heart hammering. He was a dwarf, un enano! Tiny and square, a dome of a head without hair, heavy, snow-white eyebrows under a sculptured brow, eyes disconcertingly alive, tiny wrinkles encasing the amazing eyes, eyes that knew nothing of death. The smell of the summer field, heavy and green, filled Trini's lungs, and for a dream-edged moment she felt the pull of childhood as she searched El Enano's face for recognition. Look at me! Look at me! Know me! I'm imagining again. She deliberately broke the moment, looking down at Rico, asleep on a blanket on the grass. When she looked up again, El Enano was looking at her, his voice full of curiosity, "You want to buy the land?"

"Yes."

"For your family, I hear."

"My husband Tonio will find me soon, then I'll bring my family from San Domingo . . ." Her voice had the heavy anticipation of destiny.

The hermit laughed, amused at her earnestness, then his eyes turned serious, thoughtful, as he observed, "It is good that you are not alone."

Somehow Trini knew that the words meant, "I'm alone." It was in his eyes, that long, empty clarity of living with and by oneself. His body, his expression, still lived a loneliness. His smallness tugged at Trini's heart. They were all sitting in a circle except for El Enano, who leaned against the giant elm, a wounded tree with creeping, tenacious fungus scarring the base of its trunk. His skin was weathered to the same texture and color as the tree, a mottled grey and brown, the bark grooved, meticulously scaled in spirals wearing the vastness of seasons. The little man looked at his visitors and passed his hand across his brow, his head at a slant, his forefinger to the side of his mouth, his dark skin stretched tightly over the bone. "I don't want to sell the land."

No! Trini objected inwardly. She would not be cast out from this place. This was the place cradled in her innermost self, distinct, particular. It was the coming home. It had been fated. A pleading flowed into her eyes as he looked at her, understanding, for he went on: "The land is yours. I will sell it to you for one dollar—if you stay."

"Stay?" She had never thought of leaving!

"I don't want to die alone." There was no self-pity in his voice.

Old ghosts of eternal things filled her—wild wind, the fig tree, rainbow rocks, the image of Tonantzín, four-breasted, brown, all before her, a vision in the blood. The earth and chance had woven her destiny, the love of the Virgin keeping watch. It was so wonderful to be alive! She burst out, joyously. "Of course I'll stay! You don't have to give me the land for that. I want to stay."

* * *

The hermit's name was Salvador, the savior; his life had been spent with a small traveling circus that played small towns in Mexico. He had stood in a circus ring and danced with a blind bear. He had been a spectacle to men, his smallness a strangeness to the giants of the earth. When he had felt the need to be more, he had bought the piece of land in Juárez. He had rediscovered the gods of his ancient heritage, the gods of seasons, of sky and wind.

Salvador and Trini were clearing the land around the giant elm, for she had expressed a wish for a vegetable garden. One Saturday, the Fierro family had driven her to Juárez to pick up Linda, her mamá's bultito, and her papá's seeds. She had placed these on the kitchen table and had explained the importance of the seeds to Salvador.

"These seeds have waited a long time. I want to plant them here."

"I will prepare the land," promised Salvador.

It dawned on Trini that Salvador might not be around for the planting. They pushed the thought of death aside. Salvador had to be eternal, like the seasons. Salvador took a handful of seeds, reminding her, "Spring—I will not see spring, but these seeds will breathe in the earth when spring comes. I will be part of spring . . ."

Trini struggled to understand. Salvador spoke like Perla, a language without ends. And the words always had a feeling, ample and sustained, of Salvador being time itself, someone reconciled with all things dark and all things bright. They cleared the land together, and as they worked he spoke about his belief. "There is really no dying, Trini."

She looked at him, eyes perplexed, arms full of dry stalks. Salvador laughed, breaking soil with a shovel. He stopped working for a while, leaning on the shovel. "Life is forever, Trini."

"But humans all die eventually." Her words were hesitant, not wishing to remind Salvador of his impending death.

"I am just a speck of life. You are another speck. The whole of life never dies. It's in our hearts, our minds." He was back to shoveling dirt, looking up every so often to wipe his brow. Trini questioned. "We disappear from the world, don't we, when our bodies die?"

He pointed to the giant elm. "Our bodies are the leaves on that tree. But our senses are the tree."

Trini looked up at the elm with wonder as he put aside the shovel to sit down and rest. He closed his eyes. "I think my roots are longer and deeper than those of this tree. Forever living, Trini, soundless and tongueless. So I will lose the leaves of my tree, but I will still feel the sun."

In the stillness that followed the hermit's words, Trini looked at his small erect frame, eyes wearing a live, liquid darkness. Trini remembered Tonantzín. She was eternal, green roots covering the whole of earth.

"We are all one," Salvador reminded her.

We are all one! El Enano, Manuk, Salvador—we are all one! She turned to Salvador, "Did you live thousands of years ago?"

Salvador pondered the question, his eyes intense. "I suppose so. So did you."

"Me?" The thought was disconcerting; she was thinking of El Enano, Manuk, and Salvador as magic. But Salvador was not speaking of magic. It was some kind of unknown truth. She could not help but ask, "Do you know my valley in Mexico, Bachotigori?"

"Yes."

Trini held her breath, then whispered, "Did you know me as a child?"

He looked at her quizzically, then answered softly, "I think I've known you all my life."

Trini questioned no more. All had been said.

Late that afternoon, they were under the elm watching a sunset, Rico in her arms, Linda by her side. Salvador was sitting on the now yellow grass a little distance away. He was tasting, touching, hearing the burning colors of the sun. The tangle of her emotions grasped for an understanding, an opening. What would she do without him? He was so dear. She wondered if Salvador would always be with her. She put the thought of his death out of her mind one more time.

* * *

Trini was in the kitchen of Salvador's two-room house. She was boiling coffee in an enamel pot, having set out two cups for the little man and herself. The dwarf sat on a high chair that reached the table comfortably, his legs, almost invisible in baggy trousers, dangling above the floor. Threads of light from a window spread and fell on his bald head, glowing bronze, softening the sharpness of age and the protuberance of an Indian nose. His eyes, velvet-soft, deeply alive, watched her every move. The children were still asleep in the other room. Salvador poured himself a cup of coffee and waited for Trini to sit down, waited to tell her a secret.

She sat facing him, holding up the enamel pot at the level of her face as her eyes met the dark, waiting dilation of his. Her gaze fell away, looking down at a faint streak rising from the dark liquid as she poured herself a cup. His voice broke the stillness.

"You must know about the winds."

"The winds?" she asked, her eyes somber.

"They have to do with the dying of my body."

Trini looked up, moistening her lips, a line of distress appearing on her brow. He smiled, reassuring her, "A time that has to be. Do not be afraid."

"I am not afraid. I just don't want you to die."

"I understand. You will miss your friend."

"Very much . . ."

"Do you remember the screaming wind?"

Yes, she remembered the screaming of the wind after a docile, spring-like February. The newborn winds had rushed into an open field of thistle, ragweed, and Johnson grass that choked the remnants of brown cornstalks outside the kitchen door. "I remember."

"You heard the howl of young winds, new winds." He seemed to be deep in thought for a second, then resumed. "Soon, the strong winds, those that are full of life, will be upon us, happy and wild. When they are gone, a time after, we shall listen for the moaning winds, the winds of departure. My body will die when the winds die. You will scatter my ashes before the rain."

El Enano broke a piece of bread from a plate on the table, holding the piece between two gnarled fingers, crumbs spilling; his eyes, intent and luminous, for some time saw nothing but the broken piece of bread in his hand. With a quick movement, he suddenly brought the bread to his mouth. His lips clenched, his jaws rolled slowly, then he took a sip of his coffee. He straightened his back and placed finger on finger, locking his rather large hands, and continued:

"I have made a cradle. I have built a pyre. You, my friend, will burn my body after it dies. I will show you where it is very soon. It's not far. We shall go there—the open ground among the cottonwoods, beyond the cedars. For this I have promised you my land. You and I will watch my body burn."

Burn his body—the thought clung in Trini's mind; it hung, flitting, waking an anxiety that flowed through her, forcing her to close her hand into a tight fist. Burn his body? Could she go through with it? Burn his body, burn his body—the thought swept in heavy surges through her—burn his body. She could not stop him from dying. She had made a pact with him. So be it. Still, she fell to weeping quietly as she stirred the morning cereal for the children. Through the window she watched Salvador turn the earth for her vegetable garden. The sight of him provoked a rush of memories: El Enano scampering up the hill toward the manzanilla tree, little Linda following, holding baby Rico's hand; the dwarf lugging water back and forth, running with rhythmic little soldier strides, to help bathe the children. There were the nights when they all sat outside the kitchen door and listened to his stories about his days with the circus or shared his feelings about life. Such gentle wisdom! A nourishment for her. The days without him? She did not dare to think about them.

Screaming winds drugged the whole morning as she went about her chores, feeding the children, sweeping, setting a pot of beans to cook. A busy morning, a time to forget the things to come. But the hour did come, bringing with it the little man's ritual of pain. She sat on the edge of the children's cot as they napped. She worked at her darning until she saw him in the doorway, his steps hesitant, slow, his body bent almost in half as he made his way to the corner by the stove. Salvador wished to be alone with his pain, an agony void of form that took the little body to battle.

He fought the pain in ancient ways, sitting crosslegged with an earthen jar between his legs. The jar held a slimy green fermentation of peyote. He sat and met the cutting, lusterless thrust, bones resisting the sudden jerk of flesh, mouth opened, jaw slack, displaying naked teeth. Now the jar sat between his taut, spasm-shaped loins. Trini remembered how the jar had stood on the windowsill for thirteen days. She had watched him cut off the round top surface of the cactus, exposing a spiraled, sinuous furrow with little tufts of matted, grayish fuzz. He had sliced it like a carrot, dropping the pieces into a boiling mixture of carcomera and matarique. Then the mixture was set aside on the windowsill.

She had watched him many times, raising the jar, shaking it, a hand over the top, the heavy greenish liquid spilling. Soon the muck settled to the bottom and found a new consistency, a running, paste-like composition. He stared at it with the shock of pain behind his eyeballs, then his fingers dug into the rancid thickness, coming up full of the bile-like substance, some sloshing to the floor. His hand found his chest, his stomach, rubbing with circular, trembling motions, lips tight over gnashing teeth that blew out pain, limbs rigid. He fell back prostrate on the floor, his body stretching like a root through earth. Suddenly he began to twist from side to side, to twist and twist again, like a fish on a hook. After a while, all movement stopped.

He lay there a long time while Trini sat and watched, curious, sad, tense. The children napped in the early afternoon. In time, his prostration receded and his breath came easily; his eyes blinked, then opened wide. There was peace now, creeping slowly, relaxing his face and body; the battle was temporarily stayed.

* * *

She did not believe—she could not believe—the pyre! It was made of crisscrossed cedar logs, five feet high, standing over a circular grave filled with brush and firewood. But around the grave was an old magic—a wide circle of rocks the color of the rainbow, like a rain of tiny meteors, stones in a circle, one rock balancing another, red rocks like frozen fire, black rocks creeping out of grey. Stones gleamed with morning light filtered through the tall cedars, golden-hued rays spiraling into the blue of the sky.

Mysteries! She was back in Batopilas again, thousands of miles away. She was a child again, watching her father pile rocks in the backyard to build his children a rainbow mountain, a mountain of purple-pinks, orange-gold, and dark glinting rocks gathered along the stream that cut the valley of Bachotigori. She remembered another enano that had materialized from the rocks. Had she imagined him as a child? And now there was a real enano, a circle of rainbow rocks around a pyre. The pyre! Salvador had circled his future grave with rainbow rocks. What did it mean? Trini shrugged the thought away, for the sight of the pyre made her think of Salvador's death. There it was—above her, compact, waiting. She stared at the top of the pyre covered with a reed mat interwoven with colored strips of cloth. She turned away, picked up little Rico and took Linda by the hand. They made their way to an old twisted cedar tree bent and curved by wind. She didn't want to think of death on such a beautiful day. She sat on the grass under the tree, the children by her side. She was listening to birds everywhere, their chirping sprinkling the rush of a light wind, a happy wind, a wild wind, a wind full of life. She noticed a trail of lavender verbena scattered along the wind's path, leading to the pyre where Salvador was busy putting brush into the grave. The wind played with his clothes and his shirt flew open. His body stood taut against the wind as his hands tied wood securely. Suddenly, he quit his labor and looked around at the work of many months.

Trini took the wind into her lungs as she remembered the old game and the old song played around the rainbow rocks in the valley of Bachotigori, a game played with her brother and sister under a tree whose leaves tangled the morning's quiet. The words came easily, almost joyously, to her lips. "Naranja dulce, limón partido . . . ." She stood, holding the children by the hand in an open circle. She called out, "Salvador, come play."

Salvador joined them, taking her outstretched hand and little Rico's. The circle was closed. She began to sing again, "Naranja dulce, limón partido . . ." as they went around in a circle, swaying to and fro. Trini looked at the little man as he lifted her son and danced him around. She caught the twinkle in the dwarf's eyes; feelings came together through the air, blending into sun. The dancing stopped and El Enano put Rico down almost too quickly, leaving them, walking awkwardly toward the grave. He stumbled, fell, then got up again. The pain! Breathing in gasps, he took a bottle of tequila he had rested on the rocks. With shaking hands he drank from the bottle as one drinks water. He let his body fall to the grass, then he dragged himself up against the colored rocks, his hand reaching for a clay pipe in his pocket. He filled it with dried peyote from a small bag. The wind took the flame of two matches before he was able to light it. But when he did, he sucked on it in desperation, then drank from the bottle again. Once more he sucked on the clay pipe, drawing smoke into his lungs in long, choking breaths, ventilating, a half-moan rising, a cry jumbled in his throat. Feelings churned in Trini. She wanted to run to the little man, to hold him in her arms against the pain, to take some pain from him, but the agony enclosed him, a nebula palpitating its final fires. A sob caught in her throat—God help him, Oh God, please help him, only You can help him. She dared not tread upon his pain, so she gathered Linda and Rico and made her way to a slope where wild yellows and thistles were in bloom. A wily, supple wind seemed to push them along. Suddenly, an escaped strip of colored cloth from the pyre flew right across their path.

Rico ran with baby legs after it, his little hand reaching out as the strip settled on the path before him. The wind blew it once more along the path; the baby toddled after it until Trini caught it and placed it in his tiny hands. Rico sat down to examine the orange strangeness, while Linda listened to the buzzing of invisible bees, her eyes following the tail of a lizard now lost in tall grass—a child's world of summer sounds and sights. While the children played, Trini leaned against a tree and watched Salvador still crouched in some fold of time, oblivious, consumed.

Finally he stood, finding his voice, spitting, swearing, laughing harshly. His face was bathed in sweat, his eyes burning, teeth chattering. He stared at them unseeing, through them, past them, his body slowly becoming elastic again, his feet firm on the ground. He seemed more withered, yet there remained something indomitable in him. He smiled, whole again, his eyes falling on the three of them. He walked slowly to where they were, sitting down nearby, whispering, "My blood is cold, Trini, but the pyre is finished. The rest is up to you."

Up to me, up to me—it was still a chant of indecision. A wild wind stirred in her, one without given direction, pulling every which way. The bargain must be kept. But it was more than a bargain now. He was to give her his one acre of land for having shared his last days, for promising to burn his body and close his grave. She knew that he was waiting for reassurance from her. He was waiting with persistence. The land was no longer important. How strange! The dream and struggle of many years—the promise to plant her papá's seeds on land that would belong to the family—this had been the intuitive pull to the miracle called the United States of America. Land! It didn't seem to matter anymore. She would give it up gladly if Salvador could be spared from pain, from death. But the reality could not be changed. She wanted him to know. "I don't care about the land ..."

"I know, Trini, I know."

"But I will burn your body because you wish it so."

Salvador drew his head back, throat taut, eyes to the sky, unblinking, clear. Then he looked at her, eyes moist with gratitude. His voice was calm, soothing. "After the burning, when the pyre falls, let the ashes cool."

"The wind will scatter them ..."

"There will be no winds," he reminded her gently. "The rains will come, but before they do, cover the ashes in the grave with the stones. Break the circle, make a mountain."

Then he laughed, stretching out his little legs, a child of wisdom, his features sharpened by a brightness, a fierce candor, free of pain, free of doubt. He will go, thought Trini, and I will make the mountain out of the rainbow rocks.

* * *

Trini awoke with a start. The moaning wind that had shaken the house all night still gripped the morning light, pouring through a crack in the roof, bathing the children's sleeping faces. She rose and tiptoed to the doorway leading to the kitchen. The cot in the half-shadows was empty. Salvador was gone. She knew where he had gone. She envisioned him following the moan of the wind, ascending a long, gradual slope that took a sharp bend to the right, leading to the river. She saw him walking, twisting in pain, knowing that the time had come. He would walk the long cluster of salt cedars that had been gaining ground for years. Before him would be the grove of cottonwoods, the pyre waiting for the burning. Her mind's vision saw him on the ribboned mat on top of the pyre, the wind rattling its pain cry around him, waiting with a hunger. The moan of the wind shaped the words so clearly: He's dead—he's dead. . . .

Now she must do it alone. Barefooted, she fumbled for matches in a drawer, for the can of kerosene behind the door. She left the house against the wind, dust swallowing the path. When she came to the salt cedars, the smell of water touched by dust became a taste in her mouth. The cottonwoods soon loomed before her. She began to run between clean slashes of half-breaths. She felt her tears drying on her cheeks. She looked up at the cottonwoods, at the twisted branches holding firm against the wind. She was on open ground now, the pyre before her.

The moaning winds were vanishing, becoming wisps of swirling dust hung in the air, swallowed by the coming sun. She looked toward the top of the pyre and saw him there, his still form lying on the reed mat woven in color. He was gone. Trini felt an emptiness consume her, a heavy loneliness that brought her to her knees. The ground was cold, her senses cold. He was gone. The emptiness, impeccable, dry tongued, left a ringing in her ears—or was it only the chirping of a morning cricket? She did not know; she could not tell. She sobbed wildly for a long time, then slowly got to her feet, her body aching with sadness. She made her way to the pyre, then up the narrow rope ladder leading to the top. She felt a sharp pain in her leg as she made her way up the stacked salt cedars. A sharp edge had cut into her skin. She was now sitting on the side of the cradle, high up above the world, next to Salvador's body.

He lay so still. His head seemed big and heavy on his little body. The fingers of one hand were spread out over his face like a dead brown spider. She touched the hand, then took it gently and laid it by his side, revealing his closed brown lids and the sudden glint of metal on his ear. An earring! She had never seen him wear an earring, but she remembered El Enano of her childhood wearing one so long ago—the little man of dreams, of green hills encircling the valley of Bachotigori, the legend of gentle miracles. Yes, he had worn an earring. But Salvador? Then she noticed something else. He wore only a red cloth around his groin—again El Enano of long ago . . . Ah! mysteries that warm the heart and shape our dreams!

She laid a warm hand over his cold one. She knew it was the end of a time, the end of a way. She sat next to him for a long while; then deep from a reservoir inside her rose a clean, fragrant hope, the trust in a new beginning. She looked down at the pile of stones circling the grave, at the spilling yellow of dandelions on a distant slope. The trees seemed to burn green in their closeness. She gazed peacefully at the river striking south, then north again. She felt the air, suddenly at rest. Yes, the winds were gone for certain. She felt a terror, something joyous and perplexing at the same time—the significance of death, the significance of life, both caught in the long, straight silence. Far away, the sound of churchbells rose in the immensity of stillness; then, after a while, the ringing stopped. One thought came quickly to Trini—I must start the fire.

19

Air of Farewell

José Mario, wearing a hanging sack with a pouch full of seed, stood back and looked over the plowed land, then glanced up to see Trini walking toward him wearing an old, flapping straw hat. Rico, at nine, with the sun at his back, stood silently next to his grandfather, watching the old man's concentration. Trini could feel the boy's closeness to José Mario as the old man measured the distance. He put groups of two or three seeds about a foot apart in the plowed earth, ridged to a living brown in straight rows, the moisture of a thousand years deciding texture, color, ravenous for seed. When he finished a row, he stood back to observe his work, Rico following, putting earth over the seed, repeating the ritual of his grandfather, standing back to survey his work.

The smell of turned, moist earth was the sweetest smell in the world to Trini, who felt at peace as she glanced sidelong at her father and Sabochi's son. Yes, it was a secret joy to think of him as Sabochi's son, to watch the child look at her through Sabochi's eyes, with Sabochi's smile. Her secret joy. She had come out from her cool kitchen to help them clog the small ditches that José Mario had dug at the end of each row. The three of them spent the rest of the morning burying pieces of rags and tin as stoppages, creating a series of small dams with rag gates to stop the water when José Mario rotated the irrigation of the planted rows, letting the water flood one row at a time. When they finished, Rico pumped the water, splashing, following the pathway of the long, narrow trenches. José Mario removed the rag gate when the first row was full, and another row filled with water, three ditches at a time.

The heat of noon was upon them by the time they made their way back to the house. In eight years only one room and a bathroom had been added. The house was still too small for the nine of them.

There were five children now. Aside from Linda and Rico, there were Tonito, Salva, and Tiana. Salva was short for Salvador, Tiana for Sebastiana. Trini had asked Tonio about the names, but he had not cared one way or the other, letting her keep things together for the times he came home.

The spring following Salvador's death, when Trini had been planting the land cleared by the hermit, Tonio had come home from California. He had been grateful and excited by the land she had acquired. But only for a little while. He had no interest in farming. He found work at Asarco, the copper refinery at Smeltertown. The plant had originally been designed for ore coming in from Mexico, and when that had dwindled, there had been the refining of lead and zinc and copper ore concentrates from Katanga in the Belgian Congo. Tonio sorted the ore—a tedious, exhausting, dirty job. Somehow his way of life had been stunned, denied, his spirit haltered, reined. But the job was steady and, in time, Tonio found new escapes—no, old escapes. A wandering eye—women. It became a way of life.

Trini knew about the other women. He would come back to her whenever a love affair was over, silent, morose, unable to make an apology, angry at her silences. When he was home, he spent his evenings drinking beer at the Star Dust, a bar across from the cemetery, where he played poker, sometimes losing a whole paycheck. Once in a while, when he won, he would come home with trinkets for the children. Tonio, effulgent, base, part-time father. Never a husband these days. Trini pushed past the indifference, raising the children, making a life with the help of José Mario and Tía Pancha.

He's been gone three weeks now, Trini reminded herself as she stirred the cooking beans. She stared down at the boiling brown bubbles. To stop the heartache she did no more than stare, all things erased except the dancing brown bubbles. She did this often, sometimes staring at a drop of water or feeling the textures of a leaf to stop the ache, to accept an insurmountable existence that hung, split, folding into loneliness.

The children's voices invaded her capsule of sadness, busy movements around the kitchen, all helping with the noonday meal. Trini sighed. Children belonged to children in a children's world. The child had been burned out of her with the burning of Salvador's body. It had nothing to do with his death, she had decided. The journey was over, the land had been found, the family had been gathered. The dream had come true. There had been other dreams, about her life with Tonio, dreams that would never be. Dreary days upon dreary days of hard toil, not enough money, broken furniture, the hurt because of Tonio's affairs. All these defeats diminished her. What else is there but to endure? she asked herself again and again. Oh, I mustn't be bitter! Never bitter!—even if the world had not a single thought of her. There was intimacy with the earth, with the elm tree. She worked herself numb to keep her sanity. What she needed was a new dream, the search for new substance—what? where? Yet, faintly but surely she felt the mysteries in her veins. The green blood stirred in her, looking for an ocean, but the spirit was captured in the dreary dullness of herself. She was so alone, even with her father and Tía Pancha.

Those two kept to themselves. They were their own conspiracy. José Mario had built a room in the back of the house for the two of them. They had brought their lifestyle with them to Valverde, obstinately keeping to themselves most of the time, talking about San Domingo and the past. Her sister and brother so far away, still in Mexico—Lupita married, Buti in school. Why must it all belong to the past? Trini asked herself. She stubbornly believed that the mysteries had not died with Salvador. Listening to Tía Pancha tell the cuentos of long ago, working with her father plowing and planting, somehow made her feel as if she were as old as they were. But, I'm not old! her heart protested. Still, she felt old. She knew she looked old, wearing a faded cotton dress, hair pinned severely to the back of her neck, face roughened by sun and earth, feet bare to the ground. Linda had brought a mirror into the house one day, peering for some time at her youth and beauty as thirteen-year-olds will do. Trini had caught a glimpse of herself in the mirror, a face tight and dark, eyes wearing fatigue, a squinting sadness, hair rough, dull. What has happened? she asked herself in anguish. She had been too busy surviving to look before. I look like the earth she told herself, like the earth wanting rain. So fleeting—the firm hope, the firm skin. There's more to me, she told herself fiercely, turning away from the mirror.

Tiana was crying in her crib as Tía Pancha made her way to her, tongue and teeth forming soothing sounds, arms outstretched, hands thin-fingered. Tía Pancha and José Mario were going to eat with the family this noon, so Tía Pancha had been with the baby all morning. She lifted the child onto her lap, body bent, motionless for a second, soft, liquid eyes over the little face, brown hands reaching for a clean diaper, taking off safety pins, now in her mouth, making expert folds around the child's fat free-wheeling little legs. Salva and Tonito were milling around with the frenzy of young animals. After slicing tomatoes and cheese and setting the table, Trini led the sweaty little boys to the sink to wash their hands.

They all sat buttock to buttock on long benches at an old pockmarked wooden table. The kitchen, a dim, sweet-smelling room, a single light bulb dangling from the ceiling, was a favorite place for the family. There was always a prayer when Tía Pancha ate with them. She thanked God for blessings in the old stern voice. After the prayer, Rico announced, with his teeth biting into a piece of bread: "They're getting rid of the buffalos at Washington Park."

"To make glue. They're old," Linda exclaimed, loving the clear-cut fact.

Was that the tragedy of things, being old? wondered Trini, spooning bean soup into Tiana's mouth. She had seen the buffalo, she had seen them dig the dry, cracked earth, hooves pounding until out of the dryness appeared a brown stream from some hidden depth, welling up into a small pool like a secret message from the earth. The buffalo lumbered to the water, with their shocks of black hair and coarse beards swaying to the tempo of their tread. They sniffed and dropped their heads into the water, coming up muddy, sprinkling the air. Yes, they were old, forgotten. Her voice was wistful, "It won't be the same without them."

Nothing stayed the same. Change, change, the world moving on—moving. She remembered Sabochi's words, "Move without feeling." How funny, the words meant a thousand things, different things at different times. Move without feeling. She was trying to do that, all right. But this movement was a dumb show. There was no more journey, no more dream. Then the moving had been toward something, somewhere ... What's the matter with me? She tried to listen to the children's conversations. That was hard to do, until Linda complained, "Everybody has a television set but us."

"There's no money."

That was her answer to everything the children wanted, and they wanted many things. The temptations of the world were always there. The children did not make many demands, but the world crowded in—television, houses sprouting to the edge of her property, the children's chatter in English, a war in a place called Korea, books, magazines with the American rich splashed in bright colors on every page. The dream was for the gringos, not for Mexicans. All these things were intrusions, confusions in her life. Her old, tried beliefs and customs had fallen into insensibility. The valley in Valverde had not turned out to be the valley of Bachotigori, where silences and isolation were the voices of centuries. American life had a vigor, a constant demand for money, for things.

Trini saved pennies to buy them what they wanted, never keeping up with the children's demands. It didn't matter. They found their own amusements. To see to their needs, to have them healthy and happy around the table—what more could she want?

If there was no television, there was Tía Pancha's cuentos. During the day, she gave her children to the American school, to the English language, to American ideas. But the substance of their life was the one acre, the planting, being together. Two ways of life—it must be confusing to them sometimes. She remembered Sabochi with ageless wisdom sharing her confusions as a child.

"Grow in stillness." The words grew from the sun, from the earth, from the silent green blood. "Grow in stillness." Perhaps that was the one thing she had learned to do. If only Tonio—no, Tonio was another world she could not reach. I love him, I need him, the children need him. Oh, Tonio, why must you do the things you do?

To him, it was enough to bring his paycheck home when he could, to sit at the head of the table and reprimand poor grades and arguments. He used a strap to teach his children right from wrong because he loved them in his way. When Rico got the strap, he took the punishment silently. All the children understood that this was their father's right. Trini never interfered, never comforted them after the strap, knowing that each one would find his way out of the hurt. Yes, she could rely on Tonio to rebuke, to love them in his manner, to provide for them haphazardly. But he had fallen away from her.

She still remembered the days after his return from California. The good fortune of land, of Trini's sufficiency, had kindled like a fire in his eyes. "Querida, you did all this yourself?"

Again and again he had said it, his lips warm with gratitude. Then one day he had stopped. And then there was no more Tonio to spread her long hair on the pillow with soft fingers, to spin soft tones full of plans and desires.

When she heard about his first love affair in Valverde, she had beat her fists against his breast, hating him, wanting him gone forever. He had put his hands over hers, slowly drawing them apart, raising one hand to his cheek, to his lips, the other sliding to her back, touching her body tenderly. Taut, rigid with the thought of infidelity, she had given in. Oh, the ways of Tonio! She had given in. That was what frightened her. She had given in to Tonio—the beginning of accepting defeat? No, never!

"Mamá, Tonito ate all the cheese," Salva cried.

"I'll get some more."

Trini gave the baby to Tía Pancha and went to slice more cheese. The pattern of things was clear, but there must be more than pattern, she told herself, her knife slicing cheese with purpose. There was a need for sustenance.

* * *

Trini admired her daughter, the Linda of independence and fight, and felt with her son Rico, a sensitive, quiet, strong, boy—Sabochi reborn. It was all there, the strange web of a love woven so long ago. And every time she watched her boy—gestures, eyes, smile, the tone of voice—Sabochi came to life. She had never lost Sabochi, but there was pain and joy in remembering. Someday she would tell Rico about his father. Someday . . .

She was half-awake, Tiana still sleeping in the cradle of her arm, when she saw Linda standing over Rico in his bed, nudging him awake, a finger to her lips. Trini gently took her arm away from around the baby and sat up, asking, "What is it?"

Linda covered her mouth, repressing a giggle, and motioned her and Rico to the window, pointing to Tía Pancha's open doorway. Linda whispered, "She does that every morning."

Tía Pancha was sitting in her rocking chair combing her hair, long, silver-grey, cascading down to her lap. She had undone the braids, parting the hair in halves, then braiding them again from the top down, thin fingers running swift, complicated ways until two tight braids were done. Then she deftly held them together with one brown peineta, such a small comb for so much hair. She sighed and slapped her thighs in a brushing motion, rocking back and forth as if in thought: then with a grunt she made her way to the outside faucet and washed her hands slowly, carefully, returning to the room clearly visible through the open door. Trini, hesitating, felt like calling them away from the window, but something stopped her, a catch in the throat, the memory of Tía Pancha watching the flight of birds while she combed her hair so long ago. Now Tía Pancha seemed older than her years, her body not as erect, as she put on a clean apron to start a fire in the stove. Long swirling wisps of smoke escaped after a while from the chimney, perhaps coals still alive from the night before or pieces of good wood. She was toasting chiles, singing as she worked, her tone sad, words half-forgotten, "Estas son las mañanitas que cantaba el rey David . . ." Her voice was broken by time and tears.

"Isn't it sad?" whispered Linda.

"It's not anything. Leave her alone." Rico's voice was touched by embarrassment, a sense of intrusion.

Trini stopped it then, pulling Linda away from the window, touching Rico lightly on the shoulder. Rico turned away, pulling his sister after him, Trini following. And, outside the window, Tía Pancha swept with a broom, sprinkling the floor with water, dust settling as she swept and swept as if her life depended on it, still singing snatches of the song with drawn breath.

Later in the day, Trini saw Tía Pancha chasing Linda with a pail of water, Linda's voice teasing, "La panchorriaga, le gusta la cagada . . ." The water splashed Linda quiet for the rest of the morning, at least until Tía Pancha came looking for them, asking Trini, "Are they going to get me some pigeons?"

Trini knew that Tía Pancha paid the children a penny for each pigeon they caught. The old woman was fond of making pigeon stew. It was a soup eaten only by Tía Pancha and José Mario at the privacy of their own table since everybody else hated the concoction of carrots, potatoes, and pigeon meat. Trini shook her head. "They're somewhere in the back, Tía."

Tía Pancha must have found them, for a little while later Trini saw Linda and Rico with a ladder, a sack, and a flashlight, Linda leading the way. Trini was kneading dough for tortillas when she saw the two of them from her kitchen window. Catching pigeons, indeed! She remembered well the time when food had been scarce, when the children had been small and very hungry. She, too, had climbed through the small opening into the attic. In a darkness diluted by shadowy greys, a thin light filtering into the opening, Trini had sat, sometimes for hours, on an orange crate covered with spider webs, waiting for pigeons to feed to her hungry children. She wondered if the orange crate was still there, wearing the same spider webs. She wondered if they, too, would sit on its edge, hushed and quiet, waiting for the coming of the pigeons after spreading a few kernels of corn, the flashlight dark until the clatter of wings was heard. Sometimes the pigeons had flown right into her face, a flurry of wings storming the darkness. Trini sighed over her masa, her fingers digging into the dough. Hard times, but different times, when purpose had awakened instincts had given the mind and heart occupation. Hunger—how it can fill the day!

By the time she had a pile of tortillas de harina wrapped warmly in a towel, she saw Rico and Linda coming down the ladder. Then, out of the corner of her eye, she caught what seemed to be the fluttering of wings between the fence of the chicken house and the back of an old playhouse Tonio had built many years before. Was it the glint of the sun? Trini went out into the backyard, shading her eyes from the sun, as Linda rounded the zigzag corner of the fence that circled the chicken coop. The bag slung over her shoulder was full of muffled flutters pulling every which way. Trini caught part of Linda's conversation: ". . . she'll wring their necks, pluck the feathers, slit the stomachs and clean out the goop."

Trini knew it was her way of teasing Rico, who answered somewhat angrily, "Shut up, Linda."

Trini walked past them toward the playhouse. She could hear a thumping now—thump, thump, thump—as she turned the corner. The sound rose over the muted buzzing of bees. Then she saw it, a pigeon caught between the wire mesh and the back of the playhouse. Its wings were spread apart helplessly, neck twisted, eyes staring.

"Poor little thing! What can we do?" she wondered aloud. Then she heard Linda's voice over her shoulder. "Oh, Mamá, it's just a pigeon."

Yes, just a pigeon, Trini nodded, but still, it was suffering so. Rico was trying to reach it, to no avail. He tried from every direction, but nothing could be done short of dismantling the playhouse. She turned strickened eyes to Rico. He understood. A desperate feeling lingered until Linda stated defiantly, "He'll die soon."

They stared at the pigeon, its wings pierced by the wire, its body trembling. Trini turned away, refusing to look at it. "It's hurting."

She looked up to see Linda heading toward Tía Pancha's room. Then she saw Rico chasing after her, grabbing at her elbow. Trini knew why he was stopping her even before she heard the words.

"Let them go, Linda." Rico's command was quiet.

"Why?" asked Linda, pushing him back and freeing herself from her brother. She laughed. "They're only pigeons."

Trini watched Rico's discomfort, but she dared not interfere. She wanted to say, yes, let them go, let them go. She heard the boy, so like herself, repeat the words. "Let them go."

This time Linda laughed in ridicule, demanding, "Why?"

"Because . . ." That was all that Rico said.

"You're silly!"

With those words, Linda ran, disappearing around the corner of the house as Rico stood staring after her. Trini wanted to reach out and touch her son, to let him know she understood what he felt. But she knew that he was walled in by his own confusion. She simply stood and watched him kick dust and walk away.

The pigeon was dead by evening. It looked out blankly through the wire mesh, its wings broken, its body finally hanging limp. Everybody stayed away from the backyard except Rico, who kicked the henhouse in anger. "Damn, I wish I could have . . . done something."

A few hours later, Trini listened to the children talk about the dead bird at the supper table. Tía Pancha clucked her tongue in disapproval. Trini watched Rico lost in his own silence; then suddenly he looked at her, and their eyes spoke a bond of feeling that Trini knew could only have come from those ancient mountains in her past.

* * *

Sweet peas, a rainbow of colors—lavender, white, red, pink—with ferns shooting green from the ground, and Trini remembered the day the earth had been loosened. Early in the summer, new ditches had been made leading away from the vegetables. Linda and Rico had piled up earth. After that, José Mario sent them to gather long slender branches to set in straight rows on each side of the piles of earth. Between rows Trini and her father had planted the sweet peas, the thin branches holding the growing vines, the fragrance touching the days until the coming of autumn. Now, on Halloween, they were picking the flowers for El Día de los Muertos.

The city cemetery was north of Valverde, on the outskirts of the city. It took the length of three blocks on Alameda Street. The sweet peas were a business. The day before All Souls' Day, José Mario and Trini would cut ferns, then José Mario, with swift, deft fingers, now no more than cartilage and bone, would shape "bouquets." Trini knew his pride in saying that they were not just bunches of flowers but an arrangement of art, as he placed the ferns so carefully among the blooms. He asked in a satisfied voice, "What do you think?"

"It's beautiful, abuelito," chorused the children.

Trini helped José Mario place the finished bouquets in cans of water, and very early the next morning, on El Día de los Muertos, the whole family went to set up a stand across from the cemetery to sell their flowers.

The stand was next to the Star Dust bar. Trini had allowed the children to miss school, for all the flowers had to be sold on the day the living visited the dead. A waiting chorus of cawing birds sang among the tall evergreens.

"Flores para los muertos, flowers for the dead."

And indeed, they had sold them all by early afternoon. José Mario had bargained with Americans, holding out bouquets for inspection.

"How much?"

"Cincuenta centavos," answered José Mario in Spanish.

"What?"

José Mario turned to Linda excitedly, pulling at her sleeve, asking, "How do you say it in English?"

"Fifty cents."

All day he repeated the command, "Feefty senz," until the flowers were all gone. Rico took a single pink flower and gave it to his mother, timidly placing it in her hair. The gesture touched her, giving voice to wide and varied feelings to be discovered between them. She laughed softly, raising sad eyes to the sun. Rico said, "You're so pretty, but so sad . . ."

"It's the day of the dead."

He looked at her, not believing. But for now she closed within herself, time eating time, her eyes seared with sun. His words had fallen strongly upon her. Feelings had to be sorted, reasons cleared, before . . . was it so apparent, her sadness? She only whispered softly, "Flores para los muertos."

* * *

With the thickening of autumn, Tonio made one of his abrupt appearances, to pick up where he had left off. The children were delighted, and he used them as a refuge from Trini's eyes, her questions. He had brought them candy and comic books. Trini kept herself at a distance, holding Tiana in her arms, her lips forming a lullaby, cotton-soft; inwardly she felt a sense of injustice erupting. Her eyes were compelling, demanding. Tonio's eyes flicked past her, his body speaking awareness. Why? why? why? she asked herself, why hurl the grievances of months, of years? She felt weariness as she looked at the two younger boys and Linda swarming happily around their father. Only Rico stood aside, looking intently from Tonio to Trini.

That night Tonio lay beside her, big and blunt, protected in a dreary silence, the dark wrapped around him, his back stubbornly to her. He was denying her. Shame suffocated her, but she would be as ungiving as he. How many times had she reached out for him, forgiving? She knew that he was not awake because he did not care. She felt inept for wanting him and not having him, for having lost that freedom of forgiving. Trini, at thirty, felt the youthful green blood surging.

A thought uncoiled in her mind as she watched the moon streaming down on his bare back. She turned away from him and after a while quietly got up and opened the drawer where she kept the old bultito. She opened it with trembling hands, feeling in the darkness for the smooth, round stone, the moonstone of so long ago. Then she walked out into the night, barefoot, covered by a thin, frayed robe, yellow with age. She was going toward the salt cedars, toward the cottonwoods, to Salvador's grave. She wanted to cry out, to die in that crying, and the only solace was the open space where a mound of rocks stood silent in the night. Her thoughts swayed with the tree leaves; a wind shaped the dark. Her thoughts were about a moonstone and a man. She had gone to him. And now again, she felt the pulsing of Tonantzín's green blood. The earth was all still inside her, waiting. She must go to Sabochi again, soon . . .

She grasped the trunk of a tree before she reached the rocks; the vastness of her loneliness was about to drown her. She closed her eyes, breathing deep, a hand on her temple, massaging, soothing, her senses awakened to the moon.

She heard the tread of footsteps on grass and turned to see a familiar stride. She caught her breath. It couldn't be! Sabochi?

No, of course not. It was Rico coming toward her, his lean young body shedding shadows until he was close enough to touch. He said nothing, but sat down on the grass next to her. An old joy rose as she stood listening to the air, feeling the moon, then she sat down beside him, reaching for his hand, putting the moonstone in his palm. "Your father . . ." For a moment she could say no more. She was so full, so full! But then she began once more, clearing her throat, inhaling the richness of the autumn night.

"Sabochi, your father, gave me this moonstone, the time you were conceived. There was snow and a cabin in the canyon of Tararecua. Your father, your father is the ahua of Cusihuiriachi."

The words were said simply, cleanly, in the dark. A question came just as soft, "Tonio is not my father?"

She knew that telling was partly a form of revenge, a way of striking out at Tonio, but it was also a fulfillment, a recapturing of something that had been lost with her husband. Faintly, like the moonlight filtering through trees, the flicker of a new dream was born, a strange and splendid thing to build upon, a new adventure. Sitting under the tree, she told her son the story of a man who had helped raise her, who had defended her, had loved her, a noble man, a man of freedom. She laid a hand, warm and weightless, on his, as the fire of telling rose in her body. She was alive again, life refilling time, the loneliness moving out of her body, her mind, her senses, left only to echoes. She knew that Rico would let the seed grow inside him. "You and I will go Cusihuiriachi very soon. I shall take you to your father." Her words rang true, strong.

She was breathing deeply in a new happiness. Suddenly, her arms went around the boy, his chin between her breasts, both sharing for a second the same warmth. They laughed at their secret in the darkness; then two silhouettes, whispering in muffled voices, finally made their way back to the house, the moonstone still pressed tightly in Rico's hand.

AUTHOR'S NOTE

In writing this novel I have attempted to impart some of the flavor of the language used by the Tarahumaras, including a number of vocabulary items of regional origin and use. In many cases Tarahumara words were supplied by native informants, and I have had to base my spelling solely on the pronunciation. Following are a few terms whose meaning might not be clear from the context.

bule a clay dipper or small bowl with a handle used as a cover for a water jug and as a dipper for drinking

cabaldura saddlebag

garañones wild horses

hilpa a simple housedress made of coarse cotton; chemise

pitaya flower of the carnation family, native to Mexico

revolijo fish stew made with wine

salgazanos thieves

sarso large clay bowl that holds a whole cheese